Peter Lovesey began his writing career with *Wobble to Death* in 1970, introducing Sergeant Cribb, the Victorian detective who went on to feature in seven more books and two television series. His recent novels have alternated between two contrasting detectives: Peter Diamond, and the Victorian sleuth, Bertie. Lovesey's mysteries and short stories have won him awards all over the world, including both Gold and Silver Daggers of the Crime Writers' Association.

After a career in teaching, he became a full-time author in 1975 and now lives near Bath.

D1334749

The Summons

PETER LOVESEY

WARNER BOOKS

A *Warner* Book

First published in Great Britain in 1995
by Little, Brown and Company
This edition published by Warner Books in 1996

A CIP catalogue record for this book
is available from the British Library.

ISBN 0 7515 1627 9

Printed and bound in Great Britain by Clays Ltd, St Ives plc

Warner Books
A Division of
Little, Brown and Company (UK)
Brettenham House
Lancaster Place
London WC2E 7EN

The author wishes to record his gratitude to Joseph Matthews for his advice on sailing lore; to Sue Dicker, of Bath City Council Property & Engineering Services, for showing him inside the Empire Hotel and providing substantial information; to his son Philip Lovesey for grace notes on the music business; and to Avon and Somerset Constabulary for their help over Operation Bumblebee.

The Summons

Chapter One

They say when one door shuts, another opens.

In Albany Prison, when one door opens, another shuts.

A frustrating problem.

When a judge tells a convicted man that life in his case should mean the rest of his natural span, and when he is repeatedly denied leave to appeal, that man's mind may turn to other ways of shortening the sentence. John Mountjoy was classified as Category A, *highly dangerous to the public, the police or the security of the State*. And he was thinking of moving.

Those doors. They function on an ancient principle. You pass through one and find another barring your way. Before the second can open, the first must close behind you. That was how castle gates were made a thousand years ago. But in the electronic age the mechanism is automatic.

They tell the new arrivals in Albany that they don't have maximum security. It is ultimate security. All the gates and doors are linked to a computer housed in a control room bristling with television monitors. Approach a door anywhere in Albany and you are up there on the screen. That control room really is the hub of the place. Apart from the monitors, it houses a master location panel, radio-communications system, the generator and, of course, the team of prison officers on duty. By a stroke of irony that causes no end of amusement to the inmates,

1

those screws have to be banged up more securely than anyone else in the prison. Steel doors, dogs, floodlights and a chain-link security fence all round. If anyone broke into the control room, there would be scenes like the last reel of a James Bond movie.

Mountjoy was confined in D Hall, where most of the lifers were. When leaving D Hall to visit the workshops they were escorted through the double doors, courtesy of the computer, into the central corridor where there was always an unbroken line of screws observing them.

D Hall has glass doors. Smile if you wish, but it is no laughing matter to the inmates. The glass is bandit-proof and lined with steel mesh. Those doors will not budge except at the touch of a switch in the control room. There is a seven-second delay between the closing of one and the opening of the other. Anyone wanting to enter or (more likely) exit from D Hall is compelled to stand in the hermetically sealed unit and be scrutinized. If the control team has the slightest doubt, the interval can be extended indefinitely.

It took John Mountjoy a week of observing the comings and goings to conclude that there was no chance of outsmarting the electronics. You might outwit a human. Not a microchip. The wisdom inside is that even if the power system failed, one of those doors would always remain closed.

No other escape routes beckoned. The walls are half a metre thick, the windows have manganese steel bars and every ledge and wall outside has a razor-wire topping. Tunnelling was out of the question for Mountjoy because of the rule that lifers must be housed with other cells above and below and on either side of them. Surveillance cameras are located everywhere. If he got outside the main prison block, he would still have to negotiate dog patrols, geophonic alarms, five-metre chain-link fences and massive walls lit by high-mast floodlights. Albany was built to replace Dartmoor. It is known as the British Alcatraz because they located it on the Isle of Wight. So even if a man succeeded in getting over the wall he would still have some thinking to do.

The first step Mountjoy took towards escaping was unplanned. In the corridor outside the recess (where the prisoners slop out) he found a button, a silver button with the embossed crown design, a button from a screw's uniform. You never know when you might find a use for something, so he kept it hidden in his cell for eighteen months before he acquired another.

The opportunity came one summer evening when the screws frogmarched him to the strongbox, one of the punishment cells for troublesome prisoners. He had got into a brawl, a right straightener as the old lags termed it, over a letter some cretin had snatched from him, a letter from his mother. Mountjoy wasn't pleased. He fought when the screws stripped him and threw him inside the strongbox. He ended bruised and bleeding, but in credit. In his fist he had compensation, a shining silver trophy ripped from a black serge tunic. When eventually he was returned to his cell it joined the first button in a secret space under the spine of a dictionary.

Screws hate being shown up as negligent. The slightest character flaw anyone reveals in prison is magnified many times, and the screws fear exposure as much as the men they guard. Prison lore suggests that they are worse than the prisoners at grassing on each other. Rather than admit to losing a button and making a search that everyone hears about, a screw will keep the loss to himself and have his wife sew on another. Prison culture doesn't always work in the best interests of the system.

Mountjoy began to see possibilities in this. He started actively adding to the button collection. While working in the tailoring shop a month or two later, he met a new prisoner, a kid of eighteen transferred from Parkhurst

and desperate to obtain tobacco. A deal was struck.
Everything in the prison is open to barter. Mountjoy let
the kid know that a breast-pocket button would be worth
cigarettes to him, and he told the kid truthfully that if he
got in a scuffle with the screws they'd treat him leniently
the first time. Within a month he had the button and the
youth had five roll-up butts, one match and a threat of
castration if he grassed.

One sunny afternoon a long time after this an unimagined
opportunity came Mountjoy's way. Another feud had
ended in fisticuffs and he was back in the segregation unit
under Rule 48. If they let you exercise at all in Y Hall, as
the unit is known, it has to be solitary. The yard is divided
by thermalite blocks into a series of narrow exercise bays.
The screw watching Mountjoy had just hung his tunic on
the back of a plastic chair when he was called suddenly to a
disturbance nearby. In the few seconds Mountjoy was left
unattended except by a camera, he completed his set of
buttons. Three years inside had taught him how to dodge
a camera-lens.

In the prison world certain escapes have passed into
legend. The springing of the spy George Blake from
Wormwood Scrubs in 1966 is still spoken of with awe, and
so is the helicopter grab of two men from the yard at
Gartree in 1987. John McVicar's escape from Durham was
made into a film. John Mountjoy was about to earn his
place in the hall of fame. People say it was an astonishing
gamble. It was nothing of the sort. It was a sober
calculation, the shrewd bid of a player in a poker game of
infinite duration.

How would you plan it, given that you had a full set of
buttons? Mountjoy rejected the obvious. He didn't make
himself a prison officer's uniform in the pious hope of
bluffing his way through the doors. That would run too
great a risk. Screws may not be noted for their IQs, but

they are capable of recognizing one another and spotting the flaws in a home-made uniform.

He studied art. That is to say, he gave himself a reason to work with pencils and paper, drawing abstract shapes and shading them. Nothing too ambitious. As the tutor remarked, his style was more Mondrian than Picasso. Just black and white squares. Small ones, regular in size. The tutor suspected Mountjoy was more interested in making a miniature chessboard than an abstract, and it became a long-running joke between them.

He also worked with other art materials. In secret, he experimented using paints as dyes. He wanted a mix that would blacken T-shirts. The aim was pure black. It was a painstaking process, progressing through a series of greys. He was patient. He had abundant time and a good collection of rags harvested from the security fence around the yard, where rubbish is routinely tossed from cell windows and picked off next day by cleaning squads. Only when he was satisfied with the blackness of his dyed rags did he begin immersing two prison-issue T-shirts. Then by night – using needles from the tailoring shop and a blade formed from the handle of a tooth-brush honed to razor-sharpness on his cell wall – he started the laborious process of cutting and sewing together a passable tunic. A police constable's tunic.

Black has two things going for it. First, it is an easier colour to achieve with dyes than the midnight blue of a screw's uniform. Second, the joins and the stitching are less obvious. The effect is better still when gleaming buttons divert the eye.

The police cap, curiously enough, was easier to make than the tunic, but more difficult to hide, so he left it till last. He prepared the materials without assembling them. Strips of chequered paper reinforced with card were to form the rim. The flat top would be of dyed cotton stretched over a cardboard disc and the peak would be cut from the shiny black lid of a box of Conqueror typing paper filched from the Assistant Governor's waste-bin.

There remained the cap-badge and the silver buttons and numbers on the epaulettes. As basic material for these he used a tin-foil freezer-pack discarded in the kitchen. The resulting badge was a minor masterpiece of forgery, accurately moulded into the insignia of the Hampshire Constabulary, copied from a sheet of notepaper also scavenged from the Assistant Governor's waste-bin.

Compared to that, the shirt and tie were child's play.

Obviously he had to keep his escape-kit hidden. Cell searches generally take place in the evening during association, so he removed anything liable to cause suspicion and wore it under his prison greys. Some items the screws tolerate. They wouldn't report you for possessing pieces of cloth or a needle and thread. They're more interested in finding drugs.

With everything organized except the date, Mountjoy cultivated patience. His escape could not be hurried. Outside factors would dictate the timing. Eight months passed without a whisper to encourage him. That is, three years and eight months since he started his enforced residence in Albany. Then a new prisoner was admitted to D Hall. Manny Stokesay was a murderer, which is not unusual; he was said to have snapped a man's spine with the edge of his hand, which is. Impressive. Stokesay was a body-builder, six foot three and sixteen stone in weight. And he had an evil temper.

Within a week of Stokesay's admission, Mountjoy prepared to leave. He had seen large, dangerous prisoners before, watched them systematically ground down by the screws. This one, he reckoned, was unlikely to submit without a fight. The outcome would be bloody, if not fatal. A major disturbance inside D Hall was essential to his plan and now the chance of its happening increased day by day. He finished sewing up his black trousers. He put his police cap together. So he was committed. A cell-search now would scupper him.

But he was confident of action. The new inmate was creating tension among the prisoners. Loyalties were threatened and new alliances being formed. There are no ties of friendship in prison, only of fear. Some of the old hands decided that Stokesay was too dangerous to cross and made it known that they supported him. Others who survived by their wits set themselves up as power brokers. The prison hierarchy was shaken to its foundations by so much uncertainty.

Mountjoy was a loner. He had always resisted attempts to recruit him to one group or another. He crossed nobody and unobtrusively went about his duties. In three years, eight months and twenty-three days he had managed to avoid physical contact with inmates and screws alike. Except in combat situations.

A series of small flare-ups over several days paved the way for the big one. Three times a day in Albany the toilets are heavily in use, the last at eight-thirty p.m., just before bang-up. Precisely what was said that evening Mountjoy never discovered, because he had already washed and returned to his cell, but from the shouting carried along the landing it seemed Stokesay took offence and struck a man called Harragin. This happened in the recess, where the toilets, sinks and dustbins are housed. Harragin was no match physically for Stokesay, but he was a tough specimen, a West Indian ex-boxer with a history of violence. And he had a strong following. Two of his sidekicks were in there and went to his aid. The big newcomer thrust one of them so hard against a wash-basin that he cracked his skull. Mountjoy could hear the crunch of bone from where he was. A Caribbean voice yelled, 'You've topped him, you honkie bastard!'

Mountjoy stepped out on the landing. Someone in the recess picked up a dustbin and hurled it and bedlam ensued. The two screws meant to be supervising were bundled outside by Harragin's people. At least a dozen prisoners dashed from their cells to join in; failure to assist might have been punished later.

He told himself, this is it.

His cue.

The alarms were triggered, a horrible sound that stops anyone being heard. More screws came running to assist, but their way was barred by a heap of dustbins crushed into the space between the walls. The lads in the alcove wanted to settle their dispute without interruption. If Mountjoy had learned anything about prisoners, after a bloody maul they would join forces to keep out the screws. This had all the makings of a riot.

Mountjoy didn't have long. The screws would bang up everyone not already behind the barricade. They would come in from every section of the prison. If necessary reinforcements would be summoned from Parkhurst, the neighbouring prison.

He stepped back into his cell when the alarm went, removed his police uniform from its various hiding places and tucked it into his prison-issue wash-bowl. He closed the cell door behind him. No going back. But he had hardly started along the landing when a screw downstairs shouted up to him, 'Where the bloody hell do you think you're going?'

'Back to my cell.'

Mountjoy thanked Christ that the screw didn't usually work in D Hall. He hadn't seen where Mountjoy came from and he didn't know which cell he occupied. He shouted, 'Get in there fast, then.'

'Yes, sir.'

Of course Mountjoy didn't. He moved towards the end of the landing farthest from the disturbance. The last door was open. It was the screws' office and no one was going to be in there while there was trouble along the landing.

8

After looking over his shoulder to check that he hadn't been watched, he stepped inside his changing room. There was a table with two mugs of coffee still steaming. A girlie magazine open on a chair. A row of lockers. A notice board covered with prison bumf. A portable TV set in the corner with a repeat of *Inspector Morse* under way.

This will be one hell of a test, he thought. I dare not come out until the police are admitted to the block – as they must be if there is reason to believe a man has been killed by a prisoner. I reckon I must wait at least twenty minutes hoping that the thugs in the recess hold out that long. The most unbearable stretch of my sentence. I dare not change my clothes yet.

He could count on exclusive use of this room for as long as the disturbance lasted. Riots occur so regularly in our prisons that there is a standard procedure for dealing with them. A high priority is to make sure that there is no chance of prison officers being taken hostage, so these days there are no heroics. They don't charge the barricade at once. They bang up all the cells they can reach with safety and report downstairs to the principal officer. Some of them put on MUFTI, Minimum Use of Force Tactical Intervention gear, and get issued with crash-helmets, brown overalls, perspex shields and batons and supplies of tear-gas. This was probably happening right now, Mountjoy calculated.

In his pocket was a false moustache made from his own hair, attached to Sellotape he took from a letter. You learn to scavenge everything inside. To preserve its adhesive qualities, he hadn't once tried the tash on. If it didn't feel secure, he would abandon it, which would be a pity, because it was beautifully made, a neat strip of dark whiskers of the kind favoured by the plod. Sadly, one side wouldn't adhere. He cursed and stuffed it back in his pocket.

A rhythmic banging started up. In a moment of panic

Mountjoy thought it must be the riot shields already, much sooner than he expected. Then he got a grip on his nerves and decided the noise was coming from the far end of the landing. It had to be the mob in the recess. They must have had their punch-up and now, united against authority, they were doing their best to work up some courage. They'd have ripped out most of the plumbing and armed themselves with mop-handles.

He tried the moustache again. More pathetic than ever, a giveaway. At least he could cut off his sideboards. Anything that would alter his appearance was a bonus. He got to work with the toothbrush blade. It felt as if he was tugging out more hairs than he was cutting, but it was worth persevering, and it filled some time.

After fifteen minutes in the screws' room he put on the clothes. They were tailored to fit over his regular shirt and jeans. They had no lining of their own. He drew them on gently, fearful of ripping a seam. They felt strange. He reminded himself that they had to look convincing on a control monitor, that was all. He'd got to have confidence in them, or he would be sunk. Last, he put on the cap. It fitted snugly and felt right. No one in Albany had ever seen him in a hat. He stood up straight, shoulders back. PC 121.

Ten more minutes passed. Ten empty, dispiriting minutes. He wished he could stop the ape-men drumming. It was impossible to tell what the screws were doing. He dared not step outside until he was reasonably sure there were police in the building. He opened the door a fraction and listened.

Someone was using a loud-hailer.

The mob didn't stop to listen.

Mountjoy strained to hear what was being said.

'. . . in need of medical attention. If you refuse to let the doctor see him, the consequences could be extremely serious for you all.'

That kind of talk wouldn't impress a bunch of lifers.

He pushed the door outwards just a little more and his T-shirt felt cold against his skin. He could see a raiding party in riot gear moving along the landing towards the barricade. He pulled the door shut. This was a quicker move than he had expected. Surely they wouldn't go in? Maybe they were just assessing the situation.

Some metal object clattered along the landing. Presumably the raiding party had been spotted. A chorus of swearing followed. And the sound of more missiles hitting the iron railings.

He needed to know what was happening downstairs. Twenty-five minutes must have passed since the incident began – time enough, surely? He was going to have to make his move PDQ, or the landing would be swarming with screws. The nearest staircase was about four strides from the door. He was counting on getting down without drawing attention to himself.

He took another look. The screws had retreated apparently. The Assistant Governor – it was his voice Mountjoy heard – was issuing another warning.

'. . . reason to believe a man was seriously injured, possibly killed. I have no option but to bring this disturbance to a quick end. The prison staff have been joined by a number of police officers . . .'

That was all Mountjoy wanted to hear. He took one more look and stepped outside, moving rapidly to the staircase. It was a double flight with a small landing halfway. Eight steps down, about turn and eight steps to the ground. Then it would be time to say his prayers.

The first flight was partly sheltered from view. The second offered no protection. He remembered a clip from a film called *The Last Emperor*. That little kid stepping outside the Imperial Palace and facing a mass of people. That's how I'm going to feel any minute, he thought. Conspicuous.

As he descended, his confidence drained. What am I

11

doing for Christ's sake, dressed in dyed rags and cardboard, masquerading as a policeman? How did I ever persuade myself that this was a feasible plan?

He reached the landing and turned. Keep going, he told himself. Whoever is ahead, keep going.

There were scores of dark blue uniforms down there. Fortunately most of them weren't looking his way. The landing where the barricade was built was the focus of attention. A spotlight beam moved along the ironwork. Mountjoy started going down the stairs. To his left, at the edge of his vision, someone in a suit was issuing instructions to more of the riot squad. He looked straight ahead, trying to avoid eye contact with anyone at all, fully expecting to be challenged any second.

He reached ground level and hoped to merge with the crowd. Some of the lights had been switched off down there, he supposed to confuse the rioters, which ought to be to his advantage. He estimated fifteen paces to the first security door, but the floor was too crowded to take a straight line. It was the proverbial minefield. God, he thought, will I come face to face with a screw who knows me?

Stiff back, he told himself. Walk like a copper. What I could do with now is a personal radio to thrust in front of my face and talk into if anyone approaches me. A bit bloody late to think of it.

He was in a stupor of fear. Things were registering in slow motion as if he were just an observer. He supposed it was the stage before screaming panic sets in. Although the place was seething with screws, he hadn't spotted a single one of the fuzz yet. He didn't want to meet any, but it would be useful to know that they were there.

He was sidling around a group when the loud-hailer spoke and he reacted with such a jerk that he almost lost his cardboard cap.

'Move back under the landing,' the Assistant Governor

announced. 'We need more space here.'

He wasn't speaking just to Mountjoy. The attention shifted from upstairs. A general movement began. Someone at Mountjoy's side asked him, 'Was anyone killed up there?'

'Nobody can tell yet,' he muttered, trying to move against the tide and being forced off course. He was starting to feel like a drowning man. He hated the proximity of people, and these were *screws*. He was shoulder to shoulder with them, unable to move.

He could do nothing except shake with fear.

Behind him someone said, 'They're going in again.'

It seemed that the riot squad had taken up a position on the very staircase that Mountjoy had just come down. There was a general movement forward to get a sight of them. The congestion eased slightly and he edged to his right. He was still less than halfway across the floor to the door. So eager was he to make progress that he barged into someone and practically knocked him over.

The screw turned and stared at Mountjoy. It was Grindley, one of the SOs he saw every day. There was a petrifying moment when Grindley's eyes narrowed and he appeared to have recognized him. Mountjoy was ready to surrender. Then Grindley blinked twice. It was obvious from his face that he wasn't quite sure. He couldn't believe what he was seeing and cold reason was telling him he must be mistaken. He actually said, 'Sorry, mate.'

Mountjoy dared not speak. He nodded and moved on.

He was so close to the first door now. God help me, he said to himself – a group of police were standing beside it.

He couldn't halt in his tracks. He was on camera so he would have to act the part he was supposed to be playing.

A couple of the rozzers turned his way and looked surprised, and no wonder.

They expected him to speak, to supply some explanation for his presence. He said with all the credibility he could dredge up, 'A man is dead up there. The Governor wants us to stand by.' Then he approached the door and raised a hand to signal to the screw in the control room.

Quaking in his shoes, he waited.

One of the police said, 'You from Cowes, mate?'

He answered, 'Shanklin,' and added, 'on detachment.'

'Thought I didn't recognize you. How did you get in before us? We're just down the road.'

'A tip-off,' Mountjoy answered, and then – Praise the Lord – the door swung open. He stepped inside.

This moment over which he had lost sleep every night for years seemed like an anticlimax. He had to stand there for those seven seconds and be vetted by the team in the control room. But this place was a refuge after the ordeal he had just been through.

Nothing happened.

He waited.

He counted mentally, staring ahead.

Seven seconds had passed. *Must* have passed, he thought. He's having a long look at me.

Then the second door opened and he felt the cooler air of the central corridor on his face. He stepped forward.

He could be observed all the way now if they suspected him. He walked briskly, head erect, past the entrance to C Hall on his right and the hospital on his left. He was familiar with the route because it was the way to the classrooms and the library – always under escort, of course. The main entrance was beyond the classrooms and to the left.

B Hall was coming up. The door opened and a party of screws came out just as he was reaching there. They ran towards Mountjoy and for a sickening moment he thought they must have had instructions to stop him. But they dashed straight past, heading for the hall he'd left. He moved on and turned the corner.

14

The main entrance to the prison complex is controlled by a triple system of sliding doors. The lighting here is brilliant and Mountjoy felt certain that every stitch in the rags he was wearing must show up on the monitors. There was a bell to press, quite superfluous, he was sure.

He stood to wait, trying to achieve a compromise between confident informality and the upright bearing of your typical English bobby.

Then there was the rustle of static and a voice addressed him. 'Leaving already, officer?'

He supplied the answer he'd had ready in case he met anyone. 'Hasn't the support arrived? I'm supposed to brief them.'

The first door slid across.

'Thank you.'

He stepped forward.

He waited.

The second door opened.

And the third.

In the real world it was dark by this time, but the towering floodlights made a gleaming desert of the prison yard. He had at least six shadows radiating from his feet. Parked outside the main entrance were two red-striped police cars. Knowing that he was under video-surveillance he paused by the nearer car and leaned on the window frame for a few seconds as if making a radio report. Then he started marching across the yard towards the gatehouse.

A dog barked and its handler shouted something to disabuse the animal of its conviction that John Mountjoy was an escapee. More barking followed. At least two dog-patrols were on the perimeter, by the first of the two fifteen-metre fences inside the wall. He still had to bluff his way through four gates.

And now he believed he would.

Chapter Two

'I was offered a job today.'

Stephanie Diamond lowered the evening paper sufficiently to look over the top edge and see if her husband
was serious. 'A proper job?'

'That's open to debate.'

On the kitchen table between them was a three-quarters
empty bottle of cheap red wine and a dish that had
contained shepherd's pie. The cork was already back in
the wine to keep it from turning sour by next day.
Stephanie limited them to one glass, not for reasons of
health, but housekeeping. The Diamonds had learned to
live prudently, if not frugally, in their basement flat in
Addison Road, Kensington.

Supper was a precious interval in the day, the first
chance to relax together. If anything of interest had
happened, this was when they mentioned it. They didn't
always speak. Stephanie liked to work through the quick
crossword on the back page of the *Evening Standard*. She
generally needed to unwind after her afternoon serving in
the Oxfam shop. It was difficult not to be irked by
well-to-do Knightsbridge women who ransacked the rail
for designer labels at bargain prices and still asked for a
reduction.

Peter Diamond rarely glanced at the paper these days.
Most of what they printed put him into black moods. He
had stopped watching the television except for rugby and

boxing. There was too much about the police – too much on the news and too much drama. He was trying to forget.

'But you've already got a job,' Stephanie said.

He nodded. 'This is an evening job, as a model.'

She stared. Her mind was still on the fashion trade. 'What?'

'A model. This character with a bow-tie and a tartan waistcoat approached me in Sainsbury's. They're short of male models at Chelsea College.'

She put down the paper. 'An *artist's* model?'

'Right.'

'With your figure?'

'My figure is simply crying out to be captured in charcoal, according to my new friend. I have a Rubenesque form and challenging contours.'

'Did he say that?'

'Have you ever heard me talk that way?'

'You wouldn't pose naked?'

'Why not?' This was a favourite game, starting with a doubtful premise that he proceeded to develop with high seriousness. Better still when Steph took it all as gospel. 'The pay isn't bad.'

'I don't think I want my husband exposing himself to a roomful of students.'

'You make it sound like a criminal offence.'

'Some of them are straight out of school. Young girls.'

'I'm sure they'll hold themselves in check,' he said in the same reasonable tone. 'My challenging contours may set their pulses racing, but these classes are supervised, you know.'

He had overplayed his hand. Stephanie said, 'I think you made this up.'

'I swear I didn't. He gave me his card with a phone number to ring.'

She was silent for a while. Then she said, 'What's a seven-letter word meaning "odd"?'

17

'Is that what you think of my efforts to supplement our income?'

'No, it's in the crossword.'

'I've no idea. I wouldn't waste time on it if I were you.'

She countered with, 'Perhaps if you did, you might still have a good job in the police.'

He grinned amiably. 'No, crosswords in themselves wouldn't be enough. You also have to listen to opera in the car.' Almost two years had gone by since he had rashly resigned his job as a detective superintendent in the Avon and Somerset Police. It seemed longer. Between bouts of unemployment he'd scraped a living serving in a bar, taking turns as Father Christmas, guarding Harrods, helping in a school for the handicapped, delivering newspapers and – currently – collecting supermarket trolleys from a car park. Now was not an auspicious time to be middle-aged and looking for salaried employment.

Stephanie's job as a school meals supervisor had come to an end in July, when cuts were made in local authority spending. She had tried repeatedly to find paid employment since then. She said wistfully, 'Speaking of the old days, there was a programme about the Kennet and Avon Canal the other afternoon.'

Now it was his turn to be surprised. 'I didn't know boats interested you.'

'They don't. It was the scenery. The views of Bath. You remember how elegant it could look with the sun on those long Georgian terraces? That honey-coloured glow that I've never seen anywhere else?'

Picking his words carefully, because one of the reasons why he loved her was that she had taught him to see so much he had never noticed before, he said, 'Actually, I remember being mightily relieved to get out of the centre on those warm afternoons when the place looked like a picture postcard and felt like a Turkish bath. I can't see us ever getting back there, Steph, except on a day visit. It was a phase in our lives, a reasonably happy one. Let's settle for that.'

She said, 'It's hard work. Harder than you think.'

'What is?'

'Posing for a life class.'

Something in her tone made him hesitate. 'How would you know?'

She smiled faintly. 'When I was single and needed pocket money I did some modelling at the local tech.'

She had ambushed him properly this time. He was appalled. She always spoke the truth.

'Nude, you mean?'

'Mm.'

'You've never told me that.'

She said, 'It's not the sort of thing one drops into a conversation. Anyway, I wouldn't do it now.' After a pause she added, 'But then I haven't been asked.'

He recovered his poise sufficiently to say, 'If you like, I can put in a word for you at Chelsea College.'

'Don't you dare.'

There was another silence.

'I think it's strange,' Diamond finally said.

She reddened and her eyes narrowed. 'What is?'

'The seven-letter word you wanted.'

Much later, in bed, he told her, 'It's too bloody late to say this, Steph, but I was an idiot to quit the police. That day I stormed out of the ACC's office, I had no idea we'd end up like this, in a squalid basement in the back streets.'

'Do you mind? It isn't squalid at all. I keep it clean.'

'Humble, then.'

'And I don't see how you can possibly describe Addison Road as a back street. Just listen. No, listen to the traffic. It's gone midnight and it still sounds like Piccadilly.'

He wouldn't be shaken from his confessional mood. 'If it were just my own life, fair enough, but it was yours and you had no say in the decision. It was the most selfish bloody thing I've ever done.'

She said, 'It was a question of principle.'

'Yes, mine, not yours.'

'If they didn't appreciate your worth as a detective, they didn't deserve to keep you.'

He gave a short, sardonic laugh. 'They were only too happy to get shot of me.' He sighed, turned over and talked to the wall. 'I deserved to go. I didn't fit in.'

Stephanie wriggled towards him. 'Yes, you're a brute to be with.'

'Inconsiderate,' said he.

'Tactless,' said she.

'Boorish.'

'And self-pitying.' She tugged at his pyjama trousers and slapped his exposed rear. 'Does that make you feel any better?'

'Not really.'

'Spoilsport.'

'Who's talking about sport?'

She pressed against him and whispered in his ear, 'I am.'

Apparently the fates wanted some sport as well, because at this intimate moment came the scrape of shoes on the concrete steps outside.

'What the heck . . .?'

'Some drunks, I expect,' murmured Stephanie.

'Or kids, messing about. Sounds like more than one to me.'

'Kids at this hour?'

They lay still and waited.

'Can't even find the bell,' said Diamond.

On cue, the bell was rung.

'What sort of time is this?' muttered Diamond. 'It must be after midnight.'

'It is. Are you going?'

'Sod that. I'm not at home to anyone. I'll look through

20

the curtain.' He got up and went to the window. Two youngish men in padded jackets were standing out there faintly illuminated by a streetlamp. They didn't look drunk. 'I'm foxed,' said Diamond.

Stephanie sat up and put on the bedside lamp.

'Switch it off!' Diamond hissed at her.

But the callers must have seen the light because they rang again and rattled the knocker as well.

'I'd better go.'

'Do you think you should? They can't be up to any good at this hour.'

'I'll keep the chain on.' He reached for his dressing-gown. The knocking continued, loud enough to disturb the entire house, so he shouted, 'All right, all right.'

He opened the front door the fraction the safety chain allowed, and looked out.

'Mr Peter Diamond?'

He frowned. A couple of passing drunks wouldn't have known his name. 'Yes?'

'I'm Detective Inspector Smith and this is Sergeant Brown. Avon and Somerset CID.'

'*Avon and Somerset?* You're way off your patch, aren't you?'

'Would you mind if we come in?' The man held a police identity card close enough to the crack for Diamond to see that he was, indeed, called Smith. If you'd wanted to invent a couple of names, would you seriously have chosen Smith and Brown?

'It's bloody late, you know,' Diamond complained. 'What's this about? Has somebody died?'

'No, sir.'

'Well, then?'

'Could we discuss it inside, Mr Diamond?'

He had to admit that this was authentic CID-speak for dealing with a potential witness – or humouring a dangerous suspect. 'I'm ex-CID myself. I know my rights.'

'Yes, sir.'

'If I'm under suspicion of something, I want to be told what it is.'

'You can rest assured about that, sir. We're not here to interview you.'

'But you're up from Somerset, so it isn't just a social call.'

'Right, sir. It's urgent, or we wouldn't be disturbing you.'

Diamond unfastened the chain. At the same time he called out to Stephanie, wanting to put her mind at rest and realizing as the words came out that he would not succeed, 'It's all right, love. They're CID.'

He led them into the living room. Both officers took stock of the place with expressions suggesting that they couldn't understand how a former superintendent had sunk so low.

'Coffee?'

'Please phone this number immediately, Mr Diamond.' Inspector Smith handed across a piece of paper and added in an afterthought, 'You *do* have a phone?'

Diamond walked to it.

He noticed Sergeant Brown turn and close the door, and it wasn't to stop a draught. They wanted to prevent Steph from hearing what was said. This cloak and dagger stuff was tiresome.

He pressed out the number.

It didn't have to ring more than a couple of times. A voice said, 'Yes?'

'Diamond speaking.'

'Excellent. I'm Farr-Jones, Chief Constable of Avon and Somerset. I don't believe we have met.'

If they had, they wouldn't have spent long in each other's company. Farr-Jones's voice was redolent of golf clubs and smart dinner parties that Diamond would have avoided like the plague. But the name was familiar. Patrick Farr-Jones had been appointed to Avon and Somerset about eighteen months ago after serving as ACC in Norfolk. The Chief Constable sitting up to take a call in the small hours? This had to be high level.

22

'You probably guess what has prompted this call, Mr Diamond,' the velvet tones articulated.

'No,' said Diamond.

The terse response derailed Mr Farr-Jones. He evidently wanted some co-operation, so after a short hiatus he started again with a compliment. 'Well said. A good detective assumes nothing.'

'I'm not a detective any more, Mr Farr-Jones.'

'True, but—'

'And it's debatable whether I was ever a good detective.'

'My information is that you were very good.'

'Pity nobody thought so at the time,' said Diamond. 'What should I have guessed? If it was something in the papers, I don't read them, except to look for jobs.'

'You haven't heard about Mountjoy, then?'

An image from years ago flickered in his brain: a bedroom, a woman's body on the bed in pale blue pyjamas bloodied with stab wounds. And there was a bizarre feature that had got into all the papers. Stuffed into her mouth and scattered across her body were the heads of a dozen red roses in bud. This ritualistic feature of the murder had created a sensation at the time. 'What about Mountjoy?'

'I'm surprised you haven't heard. It was all over the papers last week. He's out. He escaped from Albany.'

'God help us!'

On October 22, 1990, Diamond had arrested John Grainger Mountjoy for the murder of Britt Strand, a journalist, in a flat in Larkhall, Bath. He had been sentenced to life imprisonment.

Farr-Jones added, 'He's made his way here. An incident has occurred, an extremely serious incident.'

'And you believe it's Mountjoy?'

'We're certain.'

'How do I come into this?'

'We need you here. It's essential that you come.'

23

'Hold on, Mr Farr-Jones. I quit two years ago. I'm not on the strength any more.'

'Kindly hear me out, Mr Diamond. This is more than a dangerous man on the run. He's created an emergency, a major emergency, and I can't say any more than that over the phone except that we have asked for and achieved a press embargo. As an ex-superintendent you'll appreciate that we don't go to such lengths unless it is justified by the sensitivity of the incident.'

'And you think I can help?'

'It isn't like that.'

'What is it like, exactly?'

'Didn't I just say that I can't go into details?'

'Why not, if there's an embargo? Surely that makes it safe to talk.'

'Please don't be difficult. I know this is a wretched time to be disturbed, but take my word for it, there is an overriding necessity for you to come.'

'You mean right away?'

'The officers who are with you now have instructions to drive you here. As soon as you arrive you will be fully briefed.'

'And if I decline?'

'I would still require the officers to drive you here.'

Diamond was tempted to ask what the purpose of the phone call had been if he was being carted off to Bath willy-nilly, but he restrained himself. 'I'd better get some clothes on, then, but no obligation. You do appreciate I'm not in the police any more?'

He showed Smith and Brown where the coffee things were and went back to the bedroom to break the news of his departure to Stephanie. He told her as much as he knew; after all, she was entitled to be told and he was under no obligation of secrecy. She found it difficult to credit that the police wanted him back after the angry scene when he had quit. In his heavy-handed way he had

24

been a good detective, but no one is irreplaceable. She asked how long he would be there and he reminded her that Bath was only a couple of hours' drive. He promised to phone her in the morning.

To make light of it, he said, 'Well, I suppose it beats posing in the nude.'

Stephanie said, 'Don't count on it.'

Chapter Three

Sergeant Brown drove as if he wanted to get airborne. The streets of West London were a blur from the back seat of the red Montego heading for the M4. Peter Diamond, never comfortable in cars, tried repeatedly to get a conversation going, but neither of his escorts would be charmed or bullied into disclosing any more about the 'major emergency' being used to justify this extraordinary night exercise. By Junction Three Diamond had concluded that they were just dogsbodies who knew nothing.

He changed the subject and asked for news of the current personnel in the Avon and Somerset CID. Evidently a shake-out had taken place since the new Chief Constable had arrived. Of the murder squad of two years ago – Diamond's team – only two senior detectives remained. As many as seven had been transferred to other duties or had taken early retirement. The survivors were Keith Halliwell, charming, but a lightweight, and John Wigfull, the fast-track career man with the staff college mentality. Wigfull had been elevated to the rank of Chief Inspector. He now headed the squad.

Diamond closed his eyes and told himself it was all behind him. What did it matter to him personally if a toe-rag like Wigfull had the top job?

'Good thinking,' said Smith.

'What?'

'Getting some shut-eye while you can.'

'The speed we're going, it could be permanent.'

However, Diamond did drift off.

When he woke, prepared to find himself in intensive care, they were at Membury Services, sixty miles on. A petrol-stop.

'I don't know about you fellows, but I wouldn't say no to a coffee,' he suggested.

'We'll be there in under the hour,' said Smith.

'Under three-quarters,' said Brown. 'Have a coffee when we get there.'

'By then I'll need something stronger than coffee.'

The last stretch, over the rump of the Cotswolds on the A46 after leaving the motorway, gave Brown the opportunity to bring the experience to a heart-thumping climax, leaving tyre marks at intervals on the winding descent from Cold Ashton, beside what Diamond knew was a sheer drop of several hundred feet if the car left the road.

In other circumstances the night panorama of Bath with its myriad lights spreading out from the floodlit Abbey would have been a welcome sight. He saved his approval for the moment they turned right on to the level stretch of the London Road.

'Good.'

'Good driving, or good to be here?' said Smith.

'What time is it?'

'Just after three.'

'All of two hours. What kept us so long?'

Smith and Brown were easy targets. He looked forward to sharper exchanges presently.

'Who will I see at the nick? Who are the insomniacs on the roster?'

Smith didn't know, or didn't care to answer.

The car drew up at the entrance to Manvers Street Police Station and Diamond, buoyant after surviving the trip, went in with Smith to get the answer to his question.

The public reception area had been altered since Diamond's day, drastically reduced in size by partitioning. The silver trophies won by the force remained on display in a glass cabinet, practically daring the local smash and grab lads to have a try. A round mirror was strategically placed to give a view of anyone entering. The desk sergeant operated from behind protective glass, like a bank clerk. He was one of the old hands and his face lit up. 'Mr Diamond! It's a real tonic to see you again.' A warmer welcome than old acquaintance merited. Diamond wasn't fooled: it said more about the new regime than his own lovability.

Smith escorted him upstairs to the room the top brass used as an office when they visited. Ironically, it was the same room Diamond had stormed out of the last time he had been here. That ill-starred morning, Mr Tott, the Assistant Chief Constable, in uniform, every button fastened, had been at the far end of the oval mahogany table to inform Diamond he was being taken off the murder inquiry he was heading and replaced by Wigfull. The offence? He had allegedly caused concussion to a turbulent twelve-year-old who had kicked him in the privates. All he had done was push the boy aside, against a wall. Young Matthew had later admitted he was faking the concussion, but by then Diamond had resigned.

The door stood open.

'Go right in,' said Smith. 'Mr Tott is waiting.'

Diamond slapped a hand against the door-frame. 'Did you say Tott? I don't believe this.'

'The ACC,' Smith whispered reverentially.

'I know who he is,' Diamond said in a voice that must have carried into the room. 'I don't wish to speak to him.' He turned away from the door and started back along the corridor to the stairs. He wasn't sure where he was heading except away from that bloody man he despised. The anger he thought he had dissipated two years ago had him seething.

Smith came after him and caught him by the arm. 'What's wrong? What did I say?'

'Just enough to prevent carnage.'

'I don't understand.'

'Don't worry. It's no concern of yours.'

'But it is. I was supposed to bring you to that room. They're waiting in there to speak to you. It's the middle of the night, for pity's sake! Where are you going?'

'As far away from that dip-stick as I can. I'm a civilian. I don't have to grovel.'

He continued downstairs.

'I can't let you do this, Mr Diamond,' Smith called after him. 'You can't leave the building.'

'Try and stop me,' the ex-detective shouted back. 'Do you have a warrant?'

Upon reaching the ground floor, he walked briskly to the entrance hall, past his friend the desk sergeant without so much as a look, through the double doors and out into the night air.

Tott.

He said aloud, 'What kind of plonker do they take me for?'

He strode up Manvers Street in a state of outrage; a case of rocketing hypertension. Some way up the street he realized that spots before the eyes are not a healthy sign, and he had better talk himself into a calmer frame of mind. At least he'd had the gumption to walk out. He ought to be feeling better for asserting his independence. He would try the Francis Hotel in Queen Square; a congenial place to get his head on a pillow until morning, when he would return home by train. At lunch-times in the old days when things were quiet at the nick he had sometimes popped into the Roman Bar at the Francis for a beer. In more benevolent moods than this he had basked in the plush ambience suggestive of less stressful times. It was easy to picture city worthies in pinstripes, with waistcoats and watch-chains, entertaining flighty young ladies in cloche hats.

Bath's city centre was safer for walking than London would have been at that hour. The only people he saw were a group of homeless men huddled around the grille behind the Roman Baths where the warm air was emitted. Safe it might be, but the option of spending the rest of the night on the streets had no appeal. If the hotel wouldn't give him a room at this hour, he'd make his way to the railway station and wait for the first train.

Ahead was the glass and iron portico of the Francis, facing the stately trees and unsightly obelisk of Queen Square. He was within a few paces of the revolving door when a police car with flashing beacon screeched around the corner of Chapel Row towards him, disregarding the one-way route around the square.

There is nowhere to step out of sight on the south side of Queen Square. No lanes, passages or shop doorways. There are just the railings fronting the hotel. Diamond wasn't built for running or jumping and he didn't fancy entering the lobby with policemen in pursuit, so he stepped to the kerb and waited.

The patrol car stopped and someone in a leather jacket and jeans got out of the passenger seat. Diamond registered first that she was female and second that he recognized her. His memory for names wasn't so bad as he had feared. Julie Hargreaves had been a sergeant in the CID at Headquarters when last they'd met. She had impressed him as an able and dependable detective.

Disarmed, he relaxed his posture and grinned. 'It's a fair cop, guv. You've got me bang to rights.'

She smiled back. 'I was willing to bet you'd make for the Francis.'

'My old watering hole.'

'Smithie's checking Pratt's.'

'It takes one to know one,' he commented. 'Are you

30

going to put an arm-lock on me, Julie?'

She said, 'I ought to. You're the most wanted man in Bath.'

Sensing that she might be willing to share some information, he said seriously, 'I wish someone would tell me why. Mr Tott appears to think he still has the right to have me hauled out of bed, driven a hundred and twenty miles and dragged before him in the middle of the night. I foolishly assumed that the Gestapo was a thing of the past.'

She said, 'Pardon me, Mr Diamond. We've got a real emergency on.'

'So I was told.'

'It wasn't Mr Tott who sent for you.'

'No, that's true,' he conceded. 'It was the Great White Chief, Farr-Jones.'

'Mr Tott isn't calling the shots. He's involved, but only as a victim.'

'A *victim*?'

'In a sense. Well, strictly speaking he isn't a victim himself.' Floundering, she said finally, 'But his daughter is.'

'Tott's daughter?'

'Look, would you forget I told you that?' She glanced over her shoulder towards her driver. He was talking into the intercom, so she added, 'They mean to brief you in their own way. They're counting on your co-operation, absolutely counting on it.'

'What can I do that other people can't?'

'You've got to hear it from them, Mr Diamond. The whole incident is under wraps.'

He stopped himself from asking, 'What incident?' To pump Julie for information that he could get legitimately would be unfair. He knew what he must do. The repugnance he felt at facing Tott was a personal matter. His self-esteem had to be weighed against whatever had happened to the man's daughter and the fact that for some arcane reason his co-operation was indispensable.

Julie said simply, 'Will you come back to Manvers Street with me and hear what they have to say?'

'All right, Sarge. You win.'

In the car she told him they had made her up to inspector last November. He said it was not before time. And he meant it.

Five minutes later, practically vomiting with revulsion, he was eye to eye with Tott, that relic from the days when top policemen were indistinguishable from First World War generals. The others around the oval table were Chief Inspector John Wigfull, Inspector Julie Hargreaves and Inspector Keith Halliwell. The reception he was given was so unlikely that it was alarming. Tott got up, came around the table and said how deeply they were in his debt for coming. Not only did he grip Diamond's hand with his right, but held his elbow with his left and squeezed it like an over-zealous freemason.

Halliwell's greeting was a tilt of the head and a companionable grin. Wigfull summoned up the kind of smile the losing finalist gives at Wimbledon.

Diamond gave them all a sniff and a stare.

Tott turned to Wigfull. 'Why don't you see what happened to the coffee we ordered?'

Wigfull reddened and left the room.

Tott said immediately the door closed, 'Mr Diamond, this won't be easy for any of us. John Wigfull is the senior man now. He's running the show.'

'Seeing that I'm no longer a part of the show, I don't have any problem with that,' said Diamond.

Tott lowered his face and brought his hands together under his chin. The body language was that of a penitent at confession. 'I . . . I want to make a personal statement. It would be remarkable if you didn't harbour some resentment against me for matters I hope we can set aside tonight. I want to assure you that my involvement is quite unsought on my part. But I thought I should be here

32

when you arrived. I owed it to you.'

'To me? I can't think why.'

'And to my . . . to someone else. Avon and Somerset Police are seeking your co-operation. I, personally, want to appeal to you – no damn it – *beg* you to listen sympathetically, and as we parted on less than friendly terms when we were last in this room together, the least I can do is—'

'Point taken, Mr Tott,' said Diamond. 'I said what I felt at the time. I didn't expect to be invited back, but here I am.'

'Thank you.'

'Now will somebody tell me why?'

Tott was overwrought. His voice was faltering. He said, 'I think it best if I leave that to Chief Inspector Wigfull. He should be back any second.'

Tott and Wigfull. What a team! Diamond couldn't think of any two people outside prison he'd rather avoid.

A cadet came in with coffee and cheese and ham sandwiches. Wigfull glided in behind him and took his place at the table. Diamond noted sardonically that Wigfull's elevation to head of the murder squad had produced one interesting change: his moustache had been trimmed. These days he was more like the former English cricket captain than the Laughing Cavalier.

'I believe you're going to brief me, John.'

'Presently.' Wigfull waited for the cadet to leave. When the door was closed he glanced towards Tott, an observance of courtesy or bootlicking, depending how you viewed it, and received a nod. 'Ten days ago, as you know, that is on October the fourth, John Mountjoy escaped from Albany.'

'You say "as you know", but I know damn all,' said Diamond.

Wigfull gave him a disbelieving look. 'It's been in all the papers.'

33

'I don't see the papers. I'm a free man, John. I do as I like.'

'Well, he bluffed his way through God knows how many electronically locked doors disguised as a police officer. To be fair to the prison staff there was a disturbance in one of the halls at the time. It hasn't been established yet whether the trouble was started deliberately as a cover for the escape. Anyway, Mountjoy had up to two hours' start before the alarm was raised. He is either foolhardy or extremely cunning because instead of heading straight for the road he made his way towards the neighbouring prison at Parkhurst, which you'll know is just across a field from Albany. There, he visited the married quarters and stole a Metro belonging to a prison officer's wife. It was found abandoned two days later at Bembridge.'

'That's an odd way to go. Isn't Bembridge way out on the eastern tip of the Island?'

'This man does nothing predictable. While all places north of Albany were being combed, he stole a small sailing dinghy, a Mirror, from outside a holiday cottage near the harbour.'

'Lucky.'

'Not really. He had the choice of several. People are slaphappy with their boats on the Island. The owner left all the gear on board. All Mountjoy had to do was wheel the thing down to the beach under cover of darkness, poke under the cover and take out the sails and rig it.'

'Where did he learn to sail?'

'Does it matter?' said Tott, betraying impatience.

'It must have mattered to him when he launched the boat.'

Wigfull said as if it shouldn't be necessary to state the obvious, 'He went to school at Eastbourne. Public school.'

Diamond – the product of a grammar school – stoutly refused to take anything for granted. 'Do they teach the boys to sail?'

'Generally in Mirrors.'

Wigfull's inside knowledge of the public school system was matched by the expertise he had just acquired in sailing. 'He must have launched it under cover of darkness, and sailed hard eastward. There was a flood tide during those nights that would tend to drag him towards Portsmouth and he actually navigated it across fifteen miles of sea to West Wittering.'

'How do you know all this?'

'The owner came down from London to shut up the cottage at Bembridge and found his boat missing. Bits of the hull have been found all along the foreshore at West Wittering. He might have assumed Mountjoy had drowned if a local farmer hadn't found some sails and a lifejacket bundled in a hedge. Meanwhile there were search teams combing the Island between Albany and Cowes, every ferry was under observation and helicopters were patrolling the Solent.'

'And he made his way to Bath?'

Wigfull gave a nod. 'Everything I tell you now is under embargo. The media will have to hold off until we resolve it one way or another. Nothing was heard of Mountjoy for almost a week. Then yesterday evening a phone call was taken by the switchboard operator at the Royal Crescent Hotel. The caller was male, an educated voice. He told the girl to write down what he said and see that it reached the police as soon as possible. This is what we were given.' He handed across a sheet from a message pad with the Royal Crescent heading.

Diamond gave it a glance intended at first to demonstrate his reluctance to be involved, but the sight of his name in the message was irresistible. He picked it up and read:

Mr Tott, for the girl's sake, tell Diamond to be ready with a car tomorrow at 9 a.m. He is to be alone. No radio and no bugs and no one to follow. Remember I have nothing to lose.

'*The girl*? Is it a kidnap, then?' Diamond said, and without letting his eyes meet Julie's he went on blandly to ask, 'Do we know who she is?'

'My daughter Samantha,' said Tott, his voice breaking with emotion.

'Ah.'

After a deferential pause, Wigfull added, 'Which is why we are so concerned.'

'You'd be concerned whoever it was,' Diamond snapped back at him. 'Wouldn't you, John?'

Tott glossed over any embarrassment Wigfull may have felt by saying, 'She is a musician. She trained at the Menuhin School.'

'A stunningly attractive young woman,' said Wigfull.

'Is that significant?' said Diamond with a glance towards Julie, who might agree that sexism had just reared its head.

'Yes, it *is* significant,' said Tott. 'Everyone remarks how lovely she is, and if that sounds like a doting father speaking, so be it. About five weeks ago, the *Daily Express* magazine section ran a feature about talented musicians forced by the recession to work as street entertainers. A picture was published of Sam playing her violin in Abbey Churchyard, outside the Pump Room. I'm sure her looks must have influenced the picture editor. Unfortunately the text mentioned that she was the daughter of the Assistant Chief Constable. We assume that Mountjoy saw the paper in prison.'

'How long has she been missing?'

Wigfull answered, 'Since Saturday evening.'

'Officially missing, I mean.'

Tott coughed and said, 'Sam is rather a law unto herself. We didn't take her absence seriously until this arrived.'

'This doesn't mention her by name.'

Wigfull said, 'There are no fresh reports of missing girls. And the message takes it as read that we know who she is.'

'How old is your daughter, Mr Tott?'

'Twenty-two.'

'How would she bear up under this kind of ordeal?'

'She is pretty strong.' Tott's mouth twitched. 'But there are limits.'

Diamond pressed his hands against the edge of the table and drew back. The role of interrogator was tempting him. He examined the slip of paper again as if he needed to confirm what was written there. 'Why me?'

'You put him away,' said Wigfull. 'He's been in Albany all this time. He isn't to know that you quit two years ago.'

'Yes, but what does he want from me?'

Tott said, 'I believe he protested his innocence at the time.'

'Who doesn't at the time?' said Diamond. 'He was guilty. The man has a history of violence to women.' He turned to Tott. 'I'm sorry, but we all know this to be a fact.'

Tott nodded and closed his eyes.

Wigfull said, 'By coming here instead of holing up somewhere, he's taking a big risk. We think he must want to bargain with you.'

'Bargain over what? I can't help him. I couldn't help him if I was still on the strength. I'm not the Home Secretary. It's gone through the courts, for heaven's sake.'

Wigfull said, 'Peter, with respect I think you're missing the point.'

So it was Peter now, qualified quickly by 'with respect'. Things had moved on in two years.

'Explain,' said Diamond.

'The latest thinking about kidnap incidents is that you listen to their demands. What matters is that you establish contact and if possible build a relationship with the kidnapper. The aim is to assess the situation. Only then can you confidently form a plan to secure the release of the victim.'

What a pompous sod, thought Diamond. 'You play along with him.'

'Exactly. Find out what he wants and keep him from turning violent. His demands may be impossible – we don't know yet – but we have to appear to be willing to negotiate.'

'And I'm the fall guy?'

Wigfull shrugged. 'He asked for you. As I just said, the first principle—'

'Save it, then,' Diamond cut him short. 'You want me to humour John Mountjoy. Seeing that I sent him down, it looks a non-starter.'

'He asked for you by name.'

'How touching! Let's face it, he wants the pleasure of blowing me away. What protection would I get? None. I can see it in your eyes.'

'We don't know that he is armed,' Wigfull said.

Deciding apparently that this was not the best line to pursue, Tott said to Diamond, 'My dear fellow, I won't deny that there is a risk. Of course there's a risk. I don't know if you happen to be a father—'

'No,' said Diamond.

'Oh.' Tott wasn't up to this. His attempt at persuasion ground to a halt.

It was Julie Hargreaves who remarked quietly, 'It's going to take an act of courage to save this young girl.'

Diamond was not an obvious hero; but he had an old-fashioned dislike of appearing a coward, particularly in front of a woman. Instead of backing off completely, he said, 'Have there been any sightings of Mountjoy in this area? If his picture has been in the papers, there are going to be sightings.'

'None in Bath,' said Wigfull. 'Practically every other city up and down the land, but you know what Bath is like.'

Diamond grunted his assent. Whether the city's architecture was the distraction, he didn't know, but the public seemed to lose the capacity to recognize faces. Members of the royal family sometimes shopped in Milsom Street and rarely got a second glance.

'You'll get sod all help from the locals while you have this press embargo. Have you thought about lifting it?'

Tott gripped the arms of his chair. 'I don't think that would be wise.'

'We'd rather keep the incident under wraps for all sorts of reasons,' said Wigfull.

'Like the reputation of Avon and Somerset CID?'

Wigfull was too polished a diplomat to hit back. He gave Diamond a look that was more injured than angry. 'The main point is to deny Mountjoy the opportunity of manipulating the media. He's no fool.'

Tott added. 'And we don't want the press or the public to hamper this operation.'

'It's an operation, is it?' said Diamond.

'Investigation, then. Call it what you will.'

'I'm not bothered about the terminology, Mr Tott. I'm simply making the point that if you want me in on this, I'm entitled to know the ground plan.'

'Absolutely,' agreed Tott, straightening in his chair, grabbing at what he took to be a lifeline.

'What has happened up to now?'

With a wave of his right hand Tott invited John Wigfull to respond. 'We're following the usual procedure for a kidnapping. Extensive searches of likely places within a five-mile radius of the city centre.'

'That's a lot of places.'

'We've got a lot of men deployed. Obviously we're double-checking all reported break-ins and thefts of vehicles.'

'You believe he's in the city?'

'He must have come in to snatch Samantha. She was busking in Stall Street.'

'What do you mean by "snatch"? You wouldn't snatch a girl out of Stall Street on Saturday afternoon. It's awash with shoppers and tourists. Was she busking alone?'

'Yes.'

'Positively seen?'

Wigfull nodded. 'One of her friends saw her playing at about four-fifteen. That was Una Moon, the same young woman who told us on Monday that she was missing. Miss Tott lives with a number of other young people in a house in Widcombe.'

'A squat, do you mean?'

Tott shifted uneasily. 'Yes, it is a property occupied by unemployed young people. She left home almost a year ago, against our wishes I'm sorry to say.'

If Samantha had rebelled against Mr Tott, she was in good company and there was something to be said for her. 'Presumably your search squads have a picture.'

Julie Hargreaves produced a five-by-seven black and white print from her folder and passed it across the table. The original must have come from the Tott family album, for it showed a young girl in a taffeta evening gown with old-fashioned bouffant sleeves of the kind favoured by young musicians on the concert platform. She was dangling a violin by her right leg and a bow by her left. A striking face with large, dark eyes and a finely shaped mouth that curved upwards at the ends and so undermined the formality of the pose. Her hair was sensational – heaps upon heaps of natural curls in a triumphant version of the Afro style. Even more sensational when compared with her father's flat-to-the-head short back and sides.

'Presumably she wasn't dressed like this on Saturday?'

Julie Hargreaves answered, 'A black knitted top and blue jeans with black tights underneath. Plus long black socks. It gets cold on the streets. And a well-worn pair of Reebok trainers. She had her violin with her, of course,

40

and the case.'

'And the violin hasn't been found?'

'No.'

Diamond reached for a sandwich. Whether by accident or design he tipped two more on the table and added them to his plate. While the others watched this manoeuvre he said casually, 'What's the plan, John?'

This bolt from the blue shocked Wigfull into displacement activity: a hand dragged down the side of his face, a shuffling of shoes and some hefty throat-clearing. 'That depends whether we have your co-operation,' he said finally.

'No it doesn't,' said Diamond. 'Look we're not haggling in a Cairo bazaar. You have a plan and I'm entitled to hear it.'

'True.'

'Well?'

'Em . . .'

'Yes?'

'We, em, we recommend that you go along with whatever arrangement Mountjoy suggests. We'll supply a car for you fitted with a monitoring device.'

'Mountjoy doesn't suggest that. He prohibits it. Specifically.'

Wigfull nodded. 'But the bugs we use are so incredibly small now that it would be quite impossible for him to locate it, short of dismantling the car in a garage. We can monitor your position and keep a discreet surveillance. I emphasize discreet, Peter. There's no question of moving in while you are with him. The object will be to track him afterwards.'

'To the place where Samantha is being held?'

'Hopefully, yes.'

'I'm glad you say hopefully,' commented Diamond. 'I can't see Mountjoy falling for this. He's not so naive as to believe you wouldn't use bugs just because he asked. My

41

guess is that he'd have a stolen vehicle at the rendezvous ready to drive me off to some remote place where he'd top me before you lot blew the whistle.'

Wigfull shook his head. 'He isn't out to kill you.'

'How do you know what's in his mind?'

'It would destroy his case. He claims he was stitched up.'

The blood pressure peaked again. 'I didn't stitch him up. Are you suggesting I was corrupt as well as bloody-minded?'

Tott said, 'Take it easy, Mr Diamond.'

'I withdraw "stitched up",' said Wigfull. 'He claims there was a miscarriage of justice, that in fact he was innocent of murder. He has maintained this consistently since he was sentenced. Through his solicitor he has three times asked for leave to appeal. The governor of Albany informed us that the man is untiring in protesting his innocence. This isn't a thug who wants to murder the officer who put him away.'

'Mountjoy is a killer,' said Diamond. 'We all know it – don't we?'

'Regardless of that—'

'You're joking!'

Wigfull continued doggedly, 'He believes he has grounds for appeal. All his requests have been turned down. We think he wants to canvass your support. I know he's in cloud cuckoo land. We all remember the Britt Strand case and there wasn't any doubt. But Mountjoy has pinned his hopes on an appeal. This meeting with you is consistent with that.'

'He's a killer.'

Julie Hargreaves said, 'Which is why Samantha's life is in danger.'

Diamond gave Julie a look more surprised than reproachful. He hadn't expected her to wade in as well. She, too, had succumbed to the pressure. Never under-estimate the sisterly bond one woman feels for another in trouble.

Tott tried putting the argument into a topical context. 'All these verdicts being overturned in recent years. What publicity they get! Everyone in prison draws encouragement.'

'Mountjoy hasn't a snowball's chance in hell.'

'Agreed, but that isn't the point,' said Wigfull. 'He believes he has grounds for appeal. A few years in Albany would convince anyone that he deserves a retrial. They find any damned thing to pin their hopes on. Look, why else has he come to Bath, where it happened? He had the chance to go into hiding or leave the country. He came here.'

'This is all pie in the sky,' said Diamond. 'You don't know what's in his mind.'

'I'm interpreting his actions. We'll know what's in his mind later.'

'I can tell you now,' said Diamond. 'Violence.'

'Agreed. If he doesn't get this meeting with you he'll give Samantha a bad time.' Wigfull put a hand on Tott's arm. 'I'm sorry, sir. Shouldn't have said that.'

Without looking at Wigfull, Tott said, 'This has gone on long enough. Will you help to save my daughter, Mr Diamond? You can state your terms. We're in no position to object.'

Diamond picked up the sandwich plate and offered it to Julie Hargreaves. She shook her head, so he put it down and collected two more for himself. 'Do you still have a room with a bed in this nick? I'd like to get my head down for a couple of hours. Shall we say an eight o'clock call, with tea and a cooked breakfast? When we get word from Mountjoy I'll let you know my decision.'

Chapter Four

When Mountjoy returned from a visit to the supermarket, Samantha Tott was motionless under the tartan blanket.

Dead?

Only a few red curls were visible, ominously still against the pillow. He stood in the doorway facing the possibility that she had suffocated. To gag her he'd used a strip of linen torn from the bed-sheet instead of an adhesive strip. If it had worked its way up against her nostrils, she'd have been unable to pull it down, because her arms were tied.

He was on the point of flinging back the blanket and ripping off the gag when she stirred.

No panic after all.

Back off then, he told himself in a sharp reversal of tactics. Leave her asleep. After the supermarket, his nerves were frayed. He needed more time to himself before submitting to another bout of conversation.

He removed his shoes prior to creeping away, for the floor was like a drumskin. Gently he set down the carrier bag he had brought back. It was a long time since he had eaten, but he would wait. Waiting was one of his specialities now, the chief accomplishment he'd mastered in Albany.

As it happened, this was not unlike a cell with its foldaway furniture. In fact it was smaller. On the side opposite the bed there was a narrow bench that let down from the wall. He released the catch and drew it down, careful to avoid making the seat creak as it took his weight.

Bliss.

He sat stiffly in the silence, knowing he was safe. The shopping had been a challenge and only now did he realize how tense it had made him. He'd tried to appear as self-absorbed as everyone else in the supermarket, turning his face to take an interest in the stacks each time anyone approached. At least it had been safer than going to a corner shop. The only major risk had been the checkout. He'd looked along the cashpoints, none of which was busy, and selected a young woman chatting to a friend on the adjacent till as she was passing the goods across the sensor. He'd got through without exchanging a word. His face hadn't registered anything with the cashier, he was certain. And he'd returned to the caravan park by a devious route that involved pushing the motorbike across a field; tiring work, but necessary.

A funny kind of freedom, this. He kept coming back to the idea that he'd exchanged one cell for another. The only difference was that he shared this one with a woman. So what's wrong with that, you lucky bleeder, most of Albany would be saying if only they knew. What are you, a woofter? No, I am not. But sex isn't included in my plan. Believe it or not, you libidinous old lags, there is something more important at stake, something that requires me to respect Samantha Tott. I'm fighting for justice, and the other can wait.

The place was cold, colder than Albany, which was why he'd given her the blanket. Maybe they'd both feel warmer with some food inside them. He'd been tempted to buy vodka or whisky, which would have been ridiculous, using up all the money. He'd gone out with a little over twenty pounds. Five hard-earned in Albany and fifteen from the back pocket of Samantha's jeans; after all, he was feeding her. For the next two days they would have to subsist on corned beef, bread, powdered soup, bananas, chocolate and tea. He'd also bought milk and sugar and there was a packet of ginger biscuits, long past their sell-by date, left in the kitchen cupboard. The place was equipped with a kettle and a saucepan and there was gas left in the cylinder, thank God, and he knew where to get water. As an old lag had once told him, we'd all go bananas without a brew, a bed and a bog.

Yes, this was not a bad bolt-hole for a few days so long as he remained alert. He'd remembered the site from years back, when the farm had sold strawberries on a pick-your-own arrangement. The caravans, none of them occupied, had been lined up in the field beside the rows of fruit. The owners paid the farmer a fee to park them there. In the time Mountjoy had spent in Albany the field might have been put to some other use, so he'd driven out to check that it was still there before snatching Samantha.

Snatching Samantha. What a high-risk operation that had been, patrolling Stall Street, one of the busiest in Bath, staking out the buskers who played violins in quartets, trios, duets and sometimes solo with a recorded orchestra as backing. The city was over-stocked with classical musicians. They took two-hour turns in the most favoured pitches along the pedestrian walkway. On the first morning he'd heard enough Vivaldi to last him a lifetime. He'd practically given up hope after her ladyship didn't appear for the first two days. On the Saturday afternoon he'd spotted her. No mistake: she was just like her picture in the *Express*. Pale, soulful face that lit into a smile whenever someone dropped a coin into her violin-case. Way-out hair – literally way-out, a great frizzy mop that he hadn't realized was flaming red, but then the picture in the paper had been black and white. He'd listened many times over to the stuff she played on her fiddle, judging the best moment to approach her, just as she was about to pack up. He'd done it with conviction, told her he owned a new restaurant in Batheaston and was willing to pay twelve pounds an hour if she'd agree to play there. It might not be as much as she earned busking on a good day (he judged it finely) but in October it would be warmer indoors and more civilized, and she might get tips from the clientele if she played requests. He'd given his mythical bistro a French-sounding name and said that the waitresses were all students and invited her to come and see it straight away. Taken in by his polished spiel, she'd walked with him to the Orange Grove, climbed on the back of his bike and been driven away to her prison.

Now she moved again, turning her head on the pillow and freeing a mass of auburn curls from under the blanket. Her eyes opened, large, blue-green eyes, dark-shadowed not with mascara, but anxiety and exhaustion.

'Yes, I'm back,' Mountjoy said. 'I'll make tea.' And when she responded with a moan that was clearly asking to have the gag removed, he responded, 'Presently.'

He took a couple of items to the kitchen, or galley, or whatever they called the tiny section where the kettle and cups were. 'This is fresh milk,' he informed her. 'It should taste better than that stuff from the tin. If you want a sandwich, I can now offer you bread and corned beef.'

It wasn't malice or sadism that made him delay removing the gag; it was his conditioning. He wasn't used to people talking to him. Samantha was probably no more loquacious than any other young woman of her age. He just found it difficult to think when someone was talking.

When the tea was in the pot he went to her and untied the gag, staying at arm's distance, avoiding any more physical contact than was strictly necessary. This he had pledged himself to observe. After almost five years' celibacy there was a clear risk of some unlooked-for incident undermining his plan. To give way at this stage would be madness.

Samantha rubbed her face against her shoulder. There

47

was a band of pink where the gag had been. 'Aren't you going to untie my hands?'

'Turn over, then.'

'I don't know why you had to gag me,' she said when she was face down against the pillow. 'There can't be anybody near enough to hear me scream. Who's going to be living in a caravan park in October?'

It was a try-on, probing for information, and he didn't answer. She was constantly testing him out, trying to discover where they were. She seemed to have got over the fear and anger that was her understandable first reaction to being kidnapped and now she addressed him in almost friendly terms. That was another reason why he found conversation such a strain. He'd have coped better if she'd treated him with steady hostility. But she was clever, disarming him with a stream of apparently spontaneous remarks.

He poured her some tea. She sat up and put both hands around the cup to warm them. 'Didn't you get a newspaper?'

'In a supermarket?'

She gave him a sharp look. 'They sell them in supermarkets now. Don't you ever go shopping?'

She didn't know – or wasn't supposed to know – that he'd broken out of jail. Several times already she'd almost twigged.

He said, 'The news doesn't interest me.'

'It ought to if you're in it. There might be a picture of me in the paper. MASSIVE HUNT FOR MISSING STUDENT.'

Mountjoy said, 'You've got some hopes.'

'My Dad will see to it. He's the Assistant Chief Constable, or one of them, anyway.'

'I know.'

'You think just because he's a top dog in the police he must have buckets of money, but you're wrong. They don't get paid much. What's your job? What do you do,

48

apart from kidnapping helpless women?'

'I make them sandwiches if they're not too bloody inquisitive,' said Mountjoy.

'All right.' She tugged the blanket aside. 'And I'll need my legs untying.'

'What for?'

'Don't be so dense.'

'Again?'

The bodily functions were embarrassing on both sides. Moreover, untying her created an additional hazard. She was a strong young woman and each time she used the toilet there was a risk that it was the pretext for an escape attempt, so the door had to remain open.

He let her loosen the flex around her ankles.

She said, 'What do you think I would do if you left me untied? I'm not going to get far without shoes, am I?'

He didn't answer. Just opened the toilet door and stood with his foot against it to prevent her from closing it. In his planning this large caravan had seemed ideal for his purpose. Civilized, even. He had no wish to cause unnecessary suffering. He hadn't appreciated the physical constraints. Now they were increasingly stressful.

When she came out, she spoke his thoughts almost exactly. 'How much longer does this have to go on?'

'Depends.'

'On my father?'

He said, 'It can't end soon enough for me.'

'But it's got to end the way you want it?'

'Obviously.'

After an interval, she said, 'Sometimes in the past I fantasized about being kidnapped, but it was always by someone like Harrison Ford, and there wasn't a shortage of blankets and I didn't even think about wanting a change of clothes or a hot dinner. Being a hostage is degrading and disgusting. Have you spoken to my father on the phone?'

'No.'

'How did you contact him, then? By letter? How will he know I've been kidnapped?'

'It's under control.'

'You left a message with someone else?'

'Something like that.'

'And you're certain he knows?'

'Positive.'

She brooded on this for a while.

'Doesn't say much for my parents, does it, if they won't stomp up? Are you demanding an impossible ransom?'

He said, 'Did you, or did you not, want a corned beef sandwich?'

'I told you I did. You weren't listening. Or is this bribery now? Do I have to stop asking questions before I get fed? I can fix it myself if you let me.'

He wasn't letting her into the kitchen. He told her to get back on the bed. While he was winding flex around her ankles, she took a comb from her pocket and started working at her hair, separating the strands and teasing them out to restore the exuberant frizz.

Wanting to say something civil as he performed the unedifying task of tying her, Mountjoy commented, 'How long have you had your hair that way?'

'Six months or so. It should be softer than this. It wants shampooing.'

'It looks fine.'

'It's greasy and tangled and it feels horrible.'

'Is it natural?'

'Of course not. It takes ages in the hairdresser's.'

'I mean the colour.'

'That. Yes, I was born with it. I hated it when I was younger. You get called things all the time.'

'If you want to be one of the crowd, why have a style like that?'

'Oh, I don't mind now. It's a big plus to be noticed.'

'By men, do you mean?'

She reddened and stared at him, disturbed by the question. The sexual threat she had largely dismissed suddenly resurfaced. She said rapidly and stiffly, 'I meant as a musician. Classical music is becoming just as competitive as pop, so far as image is concerned. You have to sell yourself, as well as your talent. So I went for a style that makes a statement.'

In a casual tone that was meant to restore confidence, he told her, 'You make the statement: I'll make the sandwich.' Making the sandwich wasn't going to be much of a task – a square slice of corned beef between two slices of cut bread. No butter or mayonnaise. The cuisine didn't run to such refinements.

She continued combing the hair. She'd worked on it like a cat ever since he'd brought her here.

She asked, 'What will we do for food when the money runs out? You must have spent most of it already.'

He didn't answer.

She said, 'You'll have to take my violin and go busking. Can you play? If not, I'd better give you lessons. It will help to pass the time.'

He handed her the sandwich on a plate, and asked her if she wanted more tea. There was some left in the pot.

She said she would like some. 'I'm surprised you bought loose tea. Tea-bags are more practical. That's all I ever buy. You can get them in all varieties now – Orange Pekoe, Earl Grey, Lapsang Souchong.'

That 'now' was another dig. She'd worked out that he was on the run, he was practically certain. He told himself to be relaxed about it. It didn't matter so much now. He hadn't wanted to panic her at the beginning.

She asked, 'What else is in the carrier? Did you get anything really delicious?'

'Chocolate.'

'Brings me out in spots, I'm afraid, but if I'm really hungry I'll have some. May I see?' She dropped the comb

51

and held out her hands for the bag, which still lay on the floor with some of its contents inside.

'No.'

'Why not?' She sounded quite hurt. 'There's no harm in seeing. I'm not going to take a bite of your precious chocolate, if that's what you're afraid of.'

He picked up the bag and carried it to the kitchen.

'It was my money,' she pointed out. 'I'm entitled to know what you bought with it.'

In the kitchen he started storing the things in the tiny cupboard. Not wishing to provoke her any more than was necessary, he said, 'Two sliced loaves, four packets of chicken soup, a pint of milk, eight slices of corned beef, six bananas, some tea and some sugar. Satisfied?'

'And the chocolate.'

'And the chocolate.'

She said, 'I don't see why you have to treat a bag of shopping as a state secret.'

He said, 'Because it's boring.' And out of her line of vision he took the final item from the bag and tucked it out of sight on top of the cupboard.

It was a packet of hair tint, labelled *Mocha*.

Chapter Five

A whiff of fried bacon was in the air.

From deep in the bed came an utterance just comprehensible as, 'You can chuck my clothes off the chair and leave the tray.'

'It's five past eight, sir,' the cadet announced as he went out.

Diamond heaved himself up to a sitting position.

The breakfast had been a brilliant idea. He was less convinced about the sleep. Three hours had not been enough. He was left with a pounding headache and a mouth that tasted as if it had Hoovered the carpet. He reached for the mug on the tray.

The tea tasted good. It hadn't come from an urn. This was almost like home.

Out of curiosity he leaned towards the tray and lifted the cover. Some angel in the canteen had a long memory: two eggs coated pale pink on a slice of thick fried bread, with several strips of crisp streaky bacon, a sausage, mushrooms, tomatoes and a heap of fried potato.

Then it occurred to him that the last meal of a condemned man is supposed to be exactly what he desires. Were they telling him something?

Keith Halliwell looked around the door. 'How do you feel, chief?'

'In need of some aspirin. No, before you get it, what's new?'

53

'Damn all, really. Nothing on Mountjoy or the girl. There's a car ready in case you . . .'

'. . . want to make a getaway?'

Halliwell smiled as if a couple of aspirin might also do him some good.

Diamond asked, 'Is Tott still about?'

'Yes, and Mr Farr-Jones is in.'

'Full dress parade, is it?'

'I'll see to the aspirin for you.'

'Thanks. And, Keith . . .'

'Yes?'

'Keep the top brass out if you can. I want to eat this in peace.'

Just after eight-forty, with a clearer head and contented stomach, he looked into the nearest locker room. 'Could anyone lend me a razor?'

He meant to have a wet shave, but one of the new sergeants on the strength seemed determined to lend him an electric shaver, not knowing the jinx he put on anything mechanical.

'This is neat. How does it work – like this?'

He slid back a cover on the side and one of the batteries fell out and rolled under a locker. 'How about that? There's an arrow thing on the side. What do they expect people to do?'

'You press the switch.'

'What switch?'

'On the side, sir.'

'Doesn't work.'

'It won't. It's short of a battery now.'

'You wouldn't be taking the piss by any chance, sergeant?'

'No, sir.'

'Where did it go, then – and what happens if you press this side?'

'Don't.'

Too late, his thumb flicked off the head-guard and shot it across the room. 'Strewth.' He handed back what was left of the shaver. 'Does anyone have one in working order?'

It was ten to nine when he completed a wet shave, courtesy of Keith Halliwell, and put on a shirt and tie and ventured out to check some old haunts. His arrival in the main office was disconcerting because three or four faces he remembered from two years ago looked up and smiled. *Smiled*. The Manvers Street mob usually put their heads down when he appeared and tried not to be noticed. Something in the looks he was getting made him deeply uneasy. It was almost like admiration. It dawned on him that the entire station knew what he was being asked to take on. He was being treated like Gary Cooper in *High Noon* and he hadn't even agreed to the shoot-out.

He returned upstairs to where the Chief Constable was waiting. Farr-Jones definitely wasn't out of a Western. Short and dapper, with a rosebud in his lapel, he could have doubled for John Mills in one of his English country gentleman roles. He shook hands as if he was applying a tourniquet.

'Man of the hour, eh? Sensible, getting some sleep.'

'I don't think sense had much to do with it,' said Diamond. 'I was bushed.' He had noted the 'man of the hour' remark and let it pass.

'Yes, I think Mr Tott ought to bunk down very soon. You can't keep going for ever on black coffee.'

Tott, leaning against the wall with the back of his head against a graph of the crime statistics, certainly looked exhausted, but insisted that he would wait and see whether Mountjoy sent the promised instructions.

Farr-Jones said to Diamond, 'I don't think you have met Commander Warrilow from Hampshire. We're fortunate to have him with us.'

A silver-haired man at his side who looked as if he might

be chairman of a golf club gave a nod and said, 'I'm co-ordinating the recapture operation.' Positive thinking. A recapture, not a hunt.

Farr-Jones said to Diamond, 'The Mountjoy case was before my time, of course, but I've looked at the file. You were commended by the judge.'

'The police work was mentioned, not me,' recalled Diamond with modesty. 'It was a team effort.'

Farr-Jones turned to Wigfull, who in spite of a night's growth of stubble on his chin succeeded in looking reasonably alert. 'Were you on the team?'

'No, sir. At that time I was in CID Administration.'

'Less newsworthy, but no less important.' Farr-Jones was obviously a student of psychology. He saw the advantage in making everyone feel important.

'It was useful experience, anyway,' said Wigfull. 'But I prefer being in the front line.'

In the front line waiting to see me go over the top, thought Diamond.

'Apart from his record, what sort of man are we dealing with?' Farr-Jones asked.

Diamond realized that the question was meant for him. 'Mountjoy? A good brain. Went through university. Opened his own private college, of course. A glib talker and good-looking, which is why the ladies get taken in. Physically strong. Underneath, he's violent, as you know. He had a conviction for assaulting his girlfriend in about 1980. Badly. She had to be treated as a casualty. Sensibly the hospital reported him. Some idiot magistrate let him off with a fine and a year's remand.'

'He also assaulted his wife, I believe.'

'Several times. The marriage survived only six months and then she had to get an injunction to keep him away. Sophie Mountjoy hadn't much to say in his favour when I talked to her. She petitioned on the grounds of cruelty. He used to get into a frenzy of rage over quite trivial matters

56

and beat her.'

'Not really a sadist, then?' said Farr-Jones.

Diamond gave him a puzzled look. 'What do you mean?'

'I mean he didn't do it for sexual gratification.'

'Does that excuse it?'

'I think you're missing the point,' Farr-Jones said, indicating Mr Tott with his eyes.

Diamond understood now. The remark had been intended to allay Tott's worst fears, not to whitewash Mountjoy. He glanced across to see how his case-summary was affecting the Assistant Chief Constable. Very little, apparently – if he was taking anything in at all. 'No, I don't think it was a sex thing. He lost his cool and went berserk, which is how the unfortunate Britt Strand met her death.'

'How did he behave under questioning?'

'Denied everything.'

'Did he lose control?'

'He raised Cain when I told him we'd traced his ex-wife and girlfriend. I saw the temper then. To be fair, he was approachable ninety-five per cent of the time.'

'Would you say that you established some kind of rapport with Mountjoy?'

Diamond gave the Chief Constable a frown softened by a smile and made no reply.

Farr-Jones nodded. 'All right, that was rather obvious. I'll lay off. What time is it?'

Wigfull said, 'Five past, sir.'

'Anyone care to place a bet?'

'I give him another five minutes,' said Diamond. 'No more.'

Farr-Jones looked round at the others. 'Why don't we all sit down? My money's on nine-thirty. He'll make us suffer a little longer.'

'If he said nine, he'll get in touch at nine,' insisted Diamond. 'The delay won't be his. It will be due to the way the message comes through.'

The phone on the desk rang.

'You do have a rapport with him,' said Farr-Jones as he picked it up. 'Farr-Jones . . . Good. Put them through.' He covered the mouthpiece and said, 'He's resourceful. British Rail Passenger Inquiries this time.'

The others listened to the responses.

'Yes? . . . When was this? . . . Nine precisely? . . . If you would be so kind. Exactly as it was given.' He picked up a pen and started to write. After a moment, he said, 'Thank you. I'll read it back and I'd be obliged if you would check every word most carefully. "J.M. to Diamond. Take a taxi up to the Grenville Monument immediately and collect instructions. Alone. Carry no weapon, phone, radio or bug. If you trap me the girl will die slowly, so lay off." Is that correct? . . . And was the caller male or female? . . . A man? . . . Thank you. And – this is important – would you kindly destroy the message now and say nothing about this to the press or anyone else?' He cradled the phone and spread his hands.

'What's the Grenville Monument?' Warrilow asked.

'Off-hand, I can't say,' Farr-Jones admitted.

Wigfull was afforded his chance to shine. 'Isn't it on Lansdown? You know, where the battle was fought in the Civil War? Grenville was one of the Royalist leaders. They put up a stone pillar where he fell.'

'Lansdown, you say?' Warrilow turned to a map on the wall.

'Yes, sir. It's one of the highest points hereabouts, beyond the racecourse on the Lansdown Road.' Wigfull traced the road with his finger. 'I walked the Cotswold Way once and passed close to it. See, the monument is marked. Just here, to the east of Hanging Hill.'

'Open ground?'

'I have a vague recollection of some trees or bushes not far away, but there isn't much else up there. It still looks like a battlefield. On one side of the road you can see the ridges of earth they dug out for their defences.'

'Still deep enough to give some cover?'

'Not where the monument is.'

'Ideally I'd use a helicopter for an operation like this,' Warrilow reflected, 'but obviously we've got to be careful.'

Tott, becoming pink, said, 'I'm not prepared to see my daughter's life put at risk.'

'No question of that, Harry,' said Farr-Jones. 'Samantha's safety is paramount in our planning.'

'Which is why I'm recommending subtlety in our surveillance,' Warrilow added smoothly.

'Surveillance of what?' Diamond said.

'Your meeting with Mountjoy.'

'I haven't agreed to meet him.'

'But surely—'

'Nothing is sure,' said Diamond. 'Nothing is agreed. I'm a civilian. Remember?'

There was an uncomfortable silence.

Something had been troubling John Wigfull. Tentatively, he said, 'There's an inconsistency in the two messages from Mountjoy, isn't there? Yesterday he asked us to have a car ready. Today we're told to use a taxi.'

'And is there a car ready?' said Diamond.

'Of course. I told you.'

'Is it bugged – invisibly, of course – but bugged?'

'Yes.'

Diamond smiled. 'You won't need it. That was the decoy. Mountjoy is ahead in this game. He's had years to plan it.'

Warrilow drew in a sibilant breath and folded his arms as if to convey that he, too, had seen through this transparent ruse. 'You'll have to carry something,' he told Diamond.

The moment had arrived for Diamond to lay out his cards. 'If you want my co-operation, gentlemen, you can have it on my terms. My terms are Mountjoy's, exactly. No

59

bugs, no radios, weapons or –' His eyes locked with Warrilow's. '– surveillance. I go up to Lansdown alone to see what this is about. I'm your surveillance, right? If I come back alive, as I intend to, I'll have plenty to tell you.'

'Come on, man, you were in the police,' said Warrilow abrasively. 'We're a professional force, not the Boy Scouts. Mountjoy is an escaped convict, a lifer with a record of violence. Our job is to recapture him. We can't let this opportunity pass.'

'And if you do pick him up, what happens to Mr Tott's daughter?'

'He'll tell us where she is.'

'That's your assessment, is it?'

'He's no idiot. He's an educated man. He'll know when the game is up.'

Diamond glanced at the others, practically inviting them to support Warrilow's line of reasoning. They were silent. Speaking in a flat tone that let the story supply its own force, he said, 'There was a stick-up artist a few years back who did post offices in the Midlands and murdered three sub-postmasters. They called him the Black Panther because of the hood he wore. Remember?'

Warrilow gave a grudging nod. The case had been notorious and was frequently quoted on training courses, but no one was going to stop Diamond from pointing out its relevance.

'He got more ambitious. Kidnapped a teen-age girl from a well-off family in Kidderminster and demanded a ransom of fifty grand. Planned it like a military operation. Found an ingenious place to keep his victim. Sent his messages on strips of Dynotape. Early in the hunt, the police had a lucky break. A stolen car was found containing the girl's slippers and a tape-recording of her voice appealing to the family to co-operate. Forensic evidence provided a firm link with the Panther, so they knew they were dealing with a killer. They put terrific

60

resources into the hunt. The girl was missing for about eight weeks. When they finally found her it was too late. She was hanging naked by a wire rope in an underground drainage tunnel. Ruddy sadist. They caught up with him by chance, nine months later, about to do another post office. The point is, why did that young girl die? The answer is that the guy was a killer already. What's one more death? If the Panther had been nicked before the girl was found, do you believe he would have revealed where she was hidden?'

Warrilow said, 'There's no comparison.'

To which Diamond replied, 'You're right, of course.' Then added mildly, 'I wonder where Mr Tott's daughter is being kept.'

There was an uncomfortable silence. Tott had lowered his head. It wasn't possible to see his expression.

Abruptly Farr-Jones said, 'In the present exercise, I believe we should set aside any idea of arresting the man.'

Warrilow backtracked shamelessly. 'I don't say we need apprehend him immediately, but we have a duty to the public to take this opportunity of tracking his movements. Rest assured, Mr Diamond, he won't be aware of what is going on.'

'Fine,' said Diamond evenly. 'You go ahead with your tracking. I'll rest assured, as you put it – in the first InterCity back to London.'

Tott said in alarm, 'Don't do that!'

'He won't,' said Warrilow. 'He'd regret it for the rest of his life.'

Warrilow talked as if he had just completed a course in assertiveness, but he wasn't the one who would be putting his life on the line. Nor was he the senior officer present. Farr-Jones cleared his throat. 'This is an unusual situation, gentlemen, and it would be wise to establish some priorities. Your duty is to recapture Mountjoy, Mr Warrilow, and we shall do everything in our power to support you. However, the top consideration must be Miss Tott's safety.'

'Thank you for that, sir,' murmured Tott, while Diamond privately noted that nothing was said about his own safety.

Farr-Jones continued, 'From all that I have heard, Mr Diamond had a high rate of success in his time here.'

'Second to none,' said Tott without a trace of insincerity.

Sensitive, possibly, to the contradictions in the file he'd studied, Farr-Jones explained, 'He didn't always go by the book, but he achieved results. He knows Mountjoy. He sent him down. He's our best hope in this emergency. I'm willing to back him one hundred per cent.'

'Without surveillance?' said Diamond.

'Yes.'

'No bugs?'

'No bugs.'

Warrilow stated piously, 'I should like my dissent placed on record.'

'So be it,' said Farr-Jones without looking at him. 'Are you ready to leave at once, Mr Diamond?'

Decision time. He'd talked some sense into the police. Now was he ready to take on Mountjoy?

'If someone will call a taxi. I'm sorry about the car you had ready, John. What is it, by the way?'

Wigfull frowned. 'The make? A Vauxhall Cavalier.'

Diamond grinned.

'What's funny?' asked Farr-Jones.

'The idea of taking a Cavalier up to Lansdown. Didn't they lose the Civil War?'

A long-serving Abbey Radio cab rattled up Broad Street in a slow stream of traffic past familiar landmarks like the Moon and Sixpence and the Postal Museum, with Peter Diamond beside the driver spotting the changes. The disfiguring grime on the stonework of St Michael's had been removed, leaving an unexpectedly handsome church. Rossiter's, where Steph had always bought her greetings cards, remained, but the little café two doors up, where students used to congregate, renowned for its cheap, wholesome vegetable soup, had gone. Somehow the Bath Book Exchange had survived the recession, still displaying secondhand books with alluringly handwritten descriptions of their contents; he'd once found a fine copy of *Fabian of the Yard* there, a volume he treasured. If the city shops had changed, how much more had detective work, and not for the better in Diamond's opinion; these days it was all bureaucrats and boffins. Strange, then, that this morning the central nick, that barrack-like block in Manvers Street, had felt like his second home.

It was as well that Farr-Jones and the others hadn't been privy to his thoughts. He didn't want them getting the idea he missed the action. Far better if they imagined he had found his true vocation retrieving supermarket trolleys from car parks.

The danger in this one-man mission was real. Mountjoy could draw a gun and kill him. But as Diamond's pulse quickened and his skin prickled in anticipation he knew that the razor's edge was what he had craved for the last two years.

'Where do you want to be dropped?' the taxi-driver asked. They'd motored out of the city and the buildings were separated by stretches of open land. The enfenced Ministry of Defence buildings came up on the right and Beckford's Tower on the left.

'Slow down a bit, would you? It's only a quarter of a mile past the racecourse,' Diamond said, thinking as the countryside opened out that Mountjoy had chosen well. Any police vehicles here would be conspicuous for miles.

They started to acquire a tail of vehicles. Except on race days drivers expected to travel fast along this stretch towards the M4, but overtaking was difficult. Some speed merchant behind was repeatedly flashing his headlights.

'There's a sign ahead, if you'd take it more slowly.'

'If I go any slower, mate, you can walk in front with a red flag.'

It pointed the route of the Cotswold Way. 'There's a space on the right. Can you pull in over there?' Diamond had caught a tantalising glimpse of a stone structure not more than two hundred metres from the road.

Of course it was on the opposite side and of course they were compelled to stop for up to a minute to wait for a gap in the oncoming traffic. The procession behind them grew and when the taxi ultimately reached the sanctuary of the small space by the sign for the Cotswold Way a parade of angry faces glared at them from car windows. If anything untoward happened in the next few minutes, there would be no lack of witnesses claiming to have been the last to see Peter Diamond alive.

Ignoring them all, he settled the fare and eyed the stile he would need to climb over to reach the Grenville Monument. A man of his size had to beware of seams splitting. He got over without mishap and set off along a well-trodden grass track towards the stone memorial. No one else was visible.

Sir Bevil Grenville's monument stood twenty-five feet high and was probably no more of an eyesore than the average war memorial, but it could not be said to grace the scene. It consisted of a grey, four-sided stone on a grey, four-sided pedestal. A sculptured griffin was mounted on the top. The whole was surrounded by railings eight feet high. Diamond walked around it uncertain what he should be looking for. The eighteenth-century inscription on the side he had first approached was an encomium to the Cavalier who had fallen near this spot on a July day in 1643. If it contained some cryptic message, he was at a loss to decipher it. If this account was reliable the noble Sir Bevil hadn't much in common with John Mountjoy: '*He was indeed an excellent person . . . his Temper and Affection so publick that no Accident which happened could make any impression in him and his Example kept others from taking anything ill or at least seeming to do so. In a word a Brighter Courage and a Gentler Disposition were never marryed together to make the most chearful and innocent conversation.'* No, he didn't sound like a wife-beater and murderer.

Beneath the inscription was a modern metal plaque detailing Sir Bevil's heroic role in the Battle of Lansdown. It had been put there by an organization called the 'King's Army', one of the groups who re-enacted battles.

In all probability the people who played war games were also responsible for the potted chrysanthemum plant and the faded wreath at the foot of the monument that must have been pushed through the railings. Diamond wasn't built for bending or crouching, but he was glad he put a hand on the railings and made the effort to look more closely because he spotted the corner of a scrap of clean white paper which turned out to be a till receipt, tucked under the flower-pot. He got his arm through the bars and picked it up. On one side was a list of food items bought at Sainsbury's the previous day. On the other, a message printed neatly in pencil: D. WALK OFF SOME WEIGHT. FOLLOW THE PATH ACROSS THE FIELDS. M.

The gibe annoyed Diamond, mainly because Mountjoy knew that at this stage some personal abuse wouldn't abort the mission. He pocketed the receipt and looked to his right to see what lay ahead. Another stile, inevitably. In the low moments that sometimes troubled his conscience after stepping off scales he had never contemplated anything so drastic as a country walk. In theory he supported the Ramblers' Association in their campaigns to keep public footpaths open. He also supported the Lifeboat Association, but he didn't go to sea in a storm.

Grudging each step, he ambled towards the stile. Things could be worse, he tried telling himself. It wasn't raining.

In fact for October it was a tolerably good morning, with a pale blue sky and a light breeze. In a raw east wind this place – what, eight hundred feet above sea level – would be bleak in the extreme. Yes, how lucky I am, he thought, to be stepping out in this splendid landscape to meet a murderer I put away. Lucky, my arse.

Having heaved himself over the stile, he started through the copse, up a gentle rise with glimpses between the trees of the traffic speeding along the Lansdown Road. Common sense told him that Mountjoy would want a view of him alone in open country before he risked coming out of hiding. At the very least he faced a twenty-minute hike.

There was no chance of missing the route. Numerous signs and arrows marking the Cotswold Way sent him steadily higher to a point where he presently emerged from the wood and started along the track beside a drystone wall speckled with yellow lichen. The direction was still gently upwards, making his legs ache, but the terrain had changed to turf uncluttered by trees or bushes, a band of dark green across his vision meeting the skyline not far ahead. He must have been walking for three more minutes when a spectacular view opened to his right over the fields and across the Lam Valley to Charmy Down. The climbing was over for the time being. And there was no human being in sight.

The slight hope remained of hearing a voice at some point from behind the drystone wall that stretched ahead for a long distance. The wall was above head height, yet there were small gaps in the structure here and there that a man on the run might use, firstly to spy through and secondly as a kind of confessional screen – except that confession was probably farthest from Mountjoy's mind. Even so, when a magpie suddenly took flight on the other side Diamond stopped and crept closer and waited, ear to the wall, willing to play the part of the priest. Without result. Sheepishly he set off again and in time came to a gap in the wall. On stepping through to check, he confirmed that he was, indeed, the only living soul in that vast landscape.

Then it had to be down the steep hillside, where, no doubt, some of the less brave of the soldiery had made their escape from the conflict three hundred and fifty years before. History had not made much impression on Diamond in his schooldays and his sense of it here was slight, but he had a strong affinity with anyone of independent mind. Mostly his thoughts were less ethereal. His feet ached. This was harder on the feet than climbing. His immediate concern was at which point he should give up and turn back. There was a limit to the distance he was prepared to go along this path, pretty as the views might be.

There were farm buildings visible in the valley, so there ought to be some sort of lane or track that linked eventually to the road he had left. He didn't fancy toiling back up the hill to the monument.

Some way down the hillside he remembered his promise to phone Stephanie. She would sigh and put this down as another lapse. Over the years she had assembled quite a dossier of broken promises. He couldn't argue with most, but this time he *had* remembered. Why did it have to be in such an inconvenient place?

The descent became less steep as he approached the floor of the valley. Ahead was a stream with a ford where – he was pleased to discover – a track crossed. Good news: the crossing-point was marginally above the level of the water, so he kept his feet dry. The next obstacle was a cattle grid. Having crossed that without turning an ankle he paused for thought; he must have tramped more than a mile and a half. A decision had to be taken. The signpost by the ford invited him to continue up the other side and along the Cotswold Way, but that could mean trudging on for a hundred miles through the whole of the Cotswold

Hills into the heart of Gloucestershire.

There was a limit to his good nature and he'd reached it.

Propped against a five-barred gate, he eyed the scene. The track that snaked through the valley was not the prettiest thing he had seen since he started this excursion, but it was the most welcome. Some attempt had been made to tarmac the surface, presumably for cars, because to one side an area of grass had been levelled and laid with gravel. He'd noticed a sign that mentioned angling access, although today there were no cars and no fishermen. It all added up to a short cut back to the main road.

He was thinking he could do with a drink, wondering how pure the stream might be, when he became conscious of an engine note from the direction of the farm somewhere to his left. The sound was pitched too high for a tractor or a lorry. For one sour moment he wondered if it could be Commander Warrilow's helicopter. Then he saw it coming along the lane at speed, a motorcycle. The rider was in black leathers and a red crash-helmet with a black visor.

A volley of thoughts attacked his brain. Then the bike was skidding to a stop a few yards from him. Without lifting the visor, the rider turned and unfixed a second helmet from the passenger seat and threw the thing at Diamond's feet.

Diamond ignored it. There was no point in saying anything. The engine drowned all sound.

The rider beckoned vigorously. He seriously expected a fifteen-stone man to put it on and ride pillion.

Diamond folded his arms and looked in the other direction.

Chapter Six

It was apt that Mountjoy should have summoned Diamond to a battle-field. The strategy behind this encounter would not have disgraced a field marshal. However, as field marshals know, battle-plans have to be adjusted as events unfold.

It wasn't a case of Diamond outmanoeuvring the enemy. He hadn't any strategy of his own; he simply refused to ride pillion.

So eventually he won this skirmish because the motorcycle had to be silenced. The rider switched off and lifted his visor. Four years in Albany had given a gaunt look to the face, but the features were as Diamond remembered, more Slavonic than Anglo-Saxon, the dark brown eyes deep-set, cheek-bones high and wide, mouth and jaw uncompromising.

Diamond gave John Mountjoy the kind of indifferent nod he gave strangers who stood beside him in bars. There were a dozen questions he was keen to ask at the right opportunity. This was Mountjoy's show: let him get on with it.

'We're not talking here,' Mountjoy called across.

By saying nothing, Diamond appeared to concur.

Mountjoy shouted, 'Pick up the helmet and get on the blasted bike.'

Diamond shook his head.

'What did you say?' demanded Mountjoy.

'Nothing. I said nothing. This would be easier if you took off your helmet.'

'What?'

'I said . . . Oh, forget it.' It was obvious that Mountjoy couldn't hear a word.

Now Mountjoy tried a more persuasive tack. 'I won't take you far.'

'You won't take me anywhere,' answered Diamond, but he was speaking to himself.

'Playing for time, are you, until the mob with the guns and shields get here?'

Diamond shrugged and spread his hands in a gesture of helplessness.

'I'm bloody telling you, copper, you can write off the girl if you pull me in.'

It was strange listening to this educated voice trying to speak the language of a hard man. Mountjoy's prison years may have toughened him, but only four years ago he had been the principal of a college, and it showed. He had been vicious then, only his violence had been domestic, his victims women. He had never mixed it on the streets.

Diamond yawned conspicuously and looked away, taking an unwarranted interest in some strands of wool that a sheep had left attached to the barbed wire fence.

He seemed to get his point across, because after scanning the surrounding fields to make sure he couldn't be ambushed, Mountjoy lowered the kickstand of his motorcycle. Then he lifted the helmet from his head and rested it on the fuel tank.

Prison had added some streaks of grey to his dark hair. He raked it with his free hand. 'We'll talk here, then.'

'Suit yourself,' said Diamond as if the decision had been Mountjoy's alone.

Mountjoy understandably felt the need to assert his position. 'Did you hear me just now? If you pull me in, that's curtains for the girl.'

'It's not my job to pull you in.'

'What do you mean?'

Diamond was on the point of saying he was no longer on the police payroll. He checked himself. He might get nothing out of Mountjoy if he dashed his hopes. 'You're not my problem,' he said. 'Albany is Hampshire. They're the boys who want to find you.'

Mountjoy said, 'Correction, Superintendent. I'm still your problem. You put me away in 1990 for a murder I didn't commit.'

'Not that old line!' said Diamond with contempt, as if he hadn't been expecting it. 'Think of something better than that, John.'

Muscles twitched ominously in Mountjoy's cheeks. 'I'm telling you, Diamond. I didn't kill Britt Strand. I'm no saint, but I've never killed anyone . . . yet.'

'That's a threat, is it?'

'They won't let me appeal. What am I supposed to do to get justice?'

'You harm Samantha Tott and you're finished. You realize that?'

Mountjoy didn't answer. Instead he said, 'Think about this, then. I broke out of Albany. I could have gone anywhere and stayed out of sight, but I came back to Bath. Why? Why would I put myself at risk if I'm guilty?'

In fact this was a point Diamond had been brooding over. 'I don't know, but I'll give you some advice for nothing. If you really think you have a case, you'd be better off going to one of those television companies who make programmes showing the police as inept. Or bent. They're the people who get verdicts overturned.'

'I'm not saying you were bent. If I believed that, I wouldn't be talking to you. You were wrong, tragically wrong, and I can't forgive you for that, but I think you were honest in your mistake. You're my best hope. I've got to get you to admit that you screwed up.'

71

'Under threat?'

'Have I threatened you?'

'Samantha Tott is under threat.'

'She'll survive if you do as I tell you.'

'However you put it, John, it's a threat.'

Mountjoy glared at him. 'Can you suggest any other way of getting justice?' He seemed to have dismissed or not listened to the suggestion about television. 'I can't tell you who murdered the Strand girl. That was your job.'

'There was no other suspect.'

'I know. Everything pointed to me. I had the motive. She was out to get the dirt on me.'

'You'll have to remind me of the details,' Diamond coaxed him. Anything to get him more relaxed and more talkative. 'I've done other cases since. She was a freelance journalist, wasn't she?'

'That's the polite name for it. For pity's sake, you remember! To get her story she enrolled in my language school, pretending to be a bona fide student. It was a shabby trick. I don't think anyone disputed that.'

Diamond shrugged. 'The scam you were working was more shabby than anything she got up to.'

'Scam?'

'Oh, come on. Enrolling young Iraqis on so-called English courses all through the summer when everyone knew Saddam was about to go to war.'

He said casually, 'Fair enough. Some of them were dodging military service. Some of them were genuine students.'

'Some could have been spies. You know very well that ninety per cent of them signed on to get the piece of paper saying they were full-time students. For you, they were all fee-payers, all profit.'

'You call it a scam, but it's been going on for years in plenty of colleges I could name,' Mountjoy shifted ground. 'They sign them up for fifteen hours a week of tuition knowing they won't see them again. And it isn't just students from Middle Eastern countries. Something like seventy-five different countries issue visas on the basis of that piece of paper. I'm not defending it. I'm just saying I don't know why she hit on me.'

'Because you were here in Bath where she lived,' said Diamond. 'And because of the timing. Saddam invaded Kuwait in August. Britt Strand was a smart journalist. She saw the Gulf War coming. An exposé of your college could be sold to the tabloids as a national scandal, a private college providing a cover for potential spies.'

'It would have finished me. Well, it did, as events turned out,' said Mountjoy. 'The trial wasn't just about the killing of Britt Strand, it was the unfolding of all this school for spies nonsense.'

'Go on,' said Diamond. 'Tell me you didn't get a fair trial. The fact remains that you were with Britt Strand on the night she died. She'd been stringing you along, playing the Swedish au pair when in fact she'd been living in this country for years and spoke the language well enough to make her living as a journalist. She totally deceived you. She was gathering information. She'd got to your files. She had photocopies of enrolment forms and correspondence and class registers and attendance summaries and God knows what else. She was about to blow your reputation apart. I can't think of a stronger motive for murder.'

'But I didn't kill her.'

Diamond refused to concede anything. 'You and I know that you have a history of violence to women. Your ex-girlfriend, your wife. If any of that had been admitted as evidence—'

'You knew it,' Mountjoy broke in. 'It coloured your perception of the case.'

'Yes, and I had another advantage over the jury,' said Diamond. 'I viewed the corpse. I saw the damage you – sorry, let's say the murderer – inflicted on her. This wasn't what you'd call a cold-blooded killing. It was committed in anger. She was a mess, John.'

Mountjoy stared up at the sky. A small plane was passing over Bath, too far off to be on surveillance duty. His eyes returned to Diamond. 'Are you refusing to look at the case again?'

'Why ask me to look at it?' said Diamond. 'Surely I'm the last person to ask.'

Mountjoy was adamant. 'No. You did the work. You have files on the case. Records of interviews. Lists of suspects.'

'Which suspects? There was only you.'

'You've made my point for me,' said Mountjoy. 'You didn't look for anyone else.'

Diamond sighed, 'How long did the jury take to reach a verdict? Ten minutes, or fifteen?'

He seemed not to have heard. 'If anyone can find the killer, you can.'

'So you're not merely asking me to reverse my conclusion and prove you innocent – you expect me to pin the crime on someone else?'

'It's the only sure way to get the verdict overturned.'

Diamond couldn't stop himself smiling at the audacity of the man. 'You're the biggest optimist I've ever met. Have you thought what's in it for me, setting out to prove that I got it all wrong in 1990?'

'You're straight, or I wouldn't use you,' said Mountjoy.

Diamond noted the wording: 'use', not 'ask'. There was a whopping assumption behind it. 'Is there anything you can give me, any single item of fresh evidence, that would alter my opinion of four years ago?'

'No.'

Diamond spread his hands as if that settled matters.

'You've got to dig,' Mountjoy followed up the negative answer with passion. 'How would I have found anything new, banged up in Albany? Someone killed the woman.

Someone is still at liberty, laughing up his sleeve at you. Doesn't that bug you?' When he received no answer he added, 'He must have hated her unless he was a complete nut. She must have had lovers she dropped, professional rivals, people she elbowed out of a job.'

'We looked into that at the time,' Diamond told him.

'Yes, but once you had me as a suspect, did you pursue them with the same energy? The hell you did.'

For a short time the only sound was the movement of water trickling over stones. Mountjoy had offered nothing of substance to support his claim. The solitary thing in his favour was that he had gone to so much trouble to set up this bizarre meeting when common sense decrees that a man on the run lies low.

But with a young woman as hostage, he had to be humoured. 'Suppose I re-open the files, as you want, and still find you responsible for the murder?'

'Then you won't be any good at your job,' said Mountjoy, his eyes widening, catching a gleam from the grey October sky.

'How long do you hope to remain at liberty? Whatever happens, you can't expect us to suspend the search.'

'I can hold out.'

Diamond probed some more. 'With the girl as prisoner? What you're doing now – holding her against her will – is an offence.'

'Don't give me that crap. I want action from you, Diamond. You'd better report some progress when I see you next. I have a short fuse.'

'I know that. How would I contact you?'

'You won't. I'll find you.' He released the kickstand, turned the bike and wheeled it closer to Diamond. 'I lived in Bath for longer than you, my friend. I know the back-streets and the byways. No one is going to find Miss Cute-Arse before you deliver.' He leaned down and picked up the spare helmet. 'Get weaving.'

He kicked the engine into life, replaced his helmet and zoomed away towards Bath.

Chapter Seven

Not one of the top brass at Manvers Street showed any gratitude.

'Didn't you find out *anything* about my daughter?' Tott asked, making it obvious that he saw no further need to grovel for Diamond's co-operation. He'd snatched a few hours' sleep, and was quite his old, carping self. 'I thought that was the point of this exercise.'

Diamond answered, 'I thought the object was to find out Mountjoy's demands.'

Farr-Jones was quick to follow that with, 'And I don't care for them at all.' He spoke as if Diamond himself had framed the despised demands. 'The fellow was justly convicted. We can't reverse the verdict just because he has an aversion to prison.'

Commander Warrilow, the big cheese from Hampshire, tossed in his two cents' worth. 'We missed a golden opportunity. Diamond has told us nothing except that Johnny Mountjoy is now in possession of a motorbike.'

'And all the kit,' contributed John Wigfull from the far end of the room, not missing a chance to demonstrate his power of observation. 'Where would he have got the kit?'

Farr-Jones snapped back, 'If he can get out of Albany, he's perfectly capable of nicking a bike and leathers.'

Little Hitlers, every one, Diamond thought. How does anything ever get decided these days? Maybe on the orders of a bigger Hitler, like me.

Warrilow continued his sniping. 'If the press get wind of this, they'll have a field day. He delivers himself to us on a plate and we let him go.'

The clichés of despair continued to rain down. No glimmer penetrated the gloom. This suited Diamond. In his long trek back from the ford to the Lansdown Road (where he had thumbed a lift from a student – a nice reversal) he had decided on a strategy. He knew the psychology of police meetings. Farr-Jones and his henchmen had to eat dust for a time. They had to be thoroughly demoralized – or they would never agree to his terms. So he offered nothing yet.

Presently Warrilow tried striking a more positive note by outlining his plans for the recapture, and it was routine stuff: roadside checks of cars, a poster campaign, searches of unoccupied buildings and outlying farms. He complained that he needed more men for the operation than Avon and Somerset were willing to provide and he wanted better media coverage.

They wrangled tediously over the dilemma posed by the embargo on the news of the kidnapping. Was it enough to inform the public only that Mountjoy had been sighted in the area and that the recapture operation was concentrated there? Warrilow wanted the embargo lifted immediately. He thought Samantha's best hope – not to say his own – was full publicity. Farr-Jones and Tott insisted that to release news of the kidnap could hinder the delicate process of negotiating a release. They stressed Mountjoy's record of violence to women. They didn't want this kidnap ending in tragedy through some precipitate action by the media.

'How do you expect to make progress?' Warrilow demanded in a bitter outburst. 'You talk about negotiating, but all we have are these paranoid demands for his case to be re-examined. You don't seriously expect to humour the man by re-opening the files? What's the point if the case was cut and dried?'

'We're not idiots,' Farr-Jones rebuked him. 'The obvious way to deal with this fellow is play him along, let him believe we're working on it.'

'To what purpose?'

'To involve him in the process, set up more meetings, win his co-operation.'

'And . . .?'

'Ultimately track him to his hideaway.'

'Which we could have done this morning.'

'With a helicopter?' said Farr-Jones, twitching in annoyance. 'No, this requires subtlety, Mr Warrilow, and it's obvious that Mr Diamond has to be given a role. Mountjoy trusts him apparently.'

So the focus shifted. Warrilow stared out of the window as if he no longer expected any sanity inside the room, and all other eyes were on Diamond, who in his own way looked just as disenchanted.

Farr-Jones put a hand to his neatly groomed hair as if he needed to check that it was still immaculate. He hadn't dealt with Diamond before, and he must have been warned of his prickly personality. 'It's an intrusion on your time,' he ventured. 'Inconvenient, no doubt.'

Diamond played the Buddha.

'We can't insist that you lend a hand. We'll be in trouble if you don't, since Mountjoy appears to believe that you're still on the strength, and the only cop he can trust.' Farr-Jones paused to give an ingratiating smile. His hands were lightly clasped, eyebrows arched. 'What do you say?'

'I'd like to make a phone call.'

The mildest of requests can sound like threats when spoken by men of hard reputations. Farr-Jones stiffened his back.

'To my wife.'

'You haven't answered my question.'

'I will – after I've spoken to my wife.' Diamond nodded civilly and left the room.

Steph would be back about now from a morning's shopping. After lunch she would be leaving for the Oxfam shop, so this was the ideal time to catch her at home.

He used the wall-phone downstairs. 'Looks as if I could be here a few days,' he told her after apologizing for not having reached her before. 'Can you cope?'

'More to the point, can you?' said Steph, who never nagged, but regularly spoiled the image Diamond had of himself. 'You didn't pack an overnight bag.'

'I'll buy myself a toothbrush.'

'And a strong aftershave, I suggest, if you're not proposing to wash your shirt overnight. What have they talked you into?'

'Something came up from the old days and they can't seem to handle it themselves.'

'Unfinished business?'

'I thought it was finished. Someone has another opinion.'

'If you remember, you weren't going to have any more to do with them.'

'The "someone" isn't a copper. Can't go into details, my love.'

'No need. It's Mountjoy you're talking about, isn't it? That college principal who knifed a woman journalist. I went through the papers while I was waiting here this morning for a call that didn't come. Peter, just remember you're a civilian now. It's their job to catch him.'

'I'll remember.'

There was a pause. Then she asked, 'Aren't you going to tell me to keep all the doors and windows locked and sleep with a police whistle under my pillow?'

'He won't be coming your way.'

'So I can invite strange men home in perfect confidence, can I?'

Stephanie knew how to pierce his thick skin every time.

'What?' he said.

'What else can a lady do when the prize is snatched away? You did leave me rather suddenly, if you remember.'

'I won't be long.'

She gave an ironic laugh. 'Where are you staying?'

He was glad she asked. He hadn't thought until now. 'The Francis.'

'And I was about to say, "Take care." '

When he returned to the meeting, it was like the star performer making an entrance. Such conversation as there was ceased abruptly. 'I'd like to outline my terms,' he said, taking the chair opposite Farr-Jones and leaning forward over clasped hands. He'd never been in the position of dictating to a Chief Constable and he relished it. 'I'm prepared to remain here until Miss Tott is released.'

'Good man,' purred Farr-Jones. 'I knew we could rely upon you.'

'On the following conditions,' his voice overrode the Chief Constable's. 'First, I want access to the files on the Britt Strand murder.'

Alarmed looks were exchanged between Farr-Jones, Tott and Wigfull. Warrilow rolled his eyes upwards.

'You're not serious?' said Farr-Jones. 'You told us yourself that the man was guilty as hell.'

'If I'm to have intelligent contact with him, I have to be up with the case.'

There was some shifting in the chair at the far end of the table, 'I don't know that I can sanction this. You're not a member of the police any longer.'

'That's rich considering what you asked me to do this morning. And since I have no other duties while I'm stuck in Bath, how am I going to spend my time – sitting over coffee in Sally Lunn's?'

This was provocative stuff, even allowing that he no longer needed to touch his forelock to anybody in the room.

81

Farr-Jones, pink-faced, glanced down as if suddenly aware that his fly was unzipped. 'Very well. If it becomes necessary to inspect the files, you shall.'

'No "ifs", Chief Constable. This afternoon,' insisted Diamond. 'I need to bone up on them today. Which leads me to condition number two. I require an assistant.'

'An assistant? You mean someone to work with. You can work closely with John. You did before.'

Diamond avoided eye contact with the career man Wigfull. 'The officer I have in mind is DI Hargreaves.'

'A woman?' piped up the Chief Constable, in serious danger of flouting the Sex Discrimination Act. 'Is there a reason?'

'She's my choice.'

'But—'

'Nothing personal, but Chief Inspector Wigfull is part of the command structure now. I want full authority to act independently if necessary.'

'You can't do that.'

'I'm not just going through the motions. If I find something of interest in the files, I want the freedom to follow it up.'

'You're making this very difficult.'

'I didn't ask to come in the first place.'

Farr-Jones turned to Tott, and a short, murmured consultation took place. It was supposed to be inaudible to Diamond, but he knew it was about damage limitation. If they could find a way of humouring him without letting him interfere with the policing, they would agree to his terms.

'Very well,' Farr-Jones said finally. 'We'll assign Inspector Hargreaves to you. And you shall have an office of your own.'

Away from the centre of operations, no doubt. A cell, in effect. He didn't reject the offer. There were compensations in being tucked away.

'And a car.'

'If you need to be driven anywhere, you can mention it downstairs.'

'I mean a car for my exclusive use.'

A martyred look spread over the Chief Constable's features. 'Very well. Does that meet all your requirements?'

'Not entirely. I'd like to have this clear, my position in the hierarchy. I answer to you personally, Chief Constable, no one else.'

'We're not a monolithic organization, Mr Diamond. I delegate much of my authority to others. Mr Tott—'

'Mr Tott is personally involved.'

'We know that.'

'It's better to have this sorted now than later,' Diamond insisted. 'Decisions may need to be taken rapidly. I'm not asking to take over the entire operation.'

Warrilow murmured, 'Thank God for that.'

'What exactly are you proposing?' Farr-Jones asked tartly, signalling that his tolerance was almost at an end. 'We need to co-ordinate any action we take.'

'I'm looking ahead. If there's anything in the Britt Strand file that warrants fresh investigation, I want the freedom to follow it up without hindrance.'

Farr-Jones made a hissing sound by sucking in breath rather than exhaling. 'Dangerous.'

'I know the law. I won't masquerade as a police officer. When I need authority I'll have DI Hargreaves.'

Farr-Jones was silent.

Diamond pushed his demands to the limit. 'If you want my co-operation, there isn't anything to decide.'

'Very well. Subject to, em . . . Subject to—'

'And finally I shall need overnight accommodation.'

'That should be no problem,' Farr-Jones said in some relief, probably thinking that a section house would be available.

'At the Francis Hotel.'

'Is there a reason?'

'I like it there.'

When Julie Hargreaves reported to Diamond in his new office on the first floor she was in a black sweater and white jeans. Her blonde hair was trimmed crisply at the back and sides, the choice of a young woman confident in her femininity. 'Shall I see if I can find a couple of chairs from somewhere?' she offered.

'Good idea.'

Diamond's centre of operations was a store-room. Not a converted store-room; no attempt had been made to convert it. Hundreds of reams of paper and boxes of envelopes lined the walls on wooden stacks. A table and a filing cabinet had been pushed just inside the door.

'I'm not sure why I was chosen,' Julie said when she had returned with two stacking chairs and helped shift the furniture into position. 'I know very little about the case.'

'You've answered your question. It needs a fresh mind. I could give you my version and it would be partisan. I'd like you to read the files yourself and let me have your opinion.'

'On whether the case was watertight?'

'Nothing ever is. Look for the holes, Julie. I'll see you about three o'clock.'

He went shopping in Stall Street: two shirts, a pack of three pairs of pants, said to be XL size, and things for washing and shaving. He now regretted failing to mention expenses to Farr-Jones. After ambling to Queen Square he was on the point of claiming his room at the Francis when he thought of the bookshop only fifty yards away in Chapel Row. It didn't disappoint. He came out with a rarity for his bedtime reading: a volume he didn't know, published in 1947 and entitled *Horwell of the Yard*. Already he owned *Cherrill of the Yard, Cornish of the Yard* and *Fabian of the Yard* – not because he was a collector, but out of his hankering for the great days when the top detectives had some clout.

Having checked in and washed at the hotel, he renewed his acquaintance with the Roman Bar. A pint of Usher's, the local brew, and then duty called.

'How is it, Julie?'

'Difficult, Mr Diamond.'

'Difficult because you can't find anything, or difficult because you can and you don't know if I can take it?'

She sidestepped. 'On the face of it, this is a straightforward case. Mountjoy had his life's savings invested in this private college in Gay Street.'

'He chose a prime site,' Diamond commented as he tried his weight gingerly on the plastic stacking chair. 'A listed Georgian building in the centre of Bath. Which may help to explain why he was on the fiddle, enrolling students who just wanted a piece of paper for their embassy.'

She gave a nod. 'According to this, at the time of his arrest, there were almost two hundred enrolled full time and paying fees of three grand a year, when the place could only hold eighty at a pinch.'

'Then enter a young Swedish lady with a phrasebook in her hand and a juicy exposé in prospect.'

Julie smoothly slotted Britt Strand into her narrative. 'She signed on for part-time English language classes claiming to be an au pair. Mountjoy enrolled her.'

'He was only too pleased,' Diamond cut in again. 'After all, he needed a core of genuine students. Everything I learned about Britt suggested that she was highly intelligent and very professional. For a foreign girl to be working as a freelance in Bath and supplying the international press with major stories is impressive.'

'They don't have to work out of London these days. The

technology makes it so easy.' Julie's eyes scanned the sheet in front of her. 'She had her contacts in the right places. *Paris Match, Oggi, Stern.*'

'Plenty of contacts here, too. And I doubt if most of them knew they were being used. She was a charmer, able to mix easily with all sorts. You've got it there in the statements. To one boyfriend she was a rock chick in leather and net tights; another guy took her for one of the Badminton set, squeezing in dates between three-day events and point-to-points; and to her college friends she was the hard-up au pair fitting in her studies with doing the chores for a mythical English family.'

Julie ventured a comment in support of the dead woman. 'We all show different sides of ourselves to the sets of people we mix with.'

Diamond wasn't having it. 'Britt Strand was doing much more than that. This was deception, professional deception, and that's dangerous. Fatal, in her case.'

'Maybe.'

He said sharply, 'Do you have another explanation?'

'Wouldn't you expect it from a fresh mind?'

He glared at her briefly, recognized his own phrase and softened his expression. 'Sorry. You're telling the story. Don't let me interrupt,' he said, as if it would make any difference.

Julie picked up the thread again. 'She succeeded in convincing everybody she was a foreigner having trouble with her vocabulary.'

'When in fact she was as fluent as you or me,' said he, failing to see any irony in regard to Julie's frustrated attempts to be fluent.

Doggedly she went on, 'The staff believed her and so did the other students. But secretly she was getting the evidence she wanted for her story. She made a friend of the secretary, so she was able to be seen in the office without creating suspicion. We know she photocopied masses of documents because they were found after her death in the locked filing cabinet in her flat. She also chatted up Mountjoy, strung him along and let him think she fancied him – when all she wanted was to soften him up and get incriminating statements.'

As a recapitulation of events Diamond had immersed himself in at the time, all this couldn't be faulted – but he didn't hand out bouquets. He said brusquely, 'Let's get to the evening of the murder.'

'Well, he invited her out for a meal.'

'The first time they'd been out together.'

'Yes. They went to the French restaurant, le Beaujolais.'

'The one in Chapel Row with thousands of drawn corks heaped against the window. I passed it this afternoon.'

Julie waited a moment, just long enough to let him know that she was capable of doing this unaided. 'According to the waiter's statement, they got along well with each other. No arguments. Mountjoy paid the bill and off they went at about nine-thirty. He escorted her back to her flat in Larkhall. She invited him in for coffee. She had the top-floor flat in a three-storey house in a residential street. The people downstairs were away in Tenerife, so they had the place to themselves. There's no question that Mountjoy went in, because fingerprints and matching hairs were found, and he didn't deny it anyway. He claimed he left after the coffee. She'd asked him some pointed questions about the way he ran his language school and he was in no mood to stay.'

'And if you believe that, you'll believe anything.'

'Do you want me to carry on?' Julie asked without altering her equable tone.

'Yes.' He slid his hands under his thighs as if sitting on them would discipline him. 'Finish the story.'

'Two days later, the Billingtons, the people downstairs, returned from their holiday and found milk uncollected on the doorstep and mail for Britt on the doormat. There was no message. They were worried. They couldn't sleep for worrying. Late that night they checked her flat and found her body on the bed, dressed in blue pyjamas. Fourteen stab-wounds. And those roses that gave the press their headlines.'

'Ah, the roses.'

He recalled the image sharply, thin crimson blooms of the sort imported by florists. At least six flower heads in bud had been forced into the blonde woman's gaping mouth, tips outwards, their rich colour contrasting with the pallor of the lips and cheeks. The other half-dozen had been scattered across her corpse. A dozen red roses. The memory was so vivid that in spite of his intention to lay off, Diamond once more picked up the narrative from Julie. 'The flowers must have been in the room already. We found the cut stems on the floor. But no card and no wrapping paper. She wasn't carrying roses when she and Mountjoy arrived at the restaurant. We checked every florist in Bath and Bristol. Something over twenty bunches of a dozen red roses were bought that day or the previous one. You wouldn't think there were that many romantics about.'

'Red roses are also a way of saying sorry,' Julie informed him.

He didn't seem to think it was relevant. 'About half the bunches bought were delivered by the florists, but none to Larkhall. The best explanation is that Mountjoy had them with him when he picked her up at the house. Where he bought them, we don't know.'

Julie asked the salient question, 'What was the point of putting them in her mouth?'

He shook his head. 'It would take a shrink to answer that. Presumably all those stab thrusts didn't satisfy him. He had to add a final touch.'

'Red roses have such a strong symbolism,' Julie mused. 'It's the kind of thing a rejected lover might do.'

'Pure frustration, then, after she invited him in at the end of the evening and then refused to come across.'

'But that wasn't the motive the prosecution went for.'

'Not the prime motive,' he was forced to concede, 'but look at it from Mountjoy's point of view. He's had the come-on from this attractive student. He buys her roses and takes her out for a meal. They go back to her place and instead of what he's expecting, she gives him the third degree about his dodgy enrolment system. He gets angry, turns violent and murders her. Catching sight of the red roses he so naively bought, he rips them off the stems and stuffs them into her mouth.'

Julie pondered this scenario. 'I suppose it has to be something like that, but you'd think all that stabbing would be enough.'

'Who can say how much is enough? John Mountjoy isn't noted for self-restraint.'

She picked the pathologist's report from the stack of papers in front of her. This had given Julie her images of the killing. It ran to fifteen pages of detail accompanied by diagrams and photographs: a preamble listing information about the identification of the body by Winston Billington, the date and place of the post mortem and the identities of those present; a long account of the external examination; the internal examination; followed by the conclusions as to the cause of death. If Julie were asked by Diamond, she would have to admit to having skimmed through much of it. She didn't possess the anatomical knowledge or the clinical calm to study it fully. The wounds were described minutely, mapped and measured. Some, the report made clear, were shallow; to state that the victim had been stabbed fourteen times was true, but misleading to anyone unfamiliar with this type of attack. Three only had penetrated to any depth; the others had met resistance or been warded off in the struggle, for it was clear that Britt Strand had tried to fight off her attacker. There had been defensive wounds on the fingers of both hands and on the left wrist. No indications had been found of sexual violence. The attack was categorized as fairly typical of stabbings, the cause of death being a wound of the aorta, or principal artery of the body. It had been produced by a pointed, sharp-edged instrument several inches in length.

A photograph taken from above, before the autopsy, showed the concentration of wounds above and around the left breast. The murderer's intention could not be doubted. One thrust had left an ugly cut in the neck, but the face was unmarked, still beautiful, even with the mouth agape, forced open by the rosebuds crammed into the cavity.

Julie looked down at her hands and found she was pressing back the skin from her fingernails. 'I'm not going to find it easy.'

'What do you mean?'

'Working on this. He doesn't invite sympathy.'

'He's a shit.'

After an awkward silence she said, 'Then why are we doing it? To save Samantha's life?'

'No.'

The answer baffled her.

Diamond got up and walked to the one small window they had in the store-room. Down in Manvers Street people had their umbrellas up. 'The way I see it, the man is guilty of murder. I'm ninety-nine per cent certain. This time yesterday I would have said a hundred per cent. A chink of doubt has opened up because of the choice he has made. He could have got clean away, or at least tried. Instead he stakes everything on getting me to admit I was wrong.' He turned to face Julie. 'It may be calculated to shake my confidence.'

'Get you to look for a loophole?'

'Exactly. He's guilty and he still gets me to find him an

out. Nothing is ever totally certain in this business. Sow a seed of doubt and you might end up believing Crippen was innocent. Or Christie.'

'Could you fall for that trick?' she said.

His eyes held her a moment, moved away and then came back to her. 'I don't know. I hope not.'

'But you still think the case is worth another look?'

'The top brass would be delighted if we sat on our backsides playing dominoes all day. I'd rather spend my time and yours exploring that one per cent of uncertainty. I can't say it will make a jot of difference to Samantha; her best chance lies with Warrilow and his search-parties. It's a trivial pursuit, an intellectual puzzle. If we choose to play, we might as well play seriously. Agreed?'

Julie digested this and finally said, 'Agreed.'

In a few minutes he had confided as much in this young woman as anyone he had worked with, but then he had never been asked to work in virtual isolation with so little support from the top, or for so unpromising an outcome. The room itself, their cramped, unforgiving space, was conducive to soul-baring.

'OK. Just in theory let's see if it's possible to put anyone else in the frame,' he said. 'Suppose Britt really was alive when Mountjoy left the house that night and someone other than him came in and killed her.'

'Someone she let in herself,' contributed Julie. 'There was no evidence of a break-in.'

He nodded. 'The murder was done some time before midnight or in the small hours. The pathologist as usual can't give us an accurate time of death. So we're looking at someone she trusted enough to admit some time after Mountjoy left. When was that?'

'About ten-thirty.'

'She was already dressed in pyjamas – or changed into them while the killer was with her. You mentioned boyfriends. What did we get on her love life?'

'Those two men you mentioned were interviewed. Neither was dating her at the time of the murder.'

'They'd say that, wouldn't they?'

'Her diary said it. She last saw the horsie type on October the eighth, at his riding-school – but I gather it was purely the riding she went for.'

'The horse-riding?'

She didn't dignify his attempt at bawdiness with a smile.

He picked up the thread again. 'And the murder was. . .?'

'October the eighteenth.'

'What about the rock musician?'

'Jake Pinkerton? He isn't mentioned at all. You'd need her 1988 diary for him.'

'It wasn't a personal diary, if I remember, just a record of engagements.'

'Yes. Do you want to see it?' Julie delved into the box-file and handed across a laminated book with a Matisse reproduction on the cover.

He said as he opened it, 'The point I was making is that she would make a note of dates with boyfriends in here.'

'She did.'

'And it's tempting to assume that those were the only times she saw them. Do you see what I'm getting at? If she met someone at a party or in the street, she wouldn't write their names in here.' He turned to October. He remembered seeing the entry for the day of the murder, John Mountjoy's name and the time 7.30 inscribed in confident rounded letters in blue-green ink. Not the last entry in the diary, for there were engagements noted into December, but it was still salutary to see the name written there, on the fatal day. At the trial the sheer volume of paper evidence – including this diary entry – had made an impact – all those photocopied documents from the college files, each in its transparent folder.

He flicked back a few pages and found the name Marcus

occurring regularly in August. Marcus Martin, the horse rider. 'I interviewed this thoroughbred myself. Well connected, lives in style in a manor house the other side of Frome.'

'Your notes are here on file. He said they drifted apart.'

'When I saw him he didn't strike me as a crime-of-passion man. He wasn't suffering pangs of jealousy. There was another young woman in the house cooking him pancakes.'

'*Crêpes*, I expect.'

Diamond shot her a surprised look. Her pronunciation had thrown him. 'Don't know. Wasn't offered any.' He couldn't fathom why Julie was so quick to condemn another woman's cooking. 'The point is that Marcus was well adjusted.'

'And with an alibi for the night of the murder.'

'For what it was worth.'

'Didn't you believe it?'

'Your comment just now summed it up. The alibi was supplied by the pancake-maker. He spent the night at her flat, she claimed.'

As if that were settled, he started turning the pages of the diary again.

Julie anticipated him. 'The other boyfriend was the rock musician, Jake Pinkerton.'

'I didn't meet him. One of the others had that privilege. I don't think I rated him much.'

'As a musician?' she said and her eyes popped wide like a teenager's. 'He was something special. His first solo album went straight to number one in the British chart.'

'As a suspect.'

'Don't you like his music?'

'I'd rather listen to madrigals,' he said truthfully, though he knew precious little about madrigals. 'The music revolution passed me by. Let's confine this to his other activities.'

'He seems to have been on close terms with Britt a couple of years before. The relationship cooled during 1989, according to his statement.'

'I remember now, there was a daft theory about drugs that was given an airing at one of our meetings. Pinkerton had a couple of convictions for possessing pot and the idea was that Britt had some dirt on him she was threatening to publish. I wouldn't think it could hurt his reputation much.'

'Are you eliminating him?'

'Just the motive at this stage. He's still in the frame as an ex-boyfriend, just. Where was he on the night of the murder?'

'At home in Monkton Combe.'

'*Monkton Combe*? He must be past it Julie, burned out. Does he have anyone to back the alibi?'

'He was seen in the local pub that evening. He left about ten-thirty.'

'Plenty of time to get to Larkhall. Is that the extent of it? No more suspects? You'd better go through this diary minutely. Make a file on everyone she mentions.'

'On computer?'

'You're joking. When I say files I mean things you can handle, pieces of card, not dancing dots that make your eyes go squiffy.'

She knew his prejudice well enough not to question it.

'But before you start,' he went on, 'you were going to look for gaps in the evidence that convicted Mountjoy. Did you find any?'

She assessed him with her large blue eyes. Whatever she said was going to sound awfully like criticism of his handling of the case. 'I'm sure you were only too aware of it at the time,' she prefaced it, 'but I was surprised that no blood was found on Mountjoy's clothes.'

'It wasn't for want of trying. We sent every damned shirt he possessed to the lab. Your criminal these days watches television. Practically every night he can learn about DNA analysis and ultraviolet tests. If it isn't there in a documentary it comes up in the news or *Crimewatch* or some fictional thing. We can't blind them with science any more.'

She let him ride his favourite hobby-horse, then added, 'The murder weapon was never found.'

'Must have got rid of it like the blood-stained clothes, mustn't he?'

'I suppose he must.'

'Is that it?'

She admitted that it was. She could think of nothing else in Mountjoy's favour.

'Better see what there is in the diary, then.'

Chapter Eight

Ten days before she was murdered, Britt Strand wrote the name of a Bath city street in her diary. No house number, inconveniently, but if Peter Diamond's memory could be trusted, Trim Street was short. There couldn't be more than twenty addresses, several of them shops or businesses. It was one of those tucked-away cobbled streets east of Queen Square. If nothing else, Diamond told himself as he made his way there, he would refresh his memory of the place, a quiet visit in the fading light of an October evening. Bath, like most provincial cities, shuts early and empties fast.

He approached from Upper Borough Walls, the section of the old city defence that the Victorians decorated with battlements to make it look more medieval. In the shadow of the wall, below pavement level – just outside the ancient boundary – was one of Bath's secret places, a tiny courtyard where, a stone plaque informed the public, 238 patients from the Bath General Hospital were buried. In the year 1849 the graveyard was closed 'from regard to the health of the living' – a veiled reference to the cholera epidemic of that year. He gave it a glance and moved on. No disrespect, but the health of the living didn't interest him much.

A few steps further on was Trim Street, named not for its appearance, but, prosaically, because the land had once been owned by George Trim. In fact, the narrow street was an architectural ragbag of eighteenth-century neo-classical and 1960s so-called reconstruction. The disharmony was compounded by the way the façades of the original buildings had been treated, or neglected. One was painted pink, another, next door, cleaned to reveal the creamy Bath stone, while the next was left with two hundred years of soot and grime.

Diamond hesitated at the bottom of Trim Street. This was the end that had been reprieved from the 1960s' rebuilding; on one side, a couple of shops, an art supplier and a boutique, that had second entrances in the little graveyard under the city wall. Opposite them, looking in want of restoration, was the one house with a classical façade, and also a plaque that explained why it had escaped being turned into a coffee-shop or a wine-mart; General Wolfe, the hero of Quebec, had once resided there when his poor health required daily visits to the spa waters. There were also two businesses that suggested that the modern Trim Street was a source of vitality: a Studio of Fitness and Dance and a building intriguingly labelled *The Idea Works*. A neat play on words, he thought. Maybe the nick in Manvers Street should be called *The Investigation Works*. Maybe he would try it on John Wigfull and see what reaction he got. Maybe.

What had drawn Britt Strand here was a matter of speculation. A work-out at the studio appeared the best bet. The Swedes are an athletic race. Diamond tried the doorbell several times and had to assume that the fitness and dance was over for the day. He stood under an antique lamppost and looked elsewhere for inspiration. Just ahead where the street turned right, an electrical repair shop was still open. Perhaps a faulty kettle had prompted the entry in the diary. Surely in that case Britt would have noted the name of the shop, not just the street.

The same argument held for the boutique, only someone was in the act of bolting the door from the inside, so he had to act fast. He stepped across the cobbles and tapped on the glass. The two women within had a rapid consultation. In his raincoat and brown trilby, Diamond didn't look the class of customer worth re-opening the shop for, but who can tell whether a man has made a bold decision to buy something chic and expensive for a lady?

One of them unbolted the door.

He didn't discover whether this tall, tanned woman in black was Kimberly herself or one of her staff. It said much for her professionalism that she didn't bat an eyelid when he explained that this was a police matter and produced the photo of Britt Strand. Nor did she need telling about the murder that had created such a sensation in the city four years ago. She was quite sure she had never met Britt Strand. However, someone else might possibly have served her and if he would take a seat for a moment, darling, she would look at the mailing list.

The darling reclined in a deep settee by a Georgian fireplace thinking how shabby his shoes looked against the pink carpet and wondering how much the clothes cost. The display material seemed to be French and Italian. It was the kind of place Stephanie would make a beeline for (in their salaried days) when she was supposed to be on a ten-minute shopping trip; she once came home with a sequinned jacket and pointed out that something quick for dinner need not be edible.

The helpful saleswoman returned with the disappointing news that no Miss Strand appeared in the records. Asked which businesses had been in existence four years ago, she mentioned Minerva, the art shop, and Nixey's, the electrical shop. Then she asked if this had anything to do with the crusties.

Diamond drew himself up in the settee. 'Crusties?'

'Do you know who I mean?'

'Of course I know who you mean.' It was just that he hadn't expected the subject to come up in a smart boutique. The crusties were the begrimed and dreadlocked people who congregated in the city centre with their dogs and created alarm and despondency among the council officers responsible for tourism.

'I only mention it because at about that time we had quite a scare with them. They took over one of the houses as a squat. It was reported to the police. I mean, it was very unhelpful to anyone trying to run a business. Perhaps you remember.'

'I was up to my eyes in the murder inquiry,' said Diamond. 'What happened?'

'Luckily for us, they didn't stay long, but I heard they left the place in a disgusting state and did no end of damage.'

'And you thought it might have some connection?' he said.

'She was a journalist, wasn't she?'

'Ah, but in the big league,' said he in a way that rejected the suggestion graciously. 'She sold her stuff abroad, to some of the top magazines. I can't see that a bunch of crusties squatting in Trim Street would interest anyone in France or Italy. She wouldn't, by any chance, have written a piece about your shop?'

'If she had, I'm sure I'd have noticed her picture when the murder was in all the papers.'

Ninety-nine per cent of doorstepping gets you nowhere, but in this game, you have to be persistent, he consoled himself as he left the boutique. He tried Nixey's next, then the Trim Bridge Galleries at the top of the street.

'No joy at all,' he commented to Julie when he was back at the nick. 'I thought I might get lucky with the fitness place, but I gather it wasn't in existence at the time of the murder. No one in Trim Street remembers Britt.'

'It was a long shot,' Julie was bold enough to comment.

'I enjoyed the exercise. How did you get on with the diary?'

Julie had plotted every diary entry on a grid arrangement on a large sheet. The names and places were listed down the left side, with the weeks from January to December across the top. A tick at the intersection marked each mention. This way, the regular appointments were clearly defined.

Diamond viewed her work with some reserve; this was about as much technology as he was willing to take. He studied the grid. 'Presumably these are days she paid the rent. This is the riding. These are dates with Marcus Martin. There are some women's names here. Who was May? Her name comes up quite a bit.'

'May Tan, the hairdresser.'

'That would explain it. Britt kept up appearances.'

'And Hilary Mudd . . .?'

'. . . gave her facials.'

'Why didn't I guess?' He ran his finger down the list. 'So Prue Shorter – don't tell me – has to be a manicurist.'

If Diamond made an unsmutty joke, however feeble, it wanted encouraging. Julie humoured him by wincing. 'Actually she was the press photographer Britt sometimes worked with.'

He became serious again. 'A professional colleague? Presumably we took a statement from her at the time. Be helpful to trace her. I'd like to know what other stories Britt worked on. I imagine an investigative journalist isn't everyone's favourite person. It's possible she made enemies before she ever met Mountjoy.'

'I'll see if Miss Shorter is in the phone book.'

'She's yours, then,' he said in his old, imperious style. 'Get out and see her tonight.'

She didn't object. Anyone who worked with Diamond expected overtime. But then he added, 'I'm going to see what I can get from the rock musician.' And she did feel like objecting, but she had the sense to keep silent.

As for the man himself, he was beginning to function as

a senior detective again, and it felt agreeable. It would have felt even more agreeable in a larger vehicle than the Escort they had put at his disposal. Fortunately Monkton Combe was a mere fifteen-minute drive. Jake Pinkerton, if the records were up-to-date, lived in a cottage close to the public school.

The coach lamp that lit up automatically as Diamond approached, the trimmed lawn and pruned cordon fruit trees, didn't fit the image of a pot-smoking Heavy Metal freak. And the man who opened the door was revealed as a smart dresser in a purple designer shirt buttoned at the neck, coffee-coloured slacks and soft leather boots. He hadn't enough hair remaining to let it grow with any conviction. Around forty, well in command, slim, tall and with alert brown eyes, unfazed by the unexpected visitor.

'Sorry to spring this on you, Mr . . .?'

The man stared back. He wasn't falling for that one.

'Mr Jake Pinkerton?'

A grudging nod.

'You were good enough to help the police in regard to a murder inquiry four years back. You remember the case of the Swedish woman who was stabbed? It's come up again and we're speaking to the principal witnesses.' Diamond presented his credentials, so to speak, without actually revealing his civilian status.

Pinkerton's face took on the glazed look of a man importuned by a door-to-door evangelist.

Diamond pressed on, 'You're going to tell me a man was convicted, and I should know, because I was in charge. Peter Diamond. I don't think we met.'

'The guy is on the run,' said Pinkerton. 'It's been in all the papers.'

'Confidentially, Mr Pinkerton, we believe he's somewhere in this area.' Diamond's eyes slid sideways, as if he expected Mountjoy to come around the corner of the

101

cottage carrying a sledgehammer. 'Mind if I come in?'

The interior was straight out of *Homes & Gardens*, furnished with fine antique pieces that must have taken some finding, and some funds. Three framed gold discs were displayed in an alcove. Where were the cigarette-burns and the wine-stains, Diamond thought, the signs of head-banging and wild parties?

Pinkerton showed him to a white leather chesterfield and faced him from an adjacent window-seat.

He said, 'Let me absorb this fully. You're re-opening the Britt Strand case – is that why you're here?'

'I wouldn't put it in those terms. This is routine, in case Mountjoy attempts to contact anyone. He claims he was unjustly convicted.'

'Who doesn't these days?'

'I don't want you to think there's any reason for panic,' Diamond said, regardless that Pinkerton was totally self-composed. 'Do you know Mountjoy?'

'Never met him.'

'But you were a close friend of the victim?'

Although Pinkerton didn't quite deny this, his tone made clear that he would have liked to. 'Britt and I had something going at one time. It was over by the time she was killed. That was a couple of years later.'

'You'd stopped seeing her altogether?'

'We each found other people, but we kept in touch. I liked her.'

'But there had been an affair between you?'

Pinkerton thought about his answer. His whole manner was dismissive. 'If you want to call it that.'

'When?'

'Around 1987, through '88.'

'What was she like?' Diamond rephrased it more tastefully. 'I mean, what sort of person was she?'

'Britt? She was smart.'

'Fashionwise?'

102

'Headwise as well. She knew what she wanted and how to get it. She was an ace reporter, wasn't she? I only ever saw one thing she wrote, and that was about me, miles better than most of the stuff that gets written.'

'Where did you meet?'

'Conkwell.'

Puzzling. Pinkerton had named a hamlet deep in the Limpley Stoke Valley, south-east of Bath. 'Were you performing there?'

'Give me a break.'

'I thought perhaps there was a pub.'

Pinkerton said evenly, 'I don't perform any more and I never performed in pubs. I'm a producer.'

'You manage other musicians?'

'The hell I do. I'm a producer.' Diamond had hit a raw nerve.

'Pardon my ignorance. What's the difference?'

'I own some land at Conkwell. A big slice of the wood, if you really want to know. I built a studio there. It's . . .' He paused. '. . . Rather famous in the music business. Bands come from all over and I create unique sounds for them.'

'I see. And Britt came to Conkwell to see the studio with a view to writing about it.'

'You got it.'

'And one thing led to another . . .' said Diamond casually, as if his own life had been filled with erotic experiences with pretty Swedish journalists.

'Yep.'

'But it didn't last?'

'It didn't last.'

'Would you like to tell me about her?'

Pinkerton looked at his watch. 'She was very together. She could get enough bread for a single story to keep her living in style for months while she worked out the next story line. It wasn't just finding the material that she was so good at. She was always after the angle. Once she went

103

through a news mag pointing out all the good stories and the great items they might have been, given the right slant. Blew my mind.' He talked with more admiration than warmth, and it occurred to Diamond that this was one well-organized person praising another's capacity to work the system. Whatever Pinkerton did at his studio in Conkwell Woods, he wasn't a raver; he was making intelligent use of his know-how.

'Did she ever mention the College?'

'I didn't even know she joined a college. We'd cooled off yonks before all that.'

'Parted, you mean?'

Pinkerton looked unhappy with this interpretation. 'Cooled off, I said. We were grown-ups. We stayed friends. Why do you want to know all this?'

'I'm trying to see it from Mountjoy's point of view,' Diamond said, at full stretch to make it plausible. 'If he's in the area, either it's to settle old scores or find something out. He's got to be taken seriously.'

'He won't trouble me. Why should he trouble me?'

Diamond didn't venture a reply. 'I'd like to get a fuller picture of Britt Strand. What else do you remember about her?'

Pinkerton slid his eyes upwards, as if an image of Britt were painted on the ceiling. 'The presentation mainly. She was immaculate, blonde, a real blonde, with sensational skin. Good smile. Most probably had her teeth fixed along the way. In her business you have to be confident. She oozed it, sex and confidence. She was a great lay. Typically Swedish, with no inhibitions. Fancy a livener?' he said, drawing a line under that phase of the conversation.

Diamond shook his head.

'Britt liked her whisky straight,' Pinkerton added. 'She could put them away.'

'I thought she was TT.'

'She was a journalist.' Apparently that spoke for itself.

'Booze is bloody expensive in Sweden. They go wild when they come over here. Now you mention it, she did ask for a tonic with lemon and ice last time we met. One hangover too many, I guess.'

'Perhaps she used alcohol to put her in the mood.'

'And drank tonic water to batten the hatches? Maybe.'

'Was she romantic?'

'What do you mean?'

'Speaking of putting her in the mood.'

'Romantic?' He still treated the word as foreign.

'Well?'

'Basically, no. She didn't go in for violins and roses. Ah.' He stopped and said, 'I see what you're getting at. Roses. No, I never gave her any. Red roses played no part in our relationship. I can't believe anyone who knew her would think she liked that crap.'

'This relationship . . .'

'We didn't live together.'

'Did she come here?'

'Was it her place or mine, you mean? Always mine. Here or the studio. You're wasting your time with me.'

How often had Diamond heard that piece of advice from a suspect who wanted him off his back. For the present he was disinclined to take it. 'But you can tell me all about Britt.'

Pinkerton got up and went to a rosewood desk that opened into a drinks cabinet. He held out an empty wine glass. 'Sure you won't?' He poured himself a brandy. 'What can I tell you that I haven't already?'

'Did she mention any fears?'

'About what?'

'Other men pestering her. She was stunning to look at, you said yourself.'

'Britt could handle that.'

'She didn't handle someone with a knife and a bunch of roses.'

There was a silence that seemed not to trouble Pinkerton.

Diamond said, 'Would you mind telling me why the . . . arrangement between you and Britt cooled, as you put it?'

'No reason,' said Pinkerton.

'Come on. You slept with her. This terrific blonde who put so much into the sex. Did she dump you? Is that the expression?' Maybe he would get somewhere by goading Pinkerton.

But the self-composure was impenetrable. 'We dumped each other, if you want to put it that way. No fights. No big scenes. Nothing said, even. We just stopped screwing. If you find that hard to believe, Mr Diamond, I can't help you.'

'It didn't cross your mind at any stage that she might want to write something uncomplimentary about your past?'

Pinkerton's brown eyes regarded Diamond steadily. 'My past? A few teenage trips on resin-assisted cigarettes don't amount to hard news by today's standards. She wrote a profile that she cleared with me first. She sold it to several magazines. All about my state-of-the-art studio in the wilds of Wiltshire, in a wood where nightingales sing. No dirt, on me or anyone who works with me. The piece didn't need it. I have no other secrets, Mr Diamond. I don't date any of the royal family and I can't predict Derby-winners. Satisfied?'

After that little onslaught Diamond realized that he was ring-rusty. He was glad no one from CID was there to hear it. 'Did you go to the funeral?' he threw in finally, knowing the answer.

'Yes.'

'Why, if you didn't care that much about her?'

'I'd have looked a right flake if I hadn't. It was in all the papers that I was an ex-boyfriend. There were some ugly hints in the tabloids. I went for purely selfish reasons, if you want to know.'

Diamond accepted this with a nod.

Then Pinkerton threw in an extra. 'And I wasn't the nerd who sent a bunch of red roses to the funeral.'

Chapter Nine

It was obvious that something dramatic was happening when Diamond looked in at Manvers Street Police Station around nine-thirty the same evening. In the room where the hunt for Mountjoy was being co-ordinated, the three sergeants and their team of civilian clerks had stopped work. They were supposed to be taking information from uniformed officers reporting the results of an evening hoofing around the city checking potential hide-outs. Everyone – including the small queue waiting to report – watched Commander Warrilow, who was speaking urgently into a phone. He beckoned across the room to Diamond.

Self-congratulation spread across Warrilow's features when he had finished the call. 'You're just in time for the action,' he told Diamond. 'We're about to take Mountjoy. He's holed up at a caravan park on a farm out at Atworth. I've got a response car there already and two more on the way and we're sending in a team of marksmen.'

'When was this?'

'The sighting? Barely twenty minutes ago. Want to be in at the kill?'

Diamond let the insensitive choice of expression pass. 'All right.'

'Better move, then,' said Warrilow. 'I'll give you the state of play as we go.'

They stepped sharply along the corridor with Warrilow

broadcasting his news loudly enough for the entire second floor to hear: 'The first intimation of something was earlier this evening, about six-thirty. A farm worker saw a moving light in one of the caravans, as if someone was using a torch. He crept up close and heard voices inside. Reported it to the farmer, who did damn all about it. He was too busy with the cows, or something. Later the farmer was back in his house having supper when he heard a motor-cycle being driven up the lane and went out to investigate. No one has any business going up there. It's a farm track. None of the caravans are in use. They're locked and parked in his field for the winter, over a hundred of them. Farmer goes to have a look, finds the lock of this van has been forced and starts to go in, but Mountjoy appears at the door, shoves him in the chest and knocks him down.'

'Are we sure it was Mountjoy?'

'Positive. The farmer has just been shown the mugshot. Anyway, he didn't mix it, just hared back to the house and dialled 999.'

'Mountjoy will have scarpered by now.'

'We'll have him,' Warrilow said with confidence. 'It's way out in the country. Open fields and very little cover. We're sealing the area with road blocks.'

'Any news of Samantha?'

'Not yet. I don't want anyone approaching that van before we've checked it.'

A line of cars waited with their beacons flashing. They got into the first and it sped off northwards through the city centre. Diamond had a vague idea that Atworth was a village west of Melksham. A mercifully short ride; he hated travelling at speed, particularly when someone else was at the wheel. And there was no prospect of being distracted by conversation because Warrilow was totally absorbed issuing orders over the radio. It sounded as if the combined forces of Avon, Somerset and Wiltshire were converging on the caravan park.

They took the London Road as far as Bathford and peeled off under the railway viaduct, where a police barrier was already in operation. The roads became more narrow and from the back seat it looked impossible to pass oncoming cars. There's no law of science that says that a speeding police car is less likely to crash than any other; rather, statistics show the reverse to be true. More than once as they swung around a blind corner he braced himself and shut his eyes.

'Coming up on the left, I think,' said Warrilow.

Another blue flashing police beacon greeted them at the farm entrance. The officer standing by the response car directed theirs up the track to the farmhouse.

Warrilow was first out, keen to make his impression as the man of the hour. Diamond stayed put. He had no official role to play and if guns had been issued he would be marginally safer in the car. He didn't share Warrilow's relish for this situation. He simply wanted to know the outcome. If successful, the police operation would bring a premature end to his re-examination of the Britt Strand murder. Farr-Jones and Tott would be more than happy to give him his marching orders.

Frustrating. Just when he was starting to function again as a detective. Not much progress, of course, but things could have begun to happen. No one had satisfactorily accounted for the roses in the victim's mouth. Or the dozen red roses sent without a message to the funeral. He would have liked another crack at the case, if only to remove all doubt.

A private car drew up beside them. John Wigfull. He must have been off duty, probably relaxing at home with his train-set, Diamond thought uncharitably. He watched Wigfull stride away towards the fields where the caravans were parked.

'Not my sort of holiday, dragging one of those things down to Devon being cursed by everyone else,' he said conversationally to the driver. 'I bet you hate them. The point of going away is staying somewhere nice, seeing some decent views, eating some good food, isn't it? Buy one of those and you're stuck in a field looking out at more of the ugly things and eating pot noodles. I'd rather rent a cottage or go to a good hotel when I can afford it.'

The driver wouldn't comment. Perhaps he belonged to the Caravan Club.

Discomfort in the back of the car eventually persuaded Diamond to get out. He strolled along the lane and joined the group who seemed to think they had a safe vantage point. Among them, he presently gleaned from the conversation, was the farmer. It seemed he was worried about possible damage to the caravans in his care. He didn't want the owners coming back next spring and finding bullet-holes in the sides of their vans.

'This man in the caravan – are you sure he's the one we're looking for?' Diamond asked.

'Hundred per cent, sir.'

'You had a good look at his face?'

'I were as close to him as I am to thee.'

'Yes, but it was dark.'

'I can see in the dark.'

'What's your secret – carrots?'

'Are you being sarky, mister? You're speaking to the man who were knocked over by the bugger.'

'And did that assist identification?'

Diamond had the last word because a searchlight was switched on in the field ahead and everyone's attention focused on a white caravan standing in a row of about twenty. Curtains were drawn across the two small windows in view.

Warrilow's voice came over a loud hailer: 'Mountjoy, I want you to listen carefully. This is the police. You are surrounded and we are armed. Do exactly as I say and no one will get hurt. First, you are to release Miss Tott. Then you will come out yourself with your hands on your head. Is that clear? First, Miss Tott. Allow her to come out now.'

Another light-beam swung across the space in front of the caravans and stopped at the door. The forced lock was clearly visible. Everyone watched for a movement, but none came.

'Mountjoy, it's all over,' said Warrilow. 'Release the young lady now.'

A short time after, he added. 'You're being very unwise. You have another twenty seconds.'

Privately, Diamond thought it was Warrilow who was being unwise. Time limits are unhelpful in siege situations unless they are agreed by both sides.

At least a minute went by. Then someone in Diamond's group spotted two masked figures in black approaching the caravan from the unlit side, creeping swiftly around it, right up to the door. One rammed it open with his hand and the other lobbed something inside.

'Tear-gas,' murmured a voice.

Still no one came out.

'What happens if they aren't in there after all?' someone asked.

'There are ninety-nine other caravans to search,' said Diamond with a yawn.

'He were definitely in there,' the farmer insisted.

Nobody disputed it, but the tension had eased.

A man wearing a gas-mask and armed with a gun entered the caravan, spent a few seconds inside and then came out and spread his arms to gesture that no one was there. The search would have to widen in scope. Warrilow began issuing fresh orders.

Diamond stayed well in the background, preferring to prowl around the farm buildings. Not that he expected to find anyone. He was sure Mountjoy would have quit the area immediately after the fracas with the farmer – if, indeed, the man inside the caravan had been Mountjoy.

The impression he got of this farm was that it barely deserved being described as such. He guessed that the farmer – who must have been over sixty – relied on the caravan parking fees as a main source of income. There were no animals apart from a few chickens. The farm machinery consisted of a tractor with mould growing on the wheels from disuse. Maybe the policy known as 'set aside' had something to do with it. Diamond vaguely understood the economics that paid farmers to limit their production, but found it depressing to observe.

Emerging in the lane again, having completed his tour, he spotted the man who had checked the interior of the caravan. The gas-mask was off now.

'What was in there?' Diamond asked.

'The caravan? Definite signs of an intruder, sir. A half-eaten loaf, some apple-cores, a milk carton, a piece of rope. He can't have got far.'

'Why do you say that?'

'We found the motor-bike behind a hedge, so he doesn't have wheels any more.'

'I wouldn't count on it.'

'What did you say, Mr Diamond?' It was Warrilow himself, butting in on the conversation.

'I said I wouldn't count on Mountjoy being without wheels. There's a garage behind the farm-house with an up-and-over door which is open. Empty. If I were you, I'd ask the farmer what make of vehicle he drives.'

'Gordon Bennett!'

'Really? I'd have thought an old Cortina was more his style.'

Chapter Ten

Emerging from a satisfying sleep, he lay face up, registered after some time that there weren't any cracks in the ceiling, so it couldn't be Addison Road, which led him after some more time to recall that he was in Bath, staying at the Francis. With their Traditional Breakfast in prospect – the 'Heritage Platter' being the Trusthouse Forte term for bacon and egg with all the trimmings – he had no difficulty rising from bed. The events of the evening before surfaced in his memory and prompted quiet satisfaction at Warrilow's come-uppance. It was disloyal, but Peter Diamond grinned – a rare way for him to start the day. A stretch, a scratch and a yawn and he padded across the carpet to the window, reached for the curtain – and instantly regretted it when a needle-sharp pain drove into his thumb. In his muzzy state the shock made his skin prickle all the way down his right arm.

First he reckoned he must have touched the point of a needle or pin left in the curtain by some negligent seamstress. But the pain didn't ease. If anything, it got worse. With the curtains still closed, he couldn't see much. Flapping the hand, he hurried to the bathroom and ran cold water over it. In the better light, he examined the thumb. Around the point that hurt most it was turning white. No blood was visible.

He'd been stung.

Hotel rooms were always too warm for his liking and the

previous evening he had opened the window a little. A wasp must have flown in. At this end of the year there were still a few about.

It could still be lurking in the room, waiting to strike a second time.

You never know what infliction life holds next, he thought, back to his embittered worst, standing in the bathroom with the door closed while he tried to step into his clothes using one hand. You get up in the comfort of a good hotel ready for the Heritage Platter and the morning papers and this happens.

Downstairs he asked at the desk if they had anything for wasp-stings.

'How did you do that?' the young woman on duty asked.

'I didn't do it. It was done to me.'

'Are you sure it was a wasp, sir?' She seemed to take it as a criticism. Perhaps in a four-star hotel a queen bee would have been more fitting.

'I know I've been stung, right?'

'Did you actually see the wasp?'

Now he felt as if he were being treated as an unreliable witness. 'Don't you believe me? What do you want – a description?'

'We've got some antihistamine in the first-aid box. Do you mind if I look first?'

He held out the thumb. Some people waiting to pay their bills stepped forward to join in the diagnosis.

'That's no wasp-sting,' a small man in a tracksuit said. 'It must have been a bee. Look, the sting is still here.'

'So it is,' said an American woman. 'That's gotta be a bee. It's the way their stings are shaped, like little arrows.'

'Barbed,' said the small man.

'I can see it now,' said the receptionist.

'Well I can't,' said Diamond, thoroughly peeved.

'That was definitely a bee,' the receptionist said to justify the stand she had made.

115

'Perhaps you need glasses,' the little man suggested to Diamond. 'The eyes change at your age. Want me to take it out? It ought to come out, you know.'

'You wanna be careful with a bee-sting,' said the American woman.

'Wait a minute. I'll get some tweezers,' said the receptionist.

The operation was performed at 8.10 a.m. and the patient remained conscious throughout. Everyone had a different suggestion for the after-care: a blue-bag, bicarbonate of soda, iodine, cold water and fresh air.

'Take my advice and get your eyes tested,' the little man said in a parting shot.

'Thanks.'

He didn't fancy the Heritage Platter any more. All he wanted was strong tea and one slice of toast. The thumb was still sore, even with a coating of antihistamine ointment. Some of this came off on the *Daily Mail*, leaving a smear beside the report that a major police operation was under way to recapture John Mountjoy. The stake-out at the caravan park had happened too late to make the morning papers.

Where would Mountjoy go? he demanded of himself, trying to ignore the throbbing. The stolen car wouldn't be of use for long. Every copper in the West Country would have the number by now. Without a doubt Mountjoy would have some new bolt-hole planned. He'd lived in the area long enough to know his way about. Another caravan site would be too risky. So where?

With a friend? It seemed unlikely that anyone would run the risk of conspiring in a kidnap as well as harbouring an escaped prisoner. Friends with that degree of loyalty are rare.

Mountjoy's problem was Samantha. A man alone might wander about looking for places, or decide to sleep rough. A man with a young woman hostage wasn't going to get far without creating suspicion. An empty house was the best bet. There were plenty in and around the city with agents' boards outside.

Julie Hargreaves was already in the office when Diamond got there soon after nine. To his already jaded eye she looked depressingly top-of-the-morning.

She said brightly, 'We're still in business, then?'

'Naturally,' said he, manfully. 'It throbs a bit, but the antihistamine will take it down, no doubt.'

She said, 'I think we're at cross-purposes. I was talking about Mountjoy getting through the net at Atworth last night. What's wrong?'

This way, it sounded as if he was touting for sympathy. He told her about the sting and she made the appropriate remarks.

'How was your meeting with Jake Pinkerton?' she asked when it was clear that he wished to talk about something else than his thumb.

He summed up. 'He just confirmed what we know: he and Britt dumped each other more than a year before the murder. He reckoned it was mutual. No resentment. And she had no interest in dishing the dirt on him because it had all been done by others when he was younger. The only mildly interesting thing that came up was that he was at the funeral and remembers seeing a bunch of red roses among the floral tributes.'

'Who from?'

'No message. Pretty tasteless in the circumstances, don't you think?'

'Sick, I think.'

'So how about you?' he asked. 'Did you get to see the photographer-lady?'

'Prue Shorter – yes. She lives out at Steeple Ashton. She was certainly worth the trip. She took the pictures – or pics, as she calls them – for three stories with Britt. Well, only one, actually. The last two were never completed.'

117

'One of those being the college exposé?'

'Yes, she took some exteriors of the building and she was going to get some of Mountjoy when the opportunity came, but Britt didn't want them taken until she'd finished her investigation. She intended to confront him with her evidence on the night she was killed.'

'That's what I always assumed, but it's good to have it confirmed,' said Diamond. The case against Mountjoy wasn't crumbling. It was being reinforced. 'What was the story that did get into print?'

'She did an exclusive feature on Longleat House and Viscount Weymouth. He's Lord Bath now, of course. Well, the whole emphasis of the story was the gallery of portraits he has of his lovers, his "wifelets", as he calls them, all fifty-four of them.'

Diamond smiled. 'I once attended a meeting about security at Longleat and we were shown inside the Kama Sutra room, with its four-poster bed and the murals painted by the Viscount. Allegedly erotic.'

'Allegedly? I've seen the photos,' said Julie.

'Well, if they struck you as erotic, fine.'

She coloured.

'I mean, it's all in the mind, isn't it?' Diamond teased her.

She stayed staunchly with the story she was reporting. 'The family were extremely obliging. Prue Shorter took any number of photos while Britt got the interview with the Viscount and wrote the story. The press made a great splash out of it. She did some very big deals with continental magazines. Anything out of the ordinary about the British aristocracy sells well in Europe.'

'Out of the ordinary? Yes, I think that sums it up.' Privately he thought the Longleat story unlikely to have influenced the murder. 'You said there were three stories Prue Shorter photographed for Britt. The Longleat portraits, the Mountjoy scam and what else?'

'The other was Trim Street.'

'Really?' He leaned forward in the chair.

'Well, you found this out yourself,' said Julie. 'The crusties got into one of the empty houses and declared squatters' rights. Britt got to know them and succeeded in getting Prue inside to photograph the place.'

'When?'

'She couldn't pin down the date, but it was only a week or so before the murder. Britt's story never got written. Prue Shorter has some excellent shots of the crusties inside the place. She showed them to me.'

Diamond examined his thumb again. Every so often it gave a twinge and his face prickled as if he were sitting in a draught. 'I can't think what she hoped to do with the story. There are homeless people all over Europe occupying empty houses.' Recalling a comment of Pinkerton's, he said, 'Did she say what the angle was?'

'The angle?'

'The point the article was making.'

'I didn't ask.'

'Maybe I should meet this woman. Steeple Ashton, you said? Is she likely to be there this morning?'

Julie thought so. She had gathered that Prue Shorter worked from home these days. She had given up the photography.

They drove there together, Julie at the wheel of the Escort. So far, he was glad he had asked her to act as his assistant. The decision hadn't been taken out of any strong conviction that women deserved a better deal in the police. He judged people on their merits, and Julie was a good detective. John Wigfull was also a good detective, much more experienced than Julie, but a pain to work with.

Steeple Ashton lies east of Bath, across the county border, in Wiltshire. Strictly, he should have informed the Wilts Constabulary that he was pursuing inquiries on their patch, and Wigfull would have reminded him of the fact, but Julie had the good sense to say nothing.

Prue Shorter's cottage was stone-built and thatched, south of the village, up a lane much used by cows. There were some ancient apple-trees in the garden.

'Is she friendly?' Diamond asked.

'I think you'll find her so. With that sore thumb of yours, I wouldn't shake hands. She's big.'

'Hearty?'

'Yes.'

Smoke was coming from the chimney, a promising sign. The hearty occupant must have heard the car because she opened the door before they reached it. 'You again, love?'

'This is Mr Diamond, my boss,' said Julie, sidestepping the trifling matter of rank. 'He won't shake hands because he was stung by a bee this morning.'

'Poor lamb!' said Prue Shorter. 'Have you put something on it?'

He didn't care to start that again. 'It's under control, thanks. I wanted to meet you because you worked with Britt Strand, the woman who was murdered. I don't know how much Inspector Hargreaves told you.'

'I know Mountjoy is on the run,' she said. 'I can relax. He never met me. Doesn't even know I exist. Are you coming in? I'll get the kettle on.'

When she opened the door wider and turned, she made Diamond feel undersized, a mere tug beside an ocean liner. Such encounters were rare. She had to ease her way into the kitchen, where something rich was cooking.

Left in the living room, which was the greater part of the ground floor of the cottage, he looked around for signs of the work Miss Shorter did from home, and saw none. Maybe she had an office upstairs, he speculated, because this room was furnished for relaxation, with a chintz sofa and armchairs, a music centre and a television set. It also contained the stone hearth and a log fire. The framed pictures of Redouté roses, the vases and ornaments and the cut chrysanthemums in a glass vase were arranged with a bold sense of design. Large as she was, Prue Shorter was not ham-fisted. A violin in a white alcove was elegantly displayed.

'You're a musician, I gather?' he said sociably when she returned with a laden tray.

'What makes you say that? Ah – the fiddle. It's not full-size. It belonged to my daughter. She died.'

'Sorry – I wouldn't have . . .'

'It's all right. I'm thick-skinned. And I like to listen to music. I play things most of the time – CDs, I mean. The recorder was the only instrument I mastered, and there's not much joy playing that.'

'Music is nice as a background, if it doesn't interfere with your work,' he ventured. This was subtle stuff, and he hoped Julie was taking note.

'Oh, it's just the thing for what I do,' Prue Shorter said. 'I make and decorate cakes. There's one in the oven right now.'

'It smells irresistible. No more photography, then?'

'Only pics of the cakes.' She set down the tray. 'You can sample one I made for myself.'

'I'd love to.'

'That's the kind of man I like,' she said raising her fist in tribute. 'Sod the calories, forward the cakes.' She cut a generous slice of iced fruit cake and handed it to him. 'How about you, Inspector? Do you good.'

'Thanks, but it's a little early in the day,' Julie said.

'And last night it was too late. When *do* you eat? Never mind, love.' She went through the manoeuvre of sitting down, in free fall for the last foot or so, severely testing the frame of the sofa, never mind the springs. 'Yes, the press photography suffered in the recession – and without Britt. I was always freelance, you see. Didn't want to live in London, where the well-paid work is. So I went back to making cakes. I learned it years ago. Won competitions for my icing. The great thing about all this – and I'm not referring to my figure – is that even in a recession people get married and want wedding cakes. Whatever damn-fool things the government does to ruin the economy, babies get christened – that means more cakes – and Christmas comes up every year – and that's another batch.'

'It sounds like good sense to me,' said Diamond.

'You're in the same happy position, ducky,' she remarked. 'Crime is always going to be around. You're never going to be short of work.'

He let that pass. 'I'd like to ask you a couple of things that could be helpful without going over the ground you covered with Inspector Hargreaves. About Mountjoy. Did Britt say much to you about what she was uncovering at the college?'

'About as much as I needed to know, my dear, and that was all. She was a shrewd operator.'

'She must have admired your work.'

'I was reasonably competent,' she said. 'No – why be modest? – I'm bloody brilliant with a camera. When I showed her my book, she hired me.'

'That's how you met?'

'In that business, you have to hustle for the work, darling. I heard about this top journalist living in Bath, so I turned up on her doorstep one morning and showed her what I did. Getting photographers down from London each time she had a story to cover was a real drag, and as I was on the spot she gave me a dry run with the Longleat story. I got some nifty pics and – bingo! It sold all over the world.'

'Coming back to Mountjoy . . .'

'You wanted to know how much Britt let me in on the story, right? I knew she enrolled there as a student to dig some dirt, but I hadn't the faintest idea it was about Iraqi spies. She just wanted pics of the exterior, which I took, and she said when the time was right she'd want some of the Principal. My best guess was that the old goat was having it away with some princess from a tinpot European state who had come to learn English. Improper verbs, you might say.' She popped most of a slice of fruit cake into her mouth.

'Were you in close touch with Britt in the last days of her life?'

After some rapid work on the cake, she said, 'Not unless you count a phone call as close touch. We spoke the day before she died, updating on the projects I was doing with her. She said the college investigation was coming along nicely and I had better stand by to get some pics of the principal as soon as she gave me the word.'

'Did she sound the same as usual?'

'Absolutely. Very calm, with that precise way the Swedes have of speaking English. Always made me sound a blethering idiot by comparison.'

'Did she mention anyone she was planning to see?'

'No.'

'The dinner with Mountjoy wasn't mentioned?'

'No. She wasn't one for chatting. It was all strictly business with Britt.'

'Do I sense that you didn't like her?'

Prue Shorter weighed the question.

'Didn't like her much?' Diamond pressed.

'I liked the money she paid. We respected each other professionally. As for friendship, she was the ice maiden. Maybe she was only interested in men. She could put it on with them, for sure. I watched her in action.'

There was disapproval in the tone she used. It crossed Diamond's mind that some sort of jealousy was at work. If he hadn't heard about the daughter who had died, he might have assumed that Prue Shorter was a lesbian, frustrated in her overtures to Britt. Of course, it wasn't impossible that she was or had become one.

'Would you go so far as to say that she used her looks to further her career?'

123

She mocked this with a huge laugh. 'What is this pussyfooting "*would you go so far as to say*"? Is this what they call political correctness? Load of horseshit. Of course she maximized her assets, and good luck to her.' She turned to Julie and said, 'Don't you agree?'

Julie reddened and said ineffectually, 'Well . . .'

Diamond was tempted to point out that 'maximized her assets' was pussyfooting, too, but he wasn't there for an argument. He moved on. 'I'd like to ask about the Trim Street job that you did for her. The squat.'

'What about it?'

'How did she persuade them to let you inside with your camera?'

Prue Shorter opened her hands to stress how obvious the answer was. 'Like I said, my dear, she exercised her charm. They had a leader. He was called GB. Don't ask me why. The crusties all had made-up names like Boots and Tank, even the girls. GB used to hang around the Abbey Churchyard – you know, in front of the Abbey, right in the centre of Bath, and that's where Britt linked up with him. I don't know how she could. These people pong like a stable, you know. He had a dog on a piece of rope, a vicious-looking thing, and she would buy meat for it. Just getting GB's confidence. She knew if she could get in with him, he'd square it with the rest of them in Trim Street.'

'But why? What was the object?'

'To get into the house and get some pics.'

'I know that,' said Diamond. 'What I mean is that it's no big deal, some derelict people in a derelict house. As a piece of journalism it doesn't compare with the story she was doing on Mountjoy.'

She nodded. 'There must have been something about it that she wasn't telling. She guarded her secrets, did Britt. I remember wondering at the time if it was worth risking headlice and fleabites for, but she was very insistent. She got us in and I took five rolls of film.'

'Anything of interest?'

'You can see the prints if you want. As pics, they're bloody good, but I wouldn't know where to sell them now. Young people with rings through their noses and tattoos and punk hair-styles lying around a gracious Georgian fireplace drinking beer and cider. Rather boring.'

'Were there any objections?'

'From the crusties, you mean? A couple of the girls told me to piss off, I think, but GB gave them a mouthful back and they fell into line. No, we had the freedom of the house.'

'This GB. Is he still about?'

'In Bath? I've seen him from time to time in various states of inebriation. They moved out of Trim Street quite soon after we were there.'

'Do you know why?'

She shook her head.

'Since you mentioned it, I'd like to see your pictures of the crusties.'

'All right. Give me a hand, will you?'

She literally wanted a hand to help haul her up from the sofa. He supplied it and got a sense of the weight her legs had to support. He'd been about to take another bite of cake, but he left a piece on his plate.

Their hostess had to go upstairs for the photos. Diamond returned the cups to the tray and carried it to the kitchen. Julie offered, but he shook his head. He wanted to see that kitchen. It was orderly and well equipped, with a solid, square table, a German oven and a set of French saucepans. A cork notice-board over one of the work-surfaces was covered with the sort of ephemera that people often feel obliged to keep for a time out of sentiment or necessity: a faded drawing that a young child must have done of a stick figure apparently female with a bush of hair and hands like toasting-forks; postcards from Spain and Florida; a Gary Larson cartoon; two newspaper cuttings of local weddings; and a couple of business cards. There was also an engagement diary with every Saturday in the month marked as a wedding.

He was back in the living room when Prue Shorter came downstairs carrying a manilla folder. She took out the photos and spread them across the coffee table. 'Help yourself, folks. I'd better check that cake.'

They were eight-by-ten prints in black and white, mostly of groups of the crusties lounging in rooms, some in embraces, their dreadlocked hair inseparable and suggestive of sheep after a hard winter in the hills; others lolling in armchairs or lying full-length across the floor. There were also some striking portraits of individuals staring at the camera, their pinched faces and joyless expressions testifying to the hardship of life on the streets.

'Which one is GB?' Diamond asked when Prue Shorter came back into the room.

She picked one off the table. 'How would you like to share an icecream with that? Britt did. I wish I'd had my camera with me at the time.'

GB had a shaven head and a drooping eyelid. His teeth looked as if he had just eaten blackcurrants. It was impossible to estimate his age. He was in an army greatcoat and he had a leather necklace with pointed metal studs, the kind people used to give guard-dogs to wear. In the photo he was holding a beer-can in each hand.

'How big is he?'

'Six-three, must be. Terrific shoulders. He must have done some body-building.'

'Did you find out anything about him, his background, I mean?'

'Britt may have done. I'd say he was a Londoner by his accent. Actually he had quite an educated voice.'

'Bright?'

'Brighter than most of that boozy lot. Their brains rot with the stuff they put away.'

126

'You said Britt worked her charm on him. Was that as far as it went?'

'You mean did she do it with him? What a revolting thought!'

'Did you ask her?'

'I wouldn't have insulted her.'

'Did they kiss, embrace, or touch at all? You see what I'm getting at? I want to know whether GB could have regarded her as his girl.'

'Sweetie, I've no idea what was in his mind, but I'd be very surprised if Britt let him get up to anything. She had any amount of dishy men to choose from.'

Diamond wasn't to be distracted. 'When you were in the house in Trim Street, how did they seem with each other?'

'You mean did they go upstairs for some how's-your-father? If they had, I'd have gone with them. I was feeling very uptight among all those weird people. No, thank God, Britt was supervising me. She asked GB each time we wanted to move to another room or have some furniture shifted for a better shot, and he was very obliging, very eager to please. It was all done in less than an hour.'

'Did any money change hands?'

'Not while I was looking.'

'Might I keep this photo of GB?'

'Help yourself. I've still got the negs if I really want to remind myself of his ugly mug. How about some more cake?'

They got away without more cake.

In the car, Julie put the key in the ignition and said, 'Dare I ask?'

'What?'

'Who gets the job of finding GB?'

He said, 'It never ceases to amaze me.'

'What's that?'

'A woman's intuition.'

Chapter Eleven

He swung the door open. Then he stopped.

He had just come back to the storeroom they had given him as an office. On his desk was a bee the size of a walnut.

Anyone could see it was not a live bee.

He felt an idiot to have reacted as he did on first sight, furious at the gooseflesh that covered his arms. Grinding his teeth, he picked up the thing.

Made of black and yellow wool, with wire antennae, gauze wings and perspex eyes with black pupils that moved, it was basically a soft toy. A ridiculous object. Someone's feeble idea of a joke. Would Julie Hargreaves have planted it there? Not Julie, he decided, his investigative skills at work on something tangible at last. She hadn't had the opportunity. She had been with him ever since she'd heard about the bee-sting in his thumb and now she was – or should be – in the Abbey Churchyard, enquiring about GB the crusty.

Who would have thought it amusing? Any of the bunch he'd worked with in the old days. On arriving that morning, he'd mentioned his misfortune to the desk sergeant – a cardinal error. The story must have been passed around the entire station.

Footsteps were approaching, so he opened the top drawer, slid the bee inside, sat back and faced the door, fascinated to see if anyone came in. It is well known that the first person on the scene after a crime will often turn out to have been the perpetrator.

John Wigfull walked in.

Surely not Wigfull! He was too po-faced to stoop to something so childish.

'How's it going?' he asked Diamond innocently enough.

'Depends what you mean by going. There isn't much activity.'

'Good thing.'

'Maybe.'

'I mean that the case is cast-iron. Everyone says you sent the right man down.'

'Thanks.'

'So this is just a trip down memory lane for you.'

'A double-check,' said Diamond.

There was something faintly comical about John Wigfull foraging, like some small rodent with whiskers twitching. 'Has anything fresh come up?'

'We've seen a couple of people I didn't have time to interview the first time round.'

'With any result?'

'Nothing to get excited over.'

If Wigfull wasn't there to assess the result of the bee tease, there had to be something else he wanted to know. He wouldn't linger to indulge in casual conversation. He reached for Julie's chair and then couldn't summon the nerve to sit down, so he gripped the back and leaned over it. 'It must be boring for you, all this inactivity. It shouldn't be long before we catch up with Mountjoy.'

Diamond agreed that it shouldn't be long, privately thinking it was down to the efficiency of the searchers.

'We got damned close last night,' said Wigfull.

'I was there.'

'We've stepped up the hunt. It will help us enormously if Mountjoy gets in touch again. He said he'd want another meeting to see what progress you'd made. Is that right?'

Diamond gave a wary nod.

'You *would* let us know if he contacted you directly?'

So that was what he had been leading up to. Far from being hot on the trail, they were desperate. 'You know me, John.'

'Yes,' Wigfull looked at the shelves of blank stationery as if they would supply information as good as any Diamond gave, which was probably the case. 'If you're bored out of your skull, you might like to try some offender profiling.'

'Oh, yes?'

The voice took on a self-congratulatory note. 'Do you know about offender profiling? It was being pioneered before you, em, moved to London. It's a way of using statistics to build up the profile of an offender.'

'With a computer?'

Wigfull's face lit up. 'Yes. It's a programme called CATCHEM.'

'Called what?'

'CATCHEM. That's an acronym for the Central Analytical Team Collating Homicide Expertise and Management. The initial letters spell Catchem.'

Diamond's eyes narrowed. His face reddened. The woolly bee may not have achieved the desired reaction, but Wigfull had touched a raw nerve this time. In a tone thick with contempt came the words, 'Who do they think we are?'

Wigfull blinked nervously.

'I said who do they think we are – ruddy seven-year-olds? Who are the people who dream up these names? They seem to think dimwits like you and me will learn to love computers if they give them names. We're grown-ups, John. We're in a police force, not a play-school.'

'I don't have any problem with it,' said Wigfull.

Diamond shot him a look that told him it was not an acceptable comment. 'They think up these cutesy names and then bust a gut trying to fit rational words to justify them. There's a police computer called HOLMES.'

'Home Office Large Major Enquiry System. What's wrong with that?'

With difficulty Diamond resisted grabbing Wigfull by the tie and hauling him across the desk. 'Doesn't it strike you as puerile? Why use the words "Large" and "Major" together when they mean the same thing? I'll tell you why. Because some genius rubbed his hands and said "We'll call it Holmes – just the thing for the plod." Well, if you don't find it patronising, I do.'

Wigfull gave a slight, embarrassed shrug.

'Do you or don't you?' demanded Diamond.

'I said it doesn't bother me. I only mentioned Catchem in case you wanted to see how the Strand case measured up.'

'Catchem!'

'I'm sorry I mentioned it.' Wigfull let go of the chair and took a step backwards. 'I'd better get back to the centre of operations.'

'COMA,' said Diamond.

'I beg your pardon?'

'Centre of Operations, My Arse. Never mind, John. You get back to it. I'm sure it's all action there.'

Alone again, he spread more ointment over his itchy thumb. Wigfull had made him restless. The files wanted studying, yet he was going to find concentration difficult now. He reached for a folder and opened it, turned a couple of pages and stopped. He lifted the phone and pressed out a number on the keys. 'Is that Mrs Violet Billington? Sorry to disturb you, ma'am. I'm speaking from Bath Central Police Station. My name is Diamond. Is your husband home? . . . No? Well, I wonder if I could trouble you? There are some questions relating to the late Miss Britt Strand. Won't take long, if I could call on you in, say, twenty minutes? How very kind.'

In the corridor, he fell in behind Commander Warrilow in earnest conversation with a slim young woman with her hair in a thick, dark plait that scarcely moved as she walked, her gait was so smooth. He might have taken her for a ballet dancer were it not for the army greatcoat and boots she was wearing. The back view intrigued him so much that he followed them into the main computer room hopeful of a sight of her full face.

Luckily for Diamond, one of the computer operators had something to report and Warrilow cut across the room to look at the screen, leaving the young woman gazing uncertainly after him. She was pale, with the dark marks of tiredness around the eyes in a face that was not conventionally good-looking, but watchable – thin in structure, with a small, thin mouth and long jaw.

'Any idea who that is?' he asked Charlie Stiles, an old chum who for some arcane reason had joined the keyboard-tappers.

'The lance-corporal? Isn't she the one who reported Mr Tott's daughter as missing? They live in some kind of squat in Widcombe.'

'That'll be Una Moon, then. What's she doing here, I wonder?'

'Keeping Warrilow up to the mark, I reckon. She's a one-woman pressure group.'

'In that case, I won't ask to be introduced.'

It was one of those narrow, one-way streets in Larkhall with cars parked on one side from end to end. Diamond left the Escort on a yellow line outside the Post Office and walked back.

There was a 'For Sale' board by the front gate. Houses where murders have occurred are too commonplace these days to justify demolition or the renaming of the entire street, as was sometimes the case in times past. But it is interesting to discover what happens to them subsequently. The market value may decline somewhat, yet for every fifty potential buyers who are put off by the history of the address (if it is revealed to them before contracts are exchanged) there is usually one who has no qualms. Unfortunately for the Billingtons, that one had not yet materialized, so they were still in occupation.

Mrs Billington, who admitted Diamond, seemed still to be affected by the tragic event. At any rate, her manner was nervous. Short and plump, with softly permed silver hair and eyes of the palest blue conceivable in a creature not a cat, she had the door open before Diamond touched the bell, and summoned him inside in an urgent whisper. 'Come into the back. We'll talk there.'

The last time he had visited this place, the hallway had been decorated in some darker shade. It was emulsioned in pale pink now, the stairs painted white. Previous visits had taken him upstairs, to the top floor, where Britt Strand had lodged and been stabbed. This morning he was ushered swiftly to the Billingtons' kitchen/diner on the ground floor, a cosy room with a wood-burning stove, oatmeal-coloured walls and a dark brown carpet. A white cat was asleep in front of the stove. A collection of small dolls dressed in national costumes was ranged along the shelves of a teak dresser.

'Forgive me for hurrying you in like that,' Mrs Billington said in a normal voice after the door was closed. 'My new lodger is upstairs, a student. I'd prefer it if she wasn't told the history of the house.'

'Is she local?' Diamond asked.

'From Nottingham. Studying chemistry at the University. In her first year. Is it dishonest not to tell her or is it considerate?'

'Students are pretty tough-minded, I find,' said he, 'particularly if the rent is reasonable. I don't need to go upstairs. I called to let you know that Mountjoy is at large, unfortunately.'

She gave him a look that showed no gratitude. 'I know that.'

133

'Frankly this is the last place he's likely to come back to,' he told her, 'but we're notifying everyone connected with the case. Do you have a safety chain? Better use it until he's back behind bars, which shouldn't be long. Did you ever meet him?'

'No. The only time he visited the house I was away in Tenerife.'

'I remember. Horrible shock for you on your return.'

'Ghastly.'

'It was your husband who found the body, right?'

'Yes. Winston still has nightmares over it. He's been on tranquillizers ever since.'

'Remind me what it was that made you suspicious.'

'When we got back from Tenerife, you mean?' Mrs Billington drew her arms across the front of her lilac-coloured blouse and rubbed them as if she were cold. She was playing the silver-haired old lady even though she was scarcely ten years older than Diamond. 'She had an order for milk, and there were two bottles on the step. And she hadn't collected the mail from downstairs. First of all we didn't think it justified looking into her flat. We tapped on her door and there was no answer. She could have gone off for a few days on some reporting job to do with her work. She wrote for magazines.'

'I know.'

'We put the milk in our own fridge the first evening. Then during the night I found myself wondering if perhaps she were ill upstairs and hadn't been able to get to the door. How dreadful if we did nothing to help. So I asked Winston to take a look, and he came out looking as pale as a sheet and told me to ring the police and tell them Britt was dead. We didn't get any more sleep that night.'

'Nor did I. How long had she been living here?'

'Quite some time. Three years, at least. She was an excellent tenant. Very reliable with the rent. We were quite fond of her.' Put like that, it said as much about the

134

Billingtons as Britt Strand.

'She had her own key?'

'Oh, yes. To the front door and a separate one for her flat. As you know, the access was through our part of the house and if she was ever late she would creep upstairs like a mouse.'

'I must have asked you this before. Did anyone else possess a key to the house?'

'Apart from ourselves and Britt? No.'

'Did she have visitors?'

'From time to time. That large woman who took the photographs for her came sometimes.'

'Any men? I'm sure we've been over this, Mrs Billington, but my memory is hazy.'

'She gave us no cause for complaint. I don't recollect anyone staying the night. I'm not old-fashioned about morals, but as a landlord you always have a dread of a partner moving in when the place is let to a single person.'

Diamond explained that he wasn't asking just about overnight visitors.

'Oh, there were callers from time to time. I'd have been surprised if there weren't. She was an extremely good-looking girl.'

'Try and remember them, particularly any towards the end of her life.'

Four years on, this taxed Mrs Billington to the limit. She managed to dredge up a memory of a caller Diamond took to be Marcus Martin, the horseman. He had called two or three times. And she was positive – because she had been asked it before – that John Mountjoy had never called while she was there.

'Was she ever sent flowers?'

A frown. 'I can't remember any arriving.'

'Did she like roses specially?'

'I've no idea.'

'I see you have rose bushes in the garden.'

135

She reddened and slipped out of her old lady role to deliver a rebuke. 'Obviously you're no gardener. You wouldn't find a dozen roses in bud in my garden or any other in October. The ones found in the room obviously came from a florist.'

He asked whether Britt had ever discussed her journalistic work and got the answer he expected: she had not.

Diamond, better than most, always knew when he had outstayed his welcome. Suddenly he was getting the message that Violet Billington wanted him out as quickly as possible and not just for the sake of the new tenant upstairs. The question about the roses had unsettled her. This made him all the more interested in prolonging the interview.

'You must have got to know a certain amount about Miss Strand's relationships with men.'

'Nothing.' Curt and uncompromising.

'Come now, Mrs Billington,' he coaxed her. 'No one is going to accuse you of prying into her life. She was your tenant for three years. In that time you're bound to have seen the comings and goings and I'd have thought you're bound to have speculated about her love life. It's only human.'

'I've told you everything you have any right to know.'

'We're not exchanging gossip,' he pressed her. 'This is someone who was murdered.'

'I've nothing else to say on the matter. It's over. You took the man before the courts and he was found guilty.'

Not, simply, Mountjoy murdered her. More like a refined way of saying you clobbered him and it's your arse in a string, mate. *What did she know?*

'Should I speak to your husband? Maybe he'll feel easier talking to me.'

'You'll get nothing out of Winston.'

She gave too much away this time. Implicit in the force

of the remark was her conviction that Winston knew something and hadn't confided in her, in spite of her best efforts.

'He's out at work, I take it?'

'Yes.'

'Does he come home for lunch by any chance?'

'No.'

'So what time do you expect him home today?

'I can't say. It varies.' Her mouth pursed and those pale eyes glared in defiance.

Diamond was plumbing the depths of his memory to get a mental impression of the man. Winston Billington's testimony at the trial had been confined to describing how he had found the body. He had never been considered as a possible suspect because the holiday in Tenerife had given him an alibi. He'd appeared younger than his wife, perhaps under fifty, a slight, dapper figure in a striped suit. 'What's his job, then? I take it he has a job?'

'Sales rep.'

'Selling what?'

'Greetings cards.'

'For a local firm?'

'No.'

'So where are they based – in London?'

'Yes.'

'And he's the area rep?'

'Yes.'

'Visits the shops, does he, trying to interest them in the new designs? Have you got any samples around the house?'

She turned away and started busying herself with dishes. 'He doesn't keep them here. We wouldn't have room.'

'What does he have – an office?'

'Something like that. A place where the cards are stored.'

'But you don't have any you can show me?'

She glared. 'I already made that clear, I thought.'

His curiosity was mounting. 'What sort of cards are they, Mrs Billington?'

'What do you mean, what sort? Greetings cards.'

'The sort I might choose for my wife?'

'I've no idea.' But she had gone a shade more pink.

'Let's give you an idea then. Her preference is for country scenes, or animals. Not over-sentimental. A basket of Persian kittens would be too sappy for my Stephanie. She wouldn't mind a horse looking over a gate.'

'I said I have no idea because I don't see the blessed cards,' she told him, overriding her blushes with acrimony. 'If you've finished, I do have things to attend to. I don't wish to discuss my husband's business.'

'You're right,' said Diamond generously. 'I'd better go to the fountainhead. When can I be sure of finding him at home?'

Her entire body tensed. She said, 'I thought the reason you called was to warn us about Mountjoy. Winston knows he escaped. I don't see why you have to bother us any more. We suffered enough at the time of the murder.'

'I'm still going to speak to him.'

'He's got nothing to say.'

'What time do you suggest?'

'After eight, if you must.'

'Certainly must.' He picked his trilby off the table. There wasn't anything to thank her for.

'Not so much as a cup of weak tea, Julie,' he voiced his disapproval of Mrs Billington over a sandwich lunch in the Roman Bar at the Francis. 'She treated me as if I was something the cat brought in.'

'Is there a cat?'

'Yes, and it ignored me. So it was *worse* than being something the cat brought in.'

138

'You're not having much of a day so far. And you think Mrs Billington was keeping something back?'

He picked up the sandwich plate. 'Put some of these on your plate or I'll swipe the lot. I'm like that. It isn't gluttony, it's concentration. Working lunches have that effect. Yes, I'd lay money that she was withholding information, and it concerns the husband. Of course it could be simply that he deals in raunchy greetings cards and she's ashamed of him.'

'Does he?'

'Don't know for sure. I got the impression that they're not the sort you'd send to your aunt. Fair enough, the shops are full of them. Mrs Billington may not want the world to know, but if it's a living and within the law, I'm not condemning Winston.'

'Wicked Winnie.'

He chuckled. 'I can remember a time when a sales rep was called a commercial traveller and the butt of thousands of dirty jokes. I'm curious to find out whether Winston fits the picture.'

'Meaning what?' said Julie.

'Meaning was he laying the lodger?'

Julie's eyebrows arched.

'It's not unknown,' he added reasonably. 'Middle-aged man lusting after pretty girl upstairs. When I looked at Mrs Billington this morning—'

'Come off it, Mr Diamond,' Julie cut in sharply. 'I'm not one of your beer-drinking cronies.'

He hesitated. Once he would have waded in. But he valued Julie's support and wanted to keep it.

She repaired the conversation seamlessly. 'If he had something going with Britt, it would be interesting to discover, but where would it lead us since we know he was in Tenerife at the time of the murder?'

'I'm talking off the top of my head,' Diamond said, 'but it might provide a motive that we didn't consider at the

139

time. If Billington slept with Britt and someone else got to hear of it, we could be talking about a jealous lover as the killer.'

'Marcus Martin?'

'He claimed he'd broken up with Britt, but we only have his word for that.'

'He had an alibi for the night of the murder, didn't he?'

'Didn't they all?'

Julie was becoming inured to the big man's cynicism. 'He was at a party in Warminster until one in the morning.'

'Time of death isn't certain.'

'Yes but the woman he was with *is* certain. She said he spent the rest of the night at her flat in Walcot Street.'

'Was there corroboration, though?'

'No.'

Diamond took a long sip of bitter. 'I wouldn't place too much reliance on it, then. Let's talk to Mr Martin this afternoon if we can.'

She looked up, surprised. 'You want me to come?'

He nodded. 'Unless you need more time with the crusties. How did you get on?'

She gestured with her thumb that the morning had not been a success. 'They're too guarded to talk to anyone like me, except to give me abuse. There are nine or ten of them sitting around the Abbey Churchyard area with their dogs. To get on terms with them I'd need to shave off most of my hair and get some combat fatigues.'

'And a layer of dirt,' contributed Diamond.

'Tattoos.'

'Rings through your nose.'

Julie paused and looked at him with widening eyes as it dawned on her that what was being said might actually amount to an instruction.

'All right,' said Diamond. 'We'll leave out the nose-rings.'

Chapter Twelve

Samantha Tott said, 'It's freezing.'

John Mountjoy told her, 'It isn't. You don't get frost down here.'

'That really cheers me up! I thought the caravan was the coldest place I'd ever have to sleep in. How wrong I was!'

'This is only temporary.'

'How temporary? I can't face another night here.'

Her voice, pitched higher, echoed off the limestone walls.

The hills to the east of Bath are riddled with stone workings. In the area of Box and Corsham Down the mining was abandoned half a century ago and the main entrances blocked up, but there are numerous ways in. From time to time rescue operations are mounted for the reckless and naive who have ventured in and lost themselves in the maze of tunnels. Mountjoy was neither reckless nor naive. In his case the risk of getting lost was massively outweighed by his need for a bolt-hole.

He had brought Samantha to Quarry Hill at night after abandoning the caravan. They had stumbled through the undergrowth looking for one of the entrances. By torchlight they had picked their way down some rough-hewn steps through a sloping shaft that linked with a tunnel where they could stand upright with ease. This was one of the main arteries. A short distance on, they had discovered a recess some two metres deep in the side of the tunnel. Presumably it was the beginning of a working that for some reason had proved unsatisfactory. To Mountjoy it had felt secure and smelt all right and was more congenial as a place to rest than the main tunnel. He had led Samantha into it with all the gusto of an estate agent showing a client around. As he pointed out, with the torch and some spare batteries and food and a blanket, it was perfectly habitable. And she had slept. They had both got some sleep.

Yet this morning she wouldn't stop griping about the cold. Mountjoy's tolerance of women who complained was limited in the best of situations. He was beginning to become unhappy with Samantha's attitude. In his opinion the first two nights in the caravan had been colder than down here. She'd been too terrified that he was a rapist to speak of the cold – or possibly she thought he might interpret it as a come-on. Now that she'd survived several nights without being molested, the protests about creature comforts were mounting up.

To calm her down, he repeated a few words of consolation someone had once given him in Albany. 'Sleeping rough would be a damned sight colder.'

'What do you call this, if it isn't rough? Couldn't we go back to the caravan park? They won't be expecting us to go back.'

'The farmer will. He'll be guarding his patch now.'

'Some other site, then.'

'I've got somewhere else in mind.'

She was elated. 'Let's go, then. It can't be worse than this.'

'I have to check it first.'

'You mean *on your own?*'

'Be sensible. What do you expect?'

'Don't leave me here. Please don't leave me. I hate the dark.' The voice was on that dangerous rising note again.

'Maybe I can get something warmer for you to wear.'

'You don't have the money.'

'I didn't say I'd buy it.'

'Don't leave me here.'

'I must.'

'Why? No one would recognize me. You said when you put that disgusting stuff on my hair that it would change my looks. No one's going to spot me like this.' She flicked a strand petulantly away from her face. True, the brown dye they had used in the caravan had made a big difference and instead of standing out like a dandelion in seed, everything drooped. When she wasn't griping about the cold, she gave him hell for messing up her hair.

'You're not going out until it's necessary,' he told her. 'This is just a recce.'

'I wouldn't scream, or anything.'

'No chance. I'm doing this alone.'

'Cruel bastard.'

'If you want to stay here for ever, fine, I won't go. We'll sit here and rot.'

A pause, then, 'How long would you be?'

'I'm not going immediately.'

'I mean is it far, this other place?'

'Not far.'

She said with heavy suspicion, 'It isn't another cave, is it?'

'This isn't a cave. It's a mine, or if you want to be strictly accurate, a quarry. No, where I'm going isn't underground. Quite the reverse.'

'Couldn't I come with you?'

'Don't be daft.'

'I'll die of fright.'

'If you don't shut up about it, I'll gag you again.'

Still she wouldn't leave it. 'What if you're recaptured and I'm left down here?'

'I'd tell them, wouldn't I?'

She scanned his features for the slightest betrayal of insincerity. 'Have you heard any more from them?'

'No,' he said. 'I'm giving them time.' Seeing how she stared at him aghast, he said, 'They've got work to do, or one of them has. Did your father ever mention a detective called Diamond?'

'Daddy doesn't discuss his work with me. In fact, he doesn't discuss anything with me. He and I don't have much in common.'

'He disapproves of your busking, I expect.'

'And much more. What were you going to tell me about this detective?'

He'd caught her interest. She'd been on the verge of panic at the prospect of being left here and his only practical way of dealing with it was to distract her. He could have ignored her and walked off. No one would have heard the screams. But he knew what it is to be reduced to despair by the brutal indifference of a jailer. Causing another hapless being to suffer was no pleasure for him and no solution. It would dehumanize them both. So he fed her titbits of information as a way of reassurance. 'Diamond is one of your father's top detectives, which doesn't say much for the others. Four years ago, he led an investigation, a murder investigation, and screwed it up. He put the wrong man away. You're sure you haven't heard about this?'

A shake of the head. It was a small triumph for Mountjoy that she'd stopped complaining.

'There are bent cops and there are cops like Diamond who believe they're right,' he went on. 'He isn't bent – I think. He truly believed he'd cracked the case. He's a typical pig-headed policeman, bossy and blinkered, but there's something about the man. It can't be his charm, which escapes me, or his style of interrogation, which just stops short of red-hot needles, or his leadership qualities, because the people who work with him hate his guts. He drives them too hard. What it comes down to, his one saving grace, is that he's straight. Mistaken, but honest.

144

And I'm giving him a chance to prove it.'

'You're the man he sent to prison.'

Two days ago, careful not to alarm her, Mountjoy would have denied that he was an escaped con. Now, paradoxically, confirming it was a way of fostering confidence. He said with a fleeting smile, 'A college education isn't wasted on you.'

'You don't have to be sarcastic.'

He hadn't meant to be. 'I've got a lot of time for students.' And he almost added that he'd been principal of his own college, but he didn't want to tell too much, too soon. 'Anyway, I was talking about Superintendent bloody Diamond. He got it wrong and I've told him to do something about it.'

'After all this time?'

'After all this time.'

'What can he do? Do you know who really did the murder? Did you tell him?'

'All I know is that Diamond got it wrong. I told him so. Whether he believes me is far from certain.'

'You must have some ideas of your own. You must have thought about it while you were locked away.'

'Constantly. I got nowhere because I didn't have all the facts. No amount of thinking is going to solve a crime if you don't have the full picture.'

'Does this man Diamond?'

'Does he what?'

'Have the full picture?'

'Not up to now, but he's the only one with the means to get at the truth. He has all the original statements and he knows—'

Samantha interrupted with a little gasp, followed by, 'What's that?'

'What?'

'A sound, a scuffling.'

'I didn't hear it.'

Together they listened. It occurred to Mountjoy that if a search party had entered the mine, footsteps and voices ought to be audible, but it would be difficult to know from which direction they were approaching because there were so many entrances to this labyrinth. Choosing an escape route would be a lottery.

'There it is again!' she told him.

It didn't sound human in origin. It was a light sound, a rustle, not far away.

'And again!' said Samantha.

'That's dust falling. I felt it on my neck.' He shone the torch upwards and a dark shape fluttered across its beam. 'A bat. That was only a bat.'

'Oh, my God!'

'They won't come near you.'

'I'm terrified of bats.'

'They're not interested in us. It's their home. See that ledge up there.' He pointed the torch. 'That's where it flew from. It disturbed some tiny chips of limestone.'

She squeezed her eyes shut, folded her arms across her chest and started rocking her torso and producing a high-pitched moaning sound. He'd never heard anything like it. The fear had gripped her like an epileptic fit. Was she epileptic? he wondered. How would he deal with it? In all his planning he hadn't anticipated anything like this.

Abandoning his self-imposed pledge not to touch her, he put a hand on her upper arm and shook her. 'Stop it, will you? Don't be so ridiculous.'

She opened her eyes. 'Why don't you kill me and get it over? Yes, kill me. I'd rather die. Kill me, murderer!'

He pushed her down and forced her hands behind her back and tied them.

Chapter Thirteen

He kept Julie in suspense all the way back to Manvers Street. She was ninety-nine per cent sure he wasn't serious about transforming her into a crusty, but that one per cent was amusing to work on. She might pass muster wearing a dreadlock wig, he suggested, and if the CID's wardrobe didn't run to combat trousers she could get away with black leggings with plenty of holes. He was sure that the RSPCA could supply her with a vicious-looking pooch; she definitely needed a dog. He strolled on stolidly, embroidering the tease all the way. But behind the poker face his mood was improving and it wasn't that beer in the Roman Bar that had made the difference.

Julie wasn't spared until they reached the nick. They were crossing the reception hall when Diamond spotted something behind the protective glass at the public enquiry point.

'I don't believe this.' But he still marched over for a closer inspection.

Another of the woollen bees was positioned just behind the glass, goggling at him with its ridiculous eyes.

He rapped on the glass until the constable on duty came over.

'Who left this here?'

'What's that, Mr Diamond?'

'This bee.'

'That's a bumblebee, sir.'

'I don't care what it is. Who is responsible for it?'

The constable frowned.

Diamond had turned flamingo pink. 'Whose idea of a joke is it? That's all I'm asking.'

'It's no joke, sir.'

'You're telling me, laddie. When I find the perpetrator he won't be laughing.'

There was a pause before the constable summoned the confidence to say, 'Didn't you get a bee of your own, Mr Diamond?'

This polite enquiry went unanswered.

'Everyone should have got one this morning. It's Operation Bumblebee.'

Diamond's eyes resembled two dashes in a line of morse code. Behind him, Julie Hargreaves lowered her face and squeezed her arms across her stomach in a desperate attempt to remain serious.

'You can have this bumblebee if you like, sir,' the hapless duty constable added to his list of offences. 'We've got a box of them back here. The poster comes with it.'

Something had to be done, and fast.

Without trusting herself to speak, Julie touched Diamond on the arm and drew his attention to a large poster that dominated the cluster of notices to his right. There was a cartoon figure of a bee in a police helmet and boots. The wording ran: SUPER BEE SAYS TO BEAT THE BURGLAR WE NEED YOUR HELP. BUZZ THE BEELINE FREE ON 0800 555 111.

He studied it in silence.

Eventually Julie managed to get out the words, 'Public relations.'

The constable said, 'If you don't mind me saying so, it isn't just PR, ma'am. Since we started Bumblebee last year, the break-ins have dropped dramatically. There are five men in the team, working with Sergeant Wood, the Bumblebee officer.'

'The what?' said Diamond.

'Every report of a break-in is fed through a central hive – that's the computer, of course. Go upstairs and you can hear it humming.'

'God help us!' murmured Diamond.

'And then the villains get stung. Would you like a bee, Mr Diamond?'

Diamond shook his head and allowed Julie to lead him away.

'Four years is a heck of a time,' Marcus Martin declared in the polished accent of a fee-paying school.

And a heck of a lot of women, thought Diamond. They had found Britt Strand's last boyfriend in the paddocks behind his Elizabethan manor house, undoubtedly one of the few brick mansions in the whole county, its triple-gabled façade glowing bright orange in the afternoon sun and blood-red where the shadow of an oak fell across the wall. Marcus Martin was with a young woman who was mounted on a black mare, in a schooling ring surfaced with wood chippings and laid out with practice jumps. Immaculately kitted as the equestrienne was, in black velvet hunting cap, black coat, white stock and antelope-coloured jodhpurs, she hadn't succeeded in moving the horse and didn't seem to be trying, thus giving the impression that the riding lesson wasn't her main reason for being there. The way Martin helped her dismount with both hands around her thigh reinforced this impression. He unfastened the tack for her and sent her towards the stables with a push on her rump. She didn't object.

'But you remember me, I expect?' said Diamond.

'Too well, my friend, too well.'

He introduced Julie, who was awarded the doubtful compliment of a lingering head-to-toe inspection.

Martin said with his eyes still on her, 'It's hard to credit.'

149

'What is?' Diamond asked.

'*Inspector* Hargreaves.'

'It wouldn't be if you were evading arrest,' said Diamond in a tribute that almost made up for the teasing earlier. 'No doubt you've heard that Mountjoy is on the run from Albany?'

Martin had heard and he couldn't see how it affected him.

'It doesn't,' said Diamond. 'It affects me, though. I'm the fall-guy who may have to speak to him. He claims he's innocent, of course.'

'What does the wretched man want – a retrial?'

'He wouldn't get that.'

Martin fed the mare a couple of sugar lumps and waved to a stable-lad to take her back to her stall. Then he suggested they went inside the house, where they would be warmer.

'I'm trying to refresh my memory of the case,' Diamond told him as if the facts had all deserted him. For once he was being as amiable as the television detective Columbo, whose style of questioning he aspired to, but only rarely approached. 'You're the obvious man to ask about Britt.'

'I don't know about that,' said Martin. 'Our relationship was short and to the point. Weeks, rather than months.'

'You don't mind talking about it?'

'Not in the least. But I don't see what bearing it has.'

In the house, before a flickering log fire in a recessed stone fireplace almost as large as the office Diamond and Julie shared at the nick, Marcus Martin expanded on this. 'I respected Britt. She was a class act. Extremely pretty and considerably brighter than I am. She was a damned fine horsewoman, too.' There was genuine admiration in his tone. 'She rode regularly. They take their riding seriously in Sweden. Anyway, Britt was keen to do some jumping and someone at the stables offered to bring her out here. I have a showjumping layout – not the one you saw, but a full course – the best for miles around. Perhaps you noticed it when you drove in. That's how we met. After she had exercised my best stallion, and cooled off with a Perrier – she was TT, you know – she said she'd like to ring for a taxi. She didn't possess a car. Naturally I offered to drive her home, and I did.' He paused and gave Julie a wink. 'The next morning.'

'This was when – in September?'

'Around then. Maybe August. As I said, it was ages ago. The whole thing didn't last more than three wild and steamy weeks. It was over at least a week before she was killed.'

'You told me at the time that you drifted apart,' recalled Diamond. 'It's hard to reconcile that with three wild and steamy weeks.'

'Did I? Then I suppose it was true. Yes, I'd been through my repertoire, so to speak. I wouldn't say we were getting bored with each other by Week Three, but we only had one thing in common.'

'You mean the riding?'

He grinned. 'She was about to start college, and I had a weekend trip to Belgium as reserve to the British show-jumping team and we didn't fix another date. Simple as that. There was no argument, thank God, or I might have felt guilty later. After I got back from Brussels I started up with someone else.'

'The young lady who supplied your alibi.'

'Yes, indeed. She died, you know. Meningitis.'

'Your girlfriends don't have much luck. You met this one at a party, if I remember, and went home with her.'

'To Walcot Street, yes. A frightful slum, but I scarcely had a chance to notice. She practically dragged me to her lair and ravished me. Repeatedly.'

Diamond took a sip of the sherry the young man had provided. He suspected that the sexual bragging was targeted at Julie. He didn't remember it being so explicit

151

four years ago. All this passion was something of a mystery to Diamond considering that Marcus Martin was a short, unprepossessing man with carroty hair trained in wisps across his balding scalp, but he'd never understood how the female libido worked. Maybe the riding had something to do with it. Or the big house in the country.

'Can we go back to Britt Strand? The affair was conducted here for the most part, was it?'

'Entirely. Her place was very unsuitable. The people downstairs – I've forgotten their name—'

'Billington.'

'Right. They wouldn't have approved. Very straight-laced. Chapel, I believe. The old lady watched from downstairs like a Paris concierge.'

'You met them, then?'

'Several times. I used to call for Britt and drive her back in my Land Rover.'

'But you didn't, em . . .?'

'Not there. It was far more relaxed here at the manor.'

'The Billingtons went away for three weeks to Tenerife. Didn't you visit there when the house was empty?'

He frowned, and tapped the arm of the chair thoughtfully with one finger. 'Now that you mention it, there were a couple of occasions when I wasn't given the beady eye from downstairs. I just assumed they were out for a short time. Britt didn't mention their holiday. Presumably she preferred to come here.'

'Did she talk to you about the Billingtons at all?'

'Not much. She didn't like them particularly, but the place was convenient. She was quite sure that they let themselves into her flat when she went out sometimes. Just to nose around. That isn't unusual in lodgings, I understand. She also told me that the man fancied her a bit. She laughed it off. Most men fancied her a bit, if you ask me.'

Julie said, 'How did he show it?'

'Gave her little presents when his wife was occupied elsewhere, on the phone, or in the bath. Chocolates, flowers from the garden, things women appreciate. Britt said he always made an excuse, said he didn't care for chocolates, or he was trimming back the roses, or something.'

Diamond's attention snapped into sharper focus. 'Roses?'

'Or daffodils or sweet peas. I don't know.'

'But you said roses.'

'It was the first flower that came to mind.'

'You know why I'm interested?'

'Of course I do, and that's probably what made me mention roses. I wouldn't attach any importance to it.'

'Can't you remember what she told you?'

'After all this time? No.'

Diamond knew from experience the frustration of dealing with people whose memories were imprecise. At this distance in time the chance of learning anything new was depressingly slight. 'Did you ever actually speak to Mr Billington?'

'Only to pass the time of day.'

'Did Britt tell you anything else about him?'

'She reckoned he was glad to get out of the house. He was a sales rep, you know, greetings cards, rather vulgar, I believe, and I think he enjoyed a good laugh with some of the shop-ladies he visited. Why are you so interested in old Billington?'

Diamond ignored that. 'How do you know about the cards?'

'I saw him once doing his stuff in Frome. One of those newsagents in the pedestrian bit. The woman was practically wetting herself giggling at the cards he was trying to persuade her to take.'

'Let's get back to Britt. Did she talk to you about her work at all?'

'The journalism? Very little. I was completely in the dark about all that stuff that came out at the trial. The Iraqi connection. She told me she was enrolling at the college when the term started and that was all. I didn't even ask which course.'

'Did she mention Mountjoy in any connection?'

'None at all.'

'Have you met him?'

'Never, so far as I know.'

The same brick wall.

'During your visits to the house at Larkhall, the murder house, did you go up to her room?'

'Of course.'

'And did you ever take her flowers?'

Martin put up his hands in denial. 'Hey, what are you suggesting? Oh, no.'

'Did you send any after the friendship cooled, perhaps as a goodwill gesture?'

'A *what*?'

'Did you notice any in her flat?'

'Roses? No.'

'Did you send some to the funeral?'

'Certainly not.'

Martin made a point of looking at his watch.

It was Julie, unbidden, who picked up the questioning. 'We believe she may have been preparing some kind of article about the crusties in Bath. Did she mention it to you at any stage?'

He frowned, looked into the fire and snapped his fingers. 'As a matter of fact, she did. One afternoon we had tea in the Canary, that rather genteel café in Queen Street where they play taped classical music as you sip your Earl Grey. They insist on escorting you to your seat. We were favoured. We were given a window seat downstairs. You can watch the people walking past. I was doing my best to amuse Britt by making up stories about them as if I knew them all. This one posed for Picasso and this one is a train-spotter, or an escaped nun, and so on. Very silly when I describe it now, but it seemed amusing at the time. Then this enormous man strolled by in an army greatcoat, obviously a crusty, and to my amazement Britt waved to him and tapped on the window. He stopped and stared. For a moment I thought she was going to invite him in and so did the manageress. I mean this guy wasn't exactly teashop material. Dreadlocks, tattoos, ear-rings, hobnail boots. But Britt got up and went out to him, incidentally taking him half her toasted teacake. They were out there chatting for some time. The Canary clientele were absolutely riveted. He was an awesome sight.'

'Has to be GB,' Julie remarked to Diamond.

'Eventually he went on his way and she came back full of apologies. He was just a contact, she said, and I remember wondering how intimate a contact. I as good as asked her. You want to know the risks you're taking, if you understand me. But Britt insisted that it was purely professional. She was collecting material for a story about the crusties, something that could turn out really sensational. She was keeping the big fellow sweet until she had all the facts.'

Diamond turned to Julie. 'The Canary – that's just around the corner from Trim Street, isn't it?'

She nodded.

'Did she tell you anything else?' Diamond asked Martin.

'About the crusties? No.'

'She wasn't scared of this man?'

'She certainly didn't give that impression.'

'Have you seen him since?'

'No, I think he must have left the area.'

Summing up in the car as Julie drove back towards Bath, Diamond said, 'Not bad. We started with two men in the frame, Jake Pinkerton and Marcus Martin, and now we have two more: Wicked Winnie, as you called him, and GB, whoever he is.'

'Winston Billington had an alibi, surely?' said Julie. 'He was in Tenerife at the time of the murder.'

'I wonder if anyone checked it.'

'We must have.'

'You say "we", but you weren't part of it then. If there was any carelessness, it was my fault. Billington didn't loom very large in the inquiry, I can tell you that.' He let her negotiate a crossing and then resumed, 'He appears to have fancied his chances with her. The presents. The roses.'

'Or sweet peas,' she reminded him.

'All right, but he gave her flowers. And being the landlord, he had a key to her flat. If there's the slightest doubt about that alibi, Winston Billington has some questions to answer.'

'Surely we can check that holiday in Tenerife with the travel agent?'

'Four years on? I doubt if they keep their records that long. It's all on computer, isn't it? Dead easy to wipe.'

Julie smiled. Diamond never missed the chance of a sideswipe at computers.

'The same applies to the airlines,' he added. 'At one time we might have stood a chance of tracing a passenger list. It was all on paper. The stewardess had a clipboard with all the names. Not now.'

'Was that when Lindbergh was chief pilot?' Julie asked without taking her eyes off the road.

He gave her a quick look. 'On further consideration,' he said, 'a couple of rings through your nose might make all the difference.'

She didn't answer.

Back in Manvers Street, the same constable was still on duty behind the protective glass. He called out Diamond's name.

'What is it this time?'

'You have a visitor upstairs, sir.'

'One of your bumblebees?'

The constable was uncertain whether he was meant to smile. 'No, sir. A crusty.'

Chapter Fourteen

On the way upstairs Julie Hargreaves asked Diamond whether he wanted her to be present.

He told her brusquely, 'Of course I do. He's only here thanks to you.'

'I didn't arrange it.'

'You scattered the seedcorn.' But it wasn't said as a compliment. He had been assembling his thoughts for the interview to come, and she had disrupted them.

That was soon forgotten. In their makeshift office, a truly distracting spectacle was waiting. The crusty was asleep, feet up on the desk, head back and mouth open. Neither Julie nor Diamond had mentioned the fact, but each had expected to find someone fitting GB's description. This crusty was emphatically female.

Stirring at the sound of the door being closed, she yawned and said, 'Who are you?'

'We work here,' Diamond answered.

The statement was received with a slit-eyed, disbelieving look. Clearly they didn't look like the sort of police she was used to seeing. She would have been received downstairs by one of the uniformed officers and escorted here by another.

Diamond added, 'Plain clothes. And who are you?'

'I just looked in.'

One evasion for another. He decided to give his surname and Julie's rank and name.

The crusty responded with, 'Shirl.'

Shirl was in what looked like a wartime flying-jacket of faded brown leather with a fleece collar. She had a black T-shirt and fringed leather miniskirt, fishnet tights and badly scuffed ankle boots that she showed no inclination to remove from the desk. Her black hair was cut shorter even than Julie's and a Union Jack shape was shaved on each side of her head. Large silver rings adorned her ears, but she had no nose-decorations and no visible tattoos. Quite a conservative crusty.

'What can we get for you, Shirl? A coffee?'

She mimed the action of holding a cigarette to her lips.

Diamond exchanged a look with Julie and she went out to waylay someone who smoked.

'What brings you here?'

Shirl eyed him warily, still with her legs propped on his desk. Since the legs were so much on display it was impossible not to notice that they were stumpy. Neither the boots, nor the stockings, nor the miniskirt, could make them look anything else. Probably when she was standing no one noticed her legs, for she was generously proportioned above the waist. Deciding finally that some kind of explanation for her presence in the office had to be conceded, she told him, 'Some of the fuzz was down in Stall Street this morning asking about GB.'

'You know him?'

'Course I know him, or I wouldn't be here, would I? What do you want him for?'

'Only to help us with our inquiries.' The familiar form of words escaped Diamond's mouth before he was fully aware how sinister it would sound. Swiftly he rephrased it. 'I want to talk to him about someone he met a long time ago.'

'In Bath?'

He grinned, trying to be agreeable. 'Trim Street, actually.'

'Don't know it.'

'You know the bottom of Milsom Street, where the phones are, and that shop with the coffee machine – Carwardine's?'

Shirl said, 'It's gone.'

He frowned. 'Not Carwardine's?'

'Closed.'

'God help us.'

Shirl said helpfully, 'But I know where you mean.'

'Tucked away behind there, then. GB was living in a squat in Trim Street at one time four years ago. This woman was a journalist. She arranged with him to visit the house and take some pictures for a magazine.'

'This is that Swedish reporter who was killed, right?'

'Right.' Encouraged that she knew, he still tried to keep the same amiable tone. 'So you remember her?'

'I wasn't here then. I was still at school.'

'But you know about the murder?'

'Only what I was told.'

'And you can take me to GB?'

This caused her to gasp in alarm. 'No way! I didn't say that.'

'Then why are you here? Did he send you?'

She answered the first question, not the second. 'He's my bloke.'

Julie returned with three cigarettes and some matches. Shirl grabbed them all and lit one, slipping the others into a top pocket. Diamond told Julie what he had learned so far, cueing her to take up the questioning.

'Where are you living, love?' Julie asked.

'All over. I'm a traveller, aren't I?'

'In a van?'

'Something like that.'

'Close to Bath?'

'What's it to you?'

'We can give you a lift home.'

'Piss off.'

Diamond manfully took this as the end of the exchange with Julie and his turn to try. 'We'd like to meet GB, just to get his memories of four years ago. Do you think he'd agree to meet us?'

'Why ask me?'

'We'd ask him if he was here, but you're the next best.'

She transferred her interest to the cigarette, as if she'd won that point, too.

'He's your bloke, you said. Does he know you came? We can keep you out of it if you like.'

'I'm not scared of him,' said Shirl, but it sounded more like bravado than the truth.

'Did he send you?'

Silence.

This time Diamond let her stew for a while. She'd given no sign of wishing to leave and there had to be some reason why she had come. Crusties aren't in the habit of walking into police stations to fraternize with the fuzz.

Julie knew the tactics. She gazed steadily at the stack of stationery opposite as if her true vocation were counting envelopes.

Shirl endured the indifference for a minute or so and then became fidgety, inhaling on the cigarette several times and puffing out smoke. Finally she pinched out the lighted end and positioned it to cool on the edge of the desk. She lowered her legs to the floor and leaned forward in the chair.

'You think GB stiffed her, don't you?' Her black-lined eyes bore into Diamond. 'Don't you?'

Trying not to react at all, he stared over her head at an out-of-late notice about colorado beetles.

Shirl blurted it all out. 'You've had the wrong bloke banged up, and now he's escaped. That teacher. Mountjoy, or something. He didn't kill the woman. GB says so.'

'He told you that?' Diamond reacted eagerly, breaking his vow of silence. 'What else did he tell you?'

Interrupting her had been a tactical error. It shocked her into silence. Worse, she got up and walked to the door, pausing only to retrieve the dog-end from the edge of the desk.

Julie put a sisterly hand on her shoulder and said, 'You're going to want somewhere to sleep, love. You can't go back to him.'

'I'm not scared of him,' Shirl insisted for the second time, brushing Julie's hand away. 'He didn't do nothing – well, nothing serious.'

Some fast talking was required, so Diamond said with a firm statement of fact that rapidly gave way to an appeal and then practically a cry for help, 'It's obvious that GB sent you. Fair enough – he wants to know what we're up to. Would you give him a message from me? Tell him I'd like to meet him and talk about Britt Strand. He could be a crucial witness. Tell him I'm only interested in what happened four years ago when he was squatting in Trim Street. I'm willing to go anywhere for a friendly chat. Anywhere he cares to name.' Before he had finished, Shirl was out of the door and on her way downstairs to the street. It was by no means certain that she had heard the offer of a meeting.

'Shall I get the car?' Julie offered.

'No point. She'd lose us easily in Bath. I'm going to organize a tail. On foot.'

She looked doubtful. 'You'll have to be quick about it.'

'Yes, it's you.'

Julie gave him a startled look. 'But she knows me.'

He nodded. 'She'll expect someone to come after her, so it might as well be you. Radio in when you can.' Man management had never been Diamond's strong suit. As for woman management . . . pass.

Julie got up and went through the door without letting her eyes meet Diamond's.

*

After she'd gone, he sat back and pondered the reason for Shirl's visit. It seemed to have been dedicated to getting one point across. Having delivered the statement that Mountjoy was innocent, she couldn't get away fast enough. Did GB seriously think he would get the police off his back by sending this tantalizing message? If the man *really* knew something that hadn't been aired before, this could be a pivotal moment in the case. The most likely explanation was that Shirl had been sent solely to find out why there was police interest in GB, who was probably involved in other, unrelated crimes. She hadn't been instructed to say anything about Mountjoy. That had been a bonus.

He ambled along the corridor to check on progress in the hunt for Mountjoy. Standing among the computer terminals where civilian staff tapped steadily at the keyboards, Commander Warrilow eyed him morosely.

'Any progress?' Diamond enquired.

'It's all progress.'

'That's a positive attitude.'

'We've just had a sighting.'

'Nice work!'

'Possibly. A man of his description was seen less than an hour ago in the Circus.'

'Walking the tight-rope?' Diamond asked, knowing perfectly well that the reference was to the circle of terraces that was one of Bath's architectural glories.

Warrilow ignored the remark and said, 'The water people are working up there, inspecting the drains. Several inspection covers have been open all week.'

Diamond widened his eyes. 'And you suspect . . .?'

Warrilow gave a nod. 'The original sewage culverts go right underneath the buildings. They're large. You can stand upright in some of them. We think he could be hiding there. I've got a search party about to go in.'

Peter Diamond started to whistle the theme from *The Third Man*.

Warrilow clicked his tongue and turned his back.

Diamond moved on to the radio room and told the sergeant supervisor that he wanted to be informed when Julie Hargreaves checked in. 'Should be soon,' he said confidently. 'Can I borrow a headset?'

In a few minutes he heard Julie announce herself. She had followed Shirl to the railway station forecourt, where she had stopped to talk to a couple of crusty men, neither of whom fitted GB's description. 'Now she's leaving them, heading for the tunnel under the railway where the taxis line up. I'm following.'

Diamond turned to the sergeant. 'Do we still have a unit to monitor the movements of travellers and crusties?' One summer there had been a much publicized incident on the M5 motorway when the crusties had halted their vehicles in line and blocked the traffic for over an hour as a protest against what they termed police harassment.

'Only in the summer months, sir. They're less of a problem now.'

'Like house-flies? So we ignore them in the winter?'

'We don't have the resources to monitor them all the year round.'

Muttering, he replaced the headset. Julie didn't make contact again for twenty minutes. Then she reported that she had just reached the A36, the Warminster Road, and Shirl was by the side of the road trying to hitch-hike. 'What are my orders if she gets a lift?' she asked.

Diamond said ungraciously, 'I suppose I'd better pick you up. Where exactly are you?'

'I just gave you my position.' Julie's indignation came forcibly over the two-way radio.

He didn't apologize. He wasn't much good at street-names and chasing about in cars wasn't his favourite pastime. The sergeant in the radio room put a finger on the appropriate place on a street-map displayed on the wall. With an air of martyrdom, Diamond went to collect the Escort.

He drove it through central Bath and over Pulteney Bridge at the modest speed dictated by the traffic.

Julie was still waiting by the government buildings opposite Minster Way. She waved vigorously.

'Lost her, then?' he said.

'Not if we get weaving,' she informed him as she got in. 'She's in one of those long builder's lorries with a yellow cab. He picked her up about two minutes ago. We ought to be able to catch it.'

'We can try,' he said without much conviction. 'Not easy to overtake on this road. With this old heap, I mean.' He spoke as if all he needed were some extra horsepower. In driving away, he pulled out in the path of a BMW that was forced to brake abruptly. 'What I could really do with,' he said above the blare of the BMW's horn, 'is one of those detachable flashing beacons that Kojak used to have. You put your arm out of the window, slam it on the roof and off you go. Everyone knows it's an emergency.'

The road widened and he succeeded in overtaking a small white van. 'Did she know you were tailing her?' he asked Julie.

'I don't think so. There were a couple of hairy moments when she looked back, but I merged with other people on the street.'

The road ahead dipped and gave them a longer view. 'Any sign?' Diamond asked.

'I don't know . . . Hold on – yes! Just about to go out of sight. See?'

While he was trying to see, the white van – the only thing he had overtaken so far – trundled past him again. For the next couple of miles the oncoming traffic prevented him from making any progress. Some traffic lights at the Viaduct pub hindered him further, but Julie pointed out that there was a steep hill ahead that was obliging everyone to move at the speed of the slowest.

Soon after they reached the top, they were rewarded with the sight of the yellow lorry at the side of the road and Shirl in the act of climbing down from the cab. The stretch of road here was fringed by trees on either side.

'Watch where she goes,' ordered Diamond, the man of authority once more. 'I'm going past.'

He slowed to a crawl – to the incandescent fury of the driver of the BMW behind him – until he found a place to pull in on some even turf about a hundred yards on. In his mirror he saw the lorry flashing its direction light to move off again.

'She stayed this side of the road,' said Julie as they got out.

Shirl wasn't in sight, however. She must have headed straight into the wood, a dense, dark strip that funnelled outwards to cover a substantial area. After trekking back along the road, they found a bridle path, the only route she could have taken.

They started in pursuit. A brisk walk over frost-hard leaves brought them to a clearing occupied by up to a dozen vehicles in various states of dilapidation. A smouldering fire and a pair of barking dogs gave promise that the place was inhabited.

A woman – not Shirl – stepped out of an ancient double-decker bus and Diamond asked if GB was about.

She must have been about thirty, with a weathered, intelligent face and cropped hair. She said as her gaze moved from one to the other, assessing their potential for trouble, 'Who wants him?'

'I'm Peter Diamond. This is Julie Hargreaves. Friends of Shirl.' Which was overstating it, but worth trying.

'Shirl?'

'Shirl. You must know Shirl. Only we'd like to meet GB.'

The exchange was interrupted by a sudden shout of,

'No! Don't touch me, you bastard! Get away!' from the interior of a large black van close by. A piercing scream followed. A door in the side of the van was flung open and a young woman in just a T-shirt and knickers fell out, picked herself up and ran sobbing across the clearing to a caravan. In the doorway of the van she had left stood a man holding a broad leather belt. He slammed the door shut.

'Was that him?' Diamond enquired.

'GB?' Their informant looked more surprised by the question than the incident. 'No. Follow me.' She took them around the side of the bus and back into the wood again, or so it appeared until a short path brought them to another clearing where a large, sleek camper van was parked in isolation, a stately home on wheels, not more than two years old according to its number-plate. It had a TV dish attached to the side.

'Wait.' The woman rapped on the door with her knuckles.

It was Shirl who opened it. She looked beyond the woman, sighted Diamond and Julie and put her hand to her throat. She turned and said something inaudible inside the van. A few words were spoken and then she stepped down and said with a resentful note, 'You're to go in.' She, it seemed, had been ordered to leave.

GB civilly got up to greet his visitors when they entered. He wasn't built for life in a van; he had to dip his head, although Diamond, no midget, could stand upright with ease. Neither did the accent sound right for the travelling life. It was more Radley than Romany. 'Do find yourselves somewhere to sit down. You want some background on that Swedish woman who was murdered in Bath, I gather.'

This was the assurance GB needed, apparently. No mention of other matters. He'd wanted to agree the agenda first.

Diamond gave a nod. 'Shirl did a fine job for you. She

could have a future in the CID if she wanted.'

'Not if she steps out of line. I didn't send her to you.'

'She acted independently?'

'Women,' said GB.

No question: he had altered. Whereas his head had been shaven in the photo Diamond possessed, he now sported a crisp haircut that would not have looked out of place in a Martini commercial. His black sweater, jeans and designer trainers were straight out of GQ: the new-look GB was a dapper figure with a disarming smile. All the menace of dress and demeanour had been discarded, except the one feature he could not alter, the 'lazy' left eye that Prue Shorter's camera had caught. Recalling the photograph, and Marcus Martin's account of the greatcoated crusty who had created a sideshow at the window of the Canary café, this was a transformation to rank with the emergence of a butterfly.

The van, too, was luxuriously fitted, the curtains, cushions and seat coverings in a matching fabric that could have come from Liberty's. GB had gone upmarket, but why? Diamond's quick assessment was that this was probably a drug-pusher in the process of distancing himself from the mugs who used the stuff. It was a familiar scenario. The pusher first identifies his market by mingling with the potential buyers, dressing as they do. In time he gets rich and gives up that pretence. The crusties depended on GB now. If he'd come dressed in a bowler hat and pinstripes they'd still buy from him.

'GB – are those your initials?' Diamond asked when he had lowered himself on to a bench with as much dignity as a fat man could. He was civil in his manner to GB. The drugs connection, if any, was someone else's concern.

GB answered, 'No it's just a nickname for a patriotic fellow who used to keep a bulldog with a Union Jack coat. Tea or coffee?'

They hadn't expected the offer, but it seemed to go with

the new image. 'Tea for me.'

'Me, too,' said Julie.

'So what's your real name?'

'GB. I answer to GB,' he said smoothly. 'I've been called worse things in my time, so I settled for that.'

Diamond moved on to more urgent business. 'We didn't meet at the time of the Britt Strand murder.'

'No reason to,' GB said with his back turned, attending to the kettle.

'Except that you apparently met Miss Strand in the weeks leading up to her death and we tried to interview everyone.'

'Yes, I met her,' GB admitted, turning to face them, 'but so did hundreds of other people, I reckon. When you think about all the contacts Britt must have made in the course of a week—'

'It was our job to trace them,' Diamond said to cut him off. 'We missed you the first time around.'

GB gave a smile of sympathy. 'It must be deeply frustrating. You'll never trace everyone, particularly after so long.'

'We'll do our best.'

'Memories go slack.'

'We'll prod them, then.'

'The best of luck.'

Diamond thought as he listened that GB was trying a mite too hard to present himself as the genial, laid-back host. It was more than likely that drugs were hidden somewhere in the caravan, which could account for his behaviour, but there was always the chance it was prompted by something more relevant to the present investigation. 'Would you care to tell us how you came to meet Britt Strand?'

He said without hesitation, 'She came looking for me. This was the summer before she died. I heard that this blonde woman was chatting up the crusties outside the pump room, asking about me. I was damned sure it was some spy from the social security office, so I kept a low profile. But eventually she nailed me. I was living in a squat in Trim Street at the time and she waited on the corner and stepped out as I was going past. I remember being extremely abusive, but she wouldn't back off.'

'Did she say what she wanted?'

'Right off. She told me she was a journalist researching a story about Trim Street. Flashed her press-card. It didn't open doors with me, I can tell you. I didn't want to be written up in the tabloids.'

'But she wasn't from the tabloids.'

'Would you believe anything a press reporter told you?' GB said as he tossed teabags into three mugs. 'She insisted it wasn't me personally, it was the squat that interested her and that made me even more suspicious. When you're living in a squat, you need publicity like Custer needed more Indians. I told her exactly that and she offered me fifty quid for an exclusive, with pictures of the squat and no names to be published. She said the story wouldn't appear for six months and then only in up-market magazines selling abroad. I was mystified, I can tell you. Why the hell should someone in France or America want to read about a bunch of crusties squatting in Bath?'

Diamond dearly wanted to know. 'Did you ask?'

'Actually, no.'

'You didn't want to talk yourself out of fifty pounds?'

GB grinned. 'It was enough to keep me sweet. This lady was loaded. Smart clothes, much too snazzy for the social worker I'd first thought was on to me. When she handed me a tenner just to set up another meeting, I didn't give it back.'

'You got into negotiations?'

'I wouldn't put it as strongly as that. We met a couple of times in Victoria Park.'

'But by arrangement?'

'Naturally.'

'Why in the park? Why not in Abbey Churchyard where you people congregate?'

He said with a sly grin, 'The park was more private, wasn't it?'

'You didn't want your fellow squatters to know you were doing a deal?'

'I didn't say that.'

'But you meant it.'

The kettle had suddenly become altogether more interesting to GB than his visitors.

Diamond kept the momentum up. 'This was during the summer of 1990?'

'September or thereabouts,' GB answered without looking up. 'The weather was still okay. We sat on the grass and talked.'

'Britt sat down with you? Did she fancy a bit of rough?'

A blank stare. Even Diamond decided on consideration that it was a tactless remark.

Partly to soften it, he turned to Julie and said, 'I hope you're not a feminist.' Then he told GB, 'Let's face it, she was extremely attractive and she wanted a favour from you. You're telling me all that you two did was sit down together in Victoria Park and talked? You just said the park was private.'

'Compared to the Abbey Churchyard it is. Are you trying to pin something on me, Mr Diamond? Britt and I were not lovers. Okay, we got into a clinch once or twice and yes, I fancied her, but Victoria Park isn't *that* private.'

'I didn't know you were bashful.'

'It takes two.'

'*She* was bashful?'

'She was class.'

Diamond said after a pause, 'So the upshot was that Britt had her way, but you didn't?'

He laughed. 'You mean she screwed me? Yes, that sums it up. She got the deal she wanted.'

'I wouldn't say she screwed you if you got the fifty pounds.'

'I earned every penny. I had to talk my Trim Street mates into posing for poncy photographs. That wasn't easy. They all had a share of the fee,' GB was quick to add.

'So what happened?'

'She turned up one evening with her fat photographer and took masses of pictures.'

'We've seen some of them,' said Diamond.

'That's more than I have. She dropped me like a stone after the photo session. Black or white?'

After the tea was poured and handed out, Diamond picked up the thread again. 'Did I get the impression that you wished you'd seen her again?'

'Britt Strand was a prick-teaser,' GB said in a nonchalant way. 'She fooled me and I reckon she fooled plenty of others in her time.'

'Did you try to see her again?' Diamond pressed, increasingly convinced that there was more to come. For all his efforts to play it down, GB's vanity had been badly injured by Britt Strand.

GB took time over his response. Finally he said, 'Yes, a couple of times I tried. I found out where she lived, in Larkhall. Looked her up in the phone book. Journalists have to have phones, don't they? I tried calling the number a couple of times and all I got was an answerphone.'

'Did you leave a message?'

'No. I wanted to speak to her in person.'

'Because you were angry?'

'No, because I'm an idiot. I still thought she fancied me. It was only after she was dead that all that stuff came out about the blokes she'd strung along – the pop music man and the showjumper and that poor sod Mountjoy.'

For the moment, Diamond resisted the urge to ask about Mountjoy. 'You couldn't reach her on the phone, so what did you do about it?'

172

'I went to the house a couple of times and she wasn't in, or wasn't answering. Nobody was answering.'

'When exactly was this?'

He gave a shrug. 'Can *you* remember things from four years back?'

'The photo session in Trim Street was ten days before she died,' Diamond prompted him, 'and you say you went to the house a couple of times after that. By day?'

'Twice. And once at night.'

'At *night*?'

He sighed as if it was all too tedious to relate. 'One evening one of the crusties from the squat was in Queen Square with a couple of mates and a bottle of cider. They happened to spot Britt with some man going into that French restaurant, the Beaujolais. Thought it was a great joke, knowing I fancied my chances with her, and came back to the squat to give me a hard time.'

Julie started to say, 'This must have been—' before Diamond silenced her with a look.

GB completed the statement for her: '. . . the night she was topped. Right. Mountjoy was her date.'

'How do you know it was Mountjoy?' Diamond asked.

'I haven't finished, have I? As I explained, back at the squat those guys really took the piss, saying the bloke she was with was a middle-aged wimp and stuff like that. I walked out after a bit, said I was taking the dog for a walk, and you know where I went, of course. The restaurant is only a short walk from Trim Street. I wanted to see if it was true. I was in a foul mood and ready to make a scene, so I marched straight into the place with my dog and looked around, but she wasn't in there. This was getting on in the evening, I suppose. A couple of hours or more had passed since my so-called mates had seen the couple going in. I could see some of the tables had been cleared. I felt cheated. I wanted to know for sure if she'd started up with someone else. So I hoofed it up to Larkhall, where

173

she lived. Just to satisfy myself, okay?'

'Okay,' said Diamond. 'What happened?'

'It's about a mile to walk there and I calmed down a lot, but I was still too curious to give up. I got to the street.'

'What time?'

'No idea. I didn't carry a watch in those days.'

'Before midnight?'

'More like eleven. There was a light on upstairs, but I couldn't be sure it was Britt's flat. All I had was the house number. I sat on a wall across the street and watched. After a bit, the light went on downstairs and the front door opened and a bloke came out. I'm certain it was Mountjoy. I've seen his picture in the papers.'

If true, this really was sensational and Diamond didn't conceal the excitement he felt. 'Did anyone come to the door with him?'

'She was there, yes. I had a clear view.'

'You mean *Britt*?'

'Who else?'

'You're sure of this?'

'Hundred per cent.'

'How was she dressed?'

'In a skirt and blouse buttoned to the neck – and if that surprises you, it's nothing to the surprise I had. What's more, there was no embrace, nothing. Not even a few civil words. She shut the door fast, before he was through the gate. He didn't look back, either. Marched off up the street. That was the end of it. He didn't kill her. You banged up an innocent man, Mr Diamond.'

'And you withheld vital information from the police,' Diamond retorted, which was an agile reaction considering the force of what had just been said. 'Why didn't you come forward?'

'A crusty? You're joking. You'd have swung it on me, no problem. I'd have been the poor, benighted sod who did four years in Albany. I mean, I was there in Larkhall. I had the motive and the opportunity.'

'So what's changed? Why are you talking about it now?'

GB fielded the question smoothly. 'What's changed, Mr Diamond, is that you're sitting in my mobile home asking questions about the murder. I've got to defend myself.'

'Right. How do we know you didn't go into the house and kill her?'

'Someone else did.'

'That's easily said.'

'I saw them.'

Diamond's pulse quickened.

GB took his time over continuing, probably sensing the need to pick his words with care. 'After Mountjoy left, I thought about going in. I was still pissed off about the way she'd used me and then dropped me. I wanted a civilized discussion.'

It sounded unlikely, but Diamond observed a tactful silence.

'The thing is,' GB continued, 'I was thrown by what I'd just seen, the way her date had been shown the door. You'd think he'd insulted her mother or kicked the cat, or something. I stood about for a bit, not sure whether to go over and knock on the door or leave it for another day. I must have been deep in thought because I didn't notice this other old git walking up the street. I don't know where he came from. There he was, opening the front gate and stepping up to the door like he owned the place. He took a key from his pocket and let himself in.'

'He had a doorkey? What was he like?'

'I only had the back view. Thin. Average height. Wearing a flat cap and overcoat. Middle-aged, going by the way he moved. I saw him for about ten seconds, that's all.'

'This couldn't have been Mountjoy returning?'

'No way. He's bigger, and they were differently dressed.'

'Was he carrying anything? Like a bunch of flowers, for instance?'

'I didn't see any flowers.'

'Roses, I'm talking about.'

GB shook his head.

'And then what?' Diamond asked.

'I left. Seeing him arrive made up my mind. He was sure to come to the door if I knocked and I didn't want any hassle.'

'You assumed he was the landlord?'

'Yes.'

'What do you mean when you say you didn't want any hassle?'

GB grinned good-naturedly. 'I might have thumped him.'

'And after that a civilized discussion with Britt would have been unlikely?'

'Right. It was only later when I read about the murder in the papers that I found out that the owners were away in the Canaries. When they got back they discovered the body, so it couldn't have been the landlord I saw, could it?'

Diamond took the question as rhetorical. Mentally he was already in another place, putting questions to someone else. He went through the motions of asking GB whether he had returned directly to Trim Street on the night of these events. Then he tried for a better description of the mystery caller, but got nothing new. GB had said it all the first time.

Diamond led Julie out of the camper. He felt sick to the stomach. What he'd just heard was devastating if it was true: the confirmation that he'd blundered back in 1990 and sent down the wrong man.

'You'd better drive,' he told Julie.

Chapter Fifteen

Frank Wiggs, a television engineer living in Morford Street, one of the surviving Georgian terraces of artisan dwellings on the lower slopes of Lansdown Hill, called out to his wife Nina that he wouldn't be long. Nina called back that if he was, he'd find the door bolted. It was their usual affectionate exchange before Frank left for a night at his usual pub, the Pig and Fiddle in Saracen Street, where they served Ash Vine, 'the bitter for serious drinkers'. Nina had long ago given up going with him.

Having checked that he had some cash and a pack of cigarettes, Frank closed the front door behind him and set off at a brisk walk down the hill.

Left to her own resources for the evening, Nina was not despondent. She reached for the television remote control and silenced the inane panel game that was showing. She opened a drawer of the sideboard and took out a box of Belgian chocolates she had bought that afternoon from the little shop on Pulteney Bridge. She popped a truffle into her mouth, crushed it rapturously between her teeth, swallowed it fast and treated herself to another, followed by a violet cream. Needing something to lubricate her throat, she opened the lower section of the sideboard and reached to the back where she kept the brandy – in a place where Frank never looked except at Christmas when the family came. All he ever drank was beer. She poured herself what she thought of as a half measure – half filling a brandy glass – put it on a tray with the chocolates and the portable phone and carried them upstairs to the bathroom where she converted the cistern over the toilet into her private altar. While running the water, she tipped in some bubble-bath. Then she removed her clothes, trimmed her toenails, tried the scales and took another three truffles. Satisfied that the water was right, she stepped in and immersed herself to the shoulders. Bliss. She reached for the brandy and the phone.

Twenty minutes later, in sprightly conversation with her friend Molly in Aldershot, Nina heard a sound from downstairs like the shattering of glass. Her immediate thought was that she must have left the sideboard door open and the cat had crept inside and knocked over some wine glasses. The silly animal had got in once before and snapped the stem of their last Waterford goblet from the set her Aunt Maeve had given them as a wedding present. The damage would be done by now and the cat would have run off, so Nina scarcely paused for breath in giving Molly the story of this French film she had videoed about a rich woman who hired young men as servants and seduced them.

A short time after this she was conscious of the stairs creaking, but the central heating caused the wood to contract, so there was no reason for unease.

Then the bathroom door opened and a man looked round the door.

Nina slammed the phone against her breasts. She found the pluck to say, 'Get out!'

He said, 'Stay calm. I won't touch you.'

Molly in Aldershot said, 'I think we've got a crossed line. I can hear someone else.'

Nina lowered everything but her head under the water and in Aldershot Molly heard strange noises on the line before it went dead. She was to spend the next twenty minutes trying to get reconnected.

Meanwhile Nina said to the man, 'I'll call the police.' Considering that the phone was now under a foot of water, this was no threat. She should have said, 'I've just called the police.'

The man's brown eyes locked with Nina's. He wasn't in his teens or his twenties as most rapists are said to be. She estimated that he was around forty. He had dark, frightening eyes and a gaunt face. But he hadn't stepped fully into the room. He said, 'You'd better get out of there.'

Nina thought, like hell I will.

There was a bathrobe made of towelling hanging on the door. He unhooked it and slung it over the taps. 'Put that around you. I don't have much time. I'm John Mountjoy and I want some help.'

'Mountjoy – the man who escaped?'

'From Albany.'

Nina gave a gasp.

He said, 'Now you know why I'm here.'

She said in a whisper, 'Danny?' Her thoughts turned back ten years to the evening she had last seen Danny Boon, the night before they picked him up for shooting the postmaster. For almost a year she and Danny had held up sub-post offices in the West Country. They had become famous in the press as Bristol Bonnie and Clifton Clyde. Her nerves had been steel-hard in those days and she'd carried her own gun and would have used it, though probably not to kill. Together they'd netted a big sum and she'd bought this house from part of her share. It was Danny who had shot the Warminster postmaster who decided to 'have a go'. He hadn't meant to kill – but how do you explain that to a court of law? Someone had seen enough of Danny to provide the police with a good photofit and they found him in their records. With his name in all the papers and on TV, he had fixed a last meeting with Nina on a cold, damp February night at

Sham Castle. He had promised her he'd say nothing to the police about her and he'd kept his word. She'd kept her promise to Danny to stop when she was ahead. Not once had she visited him in prison. Their collaboration was a closed book.

Ever since that evening Nina had been an exemplary citizen, even in that long, cold winter when neither she nor Frank had been in work. She'd married Frank on the rebound, out of grief for Danny, and, it has to be said, to confuse the police, who continued to hunt for her. Frank wouldn't know an automatic from a banana, but he'd happened to step into her life at the critical time. She'd told him nothing of her past.

Mountjoy said, 'Danny's a good man.'

'You know him?' Nina whispered.

'A bit. We went to art classes. Inside, I mean. Listen, you're going to have to help me. I need food, clothes, blankets, money. And I'm going to borrow your car. I'll tell you where to find it later. Now would you get out of the bath and help me?'

Deeply shocked and disbelieving, she said, 'Danny didn't send you. He wouldn't do that. Not Danny.'

He took a step into the room. 'No. He told nobody. But I'm here. I worked it out.'

'What?'

He leaned over the bath and twisted the handle that released the plug. The water started flowing away. He picked up the bathrobe and handed it to her.

Nina drew it around her shoulders for protection and managed to stand up with what she hoped was decorum, if not dignity. Stepping out, she made an effort to sound in control. 'What kind of clothes?'

'For a woman.'

'A *woman*?'

'A complete change. Warm stuff. Trousers, sweaters, underclothes.'

180

'Is someone with you?'

'Fetch them now. *Fast*.'

'She may not be my size.'

'We'll make do.'

Tying the belt of the bathrobe tightly across her middle, she went through to the small bedroom she shared with Frank. She opened a fitted wardrobe. 'You'd better take the stretch jeans and the double-knit sweater on the top shelf.' She opened a dressing-table drawer and picked out some knickers and a packet of tights she hadn't opened yet. 'If she's on the run with you, she must be suffering. You can take whatever you need.'

She tried to sound co-operative. She would willingly give him all the clothes she possessed to buy his good will. The physical threat had receded a little, but a petrifying fear gripped her. The man knew of her involvement with Danny. He had it in his power to shop her to the police, to have her put away for murder. With the zeal of a charity worker, she delved into the wardrobe for a hold-all and started stuffing things in. Anything to humour him.

'Will this be enough? I could fill another case if you like.'

He took the two spare blankets she kept in the chest under the window. 'The man who went out just now – where was he going?'

'The pub.' She thought of adding the reassurance that Frank wouldn't be home until well after closing time, after a slow, unsteady plod up Broad Street, but she checked herself. She wanted Mountjoy out of here as quickly as possible.

He was looking out of the window. 'Where do you keep your car?'

Parking wasn't permitted in Morford Street. 'The garages at the back. It should be open.'

'What is it?'

'An old Renault Eight. Green.'

'Keys?'

181

'Downstairs. Shall I fetch them?'

'Pick up the bag. Don't try anything. I'll be right behind you.'

As she came downstairs she saw the broken window pane in the back door and the glass splinters on the doormat. He'd simply reached through and let himself in. How many times had she told Frank they were insecure?

'Car keys,' he prompted her.

She went into the back room and found her handbag.

'Now some food.'

In the kitchen they filled two carriers, emptying her fridge of everything that could be eaten fresh and then taking cans from the cupboards, and biscuits and bread.

'The man who went to the pub,' he said. 'Is he your husband, or what?'

She answered, 'Yes.'

'Husband?'

'Yes.' She added the reassurance, 'I won't tell him about you. He knows nothing about my past.'

'And I suppose Danny knows nothing about him,' Mountjoy commented with an accusing glare, and Nina, the proof of the cynical expectation of prisoners that their women will abandon them, wished she had not spoken.

Mountjoy told her, 'You'll have to explain the car being gone.'

'He won't even notice.' When she had helped him put the carriers beside the front door with the holdall and the blankets, she said, 'How is Danny coping?'

'He's all right. He's strong.'

'You said just now that he didn't tell you about me.'

Mountjoy said, 'It was in the papers, wasn't it? I lived here when you were in the news. You're the one they called Bristol Bonnie.'

'But nobody knows my name.'

'Nor do I. I know where you live, that's all.'

'How – if Danny didn't tell you?'

He took time over answering, as if uncertain whether to tell, whether he felt she deserved to know. 'They lay on classes. Education. I did art and so did he. The only picture he ever finished was an acrylic. He worked at it for months on end. It was a street scene, viewed straight on, with no perspective to mess him up. Some Georgian terraced houses on a steep slope. They had railings outside and you could just see the basement windows. The detail was pretty good. Two of the houses had a set of Venetian windows, the central one arched, with rectangular casements on each side, with small square panes. Pretty striking. There was a woman's face looking out of one of them. Sad eyes. But Danny isn't much good at painting people.'

'Me?' She sucked in her cheeks and clamped her teeth on them. With emotion heaped on to all the stress, she was afraid she might cry.

He said, 'It had to be you, didn't it? I knew you and Danny used to operate somewhere in these parts and I know the streets of Bath. The way he painted it was what they would term naive in the art world, but he took no end of trouble to get it right, the steep slope and those windows and the railings in front of the basements and the wrought-iron stands for window-boxes on the house next door that didn't have the Venetian windows. He must have a photographic memory. Of course, it could have been one of a dozen streets except for one thing: the doors. He painted them without doorknobs, or locks, or letterboxes. And to my knowledge there's only one street with front doors that never open and that's the lower half of Morford Street. You have access from the back, through the arch halfway along the terrace.'

She didn't compliment him on his powers of observation. He didn't seem to need humouring.

He said, 'I thought you would want to help me.'

She nodded, wishing with all her might that he would leave.

He rattled the keys. 'I'll leave the car in the station car park. You can pick it up in the morning. There's one other thing.'

'Yes?'

'Those post office jobs you did with Danny. You both carried guns. What happened to yours?'

'I got rid of it.'

His expression hardened. 'I don't think so. You'll have hidden it, but you won't have got rid of it.'

'Truly.'

'Lying bitch. I had a wife who lied to me. Want to know what I did to her?'

She shook her head.

He was right. She had it in the house, under the loose floorboard in the front room, covered by a carpet and a table with a bronze flower pot. She'd judged that it was safer to keep the gun all these years than risk it being found somewhere and traced back to her by forensic scientists. Up to this minute she had been right. Nina said, 'I threw it into the river.'

Mountjoy said, 'Come here.'

Chapter Sixteen

Peter Diamond had faults – more, perhaps, than most – but reticence wasn't one of them. He needed to talk. At this minute his self-esteem was at rock bottom. He'd really messed up in 1990 unless GB had invented all that stuff about the comings and goings at the murder house. A killer had escaped thanks to his inept investigation.

So when he and Julie retraced their route through the woods to the road in silence, the break in communication wasn't of his choosing. He was bursting to speak, but inconveniently the evening was closing in fast, obliging them to concentrate on their footing. All speculation as to the identity of the man GB had seen entering Britt's lodging on the night of the murder had to wait until they were back in the car.

'Winston Billington,' he finally said, struggling to persuade the buckle of the seat-belt across his middle. 'Who else could it be but the landlord, letting himself in at that time of night?'

'You're blocking my view,' Julie told him. 'I'm trying to turn the car.'

'Clear road.' He let her concentrate on the U-turn. Once they were heading in the right direction, he leaned so close to her that the brim of his trilby touched her hair. 'What do you think?'

'I thought Mr Billington had an alibi. He was in Tenerife with his wife until after the murder.'

'But did we check it?' He turned away and pummelled his thigh with his fist. 'Did we check it at the time, Julie?'

She said, 'I wasn't there.'

Diamond was talking rhetorically. 'We had this statement that the Billingtons returned – when was it, two days after? – and discovered the body. The whole shebang started from there. Did I have their flight schedules checked? Or the hotel register? I honestly don't think I did. You'll say it was negligent. I'd say the same. But Billington was never seriously considered.'

'As a suspect, you mean?'

'What a cock-up.'

'Why would he kill her?'

'Anger, because she refused to come across. We heard from Marcus Martin that Billington fancied Britt.'

'Finding excuses to give her presents of flowers and chocolates,' said Julie.

He nodded. 'The flower connection, you see.'

'Mrs Billington insisted that the roses couldn't have come from their garden,' Julie pointed out.

'That was obvious to anyone who's ever grown roses,' he said as if he constantly carried a pair of pruning shears in his pocket. Julie wasn't to know that he'd acquired his horticultural wisdom from Mrs Billington herself. 'They were definitely imported roses from a florist. The salient point is that he's the only one of her admirers who liked to say it with flowers.'

They turned left at the Viaduct to go up Brassknocker. While the Escort was making heavy work of the curving incline, Julie commented over the engine note, 'It takes some believing. I mean, would Billington kill her in his own house and report it to the police himself?'

'Yes, because that's smart,' said Diamond. 'The dumb thing to have done was dump the body somewhere else. Bodies are hellish to dispose of. They won't burn well, or stay under water for long and digging a grave is a job for a professional. No, it looks as if Billington brazened it out four years ago and I believed him.'

'You seem to have made up your mind.'

'Not at all.' He gave her a sharp look. 'I'm weighing the possibilities.' He weighed them a little longer before adding, more tentatively, 'The wife's behaviour was instructive. I'm sorry you weren't there. Where were you?'

Julie reminded him, 'Chatting up the crusties.'

He tried to break out of the despondent mood by being boisterous. 'Well, if you will insist on keeping that sort of company. . .'

The car began picking up speed at the top of the hill. 'You see,' he went on, 'Mrs Billington didn't really want me to interview Billington. She was shielding him, yet I got the feeling that she wasn't doing it out of loyalty or affection. She spoke about him in a detached way, almost disdainful. "You'll get nothing out of Winston," but said in a tone that made me think *she*'d got nothing out of him.'

A little later, she asked, 'What's Mr Billington like? Did you interview him at the time of the murder?'

'I saw them together then, and she did most of the talking. He was civil, unassertive, a quiet bloke, but they often are.'

'How do you see it, then?' Julie asked as they began the long descent into Bath.

'Assuming Billington did it? The middle-aged man lusting after the pretty young lodger who appears to share her favours widely, but won't include him, for all his overtures with sweets and flowers. He comes back early from his holiday in Tenerife – maybe some family emergency, or a crisis at work – at any rate, some excuse he concocted – and leaves his wife to follow him in a day or two. This is the opportunity he's waited for. A night alone in the house with Britt. He buys a dozen red roses at the airport and gets home around eleven.'

'At the airport?'

'There are always flowers at airports.'

'GB didn't say the man he saw was carrying flowers,' said Julie.

'He could have hidden them inside his coat. He wouldn't want the neighbours to see them, or Britt, until he was ready to surprise her.'

'And she was supposed to melt at the sight of a dozen roses?' said Julie sceptically.

'There are women who would.'

'It sounds as if you're speaking from experience.'

He said bitingly, 'We're talking about Billington. He goes to her room, gets the brush-off and goes berserk. Stabs her repeatedly. Then stuffs the flowers in her mouth.'

'And leaves her like that? For two days?'

'Certainly. He wouldn't stick around. He'd clear off fast to somewhere else, ready to claim, as he does, that he actually travelled back from Tenerife with his wife and got back two days after the murder. He had to persuade her to back him, of course.'

'Cover up for a murder?' said Julie in disbelief.

'That's not uncommon.' Now he gave her the benefit of his years in the murder squad. 'The wife who shops her husband is rare indeed, Julie. From her point of view there's always an element of doubt. A murderer doesn't admit to his wife that he's taken someone's life. She has a vested interest in believing he's innocent. She'll clutch at any straw. After all, it's a criticism of her if he fancies other women. And then to be the wife of a killer, stared at by other people, hounded by the press – that's not a pleasant prospect. So, yes, Mrs Billington stood by him and supported his alibi. She may have believed he was innocent at first, but I get the impression four years have changed her opinion. She's not going to blow the whistle on him now, but she can't disguise the contempt she feels for him. Pity you didn't meet her.'

'Meeting him will be more interesting,' said Julie.

'Well, it's already laid on for this evening.'

'What time?'

'Don't worry,' he told her. 'We'll have a bite first. In fact, if you take the next turn on the right, there's a country pub where I'm always well treated.'

This evening proved the exception. The place was not as he remembered it. For one thing, there were rows of tables covered in red cloths, with places set for dinner and plastic flower arrangements. For another, the barmaid – or waitress – asked if they had booked.

'It's supposed to be a pub, isn't it?' he said combatively. 'We can have a drink and a snack.'

'You can have a drink, by all means. No bar snacks in the evening, sir, apart from crisps. And peanuts.'

After he'd given his opinion of crisps and peanuts, they drove on to a public house Julie knew. It had a log fire and tables where you could sit without having a menu thrust in front of you by a young woman in a white apron. They ordered filled jacket potatoes at the bar.

He was still muttering about crisps and peanuts when they were seated. 'That other place won't see me again. Cheers.'

'Round here, pubs are changing their clientele in the evenings,' Julie remarked. 'There's more money to be made from running them as restaurants.'

'Everything's changing,' Diamond complained, mounting one of his favourite hobby-horses. 'Look at Bath. Carwardine's gone now, a coffee shop of character. Owen, Owen, that nice big department store in Stall Street where I used to buy my socks and shirts. What do I see there now – a Walt Disney shop. That's American. Just down the street there used to be a Woolworth's. Gone. My earliest memory is being lost in Woolworth's. Not in Bath, I mean. Another town. Woolie's is part of our heritage, Julie.'

'It's American,' she said. 'Woolworth was an American.'

He said huffily, 'You don't need to tell me that.' With a

shift of thought that was quite reasonable in his own mind, but he couldn't expect Julie to understand, he asked, 'Is there a phone here? I can call my wife while the food is coming.'

In their basement in West Kensington, Steph had been watching an Australian soap. The theme tune was going in the background. 'I was wondering if we were still talking,' she remarked. 'What's the state of play? Shall I see you tonight?'

'Doubtful,' he answered. 'Tomorrow looks more likely. However, I think I'm about to button up the case.'

'So long as you don't stitch it up.'

She couldn't know how wounding that remark was.

She said, 'Are you still there? I hope they appreciate what you're doing.'

He laughed cynically. 'Some hope of that!'

She said, 'Because I'm not sure if I do. I've had the supermarket on the phone this evening, wanting to know why you missed two days of work. What could I say, except that you got called away suddenly?'

'You could say the police came for me.'

'Oh, yes?'

'Joke.'

She said, 'Speaking of jokes, it looks to me as if you might be modelling for the art class after all.'

This time his laugh was more hollow. It came home to him how much better he had felt doing police work again, even when it turned up old mistakes.

And Steph, with her well-practised capacity to read his thoughts, said in all seriousness, 'Why don't you stay there as long as they need you? They may come to their senses and want you back – even that man you had the row with. Tott.'

He said, 'I got stung this morning.'

'By Mr Tott?'

'By a bee. On my hand.'

'That's all right, then.'

'What?'

'I said, are you all right, then? Did you put something on it?'

'Yes. I survived.'

'Teach you to be careful where you put your hands.'

He used this as the cue to say something personal that may not entirely have made up for his delay in phoning, but definitely pleased Steph. They exchanged some frivolous and private remarks before he hung up.

More mellow than he had felt all day, he went back to where Julie was sitting and said, 'Don't you have a phone call to make?'

She shook her head.

He was sorry, because she wore a wedding ring. 'Separated?'

She smiled and shook her head. 'He'll be at work. He's in the police.'

The jacket potatoes arrived and Diamond tested one of his, risking the heat on his fingertips to feel for the cracking of rusty skin. 'I like them baked the old-fashioned way, not turned into mush in a microwave,' he explained. 'These will do. A well-cooked potato beats pasta or rice or anything. I was once told that if you had to survive on only one food, you'd better choose potatoes, because they contain some of all the nutrients we need. What is more, they aren't fattening.'

'The butter is,' said Julie, noting the large chunk he was slotting between the halves.

'Don't lecture me on diet,' he said as if *she* were the one holding forth about potatoes. 'This is better for me than chips. When I was younger, I practically lived on chips, but then I was burning up the calories playing rugby.'

'You were a rugby player?'

'Played prop.'

191

'Who for?'

'The Met.'

'Metropolitan Police. That's a good team, isn't it?'

'It *was*. These days they're languishing in Division Five South.' He sprinkled chopped ham over the potato and tried some. 'I needed this. Do you want to hear a rugby story? In the mid-seventies, we were drawn away against a Welsh team in the cup. Swansea, I think it was. We had a South African playing in the second row for us. He was on attachment to the Met for six months, doing some sort of course on dog training. An enormous fellow. Bit of a bullshit artist actually. Played a lot of rugby in South Africa. Bruce was his name. Can't remember the surname. Something Afrikaans that didn't sound the way it was spelt. Anyway, four of us were driving to Wales in a Ford Anglia. No team buses then.'

'Including Bruce?'

'Including Bruce. He was a pain about his rugby. He reckoned the standard of play was much higher in South Africa and he couldn't wait to get started and show us how brilliant he was. Now, the guys in our team were great practical jokers and when we were getting close to Wales on the M4 one of them had the lovely idea of asking Bruce if he'd brought his passport with him. You should have seen his face. He said he didn't know it would be needed. Of course we wound him up then, saying how strict the Welsh were at the border crossing point and that he should forget about playing rugby that afternoon. We'd better drop him off on the English side of the Severn Bridge and pick him up on the way home. He was shattered, totally taken in by all this.

'Then someone suggested that we put Bruce into the boot and cover him over with tracksuits and shirts and things and drive across the bridge. He was touchingly grateful. So we stopped at Aust services on the English side and watched this massive South African climb in and try and make himself inconspicuous.'

'Rotten lot!'

'We closed the thing and drove across and stopped the car just beyond the tolls and walked around it pretending to be a border patrol, tapping on the bodywork.'

'Then did you let him out?'

'Not until we'd driven another ten miles. And then nobody let on, because when the match was over and we were driving back, we did the whole thing again.' He shook with laughter, remembering it. 'Well, he *had* scored a couple of jammy tries.'

Julie said, 'That's so mean! Men's humour is a mystery to me.'

One of the first people they saw on returning to Manvers Street was Chief Inspector John Wigfull, officious as usual, issuing orders along the corridor to some hapless civilian clerk who had rashly stepped out of her office.

'There you are,' he said when he'd done with her, pointing towards Diamond and Julie as if they needed to account for themselves. 'Can I have a word?'

'What about?' asked Diamond.

'Mrs Violet Billington. You interviewed her this morning, I believe.' The tone was definitely accusing.

'I did.'

'Alone?'

Diamond said, 'Yes,' trying to sound unflustered while his thoughts careered both backwards and forward seizing on alarming possibilities. Surely the old biddy hadn't made a complaint. He'd treated her fairly, for pity's sake. Once before in this place where protocol was holy writ he'd been carpeted on a trumped-up charge of assault. That was the occasion when he'd thrown up the job.

'How was she?' asked Wigfull.

'What's this about?'

'Mrs Billington. I'm asking how she was.'

He shrugged and spread his hands. 'All right.'

Wigfull said, 'Because we've got her downstairs. She's battered her husband senseless. Any idea why?'

Diamond shook his head, lost for words.

Wigfull went on to explain that less than an hour ago an emergency call had come in from the house in Larkhall. The student lodger had returned from college to discover her landlord, Winston Billington, lying unconscious in the hall bleeding from head wounds. Assuming that someone had broken in, the student had rushed through to the kitchen to see whether Mrs Billington had also been attacked. She had not. She had been sitting at the table drinking vodka. She had admitted to the student that she was responsible for the assault and had agreed that as her husband still appeared to be breathing they had better call an ambulance.

'Where is he?' Diamond asked.

'In intensive care at the RUH. We've got a man at the bedside in case he recovers.'

'He's *that* bad?'

'They say the injuries are severe. She used a plastic bag filled with copper coins. They kept it by the door and put their excess change in it to dole out to people collecting for charity. Two poundsworth of coppers can make quite a dent in someone's skull.'

'And is she talking?'

'At this minute, no. She's in the toilet, throwing up. Too much vodka. Don't worry. WPC Blinston is with her.'

Diamond turned to Julie. 'You'd better get down to the hospital.'

Wigfull said, 'Didn't you hear? There's a man at the bedside already.'

'I want Julie there.' Momentarily it threatened to become a clash of wills. In a rare act of conciliation, Diamond confided, 'We've got new information on his

194

possible involvement in the Britt Strand murder. We were all set to interview him. If he *should* come round, anything he says could be vital.'

Julie left for the hospital.

Diamond joined Wigfull in an interview room, across a table from Mrs Violet Billington, the self-confessed husband-beater. Dressed in a faded green and white cardigan that made Diamond think of overcooked cabbage, she was almost as pale as the box of tissues in front of her, yet the blue eyes conveyed the same contempt she had shown earlier in the day.

However, she was prepared to talk.

Having recited the formal preliminaries of a taped interview, Wigfull asked the tense little woman whether she was willing to describe what had happened to her husband.

She summed it up in a sentence. 'He came home and I hit him.'

'There must have been a reason.'

After a pause: 'He's a monster – that's the reason.'

'You'd better explain what you mean by that, Mrs Billington.'

Wigfull received the full force of the withering stare. 'Why ask me? You know perfectly well that he murdered our lodger.'

Considering the explosiveness of this statement, Diamond exercised commendable restraint as he took over the questioning. 'You're speaking of Britt Strand? We must have it confirmed for the record.'

'Who do you think I mean – the Queen of Sheba?'

'Britt Strand?'

'Oh, come on – of course!'

'Has he told you this himself?'

'No. But he didn't have to,' said Mrs Billington. 'I know. And you know, too. You were coming for him this evening.'

'Coming to interview him,' Diamond made clear, at pains

195

to conduct this scrupulously while the tape was running. 'If he hasn't actually confessed to you, what are your grounds for saying he murdered Britt?'

She said vehemently, 'You don't know him like I do. He's got sex on the brain – at *his* age. You'd think an old man would grow out of it. Not him. He's always been out for the main chance, flirting with girls young enough to be his daughter. I couldn't count the number of times I've caught him out. He's not even subtle about it. I've had them phoning the house asking to speak to him. I've found their cigarette-ends in the car. I've seen the hotel bills.'

'That may be so, but loose living is one thing and murder another.'

'He killed this one because she wasn't having him. She didn't succumb to his blandishments. He kept trying and she kept giving him the frost. His pride couldn't take it.'

'How do you know this?'

'I saw the evidence. He tried all his usual overtures, boxes of chocolates and bunches of flowers, but she wasn't interested.'

'He gave her presents while you were there?' Wigfull said in disbelief.

'He wasn't that obvious with it.'

'How do you know about the presents? You looked into her flat?'

'No need. She threw them out with the rubbish. Flowers from our garden and whole boxes of Milk Tray, unopened. He always gives Milk Tray. Pathetic, isn't it? That TV advert must have sunk into his brain. Anyway, they ended up in the bin, still in their wrapper. That's how much that one thought of him. She wasn't some pathetic creature in one of the shops he visits desperate for attention. She had better fish to fry.'

If Mrs Billington had any sympathy for the fate of her former lodger, she wasn't exhibiting it. The reference to 'that one' depersonalized Britt unpleasantly. She was given no credit for resisting the wayward husband. The bitterness was all-consuming.

Diamond said, 'I don't think you understood my question. How do you know that your husband murdered Miss Strand, as you allege?'

This time he drew an answer of stunning candour.

'Because he asked me to lie to you to cover up for him. He wasn't really with me in Tenerife on the night she was killed. He was already back in England. He cut short our holiday after getting a phone call. He said he had to attend a crisis meeting. It was a crisis for someone all right.'

'When was this?'

'The call?'

'The flight home.'

'The day she was killed. He doesn't realize how repulsive he's become. He still thinks he's God's gift to women. The young things round the pool weren't interested, so he made up his mind to come home and try his luck with the lodger.'

'Is this what you believed at the time?'

She lowered her eyelids. 'No. I swallowed the lie. I really believed he had an emergency at work.'

'And when you got back?'

'He met me at Bristol Airport and drove me home.'

'How did he seem?'

'Twitchy. I put it down to the problems at work. When we got home, the first thing I noticed was the milk bottles on the doorstep. Britt hadn't taken in her milk for two days. It didn't seem that important. She might have gone away in a hurry to interview someone. But I couldn't understand why Winston had left two pints going sour. He blustered about it, said he'd stayed in London for another meeting. He isn't much of a liar. I knew he was making it up.'

'Did you query it?'

'I was too tired to bother. We went to bed and I was dog-tired, but I couldn't sleep. I felt uneasy about the lodger upstairs. She really preyed on my mind, so I asked him to check, and you know the rest.'

'We don't,' said Diamond. 'We don't know what induced you to make a false statement when the police arrived.'

'I didn't.'

'I don't follow you,' said Diamond.

She turned her eyes upwards and pursed her lips. 'Winston told me he didn't want you people bothering his bosses by checking whether he was telling the truth. He was worried about his job and he thought he might lose it if the police came asking about his movements. It was simpler all round if we both said we'd travelled back together the same day. I said I refused to tell any lies, but if he wanted to speak for both of us, that was up to him, and that's what happened, if you check your statements. In mine, I stated when I returned to Bristol and I made no mention of Winston.' For a moment, Mrs Billington's eyes had a gleam of triumph.

'So he behaved as if someone else had killed Britt Strand?' said Diamond.

'That's what he wanted me to think.'

'And did you?'

'At the time, yes. I knew he was an incurable skirt-chaser, but I'd never dreamed he was dangerous.'

'When did that occur to you?'

'When you came to see me this morning. It's obvious, isn't it? You don't think Mountjoy killed her. You're on to Winston at last, asking about the sexy cards he sells and whether we grow roses in the garden. I can put two and two together.'

Ten minutes ago, Diamond had been cockahoop at putting Winston Billington into the frame. Now his elation drained. His worst apprehensions were confirmed. Whatever the rights or wrongs of it, his interview must have triggered the attack. 'But you said yourself that the roses couldn't have come from your garden,' he said limply.

'He'd given her roses in the past.'

'These were from a florist.'

'I know. What does it matter anyway,' she said. 'He killed her. I did some checking after you went. I went through his credit card statements for four years ago. He keeps everything for five years, silly mutt. The day he returned from Tenerife, the day of the murder, he spent the equivalent of ten pounds sixty-five at the florist's at Los Rodeos Airport.'

'*That*'s why we couldn't trace the shop,' Diamond said, more to himself than anyone else.

Mrs Billington hadn't finished. 'And just to be sure I phoned his head office and asked the managing director's secretary to check whether there really had been an emergency meeting on October the eighteenth, 1990, that Winston had to attend. There wasn't. The boss himself was away on business in Scotland for the whole of that week. Now do you understand why I clobbered the rat when he stepped inside the door tonight?'

Diamond understood. He also felt marginally more comfortable in his mind that he wasn't solely responsible for unleashing the avenging wife.

Chapter Seventeen

'No change, I'm afraid, dear,' the charge nurse said when Julie Hargreaves enquired about Winston Billington. The 'dear' was kindly meant; the nurse had taken her for a relative, mishearing 'DI' as Di, a common error. Julie went over to the uniformed embodiment of the police, a youthful constable who was sitting bored in the corner drumming with his fingertips on an upturned plastic coffee cup.

'Any signs of life?' she asked him.

'He groans sometimes.'

'Is that good?'

'I wouldn't know.'

'Why don't you get some air for an hour? I'll take over. Bring me some tea when you come back. Milk and no sugar.'

He nodded his thanks and left.

She ventured as close as she could to the bed. The little she could see of the patient's face was grey, the eyes closed, one forcibly, turned purple and heavily swollen. His head was bandaged and he had a ventilator over his nose and mouth. There was another tube giving him a transfusion and leads connected to his chest were monitoring his heart-rate. In all, it wasn't the ideal way to meet the principal suspect. She marvelled at the ferocity of the diminutive Mrs Billington and the power of money when it takes the form of a bunch of coins swung in a plastic bag.

She sat down to begin her vigil. For a time, at least, she'd got a break from Diamond. He wasn't easy to work with just now. She'd heard him called curmudgeonly, and she wouldn't argue with that at this stage of their working relationship. She understood the sense of personal failure that was oppressing him over what had happened four years ago. In a way though, she preferred Diamond's abrasiveness to the emollient manner of John Wigfull, her real boss. For all Diamond's bluster and boorishness, she felt secure with him. He was open in his emotions. When he smiled (which was rarely just now) it was genuine. When he was gloomy, he shared it. He consulted her and appeared to listen. Mind, he didn't confide much in anyone else. He seemed to regard the rest of the Bath CID as turnip-heads. He obviously felt deep resentment that she didn't fully understand over his resignation a couple of years ago. She'd gathered that he had always been out of sympathy with the high-ups. For all that, his reputation as a dynamic head of the Murder Squad was still spoken of with awe in Manvers Street. He'd led a strong, loyal team, now dispersed.

About his personal life she had gleaned little so far. She now knew he'd once played rugby for the Met. She'd heard from others that he had been spotted on occasions in the stand at the Recreation Ground, where Bath RFC, the best club side in the country, played their home matches. She'd also been told that he had a natural rapport with kids, in spite of having none himself. The Christmas after he'd quit the police, he'd taken a job as Father Christmas in the Colonnades shopping precinct – and proved to be a popular Santa. He wouldn't have needed padding.

She was intrigued to know what his wife was like. The woman who coped with Peter Diamond's grouchy temperament and stayed wedded to him would be fascinating to meet. Mrs D (Julie had learned) was small and independent-minded, and put a lot of energy into community work. Once she had been Brown Owl to a troop of brownies and more recently she had worked in charity shops. Some people joked that Diamond was dressed by Oxfam.

A moan from Billington interrupted her musing about the Diamonds and reminded her why she was there. She got up and looked at him. There wasn't a flicker, so she returned to the chair.

This was the first case of serious assault by a wife against her husband that Julie had come across, though the press periodically reported on battered husbands as if it was a logical consequence of the feminist revolution. She'd watched a television programme once and been amazed and sceptical that men – big fellows, some of them – allowed themselves to be hit with heavy objects. Of course, such incidents were statistically negligible compared to the domestic violence suffered by women. Julie knew: she was the automatic choice to investigate attacks on women and she'd seen some sickening injuries. More than once she'd had to defend herself from the aggressors, so she wasn't too appalled that once in a while a woman beat up a man.

Having recently looked at the police photos of Britt Strand's corpse, she couldn't raise much sympathy for Winston Billington. It wasn't compassion that made her hope he would recover entirely and be capable of answering questions. If the bastard died, it would be difficult to procure enough evidence of his guilt to satisfy an appeal court and prove that the judgment against Mountjoy had been in error. It would be so much more positive if the appeal were backed by a signed confession.

Another sound. This time the patient moved his head. Anxiously Julie looked through the glass door to see if a nurse was about. Suppose Billington recovered consciousness only for a short time. What a responsibility she would have to shoulder! She tried to think what she ought to ask him. To accuse him of murder might be enough to kill the man. Yet if she didn't ask the obvious, she'd be in breach of her duty. Imagine telling Peter Diamond, 'Well, he did recover consciousness briefly and I asked him how he was feeling. He said, "Not too good," and died.'

Damn Violet Billington for doing this.

Another disturbing scenario took shape in Julie's thoughts. If Billington *did* die, his wife's evidence became indispensable. Julie hadn't been present when Mrs Billington had shopped her husband to Diamond, so it was impossible to tell how convincing she had sounded. Was she reliable? Was it conceivable that she had invented the story to justify her vicious attack on her husband?

No. There was corroboration from an independent source. GB the crusty had seen a man of Billington's appearance enter the house in Larkhall after Mountjoy had left.

That was the clincher. But for that, you could well imagine the vindictive wife inventing the story of her rampant husband. After all, Violet Billington didn't know everything that had happened that fatal night four years ago. *Couldn't*. She'd been in Tenerife when Britt Strand had been murdered. And according to her account (relayed by Diamond) Winston had admitted nothing. She'd hit him before he gave his version of the story.

The charge nurse returned and checked that the blood was still moving evenly along the transparent tubes. 'Your Dad?' she asked.

'No,' said Julie with forbearance. 'I'm not related.'

'Just a friend?' The nurse said it sympathetically, but with a gleam of interest in her eye.

'Actually I'm on duty. I'm a detective inspector.'

'Really?' She took a longer look at Julie. 'Shouldn't you be with the wife? I thought she was the assailant.'

Around 10 p.m., Diamond phoned Julie at the hospital.

'Has he said anything yet?'

'Just a lot of groaning.'

'He's conscious, then?'

'Not really. In fact they've given him something to ease the pain, and he seems to be sleeping now.'

'Is the brain damaged?'

'They don't know. The doctor was talking about a scan, but they wouldn't do it tonight.'

'Not much point in you staying, by the sound of it. Let's both clock off. See you in the morning, early.'

'How early is early?'

'Why don't you join me for breakfast at the Francis, say about eight-thirty?'

'A working breakfast?'

'No. Just breakfast. Well, not *just* breakfast. You'll get a chance to sample the Heritage Platter. So will I. Had to miss it this morning. Don't quote me, Julie, but there have got to be some perks in this.'

He put down the phone. Across the room, Commander Warrilow was facing the wall, pressing his finger against a map of the city. Diamond in this uncharacteristically benign mood went over and perched on the desk assigned to Warrilow. 'Did you have any joy in the sewer?'

Warrilow took this as more sniping, and scowled.

'Looking for Mountjoy,' Diamond prompted him.

Without shifting his gaze from the map, Warrilow said, 'If you really want to know, we're looking at an area just a few streets away. A man answering Mountjoy's description was seen in Julian Road earlier this evening and we had another sighting about the same time in Morford Street.'

'Alone?'

'What do you expect?' said Warrilow, turning to glare at him. 'He's got the girl trussed up somewhere, poor kid. I'm told that there's quite an amount of empty property around Julian Road, sometimes used by dossers. I'm having it searched.'

204

'You're convinced he's in the city, then?'

'It's looking more and more like it. Whether Samantha is here with him – in fact, whether she's still alive – I wouldn't like to speculate. I'm getting increasingly worried about her.'

Diamond eased himself off the desk and glided to the exit. This wasn't a tactful moment to go off duty, but he'd had enough.

In twenty minutes he was in the Roman Bar at his hotel, the solitary Englishman among three groups of German and Canadian tourists. Inevitably after a few brandies he was drawn into their conversation and just as predictably he found himself having to account for the presence of the crusties in such a prosperous-seeming city.

'It's a mistake to lump them together,' he found himself pontificating. 'There are distinctly different groups. You have the so-called new age travellers, drop-outs, mostly in their twenties, usually in combat fatigues or leather. Hair either very short or very long. Never anything in between. They have dogs on string or running loose and they can seem quite threatening. Actually they ignore people like us, unless they want money. We inhabit another planet to theirs. Then there's a hard core of alkies – men about my age – always with a can or bottle in their hands. They're shabby, weather-beaten, but conventionally dressed in sports jackets and corduroys. They sometimes shout abuse. So do I when I feel brave enough.'

This earned a laugh.

'I'm serious. I could easily join them soon,' he confided as he drained the brandy glass. 'I don't have a proper job. Chucked it in two years ago. So I look at those guys and know it's only a matter of time.' Having unburdened himself of this maudlin prediction, he rose, unsteadily. 'Sleep well, my friends, and be thankful it isn't a shop doorway you're lying in.'

As he was moving off he overheard someone saying, 'Britain is just teeming with eccentrics.'

To which someone else added, 'And crazies.'

He didn't look round. He made his way ponderously to the lift. He'd talked (or drunk) himself into a melancholy mood and he knew why. The solving of the Britt Strand case was going to hurl him back into the abyss of part-time work in London. These few days had been a cruel reminder of better times and he hadn't needed to be reminded. He wanted to be back in Bath and more than anything he wanted his old job back.

Outside his room he was fumbling with the key when he became aware of a slight pressure in the small of his back. In his bosky state he didn't immediately interpret it as sinister. Assuming he must have backed into someone, he murmured, 'Beg your pardon.'

From behind him came the command, 'Open the door and step inside.'

He knew who it was.

A gun at your back is more sobering than black coffee; a gun held by a convicted murderer is doubly efficacious. Diamond's rehabilitation was immediate.

It was no bluff, either. A black automatic was levelled at him when he turned to face John Mountjoy.

'The gun isn't necessary,' Diamond said.

The change in Mountjoy was dramatic. On Lansdown a couple of days before he'd looked gaunt and pale as prisoners do, yet he'd seemed well in control. Now he was twitchy and the dark eyes had a look of desperation, as if he'd discovered that freedom is not so precious or desirable as he'd supposed. The strain of being on the run was getting to him, unless the unspeakable had happened and he was marked by violence.

Speaking in a clipped, strident voice, he ordered Diamond to remove his jacket and throw it on the bed. What did he suppose – that it contained some weapon or

206

listening device? He waved him to a chair by the window.

It would not be wise to disobey.

'What have you got to tell me?' he demanded. 'Speak up.'

'Would you mind lowering that thing?'

'I'll use it if you don't speak up.'

Whether the threat was real, Diamond didn't know, but there was real danger that he would fire it inadvertently, the way he was brandishing it like an aerosol.

'There is progress,' Diamond told him, spacing his words, doing his utmost to project calm whilst thinking how much to tell. 'Definite progress. I now have a witness who saw you leaving the house where the murder took place. At approximately eleven o'clock. More important, he's positive he saw Britt at the front door showing you—'

Mountjoy cut him short. 'Who is this?'

'Someone she knew.'

' "He", you said. What was he doing there? I didn't see him.'

Diamond continued the drip, drip of information, trying to dictate the tempo of this dangerous dialogue. 'Watching the house, he says.'

'Who was he? You must know who he was.'

'He fancied his chances as the boyfriend. Someone told him you'd taken her out for a meal. He was jealous. He went to the house to see for himself if it was true. Stood outside in the street. He says you left without even shaking her hand and moved off fast.'

'That much is true,' Mountjoy admitted. 'Is he the killer? Why did he tell you this? Who is he?'

The advantage had shifted. Mountjoy's hunger to have the name was making him just a shade more conciliatory. Diamond was far too experienced to miss the opportunity to trade. 'What's happening to Samantha? Is she all right?'

'Don't mess with me,' said Mountjoy, touchy at the mention of Samantha. 'I want the name of this toe-rag.'

'Better not abuse him,' Diamond cautioned. 'He's your best hope so far.'

'Who is he?'

'Is Sam still alive?'

No response.

'You know if you hurt her, laid a finger on her, they'd get you.'

'What do you mean – "they"? You're one of them.'

A slip of the tongue. He said, 'The top brass.'

'They will anyway.'

'If you play it right,' Diamond broached a more positive offer, 'you ought to survive. The gun isn't going to help. I don't know where you got it, but you'd be safer without it.'

The warning seemed timely when Mountjoy used the back of the hand that was holding the gun to wipe his mouth. Whatever the man's misdemeanours, he was no gunman.

Diamond sensed that he was on the brink of getting some information about Samantha. It was worth giving more. 'As a matter of fact,' he volunteered, 'I don't have the name of this witness who saw you leaving the house. He's a crusty, a traveller.'

'One of that lot? Who's going to believe him?'

'I do, for one.'

This caused Mountjoy to frown. 'You do?'

'Yes.'

'You sent me down. Are you actually admitting you got it wrong?'

'It's beginning to look that way.'

'Was this crusty the killer?'

'Probably not.'

This wasn't the answer Mountjoy had expected. The muscles in his face tensed and he said thickly, 'Who the hell is it, then?'

'I don't know yet.'

'What?'

'–but I'm closing in,' Diamond added quickly. 'That's why it's so important that Samantha is released unhurt. She *is* all right still, isn't she?' And after receiving no reply, he said, 'Look, the people who are running the manhunt are getting anxious. If you could give them some proof that she is still alive, it might buy us both some time. If not' – he glanced at the gun – 'it could end very soon, John, and in a bloody shoot-out.'

Mountjoy's troubled eyes held his for a moment, but he gave no response.

'Will you tell me something else?' Diamond asked him, his brain in overdrive. 'That last evening you spent with Britt: did she mention anyone she was seeing?'

'Other men, you mean? I don't remember.'

'Try.'

'I mean no. Why would she want to talk to me about boyfriends?'

'Perhaps to give you the message that she was already dating someone.'

'Well, she didn't. I did most of the talking, chatting her up, you could say.'

'Didn't that involve asking her questions about herself?'

'Yes, but you don't ask a woman who else she's sleeping with.'

Fair point. Diamond was compelled to admit that on a first date the conversation was unlikely to venture down such byways. It was a long time since he'd been on a first date. 'Who paid for the meal in the Beaujolais?'

'I used my credit card, but she insisted on giving me money to cover her share. She said something about modern women valuing their independence.'

'You must have expected her to offer.' Diamond moved on – smoothly, considering the circumstances – to the real point that interested him. 'Did you by any chance give her some flowers?'

Mountjoy was annoyed by the question. Muscles tensed

in his cheek. 'The roses? No. Will you get it into your thick head that I didn't murder her?'

'There's a big difference between buying flowers for a lady and murdering her,' Diamond said. 'Someone else could have seen your flowers and taken it to mean she was two-timing.'

'They were not my flowers.'

'Pity. It would have made a nice gesture, the kind of gift a woman would appreciate from a mature man such as yourself. You wouldn't have to arrive at the restaurant with them. You could have had them delivered to the house.'

'I didn't.'

'So did you notice any roses in the flat when you went back there?'

'No.'

'*Would* you have noticed?'

'Probably.'

'So – getting back to your conversation over dinner – did you talk about her work?'

'Hardly at all. Mostly we discussed Swedish cooking and various cars I've owned.'

Heady stuff! Diamond thought. 'You're a keen driver?'

'Used to be.'

'Was she?' He already knew the answer, but he wanted to keep the man talking.

'She seemed to understand what I was on about, only I don't think she owned a car. She said you could manage easily in Bath without one, what with the minibuses and the trains.'

'And friends with cars. You drove her back to Larkhall after the meal in the Beaujolais?'

'Yes.' Mountjoy was becoming twitchy again, rubbing the gun against his sleeve.

'Did you get the impression that the house was empty?'

'It was. It was in darkness. We had it to ourselves. I

210

thought I had it made until she started on about the Iraqi students I was enrolling. Then I knew she'd set me up. I was pretty sure she had a tape-recorder running somewhere.'

'Of course,' Diamond said aloud, and it sounded as if he'd expected nothing less, whereas in reality he spoke the words self-critically. Of course she would have used a tape-recorder, a top journalist. 'Did you look for it?'

'There was no need. She went on about evidence and pictures and documentation, but I admitted nothing. Didn't even finish the coffee. I got up and left. I was pretty upset, but I saw no point in giving her abuse.'

'She saw you to the door?'

'If you mean she followed me downstairs saying she'd got all the evidence she wanted and I deserved everything that was coming to me, yes. She slammed the door after me. I walked to where I'd parked my car in St Saviours Road and drove home.'

'Did you see anybody along the street?'

For some reason this inflamed Mountjoy. 'I was too bloody angry to notice. Look, I've told you all this at least a dozen times before, you fat slob. You're just trying to fob me off with this horseshit about the crusty. Britt Strand was a class act. She wouldn't mix with rubbish.'

'She didn't normally. She was using him, the same as she used you.'

'What for?'

'A story about a squat in Bath.'

'That's no story. That wouldn't even make an inside page in the local paper. I'm not satisfied, Diamond. We had an arrangement. I trusted you. When are you going to deliver?'

'Soon.'

'Tomorrow.'

Diamond thought fleetingly of the man lying unconscious in the RUH. 'That's too soon.'

211

'Tomorrow – or never.' He tugged open the door and was gone.

All Diamond had to do was pick up the phone and tip off Warrilow. Instead, he went to the kettle and switched it on, picked a sachet of coffee from the bowl and emptied it into a cup. He spilt some of the Nescafé, not because he was in a state of shock, but because he was cack-handed. Always had been. Couldn't help it. He could handle an interview.

Well, considering his interview wasn't planned, he hadn't done too badly. True, he hadn't confirmed whether Samantha Tott was still alive, but he had just teased out the clue that would transform the investigation.

If there was time.

His elation was short-lived. There was a strange sound in the room, a whine, rising to a fast crescendo, followed by a click. Acrid fumes invaded his nose. There was no water in the kettle and he'd burnt out the element.

Chapter Eighteen

Regardless of Peter Diamond's warning that the day ahead promised to be a demanding one, his assistant Julie turned down the offer of the Heritage Platter. She breakfasted on muesli and tea, refusing to be tempted by the appetizing smells of crisp bacon and fried eggs wafting across the table. Diamond had once heard muesli likened to the sweepings from a hamster's cage and had never touched the stuff since. He decently refrained from saying so.

They had a window table overlooking the lawn of Queen Square with its mighty plane trees. A table with starched linen cloth, silver tea service, silver cutlery and fresh flowers. Never mind the grey sky outside; the big, bald ex-detective, chatting affably to his attractive escort, was oblivious of the weather. He was basking in the interested glances of the Germans and Americans he had met in the bar the previous evening, for none of them had seen Julie arrive at the hotel entrance at 8.30.

'Brought my wife here for a meal once,' he reminisced with her. 'Bit of a scene I caused. We must have had something to celebrate. Maybe it was when I got promoted to superintendent. Well, we ate a good meal and I asked Steph if she wanted a liqueur with her coffee. We're not liqueur-drinking people normally. She likes to surprise me, though. She said she'd like a glass of that Italian stuff they set alight and serve with a coffee bean floating in it. We'd seen it once and she'd been keen to try.'

'Sambuca.'

'That's right. Sambuca. It smells of aniseed. I wouldn't touch it myself, but I was feeling chuffed that night and willing to order whatever the love of my life requested. It duly arrived at the table flaming merrily. We watched it for a bit and then Steph asked how long it would go on burning, because she wanted a taste. I said I thought you had to put the flame out. There wasn't anything to hand except an empty wine glass, so, having told her the scientific principle that a flame needs air to keep it alight, I put the bottom of the wine glass over the liqueur glass. Result: the flame disappeared. I lifted up the wine glass. What I'd forgotten is that liqueurs are sticky. The rim of the glass stuck to the wine glass and it came up with it –'

'Oh God!' said Julie, beginning to laugh.

'– and then dropped on the table and tipped over.'

'No!'

'Unfortunately the flame hadn't gone out completely. Next thing we had a fire going. Flames leaping up in front of me. I had to grab a soda syphon to put it out. The table-cloth was scorched and we had to be moved to another table to finish our coffee.'

Tears of amusement ran down Julie's face. 'I heard you were accident-prone.'

'Who told you that?'

She wiped her eyes. 'We've all got our weak points. My trouble is, I can never remember who told me things.'

True to his promise, he said nothing about the investigation until they had finished eating. Then he gave her a near-verbatim account of his latest brush with Mountjoy. 'And now I've got a real problem,' he confided. 'A jumbo-sized dilemma. Do I report all this to the top brass at Manvers Street? You'll say I'm duty bound.'

'I think you are,' said she.

'But I've got nothing of substance to pass on except the fact that he is armed.'

'That's more than enough.'

He continued as if Julie hadn't spoken, 'I learned sweet FA about Samantha, or where they are holed up. If I tell Warrilow that Mountjoy is carrying a hand-gun, he'll issue weapons and some idiot will shoot him on sight.'

'You can't *not* tell them,' she argued. 'He could shoot an officer and you'd have to live with that knowledge.'

He sighed heavily. 'He's an idiot. He's supposed to be trying to prove his innocence. Why does he need a bloody gun? I wasn't going to jump him.'

'I suppose he wanted to give you a fright. He wants quick results.'

'In his shoes, so would I. But he's getting good value from me. We're in there pitching, Julie.' He spotted an uneaten slice of toast on the next table and reached for it. 'I don't need a gun at my head.'

She nudged the conversation forward. 'You spoke of something Mountjoy said that throws the whole inquiry into uncertainty again.'

'Right.' Diamond's mood improved; with a return to London looming, any delay in the unravelling of the mystery was to be welcomed. 'Picture it, Julie. He's back at the house with Britt, right?'

'This is the night of the murder?'

'Yes. They've had a pleasant meal and he thinks he's been invited back for some action. But instead, she has chosen this moment to hit him with her evidence about the Iraqis he was enrolling. It's a set-up. He said to me last night that he reckoned she was taping the conversation. Of course she was! She was a smart journalist collecting evidence. We know she used tapes in her work. She had two recorders, one of those heavy-duty things that you stack up in your living room—'

'A music centre?'

'Right. And a neat little Japanese thing dinky enough to fit into a pocket or a handbag. After the murder we carted

215

off boxes of her stuff, including tapes. The question is what happened to the Mountjoy tape?'

'If one existed,' said Julie.

'You can bet your life it existed.'

'I've been through the inventory of her material,' she said. 'She was well organized. There were upwards of fifty cassettes, every one dated and labelled, but nothing for the date of the murder. I'm sure I would have noticed.'

'The only person with an interest in possessing such a tape would be Mountjoy himself.'

'Unless it was still recording when the murder took place,' said Julie.

Diamond stared at her and snapped his fingers. 'Brilliant! The killer may have taken it.'

'Cool – after killing someone, to check the tape-recorder.'

'Very.'

'Unless . . .'

'Unless what?'

'. . . he had the opportunity to collect it later.'

He stared out across the Square. 'We're back to Billington.' The disappointment was clear in his voice. 'He was the one on the scene.'

Nothing was said for some time.

Finally, Julie spoke. 'You don't *want* Billington to be proved the killer, do you?'

'It's so obvious. Why didn't I pay him more attention at the time?'

'Because of his alibi, you told me. Any news of his condition?'

'I phoned the hospital first thing this morning. He's improving slowly, but they don't think he's capable of answering questions yet. Meanwhile if we could find that missing tape in his house—'

'Won't he have destroyed it by now – or just erased the recording? I certainly would.'

'The chances are that he did,' Diamond agreed, but with reluctance.

'Should we search the house, just the same?'

'Without a warrant?'

'To examine the scene of yesterday's assault.'

Julie was giving top value for her muesli breakfast.

He grinned. 'Let's do that.'

Realistic about his own limitations, Diamond assigned Julie to conduct the search of the Billingtons' house unaided. As a constitutionally clumsy man, in a search he was more likely to destroy clues than find them. Instead, he resolved to find out more about Britt Strand's investigative journalism. Interviewing was his forte. He drove to Steeple Ashton.

In time for elevenses.

The cottage was rich with the aroma of two fruit cakes recently out of the oven. The bounteous Prue Shorter explained that they were destined to be tiers of a wedding cake, and if Diamond didn't mind having the trimmings that had overlapped the tins, there were plenty of crisp bits to sample.

She made coffee and handed him a well-filled plate. 'How's the finger?' she enquired.

'Finger?'

'Was it a thumb, then?'

'Ah – my bee-sting.' He glanced down at his hand. 'The agony I put up with! I'd forgotten all about it, so it must be all right.'

'And you haven't found that convict yet? He isn't here, you know.'

'No, he's someone else's job. I'm still tidying up the facts about your former colleague.'

'Britt? I told you all I know, ducky.'

'You won't have heard that her former landlord is in hospital after a fracas with his wife.'

217

'*He*'s in hospital?'

'She cracked him over the head with a bagful of coins and now she's accused him of murdering Britt.'

'God Almighty!' She gave a huge, wheezy laugh and took a seat opposite Diamond at the kitchen table.

Cutting the merriment short, he broached the main business of his visit. 'You called at the house a few times, I believe. Did you meet the Billingtons?'

She was shaking her head, not as a response, but a reaction to the latest twist in the Britt Strand saga. 'Did I meet them? Yes, miserable buggers, both of them. Nary a smile between them. You pass the time of day and they treat it as a personal insult.'

'They remember you calling. At least, she does.'

'I don't exactly merge into the background, do I?'

'So you didn't have much conversation?'

'In a word, zilch.'

'I'm interested to know what Britt had to say about them, if anything. The man in particular.'

'Him? Silly old tosser! He fancied her, of course. Tell me a man who didn't. She told me he used to chat her up, or try to, when his wife wasn't about. Gave her the odd present. Is he really under suspicion?'

'Did he ever try anything?' Diamond persevered.

'You mean with Britt?'

What else did she think he meant? 'Yes.'

She paused before replying. 'Who knows? I didn't know her *that* well. There were other men, weren't there? It came out at the trial. She wasn't unapproachable, but I think she'd draw the line at old Billington. She could do better than that. Are you married, Mr Diamond?'

Annoyingly, he felt himself go pink. 'As a matter of fact, I am,' he told her in a shirty tone.

'Kids?'

'No. Is this of any relevance?'

'I'm just interested. You don't wear a ring, I notice.'

218

'Maybe you should be doing my job.' He recovered his poise. 'You don't wear one either.'

'That doesn't mean a thing these days, ducky,' she said with a laugh that was more guarded than usual.

'But you were married once?'

She nodded. 'It's an unfair world, isn't it? You probably wanted a kid and I got mine through a slip-up. The father did the decent thing, as they say, and it lasted just over a year.'

'Did he get custody?'

'No. Johnny was happy for me to keep her, because he was clearing off to Northern Ireland.' She gave a belly laugh. 'He's been stuck in Belfast with his mother and the troubles since 1982, and the best of luck. Men? You can keep them. I went back to my maiden name. Why should I put up with his for the rest of my life?'

'So you became – what's the current expression? – a lone parent.'

She hesitated and her tone of voice altered. 'I won't pretend it was easy, but if I could have the time back, I would. Sometimes I'm asked to make birthday cakes for other people's kids. I usually shed a few tears.'

'And now?' said Diamond, to steer the conversation back to a less distressing topic.

'Now?'

'Is there anyone else?'

She said sharply, 'If you're about to ask me if I'm a dyke, save your breath. I saw it in your eyes the first time you came here. Just because I don't diet or wear pretty clothes, it doesn't mean I was always built like a planet.'

Diamond said, 'I wasn't probing. Just now you asked me if I was married and I responded.'

The face relaxed slightly. 'Fair enough. I'm unattached. I'm straight. And interested in other people. We chubbies have a lot in common, right?'

He wasn't happy with 'chubby'. 'Burly' was how he

preferred to think of himself. She pushed more cake towards him to show solidarity, only at that moment he wanted to appear less solid. 'Did Britt ever discuss her sex life with you?' This was a question he could ask more easily now.

'The men she had? No. I told you when you came before, she didn't gossip. What I learned, I picked up here and there. The last boyfriend – I hate that word, but "lover" sounds even more outdated – was that showjumper.'

'Marcus Martin. Did you meet him?'

'No. She was watching him on telly one day when I called. Frankly, he's the last one I would have picked out of all the riders. Little red-haired runt.'

'But a rich red-headed runt,' said Diamond. 'And GB? Last time we spoke, you weren't willing to rate him as a boyfriend. I've met him since. He admitted to being keen at the time.'

'You're telling me. He was undressing her with his eyes when we did the shoot in Trim Street,' she confirmed. 'He certainly fancied his chances. She certainly didn't. She was just toying with him.'

'That's what he says now.'

'Men are so gullible.'

He gave a shrug. 'If I may, I'd like to take another look at the, em, pics you took.'

'The Trim Street set? No problem.'

She went upstairs to fetch them. The smell of fruit cake was undermining Diamond's defences, so he stepped out of the kitchen. She had moved things round in the living room since his first visit. The alcove where the small violin had been displayed now had a green porcelain bowl, a special piece, no doubt, but of less appeal to Diamond, who warmed to children's things in a house – with the exception of samplers, which tended to depress him when he thought of the forced labour involved. There were none here. Some of the pictures had been changed, however; instead of the Redouté roses, she had hung woodland scenes that weren't much to his taste.

'What do you think?' she asked, on her way downstairs with the photos. 'I found them in an antique shop in Bradford-on-Avon.'

'You collect Corots then?'

She shrilled in surprise, 'You know about art?'

'I know he writes his name very clearly in the corner.'

'Ah.'

Smarting at the contempt in that 'Ah', Diamond went on to say, 'But I'll tell you something about Corot. For every one of his paintings there are over a hundred forgeries. He's the most forged painter in the world.' This useful piece of trivia had lodged in his memory thanks to a lecture at police training college. 'These, I'm sure, must be genuine.'

'Genuine prints, ducky.' She handed him the manilla folder of photos. 'What are you looking for this time?'

'Some reason why Britt went to the trouble of visiting a squat,' he answered truthfully. 'I still haven't worked it out and GB was no help.'

'At least you caught up with him.'

'Yes. He's a bright lad, but he couldn't help.'

'Why is it important?'

He started working his way slowly through the photographs. 'Because it may yet provide the answer to why she was murdered.'

'Isn't old man Billington the answer?'

'We don't know for sure.'

'You think Britt stumbled into something dangerous?'

He shook his head. 'I don't think Britt ever stumbled into anything. She knew precisely what she was up to, and why. I wish we did.'

'She could still have given one of the crusties a fright without knowing it,' Prue Shorter speculated, standing close to Diamond. 'Just look at this lot! There really were some hard cases among them. God knows what unspeakable things they got up to. It only wanted one of them to think his past was about to be resurrected. I tell you, ducky, they scared me.'

He studied each photograph, characterizing the hard-faced people as individuals rather than an amorphous mob. Certain of them had obviously appealed to Prue as subjects, for they were prominent in the majority of the shots: a man with a Mohican bar of hair down the centre of an otherwise shaven skull; a woman with a cropped head and round glasses; a heavily tattooed man clutching a bottle of cider and lying with his eyes closed in most of the pictures; and of course GB, dominant in height and personality, judged by the attitudes others around him struck. Having established the leading players, Diamond took stock of the others, the less photogenic, sometimes just out of focus, or half obscured by furniture or bisected by the frame of the picture.

'This one,' he said, his finger on a slim, large-eyed girl with dark hair in a plait, 'do you remember her?'

'I remember them all,' said Prue, 'but I've no idea of their names, if that's what you're asking. Introductions weren't encouraged.'

'I think I know this one's name,' said Diamond.

'The thin woman?'

'Can you remember her?'

'Only vaguely. She stayed in the background. One of the squaws. Who is she?'

'Her name is Una Moon.'

'Should I have heard of her?'

'No.' And he didn't enlighten her. Una Moon was the young woman he had last seen at the nick with Warrilow, the one who had first reported that Samantha Tott was missing.

Chapter Nineteen

Mountjoy's barely functioning brain struggled to explain how it was possible that a woman was with him in his cell in Albany. He could definitely hear her moaning quite close to him. A conjugal visit – that great myth so often spoken of by the wishful thinkers? Conjugal visits – in Albany? About as likely as balloon-trips. Even if they *were* permitted, who in the world would want to be conjugal with him? Sophie had sworn never to speak to him again after the divorce, let alone visit him in jail for what she would surely regard as the ultimate degradation.

And why was he lying on the floor instead of in bed? The thin mattress they provided was bloody uncomfortable and sometimes you could hardly tell the bed from the floor, only this felt cold as well as solid. And there *was* a woman somewhere close.

He shifted slightly, freeing his right arm and confirming that he was lying on a flat, smooth surface that had to be lino. His fingertips ran across one of the joins. He lifted the corner of the lino and felt underneath and traced the join between two floorboards. No prison he knew had a board floor.

He opened his eyes, saw an old-fashioned fireplace and a window without bars and remembered where he was. He cursed himself for falling asleep.

He told Samantha, 'Stop moaning, will you?'

'I hate it here.'

'What?'

'This place.' She was sitting in the centre of the floor wrapped in blankets, rubbing at her face with the back of her tied hands. 'It's giving me the creeps. I've never been anywhere so musty and horrible.'

'For God's sake, I got you out of that cave, didn't I?' Mountjoy said. 'I brought you blankets, food, drink. I let you keep your precious violin.'

None of that counted, apparently. 'It feels as if no one's been in here for a hundred years. The toilet, with that wooden seat. That's antique. This old fireplace with the iron grate. It's bizarre, like being in a time warp.'

'Give it a rest, will you?'

'Where are we?' she asked. 'I can hear traffic. Why won't you tell me where we are?'

'You hungry?'

'No.'

'Cold?'

'Not really.'

'Well, then.'

'I'd like to know where I am.'

'Wouldn't you just?'

'I've lived nearly all my life in Bath. I wouldn't have believed a place like this still existed.'

'You live and learn.' Mountjoy yawned. Needing to stop himself drifting into sleep again, he got up and went to the window. Below, a long way below, the traffic moved tidily around the one-way system of the Orange Grove, past Bog Island and up Pierrepont Street towards the railway station. The view from this height was unmatched anywhere in the city because there was no obstruction except for the great square tower of the Abbey to his right. He could see the gleam of the Avon and the lawns of the Parade Gardens. Further off, beyond the spire of the Catholic Church, rising above Brunel's railway viaduct, was the wooded slope of Lyncombe Hill, leading the eye to

224

Beechen Cliff. And out to the left was Bathampton Down; last night, out on the balcony, he'd seen Sham Castle floodlit. For Mountjoy's purposes, this bolt-hole had certain merits, but he would still have favoured the caravan park if only bad luck hadn't forced them out. The stone mine was always going to be unsuitable, an overnight stop, no more. He'd seriously considered taking over the house in Morford Street, but that would have compelled him to take two more hostages. What a prospect! So he'd brought Samantha here. She would have to put up with the Edwardian plumbing.

He knew what she meant about the time warp. It was slightly eerie here. The place *did* seem remote from modern life and it wasn't merely the dust and cobwebs. Down there, somewhere, that fat detective Diamond ought to be working his butt off to get to the truth of the Britt Strand murder, yet here, six floors up, in another age, there were hours of waiting to be endured, hours when confidence drained.

How much longer?

Mountjoy yawned again. Chronic fatigue was his problem. He kept Samantha tied hand and foot and still didn't allow himself proper rest because of the risk of being ambushed by the police. It was making him twitchy, shivery and depressed; if he hadn't planned and worked so single-mindedly for justice – if he'd merely escaped – he would have traded his freedom right now for an undisturbed night in his cell in Albany. When it was over, whatever the outcome, he was going to sleep. For days.

He felt his head sinking. Cat-naps were dangerous, yet he craved them like a fix. Deciding to sit rather than stand, he settled against the wall. His lids drooped.

Minutes must have passed when he opened his eyes next. How many, he couldn't tell. The one thing he could see for sure was that Samantha was no longer in the room.

Gone.

The blankets lay in a heap beside her violin case. The rope that had bound her wrists was on the floor with the flex he used for her ankles.

He got up and dashed to the door.

It wouldn't open. Locked. Momentarily he concluded that she had locked him in after escaping. Then he felt in his pocket and found the key still there. He'd locked the door himself. Where was she, then? He crossed to the second door that connected with the next room. The door was slightly ajar. Before flinging it fully open, he hesitated. What if she were waiting inside, poised to strike him?

He took the gun from his pocket and said, 'Get out of there. I want you in here fast.'

She didn't make a sound.

'Samantha.'

He kicked the door inwards.

Still she made no move.

He said, 'You'd better know that I have a gun in my hand.' Then he stepped inside.

The room was empty.

Mystified and in a panic, he stared around him. If she wasn't inside and she hadn't gone through the door, she must have used the balcony window. Must have – for it was unfastened.

He pushed open the window and stepped outside. Samantha was there, to the left of the windows where she couldn't be seen from inside. She was half-naked. She'd stripped off the white T-shirt he had given her and she was waving it frantically.

She turned and saw him and took it as the cue to start screaming for help. Up to now, the waving had been a dumb-show. Yelling at the top of her voice, she leaned over the stone balustrade like a ship's figurehead, her bared breasts pale and pointed in the crisp October air, and continued to flap the T-shirt.

Mountjoy pocketed the gun; it was useless when she was

in this hysterical state. Up to this time he'd been scrupulous in the physical contact he'd had with her, avoiding any kind of handling she could object to as indecent. The tying and untying had been necessary, but not once had his hand strayed. All that went out of the window, literally.

He had to get her off the balcony, and gentle persuasion wasn't an option. He grabbed her from behind, one arm around her ribs, the other prising her fingers from the balustrade she was trying to anchor herself to. She continued to scream. And she was strong. When her grip on the stonework was loosened, she forced her foot against it and braced her leg, forcing him back against the window. One of the panes cracked and shattered under the weight of his shoulder. He fell and took her with him.

They were in a wrestling match now and Samantha was on top, but with her back against Mountjoy's chest, her buttocks mashing his stomach, her hair pressing into his face. To stop her from getting up, he swung his left arm across her chest and felt his fingers sink into the flesh of her right breast. In a frenzy, she pummelled his ribs with one hand and tried to bend back his fingers with the other. Her thrashing legs threatened to get some leverage on the balustrade until he succeeded in clamping one with his right leg. Then he held on in the hope that she would give up the struggle at some stage.

It was as well that they were locked like this, using up their strength. He was angry enough to have beaten her senseless.

Chapter Twenty

Two police cars with beacons flashing swung out into Manvers Street just as Diamond was about to make the turn into the yard. Commander Warrilow, with patrician self-importance etched all over his features, was seated beside the driver in the second vehicle. Yet another 'sighting' of Mountjoy, Diamond presumed, and yawned.

When he had parked, he went in and tracked Julie to the canteen, where she rose without obvious haste from a table of CID lads and came to meet him.

With a tolerant grin meant to soften the edge of his sarcasm, he said, 'High level discussions, Inspector?'

'Just getting the latest buzz,' she responded evenly. 'They're the Bumblebee squad.'

The grin faded.

Julie added, 'Want to whisk me away?' She was learning how to deal with his irony. Too well.

He said, 'That's why I'm here.'

'Have you got time for a coffee?'

'Do you drink the coffee in this place?'

Her eyes widened. 'There isn't anything the matter with it, is there?' She hadn't entirely got his measure.

Of course he left her to wonder about the coffee. He now felt he'd given as good as he'd got. 'Get me a tea and we'll update each other.'

Presently they had a table to themselves and Julie reported on her search of the Billington residence. 'If the cassette I was looking for was there, I'm afraid it eluded me. I searched everywhere I could think and I had a SOCO to help. It's safe to say that Winston Billington got rid of it, if he ever acquired it at all.'

'Find anything else?'

'A packet of raunchy pictures stuffed into an envelope in the secret drawer of an antique writing-desk. What a let-down! I thought I'd struck gold and all I found was backsides.'

'Whose backsides?' Diamond solemnly asked. 'Any we know?'

She shook her head. 'How could I tell? Facés didn't feature at all.'

'Pictures, you say. Photos?'

'Scraps of paper clipped out of soft-porn mags. Pathetic, really.'

'We all get our thrills some way,' he said philosophically.

'Well, I found it sad.'

'You're not sorry for him?'

'Sorry for the women in the pictures, reduced to that.'

'They don't need your sympathy. It pays better than the police.'

'I wouldn't do it for anything.'

Fleetingly, he was reminded of the modelling offer he'd been made by Chelsea College, and chose not to mention it. That was for Art, not pornography, and he hadn't signed up – yet. 'And you found nothing else of interest?'

'No.'

'Letters, a diary?'

'We were looking for something the shape and size of an audio-cassette,' she reminded him. 'We didn't want to get sidetracked.'

'Understood.' He summarized his interview with Prue Shorter, taking care not to understate his astuteness in recognizing Una Moon in one of the photos of the Trim Street squatters. 'Beautiful how things link up.'

'Just a coincidence, I expect,' Julie commented with serious want of tact.

'Coincidence, be buggered!' said he in an injured tone. 'She's living in a squat in Widcombe, so it's quite logical that she should have been in squats before. I wasn't surprised to spot her there. These crusties all know each other. They represent – what's the jargon I'm groping for? – a whole sub-culture.'

'Are you going to question her?' asked Julie, adding, when he didn't answer, 'Correction. Am I going to?'

'One of us is, for sure. My big mistake four years ago was that I didn't follow all the leads we had.'

'You can't possibly follow up every lead in a murder investigation. And now with only two of us . . .'

'Una Moon may be a crucial witness,' he stated with an oracular air.

'But if Winston Billington is the murderer, where does she fit in?'

'I'm far from certain that he *is*.'

She waited interestedly for him to say more. It wasn't often that Peter Diamond admitted to doubts of any sort.

'We shouldn't count on a confession when he recovers consciousness,' was all he added.

'He was *seen* going into the house.'

'If you believe GB.'

'Don't you?'

'GB is, or was, a drugs-dealer. Telling lies goes with the job.'

Julie was plainly unsettled by all this. Diamond seemed ready to jettison most of the progress they had made, and she didn't understand why. 'But we have it confirmed by Mrs Billington that her husband came back early from Tenerife. That checks with GB's statement.'

'Checks with it, yes. Confirms it, no.'

She didn't appreciate the distinction. 'We know Billington perjured himself in court.'

'But we don't know why.'

She sighed and said, 'Something is going over my head here.'

He explained. 'The point is this. Billington cut short his holiday and returned early. We don't have copper-bottomed proof yet, but since we have corroboration from two sources we'll take this as more than likely true. It's the most interesting thing to emerge since you and I started on this. Now suppose GB also got to know this information, either back in 1990 when it happened, or some time since. He could easily have concocted a story to implicate Billington in the murder.'

'I understand that. But why?'

'To shift the suspicion.'

'Away from himself, you mean?'

'Or someone he wants to protect.'

She was still sceptical. 'How would GB have found out about Billington's holiday arrangements?'

'Through the grapevine. All those crusties at the Trim Street squat had met Britt when she came to do her story on the place. There was a lot of interest in the murder. Billington's evidence at the trial was written up in the press. His picture was in the local papers at the time of the inquest. It only wanted one person to recall seeing him here in Bath at the time he was supposed to have been in Tenerife.'

She pondered the matter. 'But we've been assuming that Billington returned early because he fancied his chance of some action with Britt. He bought flowers at Tenerife Airport, remember.'

'So Mrs Billington told us.'

'We can check the credit card records.'

'Yes.'

'Are you saying all this may not have happened?'

'I'm saying there may be another explanation.'

'He told his wife the story of the emergency meeting in London.'

'*She* told us he told her.'

'Don't you believe her either?'

'Not until we've checked it ourselves. I've got a list of things that need following up a.s.a.p., and one of them is that meeting. Get on the phone to Billington's head office and see if they have any record of it. I also want to know if Una Moon has any form.'

'I'll run her name through the PNC,' said Julie, forgetting Diamond's computer phobia.

'Don't we keep records of our own in this Constabulary?' he said peevishly.

'The PNC is quicker.'

Rather than arguing, he said, 'As it's so quick, see what you can find on the rest of the bunch: Billington, Marcus Martin, Jake Pinkerton and GB.'

She didn't protest. 'Do we have a surname for GB?'

This wrongfooted him. He remembered trying to tease out the name, and failing. Annoyed with himself, he fired one of his regular broadsides: 'It's all initials these days. We don't need words any more. PNC, SOCO, CPS, PACE. Three days back in Bath and my brain is clogged with letters of the alphabet.'

'What do you suggest I do, then?'

'About the Police National Computer? Do you really want me to answer that?'

She smiled faintly. 'I meant about GB.'

When really taxed, he could sometimes dip deep into his memory. 'There's a unit to monitor the crusties over that midsummer festival nonsense every year. Operation Stonehenge, or whatever they call themselves. OS, no doubt. They ought to know his name.'

'I'll try them. Shall I check Prue Shorter while I'm at it?'

'On the computer? Yes.'

'She's still a suspect?'

He nodded, as if the question were superfluous.

Julie said, 'I wasn't sure if you'd ruled her out.'

'Why should I?'

'You thought originally that she might be a lesbian, jealous about Britt's affairs with men, but now we know she had a daughter, that motive is out.'

He said, 'I don't see why. Did the sexual revolution pass you by? There are plenty of lesbian mothers about. Haven't you heard the expression AC/DC?'

Julie exercised restraint, refraining from pointing out that he was now using initials himself. 'Fair enough. I'll check her, too.'

He finished his tea. 'Whilst you expose yourself to gamma radiation, I'm going to look for John Wigfull. I want to know whether they've charged Mrs Billington yet.'

Wigfull was in the main control room using the phone. Several others were speaking into head-sets. In fact, a major alert seemed to be on. Briefly, he moved the phone away from his mouth and muffled it against his chest. 'Have you heard?' he asked Diamond. 'We're about to move in on Mountjoy.'

'Where?'

Wigfull put up his hand to interrupt and spoke into the mouthpiece again. 'Look, we're fully stretched here. If I can't get something sorted soon, I'm trying Wilts.'

'Is this another of Warrilow's wild goose chases?' Diamond asked.

Wigfull shook his head and said down the line, 'Thanks. Just as soon as you possibly can.'

'In Bath?' Diamond asked.

He put down the phone. 'The Empire Hotel.'

'A *hotel*?' He plucked the name out of his past, clicked his fingers, and said, 'Right. You mean that enormous place behind the Guildhall that's been empty for years.'

'They're in one of the top-floor rooms overlooking Orange Grove. Young Samantha was spotted forty minutes ago on the balcony trying to attract attention.'

'Are you sure it was her?'

233

'Totally. She was topless and waving a T-shirt like a flag.'

'You know her as well as that?'

'I'm telling you,' said Wigfull blushing scarlet, more in anger than embarrassment. 'A Japanese tourist was taking a video from the top storey of the Ham Gardens car park. He brought it straight here. On the zoom you can see it's Samantha, even though her hair has been dyed.'

'Any sign of Mountjoy?'

'Hard to see.'

'So what's happening?'

'Warrilow is there, directing operations.'

'You'd better warn him that Mountjoy is armed.'

'What?' Wigfull swayed towards Diamond. 'What did you say?'

'He has a gun, a hand-gun. If they're moving in, they ought to be told.'

'Bloody hell!' Wigfull snatched up the phone again. 'Get me Mr Warrilow, fast.' To Diamond, he said, 'For crying out loud! Why didn't you tell me this before?'

Diamond treated the question as less urgent than Wigfull's business on the phone, and, sure enough, in less than the time it would have taken to answer, the vital information was being relayed to Warrilow.

'Yes, with a hand-gun . . . Peter Diamond tells me . . . I don't know, sir. I haven't had a chance to ask him . . . Of course . . . In the meantime, will you . . . ? . . . Yes, I think that's essential. ' To Diamond, he said, 'I'm lost for words. People could have been killed.'

'Is he pulling them back?'

'Of course he is. My God, Peter, you'd better fill me in fast.'

That was what Diamond proceeded to do, explaining succinctly how Mountjoy had ambushed him in the Francis the previous evening at the point of an automatic. 'Don't ask me where he got it from, or whether it's loaded. That didn't emerge. We talked. He told me he was becoming impatient. He wanted results.' He paused to receive the heat of Wigfull's outrage.

'All this was last night. Last night, for crying out loud? I simply don't understand why you didn't report it.'

'Frankly, John, because I believe Warrilow will have him shot. Now that he knows the man is armed, he's justified in taking his life. You know the form. You know how sieges end.'

'If it's Mountjoy's life or one of ours, we'll shoot the bastard,' Wigfull declared.

'And I can't fault your logic.'

This sounded like capitulation and caught Wigfull off balance. His next remark was couched less aggressively. 'But you were willing to expose police officers to fire without warning them.'

'No. The minute I heard they were moving in, I told you what I know.'

'Why not last night?'

'I just explained.'

'What's so special about Mountjoy, that you want him kept alive?'

Diamond insisted gently, 'I'm almost certain that he's an innocent man.'

'*Innocent*? He's kidnapped Mr Tott's daughter. That's a serious crime.'

'I mean innocent of murder, the murder I sent him down for.'

'I see! You believe what Mrs Billington told us last night, that stuff about her husband killing Britt Strand?'

'All I'm saying is that Mountjoy appears to have suffered a miscarriage of justice. I was chiefly responsible and I want to see him cleared.'

'If he is, it won't reflect credit on you.'

At this, Diamond erupted. 'Do you think I'm looking for bloody credit? I spent long enough in the police to know what that amounts to. I had a pretty good record as a detective, but I wasn't infallible, and when I make a mistake I have the guts to admit it and do something about it.'

'I don't understand this,' said Wigfull, raking a hand through his dark hair. 'I just don't understand. You were brought in because of Samantha Tott, not Mountjoy. Her life was under threat and Mountjoy was making demands. We had you brought here to keep him sweet while we recaptured him.'

'I made it crystal clear that if I stayed, I would look at the case again. Keeping people sweet doesn't come naturally to me, in case you haven't noticed.'

'I don't know how you hoped to get anywhere, just two of you.' A thought struck Wigfull and it was almost possible to see it strike. 'Did Inspector Hargreaves know that Mountjoy is armed?'

'She wasn't there,' Diamond said, wanting to cut off that avenue.

'But did you inform her?'

'Keep Julie out of this.'

'You may think because you're no longer on the strength that you can take chances with men's lives, but she's one of us. If she knew about that gun—'

'She didn't,' Diamond lied and then deflected the attack. 'What you need is someone who knows the building. It's a rabbit warren by the look of it. Have you got hold of the plans yet?'

'We've only just had the alert.'

'Try the City Council. Property and Engineering Services. It's their baby. They must have a set of plans. With any luck, someone there will know exactly what it's like inside the building.'

'I was getting round to that.'

'I'd get round to it pronto if I were you, John.' He waited while Wigfull made another phone call.

As soon as the call was finished, Diamond started along

another devious trail. 'Mountjoy is doing his cause no good at all by carrying a weapon. I accept that. We're bound to use marksmen now and a handgun is no use against a high velocity rifle. His chance of survival is small.'

'It would be simple if he didn't have Samantha with him,' Wigfull reflected, exactly as he was meant to.

Diamond gave a nod. 'You've got a hostage situation, and it wants delicate handling. Can you trust Warrilow not to take any risks? Speaking personally, I'm far from confident that he can handle an armed siege.'

'That's not a matter for me,' Wigfull said, ever mindful of rank.

'Has Mr Farr-Jones been informed? Mr Tott?'

'It's only just happened.'

'If I were you, I'd cover myself, make sure they were fully briefed.' The trail was opening out and the way ahead was clear.

Wigfull acted on the advice and got on the phone again. After speaking to both of the top brass, he informed Diamond, 'We're to proceed to the hotel at once. The Chief wants a meeting.'

'With Warrilow present?'

'Yes. Shall we go?'

An interested crowd had gathered, attracted by the pulsing blue beacons on the police cars parked in front of the ornate façade of the once-gracious hotel in the centre of Bath. The construction of the Empire had spanned the last years of Queen Victoria's reign and the first of King Edward VII's and its design seemed to epitomize the change of monarchs; five storeys were formal in style, typical of late Victorian public buildings, while the sixth burst into a rollicking joke. The top of the hotel celebrated three disparate styles: a red-tiled twin gable that might have been borrowed from a suburban villa; a Dutch gable defined in gracious curves; and a turret, seven-sided and castellated. In consequence it was the most vilified building in Bath, variously described in books about the city as 'huge and execrable'; 'a monolithic monster'; 'an eclectic piece of nonsense'; 'a prime example of Edwardian bad taste'; 'crazy round the tops'; 'a fearful mock-Jacobean skyscraper with a touch of Lacock Abbey in the top corner'; and 'as bad in this setting as a gasometer'. But Peter Diamond had an affection for it amounting to empathy; often his own appearance drew comments almost as harsh.

Tott had already arrived and was standing on the turf of the Orange Grove roundabout staring up at the end of the building where his daughter had been sighted, the twin gables to the left. Warrilow was speaking earnestly to him – the man whose opinion would probably hold sway – getting in his five-cents' worth before the crucial decisions were debated. Wigfull marched over to join in the decision-making.

Seeing that the Chief Constable hadn't yet appeared, Diamond didn't immediately join the party. Nothing constructive could come from a shouting-match with Warrilow, who no doubt blamed him for ruining the recapture operation. Warrilow, another career man like Wigfull, could be counted on to conduct himself decorously when Farr-Jones was present.

Instead, he took a walk around the perimeter of the Empire, faintly interested to discover how Mountjoy had got in, but mainly to gain a few moments' quiet thought. What was decided presently would settle far more than John Mountjoy's fate.

The hotel entrances had been made secure with padlocks. Along the sides facing the street, a thirty-foot-deep stone gully behind railings and covered with an iron grille made things difficult for potential intruders. He guessed that the weak points were at the back. Turning left into Boat Stall Lane, the narrow passage dividing the rear of the hotel and the Rummer public house, he came to the ramp descending to Eastgate, the medieval arch below street level that had once formed part of the city boundary. There, in a murky, evil-smelling passage looking like a left-over set from a Hammer horror film, was the Empire's delivery bay.

By a barred window he happened to notice cut into the wall several initials and dates. D.P.D., RN GUARD, 1940 was one. It was not totally inconceivable that this was his own Uncle Don, who had served in the navy during the war. Most of the carvings were made by navy guards, a reminder that the building had been taken over by the Admiralty at the outbreak of war and remained in the hands of the Ministry of Defence until 1989. The Empire hadn't functioned as a hotel for over half a century.

Progressing along the passage to a stretch white with pigeon-droppings, he examined the double doors leading to the Empire's cellars. The doors were sturdy enough, but one of the bolts securing them had been forced from the wood. A single padlock remained. This, he guessed, was a likely point of entry for Mountjoy. Whilst looking at the padlock to see if anyone had tampered with it he was surprised by a voice at his shoulder saying, 'What do you think you're doing, squire?'

Turning, he found himself in the presence of a large, young, bearded constable in uniform.

Chastened, Diamond said, 'You don't know me? I'm Peter Diamond.'

'Are you now?'

'I just got here with Inspector – sorry, Chief-Inspector – Wigfull.'

It was a consolation to discover that the name of his successor didn't make much more impression than his own. 'In what capacity, sir?'

Difficult to answer. 'A, em, negotiator. I'm here to negotiate with the kidnapper.'

'Well, I'm here to keep the public away from this part of the building, sir.'

'Keep it up, then.' He thought of adding that guarding the doors was a long tradition; only the constable didn't look as if he had a sense of history. So Diamond moved back up the ramp and into the yard at the rear of the Guildhall where the mayor and other VIPs parked their cars. His thoughts were still with those navy guardsmen. They would be in their mid-seventies now, at least – if they had survived. Was that scraping on the wall the only mark in life they had ever made? In the services in wartime their destiny was out of their control. They might have gone down with the *Ark Royal*, as Uncle Don had. But Peter Diamond in 1994 was a free agent, thank God. He'd given up all that nonsense about duty and rank and yes, sir, no, sir. Hadn't he? Deep down, did he want to enlist again?

Better focus on the present problem, he decided, and face the logic of this siege: as soon as Mountjoy was recaptured or shot, the re-investigation of the Britt Strand murder would be terminated. None of the top brass wanted the original verdict overturned. Avon and Somerset had avoided all the bad publicity that other forces had reaped in recent years through unsafe verdicts and evidence of corruption. They would be mightily relieved to pack him off to London and forget about him. He'd always known it would be so.

Recalling the start, when he had been press-ganged into this bizarre assignment, he thanked his stars that he'd had the sense to realize that he had scope for bargaining, and insisted on a genuine investigation. He'd felt deprived for too long of the work he did best. He hadn't gone into it expecting to uncover a miscarriage of justice – least of all in a case he'd handled himself. Yet now that flaws in the original investigation were revealed, he was personally committed to discovering the truth. If in the process he exposed his own mistakes the first time around, so what?

To his knowledge, he'd never once sent down an innocent man. Until, possibly, now. It was one thing to make a mistake; quite another to cover it up. If he was going to live with himself in future, he had to reveal the truth about the death of Britt Strand.

He needed more time. How long, he didn't know.

Hold on, mate, he thought suddenly, audaciously. I *do* know. I need indefinite time. I must have my old job back, nothing less. I must have it for Steph and for myself. I'm a detective, tried and tested, a good sleuth, not infallible, but better than John Wigfull will ever be. I was never cut out to be an artists' model, or a supermarket-trolley man, or a barman, or a Father Christmas. I catch villains. That's what I do best. And I can do it again. I have a unique opportunity to get what I want.

My job back.

He had come right around the hotel to the Orange Grove again. He felt resolute, positive, ready to take on the high command. There was only one drawback: the high command had vanished. Nobody was standing on the roundabout.

He walked over to one of the police cars and spoke to a sergeant he knew. 'Any idea what happened to Commander Warrilow and the others?'

'They decided to pull back, Mr Diamond, out of the line of fire.'

'For heaven's sake, he's only got a small hand-gun. He's not likely to hit anyone from there!'

'You'll find them up the street, sir.' He pointed and said with a touch of embarrassment, 'On Bog Island.'

And where better to spout opinions, Diamond observed to himself, than on the triangle of pavement given its local name because of the underground public toilets once sited there?

Bog Island was a further hundred yards or so from the hotel. He set off at the double.

241

The Chief Constable had already arrived. The four faces turned to look at him and the message they conveyed was not friendly. They could not have looked more disapproving if he had personally supplied Mountjoy with the gun. Farr-Jones remarked, 'I'm not surprised you're the last to arrive.'

Wigfull, the creep, hadn't passed on the news that he was already on the scene.

'I was checking the rear of the building,' Diamond informed them. 'Just making sure there's an officer there – and there is. Haven't had time to look at the Parade Gardens. There's a way into the cellars under the road. I presume you've covered it,' he said directly to Warrilow, whose face was quick to register a satisfying doubt.

'Have you?' Farr-Jones asked.

Warrilow stood back and passed a hand around his chin, as though checking when he had last shaved. 'I'm not entirely sure, sir. I delegated this to the inspector I am using, Inspector Belshaw. No doubt he will have posted his men strategically. He's one of yours, of course.'

'I wouldn't count on Belshaw,' Diamond said, pressing his advantage. 'He's a Bristol man. Not many locals know that way into the hotel.'

'Better check,' Farr-Jones instructed Warrilow, who gave Diamond a murderous glare and went off to deal with the matter. Then there was a question for Diamond, '*Is* there a way in from Parade Gardens?'

'In theory, yes. You could get in from the colonnade overlooking the weir. But you'd have to break through armour-plate doors. It will take him four or five minutes to check.'

'Hm. I understand your motive, Mr Diamond, only I wouldn't want you to think I support it. Now that we're family, so to speak,' the Chief Constable smoothly went on to say, 'you had better explain why the devil you didn't inform us last night that the man is armed.'

242

He gave the explanation he'd given to Wigfull, adding, mainly to get support from Tott, 'God help Samantha when the shooting starts.'

Farr-Jones said, 'You're not seriously suggesting that we handle this without issuing firearms?'

'I'm suggesting that some idiot with a telescopic rifle could cause a tragedy. Mountjoy has a small hand-gun, an automatic. We're not in much danger down here. Samantha's the one I fear for. I think we should play this in a way that doesn't panic Mountjoy. Nothing provocative. No threats and certainly no shooting.'

Tott gave an affirmative grunt and nodded his head.

Farr-Jones wasn't convinced yet. 'In the last analysis, if the man has a weapon, he can hold it to Samantha's head and walk out of there. He can make idiots of us all.'

'Rather that than blow her brains out,' said Diamond.

Tott shut his eyes.

Diamond went on, 'It's looking increasingly likely that Mountjoy didn't commit murder in 1990. He's a desperate man trying to establish his innocence.'

'At the point of a gun?' said Farr-Jones.

'Yes, he's an idiot,' Diamond admitted. 'The point is that he won't use that gun unless someone else fires first. He's exhausted, under extreme stress, yet he knows that his world collapses altogether if he shoots anyone. If I can prove beyond doubt that someone other than Mountjoy murdered Britt Strand, we can end this siege without bloodshed.'

'Can you?'

Diamond wanted to sound positive. 'I'm getting close. I know enough already to believe in Mountjoy's innocence. Proving it is more difficult.'

'Would you be willing to talk to the man – negotiate if necessary?'

'I have, more than once. He wants something more tangible than my good will. If I get the proof I'm looking for, yes, I'll be willing to talk to him again. Without it, there's no point. He's not going to surrender on some vague promise that I'll keep beavering away.'

'No more than we can hold off,' said Farr-Jones. 'You're going to have to produce the rabbit out of the hat, Mr Diamond, and produce it fast.'

There was a silence, deliberate on Diamond's part, while he picked his words. What was said now would amount to one of the most crucial statements he would ever make. 'Chief Constable, I must remind you that I'm a civilian. I'm under no obligation to do anything. I can walk away now, straight up Pierrepont Street to the station and get on the next train to London.'

'You wouldn't do that?' said Farr-Jones, meaning it to sound like a statement, and not succeeding.

Tott said huskily, 'You can't. My daughter's up there with a gunman. You can't abandon her.'

Without betraying the least compassion, Diamond remarked, 'It will get resolved without my help, one way or another.'

'No!' said Tott, grabbing his arm.

Farr-Jones said more shrewdly, 'This is a negotiating position, isn't it? What are your terms?'

Diamond kept them waiting, as if taking a long view of the mountain of choice that was before him. 'First, we stand off. No shooting. No storming the building. Nothing that panics Mountjoy.'

'For how long?'

He glanced at his watch. 'Until midnight. That gives me almost twelve hours.'

'Twelve hours!' said Tott in desperation.

It wasn't in Diamond's plan to bring comfort to the Assistant Chief Constable. 'This must be given in the form of an order to Commander Warrilow.'

Farr-Jones took a deep, audible breath. 'Very well – if you undertake to talk Mountjoy down and secure

Samantha's release. I appreciate that you need time to get the evidence to satisfy the man.'

'And there's another condition,' said Diamond. 'I must be reinstated.'

After a pause while he took in the sense of what had been suggested, Farr-Jones said, 'That's not on.'

Ignoring him, Diamond added, 'As Head of the Murder Squad.'

'Impossible.'

'Why?'

'You were dismissed.'

'No, Chief Constable, I resigned on a matter of principle. I made my protest. Now you need me back.'

'It isn't a question of *need*—' said Farr-Jones.

'Fine,' said Diamond nonchalantly, 'I'll be off, then.' He raised his trilby.

'Wait.' There was an awkward silence, whilst Farr-Jones grappled with the implications. 'We're up to strength in senior posts. I might be able to speak to the Chairman of the Police Authority. It's fraught with problems. If we took you back, Lord knows what the press would make of it when this Mountjoy business hits the headlines. It's going to look as if we're rewarding you for mishandling the case in the first place.'

'They'll have a field day,' Diamond cheerfully concurred.

'If I said I would give it serious consideration . . .'

'. . . I would say you're on your own, gentlemen. I think the next train leaves at 1.27.' He started to turn away and spotted that John Wigfull's face had drained of colour.

'All right,' Farr-Jones decided. 'You can have what you're asking for, Diamond. You bring this siege to a peaceful end by midnight and you can have your job back. I guarantee it.'

Diamond held out his hand for Farr-Jones to grip.

245

Chapter Twenty-One

'About Una Moon . . .' said Julie as she drove the Escort west of the city, past the golf course on the Weston Road.

'Yes?' But it was 'Yes?' in a faraway tone. Peter Diamond, seated beside her, was preoccupied.

She pressed on. 'You asked me to check her form on the PNC, remember? Well, she's been bound over a couple of times for possession of cannabis. Once for obstruction. Nothing more serious than that. Are you listening, Mr Diamond?'

'Mm.'

'As for the others,' she went on, 'Jake Pinkerton and Marcus Martin had clean sheets and so did Prue Shorter. I still haven't discovered GB's real name.'

She was so certain that he hadn't taken in a word of it that she added, 'And I also checked up on Mr Farr-Jones. He was convicted of stealing underwear from clothes-lines.'

'Ah.' No more reaction than that.

She glanced his way and added. 'He asked for fifteen similar offences to be taken into consideration.'

Diamond managed a response. 'Good.'

'Good?'

'Now we know where he got the shorts he wears for the synchronized swimming.'

After a moment to take it in, she giggled. His sense of humour took some getting used to. 'You *were* listening.'

'I heard every word.'

Like hell you did, she thought. She said as if bringing it up for the first time, 'So would you like to know what the PNC has on Una Moon?'

'Of course! And all the others.'

This time it seemed that the information penetrated, because when she had finished, he said, 'I don't know how I'm going to fit it in, but I've got to see Miss Moon myself.'

She took the sharp left turn into Combe Park, where the hospital entrance was. They were responding to a message from the constable on duty at the RUH: Winston Billington had recovered consciousness and was considered to be capable of making a statement.

Diamond asked what time it was.

He could have got it from the clock on the dashboard as she did, but Julie didn't mention this. 'One-thirty, almost.'

'Too late for lunch.'

'I never have much, anyway.'

'Just as well. We have ten and a half hours to nail the killer, Julie.'

They found the patient sitting up, in conversation with a woman in a dark red quilted coat.

'Who's the visitor?' Diamond muttered to the constable on duty in the corner.

'His sister.'

'Did they say he could have visitors?'

'They didn't say he couldn't, sir. She just walked in.'

He rolled his eyes upwards. 'What do you think your job is, then – watching the nurses?'

As soon as he approached the bed the woman got up from the chair, blushing scarlet. She was wearing a perfume that more than cancelled out the hospital smells. She must have been in her mid-forties, with dark, dyed hair and a small, pretty, round face of a type that had been common-place in the fifties, but you didn't see so often now.

'Pardon me,' Diamond said, 'but we're from the police.'

'Of course.' She leaned over Billington, said, 'I'll come again, Win. Take care, love,' and planted a kiss on his forehead that left a lipstick mark.

In stepping aside to let her pass, Diamond backed into a screen and had to steady it. In the confusion he murmured to Julie, 'Follow her.' Then he gave his total attention to the patient. Billington's head was bandaged, yet he was no longer linked to a ventilator or a drip-feed. The bed had been raised a few turns to bring him up from the horizontal. Was this frail figure with watery eyes the killer who had bluffed his way through the police investigation four years ago, the bottom-fancier with sex on the brain and a steady supply of Milk Tray to help achieve it? 'Remember me, sir? Peter Diamond, Bath CID. We met some years ago. Are you ready to tell me what happened?'

Billington said something inaudible.

'Can you speak up?'

'. . . very hazy.'

'I'm not surprised. You were out cold for a day. Can you recall anything at all?'

'. . . don't see how I can help.'

The phrase triggered a memory. Four years ago in court Billington had been more articulate, yet the essential message had been similar: he was a decent citizen anxious to co-operate, only puzzled as to his part in the proceedings. Diamond reflected cynically that the same air of innocence probably worked a treat in selling saucy greetings-cards.

'What happened, Mr Billington?'

'My wife . . .'

'Yes?'

'. . . spoken to you?' Hazy he might be, but he was smart enough to test the water first.

'She has.'

'We had a falling-out. She tell you that?'

248

'I'd like to hear your version, sir.'

'. . . got rather out of hand this time. She must have struck me. Couldn't say what she used.'

'A bag of coins, she told us.'

'Just coins?'

'A solid mass of them can weigh quite heavy. Enough to do serious damage.'

'Mm. Awfully sore.'

'You're lucky to be alive. What was the cause of this falling-out?'

He pondered this for a considerable time. 'Something she imagined.'

Diamond looked at the lipstick imprint on Billington's forehead. 'You didn't provoke her?'

'All in her mind.'

'You can't say for certain why your wife attacked you?'

'Don't wish . . .'

'Yes?'

'Don't wish to press charges. Sort this out in our own way.'

'It was a serious assault, sir. She damn near killed you.'

'Poor old me.'

You'll feel even worse when you know what she's accusing you of, thought Diamond. 'Mrs Billington told us that the reason for her anger went back four years, to the time the Swedish woman was murdered in your house.'

'Yes?' The voice was hollow and the eyes slid aside, as if he was unwilling to make the effort of thinking back four years.

'She stated that you returned home from Tenerife before Britt Strand was killed. That wasn't what you said in your statement to us at the time, or in court.'

Billington mumbled, 'This important?'

'It's bloody important,' Diamond told him, trying to speak the words calmly.

'Long time ago.'

'I must know what really happened.'

249

Billington's eyes made contact with Diamond's again and he said in a surprisingly lucid utterance, 'I don't wish to testify against my wife. The reason why she attacked me is academic.'

'I'm not particularly interested in what happened yesterday, sir. I want to know about 1990. Your wife has accused you of murdering Britt Strand.'

He digested this and then summoned up a smile. 'Bit over the top, isn't it?'

'Did you return from Tenerife two days before your holiday was due to end?'

'Don't think I should answer that.'

'Mr Billington, you won't know this, but John Mountjoy, the man convicted of Britt Strand's murder in 1990, has escaped and is at this minute holding a young woman hostage. He swears he's innocent of that murder. Your wife has named you as the killer.'

This elicited a long interval of silence.

'Shows how much she knows,' Billington was finally spurred to say. 'She wasn't even in this country when Britt was killed.'

'But you were. What your wife told me is true.'

'Yes.'

'She also told me you bought some flowers at Tenerife Airport.'

'How did she know that?'

'Credit card statement.'

Billington made no response.

'Why? Why did you come back early?'

'A business meeting. In London.'

That mythical meeting. Diamond looked over his shoulder for Julie, but of course he'd sent her in pursuit of the woman visitor. He'd asked her to check whether such a meeting ever took place. Was that what she'd been trying to tell him in the car on the way here? He took a chance. 'There wasn't any meeting. You came back to Bath with

250

those flowers. You were seen on the night of the murder entering the house.'

'It is my house.'

'You don't deny it, then?'

'I deny murdering Britt.'

'But you were there when she was killed.'

'No, I wasn't.'

Breaking the news considerately, Diamond said, 'There's something you ought to know, Mr Billington. We have a witness who saw a man answering to your description let himself into the house some time between eleven and midnight. This witness went so far as to say that the person looked as if he owned the place. He had a doorkey. And only a few minutes before, Britt Strand came to the door to show Mountjoy out. Do you understand what I'm saying? Mountjoy – the man convicted of murder – left the house and, shortly after that, you went in. She was still alive when you went in.'

Billington's moist brown eyes held Diamond's steadily. He said with clarity, 'And did this eagle-eyed witness also see me leave the house a few minutes later?'

These occasional bursts of articulate speech had Diamond convinced that the vagueness was a convenient bluff. Billington was in full possession of his mental powers.

'*Leave the house*? No, Mr Billington. He didn't mention it.'

'But was he still there?'

The question deflected Diamond. He cast his mind back to what GB had said. Had he remained watching any longer after the second caller arrived? Diamond dredged deep for the words GB had used. '*I left. Seeing him arrive made up my mind. He was sure to come to the door if I knocked and I didn't want any hassle.*' So Billington's story matched GB's in that particular. There was more to crosscheck. He removed his hat and placed it on the bed.

Immediately a voice behind him said, 'You needn't think you're staying. Mr Billington has had one visitor for twenty minutes before you arrived. We can't have him getting tired.'

He half turned and got a faint impression of a dark blue uniform at the edge of his vision. Judged by her voice, the ward sister wasn't the sort to respond to persuasion.

Diamond nodded, neither conceding nor defying. He leaned closer to Billington. 'Where did you go?'

Billington chose silence, probably relying on the sister to bring this to a quick conclusion.

'If you left the house as you just suggested, where did you go?'

He shook his head.

'Can anyone vouch for this? Where did you spend the rest of the night if it wasn't in your own house?'

Billington looked away.

'If you won't answer, I'll have to assume that you can't because you made it up.'

'Assume what you like.'

'That night I'm talking about, did you try anything with Britt?'

Billington frowned. 'What do you mean – try anything?'

Diamond turned his head to satisfy himself that the sister had moved on. 'A bit of slap and tickle.'

A faint trace of colour rose in the patient's cheeks. 'I didn't even see her. She was upstairs. We live on the ground floor.'

'How do you know she was upstairs? Did you hear her?'

'I saw the light at her window as I came along the street.'

A plausible answer. 'You're telling me you didn't go into her flat that night? Didn't even knock on the door?'

'Definitely not.'

'It's no secret that you fancied her, used to give her chocolates and flowers. There you were, alone in the house with her for once. Don't tell me you missed your chance.'

252

'I wasn't in the house five minutes.'

'Ah, yes. This unlikely story that you went out again. If you won't tell me where you spent the rest of the night, perhaps you'll say what you did in that five minutes.'

'Collected my car key. Went to the toilet.'

'Then you left the house again?'

'Yes.'

'After collecting your car key. So you drove somewhere?'

The assumption was rather obvious. In Billington's supposedly depleted state a sarcastic comment would sound too sharp, so he gave Diamond a despising look. 'Yes. I didn't need my car keys on holiday so I left them in the house. My old motor was parked in the street for a couple of weeks. I called home because I wanted to use it. Is that what you want to know?'

'Why won't you tell me where you spent the rest of that night? Did you return to your house at any time?'

'No.'

'Were you with a woman?'

He gave no answer.

If this had been an interview room at the nick, Diamond would have come down harder. There were people who coughed at the first hint of the third degree and Billington gave every indication of being one, but this wasn't the time and place.

Instead, the oblique approach. 'Let's talk about Britt. We know of several men friends she knew over the period she was lodging in your house. Did you meet that rock musician – what was his name? – Jake, em . . .'

'Pinkerton.'

'So you did.'

'I'm getting tired,' said Billington.

'Bright lad, that one. Sussed the pop music industry and invested in production when he'd made his millions performing. Did he come to the house?'

'If you want to chat to someone, why don't you try another ward?'

'Did you meet Jake Pinkerton?'

A heavy sigh.

'When he came to the house, it must have registered with you. He's a famous name. Mega-famous. Always on the telly. You do remember?'

A yawn.

Diamond persevered. 'They had a fling, I gather, Britt and her millionaire muso, a few steamy nights at his place, but they were free spirits, both of them. Not the sort of people who move in together.'

Billington's eyelids drooped.

This was going nowhere, and it didn't seem worthwhile starting on Britt's other lovers. 'Your car, Mr Billington. What was it?'

'MGB.'

'What?'

The eyes opened. 'MGB, I said.'

Even Peter Diamond, no car buff, knew that these days the MGB was regarded as a classic. They'd stopped building them about 1980. He wouldn't have thought a colourless character like this would own an MGB. 'Are you telling me you left an MG sports car on the street for two weeks while you went on holiday?'

Billington blinked and stared. 'Didn't say that.'

'You told me a moment ago that this was the reason you went back to the house on the night of the murder: to collect your car key.'

'We weren't talking about my car. Mine's an old Vauxhall.'

Confusion, then. Real, or contrived?

'What's this about an MGB, then?'

'That was Britt's – when she was seeing Pinkerton. Red. Beautiful little car.'

'I didn't think she drove.'

254

'She got rid of it later. Didn't get another, far as I know.'

'So we're talking about some time back?'

'I was. What were you on about?' He made it sound as if Diamond was the one suffering post-concussional effects.

'How long before the murder?'

'Couple of years. I don't know. It wasn't my business, was it?'

'But you'd know if she owned another car after she got rid of the MGB.'

'She didn't.'

'So she was without wheels. Did you ever give her lifts in your old Vauxhall?'

'A couple of times to the station.'

'Did you ever meet her train to drive her home?'

'No.'

'Ever buy her flowers?'

'*Buy* them? No.'

'You picked them from the garden.'

'Why not?' said Billington. 'She was living in my house. People can be civil to each other without ulterior motives.'

The way this pat little speech came out told Diamond it was well rehearsed. The civilized behaviour card. He was tempted to trump it with a blunt mention of the bum-shot clippings Julie had found. But as the ward sister was likely to bring this interview to a premature end any time, he moved on fast to a topic of more urgency. 'There was another man Britt was seeing shortly before she was killed. Quite a celebrity in his own way, wasn't he? That show-jumper, Marcus Martin. Did he visit the house?'

Billington perked up, the adrenaline flowing now that someone else might be under suspicion. 'He was calling right up to the time we went on holiday.'

'You met him, then? When did he first appear?'

'Only a week or so before we left for Tenerife. He was an arrogant bastard. Treated us like servants.'

'In what way?'

255

He proceeded to tell the story. 'Once I remember he had a dog with him. Big, spotted thing. I don't know what breed it was or what it was called. He hooked the lead over our hallstand and told me to keep an eye on it, without so much as a "please". We had a polished wooden floor and I could hear the claws scratching it, ruining the surface, while Mr Martin, cool as you like, started up the stairs to Britt's rooms. I asked him politely to leave the dog outside the front door. Apart from anything else, we keep a cat. But Lord Muck took not the blindest notice. So presently I took the dog outside myself and tied it to the railings.' The incident must have made a deep impression, more than four years on, for Billington to have recalled it. And his concussion had miraculously lifted to do justice to the outrage he obviously felt.

'What happened when he found the dog had moved?'

'He came downstairs because it started howling, making a God-awful racket. The next thing, this bumptious fathead marched into our private flat with the dog and said I had no right. Cheek. He got more than he bargained for when Snowy started on him.'

'Snowy?'

'The cat. She felt cornered, you see. The dog came in and hurled itself towards her. Snowy clawed its nose. She's fearless. You never heard such yelping. That was the last time he brought the dog into our place, I can tell you.'

'Did Britt have anything to say?'

'She had the good sense to keep out of it.'

A thought occurred to Diamond. 'What happens to your cat when you go on holiday?'

'It goes next door. That's always been open house for Snowy. They've got an old tabby who clears off upstairs and leaves the food-trough to Snowy.'

The cat's welfare ceased to be of interest. 'Britt's friendship with this man started only a few weeks before she died, am I right?'

256

'As far as I know.'

'They were still seeing each other at the time you went on holiday?'

'I believe so.'

'Did Martin bring flowers for Britt?'

He shook his head. 'That one was far too mean.'

'Did anyone? Did bouquets ever get delivered to your door?'

'I can't remember any.'

'Did Martin ever stay the night?'

'No one did. We made that very clear to Britt and she respected it.'

'Did you respect *her*?'

Billington frowned. 'How do you mean?'

'Her privacy. Did you ever go into her flat when she was out?'

'Only for maintenance.'

'What maintenance is that?'

'Checking the radiators for leaks, changing light bulbs, inspecting the fabric – the usual things, you know.'

'I can guess,' said Diamond, and he could.

'She had nothing to complain of.'

'That night you found her dead. What time was it you went into her flat – about one a.m., wasn't it? Was that maintenance, or what?'

'That isn't funny.'

'But I want an answer.'

Billington's gaze shifted to the ceiling as he recollected that evening. He was still talking lucidly. 'It had been so quiet. Usually we could hear her moving about. She always took a shower before going to bed, and we'd hear the water going through the system. We'd hear her footsteps across the floor. That night, nothing.'

'But there must have been times when she spent the night in other places. She had lovers. What made this night so special that you decided to check?'

'It was coming back after being away. You're more aware of things, sounds and that. Of course we noticed the milk hadn't been taken in. We assumed she was away, but it wasn't like her to go off without telling the milkman. She was such a well-organized person. Violet started worrying about her, and couldn't get off to sleep. In the end she nagged me into checking.'

Knowing Violet Billington, Diamond thought it likely that the worry wasn't so much over Britt Strand's welfare as the possibility that she had done a flit without paying her rent. 'Tell me what you found.'

'I've told you before. I've told it in court. I've told it dozens of times.'

'Refresh my memory.'

He screwed his face into a resentful look and turned his eyes towards the end of the ward where the sister had gone. 'Well,' he said after a time, seeing no one coming to his aid, 'I let myself into the flat and spoke her name. I had a sense that the place was empty and yet not empty. It was a strange sensation. As far as I can remember I went straight to the bedroom. The door was open. I didn't switch on the light at first. I could just about see that the bed was occupied, but there was a smell that wasn't healthy. I asked if she was all right. There wasn't even a movement from the bed. So I stepped out into the passage and put that light on, which gave me enough to see what had happened. It was the worst moment of my life. I still get nightmares.'

'What did you do?'

'Went downstairs and told Violet. She came up to have a look. Then we phoned the emergency number. That's all.'

'Tell me about Britt's appearance.'

He gave a shrug. 'What do you mean – appearance? She was dead.'

'Describe the scene.'

'You saw it. You were one of the first.'

'I need to hear it from you.'

He closed his eyes and started to speak like a medium in trance. 'The curtains are drawn. Her clothes are lying on a chair by the dressing table, folded. Shoes together on the floor, neat-like. She's lying face up on top of the bed, not in it, in a white dressing gown and pyjamas. Blue pyjamas. The dressing gown is made of towel stuff. It's open at the front. The pyjamas are stained with blood, pretty bad, but dry and more brown than red, and so is the quilt she's lying on. One arm – the right – is stretched out across the bed. The other is bent across her stomach. She's turned a sallow colour and her mouth is horrible. Deep red. Filled with dead roses.' He opened his eyes. 'If Mountjoy didn't do this, you've got to get the brute who did.'

'Your time's up, inspector, more than up,' a voice broke in. The redoubtable sister had reappeared.

'I hope not,' said Diamond.

'What?'

He gave her a smile. 'I've still got things to do. But I'm leaving.'

Chapter Twenty-Two

Events were not running smoothly for Diamond. First, when he went to look for the Escort it had gone; Julie had taken it to pursue the woman who had visited Billington. Second, he carried no personal radio; hadn't even thought of asking for one. So he had to use a public phone to get a taxi back to Bath. But there was a consolation: the driver recognized him from the old days. They had a satisfying to-and-fro listing the inflictions they considered were ruining the character of the city: black London-style cabs, sightseeing buses, tourism, ram-raids, 'new age' travellers, shopping malls, traffic wardens, busking, Christmas decorations, students, old people, school-children, councillors, pigeons, surveys, horse-drawn carriages and opera-singing in front of the Royal Crescent. Diamond felt much better for it by the time the cab drew up in front of the shabby end-terrace near the bottom of Widcome Hill where Una Moon, and, until recently, Samantha Tott, were squatters.

His spirits plummeted again on learning from a hairy young man in army fatigues that Una had moved out.

'Where can I find her?'

'Who are you, then?'

'A friend.'

'What time is it?'

Diamond usually asked that himself, and expected to be told. 'Around two-thirty, I imagine. Where will I find her at this time?'

'Up the uni.'

'The university?'

'Unicycle.'

'Ah.' Diamond's face registered the strain of this mental leap.

'Down by the Abbey,' his informant volunteered, and then asked, 'If you're a friend, how come you don't know she juggles?'

Diamond got back in the cab.

A crowd of perhaps eighty had formed a semi circle around two performers in the Abbey Churchyard, close to the Pump Room. A man in a scruffy evening suit and top hat was doing a fire-eating act before handing the lighted torches to a young woman wobbling on a unicycle, who juggled with them. Not a convenient moment to question her about the Trim Street squat.

She was as thin as a reed, with a face like a ballerina's and fine, dark hair in a plait that flicked about on her back with her movements controlling her bike. Ms Moon, beyond any doubt.

A church clock chimed the third quarter and Diamond seriously considered interrupting the performance, regardless that it wouldn't be a popular move, and might be dangerous. He decided to give them two minutes more, two minutes he could use to update himself on the siege, for the north end of the Abbey Churchyard led to Orange Grove. He strode in that direction.

Street barriers had been placed across the pedestrian crossing by the Guildhall, blocking the access to Orange Grove. A constable was stretching a band of chequered tape across the pavement.

Diamond explained who he was and asked what was happening now. On Commander Warrilow's orders, he learned, the area in front of the Empire Hotel had been closed to traffic and pedestrians. Sensitive listening equipment had been set up and certain landmarks around Orange Grove were being used as observation points. Someone was posted on the roof of the Abbey in the tower at the north-east end; not a marksman, the constable thought. It wouldn't be good public relations, would it, to use a place of worship as a gun emplacement?

'Have they appeared at the window at all since the girl was spotted?' Diamond asked.

'Not so far as I know, sir. He won't let her do that again, will he? He's got the whole hotel to himself, so he might as well keep her in a room at the back. There's plenty of choice.' This policeman seemed to be making a bid for CID work.

'Yes, but he'll want to see what's going on down here,' Diamond pointed out.

'He'd do better to watch the stairs inside the building. That's how we'll reach him – unless Mr Warrilow is planning something dramatic with a helicopter.'

'That wouldn't surprise me.'

It was time he returned to the buskers. The crowd was clapping as he crossed the yard. Evidently the show was ending. People on the fringe started moving away. A few generous souls stayed long enough to throw coins into the top hat. The next act, a string quartet, was waiting to take over the pitch.

Una Moon was gathering up smoking torches when Diamond approached her and introduced himself. The moment Samantha was mentioned she stood up and said earnestly, 'Is she all right? Have you found her?'

'Let me get you some tea and we can talk,' he offered without answering the question. 'There's a café in the covered market with a place to sit down, or used to be.'

She asked if her friend the fire-eater could join them. Buskers stick together when hospitality is on offer. The fellow in the top hat winked companionably.

Diamond fished in his pocket for a few silver coins and

asked the fire-eater to cool his mouth somewhere else. And returned the wink.

He offered to carry the unicycle the short way to the Guildhall market, which is hidden behind the Empire Hotel and the Guildhall. The market café wasn't quite in the class of the Pump Room for afternoon tea, but it was almost as convenient, and a better place to interview a busker. Seated opposite Diamond, across a table with a green Formica top, she warmed her hands around the thick china mug and watched him speculatively with her dark brown eyes.

'You ought to wear more in this weather,' he told her, eyeing the thin black sweatshirt she had on.

She ignored that. 'Tell me about Sam.'

He could ignore things, too, when it suited him. 'We don't have much time. Una Moon. That's your real name, is it?'

She frowned. 'What's it to you?'

'Not many of you people use your real names, do you?'

'Why should we?' she rounded on him. 'It's a free world. We have a right to protect ourselves from goons like you slotting us into the system. I want to be an individual, not a piece of computer data.'

'But Una Moon is your own name?'

'How do you know that?'

'From a computer. And before you protest about your civil liberty, it's a national computer. I'm on it, too, and so is the Prime Minister and everyone who keeps a car.'

She scowled. 'I don't keep a car.'

He said, 'We needn't go into the reason why you appear.' He'd decided a touch of intimidation would speed the process.

She stared defiantly.

'Sam also uses her own name,' he pointed out.

'She's new to this. She'll learn – if she survives. It's bloody disgraceful that you haven't caught the bloke by now.' Una was more aggressive than the girlish features and plait suggested.

He remarked, 'I sense that you're not comfortable with somebody like me knowing your name.'

'Piss off, copper.'

'By the way you speak, you had a middle-class upbringing and a good education. Were you at university?'

'Listen,' she said. 'Whether I went to university doesn't matter a toss. What are you – trying to relate to me, or something? There are more important things to do, you know.'

'You've been living this life for some years, I take it?'

'What do you mean – "this life"? The squatting? Of course I bloody have, ever since I dropped out of Oxford. Now I've told you – I was in college for a year and a bit. Can we move on to some more useful topic, like what you're going to do about Sam?'

He persisted. 'You were living in the Trim Street squat at the time Britt Strand was murdered. I've seen your photo.'

She became more defensive. 'She wasn't killed in that house. None of us had anything to do with that.'

'She visited the squat to research an article and have the pictures taken. That was only ten days before she died. How much do you remember about it?'

'Have you got a cigarette?'

He shook his head. 'Have to use one of your own.'

She produced a matchbox from her pocket and took out a half-smoked cigarette and a match and lit up. 'Britt Strand knew what she wanted and how to get it. She picked up one of the guys in the squat – well, the number one guy really, and got to work on him to soften up the rest of us for this piece she was going to write.'

'You mean GB?'

She nodded.

'Another one who prefers to be nameless,' commented Diamond.

'That's his choice.'

'Fine, but I'm willing to bet he doesn't have GB written on his social security documents.'

'I wouldn't know.'

'Were you ever his girl?'

She gave him a glare. 'That's typical of the way you people see us. Just because we lived in the same building it doesn't mean we screwed. There were other people around, you know. It was a community, right?'

'So nobody minded him bringing this smart Swedish blonde to write up the story of your squat?'

'I wouldn't say nobody minded, but it was GB's gaff. He staked it out and made sure it was empty.'

'How's that done?'

'Lots of ways. You slide dry leaves in the slits in the door and check if they've moved in a couple of days. You can shove fly posters through the letter box and see if they get picked up. Of course you go back and see if there are lights at night. GB did all that. He was the first one in. It was thanks to him we had a place to doss down.'

'GB is a bright lad.'

'He's switched on, but he lost cred with some of us when it was obvious the Swedish bird had him on a string. He really got it bad.'

'How do you know?'

She sighed and glared. 'They'd been seen around. There isn't much you can do in this poky town without everyone knowing about it.'

'But he consulted you all about bringing her to the house, didn't he?'

'Yes, he told us what she was asking. We talked it through. Some of our crowd didn't want their faces in the papers. GB said the piece Britt was supposed to be writing wasn't for a British magazine. She was going to sell it abroad, so in the end we agreed. After all, she was willing to pay for it.'

'No one had second thoughts?'

'What do you mean?'

'After the visit, was anyone nervous over what she would write?'

'Like what – getting labelled as scroungers, or something? We're used to that.'

'Did she ask any personal questions?'

'Not to me.' Una reached for the tin ash-tray between them. 'What are you driving at? Do you think one of our lot topped her?'

'It's possible. Maybe – as you said – someone objected to being photographed.'

'If they did, they should have topped the photographer, not the writer.'

'Too late. The pictures were taken,' said Diamond. 'The article was never written, so the pictures were never published.'

'Where did you see them?' she asked.

'At the photographer's. Do you remember Prue Shorter, a large lady?'

She gave a nod, eyed his physique and seemed on the point of saying something, before thinking better of it and putting the cigarette to her lips instead.

'I've seen all the shots that were taken that afternoon,' he went on. 'Not the kind of stuff you find in glossy magazines. I've been trying to work out why Britt was so interested in you lot. There isn't much glamour in a bunch of crusties and their dogs and a heap of beer cans in a back street in Bath.'

'Some of us cleaned the place up for those pictures,' Una recalled.

'I beg your pardon. But it wasn't long after the murder that you all moved out, am I right?'

'Not long.'

'Any reason?'

'GB,' she said. 'Trim Street was his gaff. He got

266

depressed. The entire house was pit city when he was feeling low. There were rows all the time. Some of us couldn't stand it and shoved off. I must have been in six different gaffs since then.'

'With some of the old crowd?'

'Here and there.'

'GB is still about.'

'Yes.' She grinned. 'He's got it made. He's a cool cat now.'

'You're not bitter towards him?'

'GB is all right.' The words didn't convey the way she spoke. This was a high compliment.

'A regular guy?'

'Better than that. He could have made us pay. I've heard of guys who open up empty houses and act as squat brokers. GB never asked for a penny.'

'I think he makes his money pushing drugs,' said Diamond.

She blew out smoke and looked up into the domed roof.

'How about Samantha?' he switched the subject. 'When did she move in?'

'To Widcombe Hill? Not so long ago. In the summer. She had a bust-up with her parents. The usual story. She's younger than I am, hasn't had the corners knocked off yet, if you know what I mean, but I like Sam. It was bloody irresponsible when the papers printed that stuff about her busking – her old man being in the police and all that.'

'You can't blame the press for what happened.'

'I can and I do.' Her small mouth tightened so hard that the colour drained from her lips.

'You know her,' said Diamond. 'How will she stand up to this kidnapping?'

'She's quite strong mentally. She'll hold out if she gets the chance. My fear is that this Mountjoy guy will get heavy with her. The asshole has been violent to women before. I remember reading about him after he was sentenced. His marriage broke up through the way he treated his wife. And there was some other woman he beat up.' Una jabbed her cigarette into the ash-tray. 'You've got to find her fast.'

'Oh, but we have. She's in the next building to this.' While Diamond told her about the incident at the window of the Empire Hotel, Una stared like an extra overacting in a silent film. 'What we've got now,' he summed it up, 'is a siege, an armed siege.'

'He's *armed*?' she whispered.

'If we want to avert a tragedy, someone must talk him down, and that's me. But he isn't interested unless I crack the Britt Strand case. I'm ninety-nine per cent sure Mountjoy wasn't the murderer. It's down to a handful of suspects, which is why I'm talking to you.'

'You suspect *me*?'

Under her anxious scrutiny, he answered candidly, 'I've no reason to, but you're one of the people I didn't question four years ago. You may know something nobody else does.'

'Is that why you asked me about GB? You suspect him?'

He swirled the dregs of his tea and put the mug to his mouth.

'He's not violent,' she said, the outraged words tumbling so fast from her lips that they merged and practically lost their sense. 'I've never known GB to attack anyone. Never. Just because he's big doesn't mean he's dangerous. You're so wrong about this.'

He sat back and passed a hand over his smooth head. 'I haven't made up my mind.'

She said, 'GB had a thing for Britt. He wouldn't have harmed her.'

He didn't spell out the logic that a man in love, even a man with no violent tendencies, might be driven to kill if he learned that his lover was entertaining someone else. 'What I'd really like to discover,' he said, 'was why Britt

268

Strand went stalking GB in the first place.'

'Obviously she was using him to get inside the house.'

'But why? As I said just now, what was so special about you lot?'

'It wasn't us,' said Una. 'It was a previous tenant.'

Intrigued, he waited for her to elaborate.

And she waited, before saying, 'Well, you know who lived in Trim Street.'

'I'm afraid I don't.'

'Jane Austen.'

He frowned. 'The writer?' It was a dumb thing to say, but he had been thinking in terms of the twentieth century.

'Well, she did produce four or five of the greatest novels in the English language, yes.'

'Jane Austen once lived in the house you squatted in? Are you sure?' Here it was, apparently, the answer he'd been seeking for days.

'No,' she answered. 'I'm not sure, and nobody can be, because the house number isn't mentioned in the letters. The only certain thing is that she and her mother had to take lodgings in Trim Street after her father died. It was a poor address and they hated it.'

He felt elated. He couldn't take much credit for rooting out the information, but it was one part of the mystery solved apparently. 'How do you know all this?'

'Before I dropped out of Oxford I read Jane Austen. She was the only author I could stomach. I devoured all the novels and the juvenilia and the collected letters. I thought I remembered Trim Street and after we moved in, I went to the Central Library to check. In one letter, before the family even moved to Bath, Jane wrote that her mother would do everything in her power to avoid Trim Street, so you can imagine their feelings when they ended up there, in 1806. It must have been hell. But you can see why it interested Britt Strand.'

He was trying to contain his excitement, and not succeeding. 'A Jane Austen house taken over by squatters? Yes, I can. It was the hook to hang her story on.'

Una had obviously reached this conclusion some time ago. 'It isn't known which house in Trim Street the Austen family actually lived in, so Britt could pick on our squat in the certainty that nobody could prove her wrong. It was as likely as any other.'

'Dead right,' he agreed. 'You see those photos and you need no persuading. Gracious Georgian fireplaces heaped with beercans. Graffiti. Crusties and their dogs sprawled around. Jane Austen's home desecrated.'

This was a touch too strong for Una. 'Hold on, we didn't *desecrate* anything. We used the toilets properly. We didn't smash windows or start a fire.'

'The point isn't how you behaved. It's how the story would have read in the magazine. Jane Austen—'

She cut in savagely, 'Bugger Jane Austen. While you sit here talking about some dead writer, Sam is tied up in that hotel with a gun at her head waiting for you to do something.'

He was unmoved. 'This isn't a one-man show. The place is under surveillance. What you've just told me is more important than you realize. I needed to know this. Who else have you told.'

'Nobody. Who's interested, for God's sake?'

'GB? Are you sure you didn't tell GB?'

She shook her head.

'Positive?'

'Why give him unnecessary grief?' she asked.

'Grief? Why should it grieve him?'

'He thought Britt fancied him, poor sap.'

Julie was in their office at Manvers Street when Diamond walked in. 'I couldn't trace you,' she said, and when it sounded like a lame excuse she added more assertively,

'Don't you think you ought to carry a personal radio or a mobile phone?'

If it was meant as a serious suggestion, she could have saved her breath. 'Did you follow that woman, Billington's visitor?' he asked.

'I did.'

'And. . .?'

'She isn't his sister.'

'Who is she?'

'Her name is Denise Hathaway and she runs the sub-post office in Iford.'

'Near Bradford-on-Avon?'

'Yes. I followed her home.'

'And spoke to her, I hope?'

'Of course.' Julie paused and changed the tempo of question and answer. 'I don't know if this is good news, or bad. She confirmed Winston Billington's alibi. On the night of the murder, they both stayed at the Brunel Hotel in Bristol. They'd been lovers for about a year, ever since he chatted her up trying to persuade her to stock his greetings cards in the post office.'

Diamond was frowning. 'On the night of the murder, Billington was in Bath.'

'It all fits in, if you'll let me finish. He was in Bath, as you say. He called at his house to collect his car keys, just as he claimed. Mrs Hathaway—'

'She's married, then?'

'Yes. She's tried to keep this relationship a secret. She has a horror of all her customers in Iford finding out about her infidelity.'

'What about her husband?'

'He works nights at the post office in Bath. She doesn't seem so worried about him. It's the neighbours who alarm her. I had no end of a task wheedling out the truth by threats and promises. It's a real hush-hush affair. She insists that they use separate cars and check in at the hotel

271

at different times. They each book single rooms and he creeps along the corridor to her room when the hotel is quiet.'

'Sounds like a scene from a Victorian novel.'

'This is English village life in 1994, the way Mrs Hathaway lives it, at any rate. On October the eighteenth, Winston was back from Tenerife and they planned to spend the night together in Bristol. She checked in at the Brunel about eight in the evening and had a meal served in her room. Winston phoned her from Bath to find out the room number and then went to his house and collected his car key, before driving to Bristol. About half-past midnight, he tapped on her door. And he had some flowers with him, from Tenerife.'

'So he bought them for her?'

'Yes.'

'Roses?'

'Carnations. She loves carnations. Next morning, they breakfasted separately and left in their different cars.'

'Discreet.'

'They are.'

'I meant the way you put it.'

'Thank you.'

'But is it really an alibi?' said Diamond.

'It fits with Billington's own statement and GB's. I've checked with the hotel and he signed the register at 12.15 a.m.'

'His own name?'

'Yes.'

'It takes us one step further,' he conceded, 'only it isn't an alibi. Remember the timing. GB told us it was around eleven when he saw Mountjoy leave the house and Billington enter it soon after. Let's say 11.15. He could have killed Britt and been on the road to Bristol by 11.30. How long does it take to Bristol?'

'That depends on the traffic. All right,' she admitted,

'late in the evening, on quiet roads, he could have driven there in the time.'

'Easily.'

'But is it likely that he'd make love to Mrs Hathaway after committing a murder?'

'Who knows?' Diamond threw in. 'The excitement may have turned him on.'

'Oh, come on,' she said. 'We're talking about Winston Billington, not Jack the Ripper.'

He smiled faintly. 'Fair enough. Did Mrs Hathaway tell you what kind of performance Winston gave after tapping on her door?'

She was unamused. 'Of course not. She's acutely embarrassed about all this.'

'You didn't press her?'

'No, I didn't.'

'Maybe Winston didn't, either.'

Julie made a sideward twitch of her mouth and flicked her eyes upwards – her way of registering disdain when the Manvers Street men made sexually ambiguous remarks.

'But you've solved one mystery.' Diamond picked up the thread before Julie said any more. 'We know where Winston Billington spent the rest of that night. Meanwhile, I've solved another.' He told her what he had learned from Una Moon about Jane Austen's connection with Trim Street.

'Where does it get us?' she asked, when he had finished. 'It doesn't give anyone a motive for murder, does it? I feel as if we're picking at scabs when we should be performing a major operation.'

For once he was undefended. He pulled out the chair from his desk and sat opposite her. 'Julie, I can't argue with that. Let's face it, we're short-handed. This isn't a murder inquiry as we know it.'

'Let's get reinforcements, then,' she said.

He shook his head. 'They'd be better employed on the stake-out. We've got until midnight – barely eight hours – and that's only if Farr-Jones keeps his word. With Warrilow champing at the bit, I'm not counting on it. We simply don't have time to brief people who know damn-all about the case.'

'So what's next?' said Julie bleakly. 'We've interviewed all the suspects we can dredge up. The only one we've been able to eliminate is Mrs Billington because she was out of the country. I put everyone through the PNC as you asked, and it got us no further.'

'Everyone?' Diamond repeated, seeming to expect some fresh insight.

'Jake Pinkerton, Marcus Martin, Winston Billington, Prue Shorter, Una Moon. As I told you, I didn't solve the mystery of GB's name, so I couldn't access him. Is that what we should be working on?'

He was silent, his face set, his expression anxious. Finally he said, 'It all originated with Britt. She's the one we should be concentrating on. Is she on the computer?'

'*Britt?*' Julie gave him a disbelieving look. 'She shouldn't be. She's dead.'

'Did we look her up on the ruddy computer at the time of her death?'

'Would she have been on it, as a foreign national?'

'She kept a car at one time, an MGB.'

'In that case, she ought to be. There could be a print-out. It should have been done as a matter of routine,' Julie said, 'but I wasn't around. I can look through the file if you wish.'

'Yes,' said he. 'Do that.'

'At this minute?'

He nodded.

Julie reached for the box-files containing all the papers. While she sifted through the material, Diamond sat back, brooding, rocking the chair on its back legs. He was profoundly grateful for Julie's calm support in these critical hours. She was on the receiving end of the taunts and rebukes intrinsic to his way of working. Usually the entire murder squad shared the suffering.

'It *is* here,' she said, taking a sheet of computer paper from the file and handing it across. 'But there isn't much.'

He examined it.

Below Britt Strand's name and address were the details of the car, a private MGB, registration VPL 294S, licensed from 01.08.88 for twelve months.

Diamond tugged at the chunk of flesh under his chin. 'So she was still the owner of the car at the time she died. Is that what this means?'

'May I see?' Julie looked at it. 'Apparently, yes. If she'd sold it, the data would have been transferred to the new registered keeper.'

'What happened to it, then? I didn't hear anything about a car when we investigated the murder. We'd have examined it, obviously.'

'It could be a computer error,' Julie said. 'The licence isn't updated. According to this, it would have expired in August, 1989, more than a year before this print-out. If you like I can get the current owner checked against the registration.'

He nodded and Julie went out to check with the PNC.

Instead of feeling encouraged that more pieces of the puzzle were in place – he now knew the reason why Britt had taken such an interest in the Trim Street squat and he also knew where Billington had spent the night of the murder – he was nervous. He wasn't used to working like this. In his murder squad days he would have had his best detectives simultaneously at work on several lines of investigation. It didn't matter that nine-tenths of it came to nothing. The team would get results and he'd interpret them. His skill – and it was a skill – was panning the gold, picking out the nuggets from the silt. But in the present case he was doing all his own digging. With only Julie to help and the time running out, he had to be damned sure the spadework was productive. The pressure was intense. There could be no error.

Julie returned, shaking her head. 'It's strange. I checked VPL 294S and Britt is still registered as the keeper.'

Diamond's contempt for computers was reinforced. 'She's been dead since 1990.'

'The computer hasn't got that information. That isn't so uncommon. What is surprising is that no one else took over the car. What became of it after she died?'

'Surely sombody must have thought an MGB was worth owning,' said Diamond.

'Stolen?'

'If it was, there ought to be something on the computer entry.'

'Well, there isn't.'

'Let's think this through, Julie. The car was last licensed on the first of August, 1988, for a year. The licence expired fourteen months before she was killed. She didn't renew it. No one else appears to own it. So where is it?' As he was speaking, a supplementary question bombarded his thoughts: *Is the red MG just a red herring?* In a piece of lateral thinking that must have bewildered Julie, he said, 'Those damned roses. We've never traced them.'

She waited for him to go on.

'A car that vanishes. A dozen roses that come from nowhere. We need answers Julie.'

She said, 'We seem to have reached a stop with the car.'

'All right. Let's think about the roses, then. Someone sends you a dozen red roses. As a woman, how do you react?'

'I'm pleased. Most probably it's Valentine's Day and I have an admirer.'

He said, 'It isn't and you don't.'

'Thanks,' she said acidly. 'I really needed that.'

'Don't take it personally. We're hypothesizing. The murder was October the eighteenth, not February the fourteenth. Was there anything special about the date? Her birthday?'

Julie went to the file again. 'She was born on April the twelfth.'

'No help there. Red roses are a token of love, am I right? Even a slob like me knows that's the language of the flowers.'

'They can be a way of saying sorry,' Julie suggested.

'I don't see how that helps us.'

'I'm just considering other possibilities.'

He didn't sound grateful. 'What do we know for sure? Every florist in the city and in all the towns around was checked to see if they made a delivery of roses, and we drew a blank. It's likely that someone bought them in a shop without leaving a name and took them to the house in person.'

'And it's safe to assume it was someone she knew,' added Julie. 'She wouldn't have let a stranger into the house so late.'

'Agreed. Let's go through her visitors. Mountjoy is the obvious man, going on a date, but he didn't bring the roses, or claims he didn't. He doesn't remember seeing any in the flat. Billington bought flowers, but for another woman.'

'And they weren't roses.'

'And GB claims he didn't call at all.'

Julie said, 'Why would anyone want to lie about giving her a bunch of red roses? Surely the killer isn't the person who gave her the flowers. It's someone else.'

'Why?'

'It must be. Surely. Someone made jealous by them.'

Diamond pondered this briefly, then said, 'You could be wrong there. Let's assume for a moment that nobody is lying.'

'The flowers were already in the flat?'

'No. We already established that they weren't delivered by a florist and Mountjoy didn't see any when he visited. I think we must face the possibility that the killer *was* the bringer of the roses.'

'Why?'

'We couldn't trace them back to any shop. There's no record of any transaction, no memory of anyone remotely like our suspects buying roses that day. What does that mean? Probably that the person who took the roses to the house went to some trouble to conceal his identity. Maybe he bought them in some other town, too far away to trace.'

'That would mean he had murder in mind before he bought the flowers.'

Diamond held up a finger in confirmation. 'You're with me now. A premeditated murder.'

It was plain from Julie's puzzled expression that she wasn't totally with him. 'Are you saying that someone bought red roses and took them to the house meaning to commit murder? Why? What would be the point?'

'To make a point.'

'You've lost me altogether now,' she told him.

'Instead of a token of love, the roses were a token of revenge that Britt understood.' He appealed to her visual imagination. 'Think of the scene — the cut rosebuds stuffed into her mouth. That's indicative of something else besides murderous intent. The flowers meant something, Julie.'

'You mean they were symbolic?'

'They had some significance known to the victim and the killer. Maybe there had been a gift of roses at some point in the past, when there was love and trust that the killer now felt was betrayed.'

'It's possible.'

'It's ugly,' said Diamond, 'but it does make sense. We've always assumed that the killer found the flowers at the scene and took them to be a gift from a lover and couldn't resist mutilating them and desecrating the body with them. I'm suggesting that they were always intended to be part of the murder scene. The killer went to some lengths to buy the flowers at some place miles away from Bath. It was a premeditated killing, not some sudden outbreak of violence. If I'm right, Britt Strand wasn't killed because of something that happened that evening, but as a coldly planned act.'

Julie absorbed this. 'Because of something that happened previously? Is that what you're saying?'

He gave a nod. 'We've given most of our attention to the evening of the murder and the people we know were in Larkhall that night: Mountjoy, Billington and GB, each of them attracted to Britt and willing to admit it. But there are two others who pointedly claim their affairs with the lady were over.'

'Jake Pinkerton and Marcus Martin.'

'Yes. They become rather more interesting now.'

'But if they weren't at the scene—'

'Do they have alibis?'

She hesitated.

Diamond reached for his hat. 'Let's start with Marcus Martin.'

Chapter Twenty-Three

It was a good thing Julie suggested phoning Marcus Martin first. His housekeeper passed on the information that he wasn't at home that afternoon; he was attending a funeral.

Instead of uttering appropriate words of condolence, Diamond ranted down the phone, 'Hell's bells, what next? Where's it taking place?'

Clearly the housekeeper judged that this loudmouth shouldn't be let anywhere near a funeral. 'Mr Martin should be home early this evening.'

'I can't wait that long. Which cemetery?'

'I'm sorry, it wouldn't be convenient.'

'Convenience doesn't come into it, madam. You're speaking to the police.'

'Oh.' Followed by a silence. Then: 'I believe it's a turning off the Lower Bristol Road.'

'Haycombe Cemetery?'

'No. The Last Post.'

'Would you say that again, ma'am?'

'The Last Post. I'm sure that's what it's known as.'

'Never heard of it,' muttered Diamond. 'Is this a pub near the cemetery, or what?'

She said, 'It's the name of the place. Haven't you seen the papers? The funeral is for Horatio.'

'Horatio who?'

'Horatio the showjumper. I thought everyone in the

country remembered Horatio at the Olympics, even though he's been retired a few years now. He was put to sleep the day before yesterday after a tragic accident hunting with the Beaufort.'

'A horse? A funeral for a *horse*?'

'Horatio was a champion, an exceptional horse. Almost a national treasure. The phone has hardly stopped ringing. He is being laid to rest at three-thirty.'

In the car he refrained from airing his opinions on horse funerals. Instead, he asked Julie what impressions she'd formed of Marcus Martin, which was a transparent way of refreshing his own memory, because she had a remarkable recall for the salient information.

She said, 'He's a type certain women get taken in by. The posh accent, the lord of the manor stuff.'

'You'd stay well clear, would you?'

From the way she paused before answering, she didn't like having it made personal. 'Well, yes.'

'You think Britt was taken in?'

'No way, knowing what we do about her.'

'Too bad we've only got his version of the affair.'

She nodded. 'And what an unlikely version.'

'Explain.'

'He said their relationship was "short and to the point", as if it was purely physical, like going with a prostitute.'

'Could have been just his way of thinking.'

'Like "Three wild and steamy weeks" – after which he went on to say that they "drifted apart" – which sounded like a contradiction. You remarked on it at the time, and his answer wasn't convincing.'

'Do you think she dropped him?'

'I wonder if she ever took him on board. Some of these men who brag about their sex-life aren't up to it.'

'Don't you believe they were lovers at all?'

'I don't believe in three wild and steamy weeks. Any woman knows the type. It's all on the surface. Bedroom

281

eyes. Wandering hands. They're trying to prove something.'

'All mouth and trousers?'

She smiled.

'I must say, Julie, you're banking a lot on intuition here.'

'Judgement.'

'Experience?'

'Judgement,' she repeated firmly without shifting her eyes from the road ahead.

'To be fair to the guy, when I questioned him four years ago, he told the same story.'

'I bet he used the same words exactly.'

Diamond thought about this. 'Let's suppose you're right. Wouldn't he have told the truth when he knew he was a witness in a murder inquiry?'

'Men are incurable liars about their sex lives.'

'Now you're talking like one of they feminists.'

'Talking sense, you mean.'

He let this pass. They were both letting things pass in the interest of the case. 'There could be another explanation. He tried coming on strong with Britt and got the brush-off. It rankled. No, worse than that, it bruised his ego. He was angry, maybe angry enough to kill.'

Julie was looking doubtful. 'Would she have let him into the house?'

'That's why he took the roses. She'd find it difficult to slam the door in his face.'

'That late at night?' she said. 'I wouldn't.'

'You're police trained. She was a fun-loving Swedish girl.'

She took a breath prior to reacting to this and then thought better of it and said, 'Do you want another theory? He kept trying to chat her up and the roses finally did the trick. She went to bed with him. When it came to the action, he couldn't perform.'

There was a pause while Diamond assessed this new

scenario. They crossed the Churchill Bridge over the Avon and got as far as the traffic lights at Midland Bridge Road before he said, 'I like that. It's better. It fits their characters.' Speaking almost to himself, he rephrased what Julie had said. 'He makes one more attempt. Takes the roses. She lets him in. She's in the mood and he can't manage it. Kills her out of frustration. It's the best we've thought of.' He sighed. 'But it's only speculation, Julie. We've got nothing positive on this creep, not so much as a ruddy parking offence.'

'So how do you want to handle this?' she asked, as if that were all that remained to be said on the matter. 'You might do better on your own. With me listening, he's less likely to admit he isn't the stud he claims to be.'

'No, I want you there. Just back up everything I say. He'll sing, and we'll see if it's the tune we want to hear. Left at the next junction.'

They took the Locksbrook Road turning, the gateway to Bath's trading estates and the austere rows of Victorian terraced housing that have little to do with the popular image of the city. The road merged into Brassmill Lane, past factories and warehouses. Towards the Newbridge end, beyond a caravan park, lay a stretch of open ground where a couple of goats looked up from their grazing. Beside it was a garden with a low wall.

'There.'

The sign over the gate in gothic lettering read:

The Last Post
Pet Crematorium and Memorial Garden

A line of cars in the street outside suggested that the obsequies for Horatio were not yet over.

'Popular horse,' Diamond commented as they got out.

'How did they bring it here?' Julie asked, looking along the line of vehicles. 'I don't see anything large enough.'

'Maybe they delivered it earlier.'

Inside was a stretch of lawn patterned with flowerbeds in a herringbone formation. At this stage of the year the few surviving roses were limp and brown-stained. Small plaques mounted on posts were ranged at intervals in the soil, each bearing the name and years of birth and death of a deceased animal and sometimes a few lines of verse as well. There were plastic and metal models of cats and dogs, framed photographs faded by the weather, decaying wreaths and, here and there, fresh flowers.

At the far end was the funeral party, at least forty, perhaps more, among them a priest in a black cassock. Most of them seemed to be young women, several carrying bunches of flowers. Marcus Martin, with strands of his red hair lifted intermittently from his bald patch by the light breeze, was to the left holding a wooden casket the size of a shoebox.

'Small horse,' Diamond murmured to Julie.

She gave him a glare.

The funeral party lowered their heads as if in prayer.

From behind Diamond's back a voice announced in a stage whisper, 'It would be quite all right to join in. It isn't too late.'

The speaker was a bearded man in a dark suit.

'Are you the undertaker?' Diamond asked.

'The owner of the gardens.'

'Ah. Ever had such a turn-out for one animal before?'

He fingered his collar. 'It is, I think, a unique occasion.'

'Was the horse cremated here?'

'No, in Frome. But that's where the incinerator happens to be. It isn't a consecrated place. The ashes were collected and brought here for disposal. Seeing that Horatio was such a well-known and popular horse, the owner thought it right that his ashes should be interred in a garden like this where his many admirers may freely visit. The gate is always open here.'

284

One of Diamond's most useful talents was his ability to sustain a serious conversation regardless of the subject. 'Is this your first horse funeral?'

'Actually, yes.'

'You generally cater for cats and dogs?'

'That's why we call our memorial garden The Last Post. Most cats have a scratching post somewhere and dogs have a lifelong interest in lampposts.'

'Not to mention postmen,' said Diamond.

This was received with a solemn nod. 'We also take on the occasional rabbit. We couldn't cremate a horse here. But there's no reason why it shouldn't be done elsewhere. It's just that a large animal like that entails a certain amount of trouble and expense.'

'Normally they'd sell the carcase for cats' meat, I suppose,' Diamond remarked. 'Or to the hunt.'

The man cleared his throat, concerned, apparently, in case Diamond's words were carrying across the lawn to the funeral party.

'How about burial?'

The answer required a hand over the mouth. 'We couldn't do that here. You'd need a mechanical digger. Mind, the Queen has her favourite horses interred on the Royal estate.'

Diamond's attention had shifted to where the funeral was going on. He remarked to Julie, 'Some of those young girls are carrying red roses.'

The owner of the memorial garden told them, 'They feel it as a personal loss, the young girls.'

'Never considered red roses as an emblem of grief,' said Diamond, more to himself than anyone else. 'No offence meant,' he picked up the conversation, 'but some people would think it stretching religion too far, having funerals for animals.'

'It's not a funeral in the strict sense of the word, more a thanksgiving for the life of the departed one and the

285

pleasure it gave us. If you have a pet of your own you may be sure that when the parting comes, as it must eventually, we can offer you peace of mind and a permanent memorial.'

Julie thanked him.

Diamond said, 'You should get one of those Queen's Awards for Enterprise.'

The man's eyes gleamed at the prospect.

There were signs of progress across the lawn. Marcus Martin had lowered the casket into a hole in the ground and some of the funeral party were stooping to place their flowers in or around the grave. A camera flashed. The priest stepped back and snagged his cassock on a rose.

Martin turned and undoubtedly spotted Diamond and Julie striding towards him, although he looked away at once and started a conversation with another mourner.

'You don't mind?' Diamond said, at Martin's shoulder. 'We need another bite at the cherry.'

'I've nothing to add to what I told you before,' Martin responded. 'And this is hardly the occasion—'

'So we'll take you to the car,' Diamond told him firmly.

Uncomfortably wedged beside Martin in the back seat of the Escort, Diamond said, 'We're pushed for time. In your steamy relationship with Britt Strand, did you ever see her naked?'

Marcus Martin was entitled to be startled by the directness of the question, but he answered it smoothly enough. 'Of course.'

'More than once?'

'Frequently.'

'So she wasn't shy about her body?'

'Certainly not. Why do you ask?'

'Because you're obviously the man to ask about the butterfly tattoo on her left buttock.'

The trap wasn't over-subtle, but it worked.

286

'Oh, that,' said Martin in as off-hand a manner as he could manage.

'Must have looked cute when she walked,' said Diamond. 'Was it a red admiral or a peacock?'

'I couldn't tell you,' Martin said. 'I know nothing about butterflies.'

'You know nothing about Britt's butt, full stop,' said Diamond. 'There was no tattoo, my friend. I imagined it, just as you imagined your affair with the lady.'

'Oh, but—'

'Let's have it straight. She turned you down, right? The wild and steamy three weeks never happened.'

'Em. . .'

'Should have realized you're a specialist in horseshit. We could do you for making a false statement, do you know that? Better not push your luck, chum. Can we rely on anything you told us? She came to you to get some riding in, strictly with the horses. Is that right?'

Diamond was fizzing. Nothing could equal the satisfaction of snaring a liar. To have caught the glib, golden-tongued Marcus Martin was a particular pleasure.

Martin leaned back and closed his eyes, trying to appear calm. 'Broadly.'

'You made a play for her and she wasn't having any?'

'You policemen make things sound so crude.'

'Yet according to previous statements you visited the house in Larkhall on more than one occasion.'

'That was true,' he insisted, opening his eyes and sitting forward. 'She had no transport. I used to drive her back in my Range Rover.'

'Hope springs eternal. But she gave you the frost each time, did she? Afternoon tea in the Canary was part of the campaign, was it not?'

Martin's voice was a semitone higher. 'No, it was quite un-planned, in fact. She wanted to do some shopping that after-noon, so I parked the car in town and joined her for tea.'

287

'That was when you saw GB and got nervous of the company she kept, or so you claimed.'

'I was speaking the truth. I still nourished hopes of er. . .'

'Getting inside her joddies?'

'Joddies?'

'Jodhpurs.'

'I suppose that sums it up, if vulgarly.'

Diamond picked up on the part of the answer that mattered. 'You didn't give up? You didn't take no for an answer?'

'Who does?' said Martin, seizing the opportunity to make a general point. 'They all say no at the beginning.'

'And mean, "yes"?' said Diamond. 'Better watch what you say, my friend. DI Hargreaves here is a rampant feminist.'

Julie, motionless in the front seat, made no comment, but the look she was giving both of them in the driving mirror made her disapproval clear.

'You persisted,' Diamond continued with his demolition of Marcus Martin. 'You couldn't believe she'd turned down an offer from you, the international showjumper, adored by all those little girls who muck out the stables. Are you sure you never bought her flowers? Have a care. We've caught you out in one lie already.'

'Absolutely not.'

'A bunch of roses would be more your style than some fellows'. We checked every florist for miles around. Care to reconsider?'

'I didn't buy her flowers of any sort, ever.' Martin's voice was taut, under strain. There could be no question that he knew the significance of what was being asked, but was he lying?

'When was the last occasion you saw her?'

'I've told you this before.'

'And I'm giving you this chance to tell it as it really happened.'

Martin shook his head wearily. 'The weekend before she

288

was killed I travelled to Brussels with the national show-jumping team. On, I think, the Thursday before that she came out for an afternoon at the jumps. She said it would be her last opportunity, as she'd recently enrolled on a college course that would take up all her time. I offered to drive her back to Bath as usual. She said she'd arranged a taxi. The message was loud and clear. We didn't even shake hands at the end of the session.'

'When did you return from Brussels?'

'The Sunday evening, late.'

'And you didn't see Britt again?'

'No.'

'Nor have any contact?'

'None whatsoever.'

'Remind me of your movements on Thursday, the eighteenth of October, 1990, the last evening of Britt Strand's life.'

'I spent the evening quietly with a friend.'

'The young woman who died shortly after of meningitis?'

'That's correct. Had she lived—'

'We wouldn't be having this conversation, sir. You'd have a cast-iron alibi.' Diamond was at his combative best. The danger, he knew, was that he could dominate too much and shock his adversary into quiescence. 'Your statement of four years ago had you in the flat in Walcot Street on the crucial evening with this young woman. What was her name?'

'Kelly McClure.'

'Could anyone else vouch for this?'

'I told you at the time. No.'

'Pity. I'm doing my best for you. You gave me some indispensable information that proved to be correct and the least I can do is help you out.'

'What information was that?' Martin asked, suspicious of this change of tactics.

'Things Britt confided, about her landlord pestering her, giving her presents and so forth. It was true. I verified it. You must have been a good listener for Britt to have talked so frankly.'

Martin didn't accept the compliment. 'It was only her way of telling me to keep off. She was being uncomplimentary about men in general when she said it.'

'You also put us on to another man in her life: GB, the crusty.'

'He wasn't a serious boyfriend,' said Martin. 'She was using him.'

'She told you that?'

'Couldn't have made it plainer.' He was more willing to talk now the spotlight had moved elsewhere. 'She was a bloody good journalist doing the professional thing, buttering up a contact. She was writing this article about the crusties in Bath.'

'I know. You're sure she wasn't playing the same game with you?'

He frowned. 'What game?'

Diamond unfolded a theory that he had not discussed with Julie, or anyone, for the very good reason that it had only just occurred to him. 'You just said it: buttering up a contact.'

'What could I tell her?'

'You tell me, Mr Martin. Showjumping is an upper-crust sport that I'm sure has a place in the glossy magazines she wrote for. She was a good rider herself, so she probably followed the careers of international riders like yourself. No professional sport is without its scandals and you're well placed to tell all.'

Martin sounded sceptical. 'Oh, yes?'

Dredging deep – because he was ignorant about the horse world – Diamond said, 'The doping of horses, for instance. What's that pain-killing drug they give them – Bute, is it called?'

'You're way behind the times.' Martin scathingly dismissed the suggestion.

Unperturbed, Diamond said, 'But what sells magazines – the sort she wrote for – is human interest, never mind our four-legged friends. People-trading. Present company excepted, the things people are willing to do to make it big in show-jumping or eventing. I bet you can tell some tales.'

'If I did,' said he, 'I'd be out. Do you think I'd chuck in my career?'

'If you did, you'd have a motive for murder.'

'What?'

'You give her the dirt, regret it later, go back and silence her.'

'No.' Martin hammered the seat in front with his fist. 'I've told you the truth. Britt wasn't interested in me or my career. She simply came to my place to ride. I fancied her, drove her home a few times, but she left me in no doubt that she wanted to be left alone. Is that too difficult for you to grasp?'

Outside, the daylight had gone. Dusk is a non-event on some October evenings. All the other cars had left except a Range Rover that must have belonged to Martin. And still nothing of substance had emerged from this interview. Stubbornly Diamond began casting the net for one more trawl.

'All right, Mr Martin. I'm accepting what you've told me. You didn't make love to her. You didn't give her material for a story. You didn't kill her.' He let that sink in before saying, 'You're still a witness, and you could be a crucial one. You spoke to her several times in the last month of her life. You've told me about other men she mentioned – Billington and GB. Was there anyone else?'

Martin thought a moment and said, 'No.'

Diamond continued to probe. 'I asked you once before if she ever mentioned John Mountjoy.'

'I didn't know of his existence until I heard he was arrested.'

'Right. Did she speak of anyone else indirectly, without speaking his name, any other man she was seeing?'

'No.'

'Someone, perhaps, who was watching her, someone she didn't even know? Did you get the impression that she knew she was under threat?'

'No. Quite the contrary. She had this air of confidence.'

'As if she was in control of her life?'

'Yes. Well. . .' He stopped.

At Martin's side in the darkness, Peter Diamond waited.

'She did once confide that she – how did she express it? – that she didn't want to be under an obligation to anyone. I think I offered to forget the fee she owed me for the riding. She insisted on paying. She said once a friend had helped her out at a difficult time. She said something about acts of kindness putting the recipient under an obligation.'

'Did she tell you the name?'

'No.'

'A man?'

'Yes, I got that impression.'

'And he was troubling her?'

Martin shook his head. 'She didn't put it like that. I'm trying to remember what she did say. The sense I got was that she'd been through some major crisis a couple of years back.'

'Here – in this country?'

'I think so. It must have been here, because she talked about him as if he was still about, somewhere close. Anyway, he helped her through the crisis, and this involved some kind of risk on his part. She felt obligated and she wasn't comfortable with that.'

'She was worried that he'd call in the debt, so to speak?'

'I don't know.'

'And that was all?'

'It may be that I've got it out of proportion. It was only said to—'

Diamond closed him down abruptly. 'You can leave now.' He leaned across and pushed open the car door.

When it was shut again, Diamond told Julie, 'Conkwell. We're going to Conkwell.'

She asked if he wished to move into the front seat.

'No,' he said. 'We've got to be quick. We don't have as much time as I thought.'

Chapter Twenty-Four

Approaching the pub called the Weston, they saw brakelights coming on and remembered the tailback caused every evening along that section of the Upper Bristol Road. Diamond was fretting. He asked if there wasn't some short cut.

'The best I can do is cross the river at Windsor Bridge,' Julie offered. 'I was going that way anyway. Why Conkwell?'

'Mm?'

'You did say you wanted to be driven to Conkwell. I was asking why, that's all.'

'Don't you remember anything?' he chided her. 'It's where Jake Pinkerton has his recording studio. In the woods at Conkwell.'

She said icily, 'I wasn't there when you interviewed Pinkerton.'

'Where were you, then?'

'Don't you remember?' she echoed his words of a moment before, without adding the 'anything'. 'I was sent to meet Prue Shorter, much to my disappointment. I haven't ever spoken to a pop star.'

'You didn't miss anything special,' he said.

She inhaled sharply. 'Ten years ago I would have scratched your eyes out for saying that. I had him on a poster in my bedroom.'

'Was that a four-poster?'

She thawed and laughed. 'At the time, I wouldn't have minded.'

'They're dumbos, most of these pop stars.'

'He must know how many beans make five to have survived this long.' She joined the right-hand stream of traffic that was waiting to cross the bridge. 'So you're willing to gamble that Jake Pinkerton is the fellow who helped Britt over this problem, whatever it was?'

'Gamble – no,' said he. 'It's a mathematical certainty. We know this person was a friend, male, lives locally, was in a position to help and knew Britt a couple of years before the murder. How many points of similarity is that?'

She declined to answer.

'It's all coming together,' Diamond said. 'Seeing those young girls with their roses at the horse funeral reminded me of something Pinkerton told me. He said some idiot – some *nerd*, I think, was the word he used – sent a dozen red roses to Britt's funeral. So Pinkerton was in my mind, you see.'

' "Nerd" is probably right,' said Julie. 'How insensitive!'

'Unless it was deliberate,' Diamond said. 'Unless the murderer sent them.'

'Is that likely?'

'I don't know about likely, but it's possible.' He looked ahead, at the line of cars. 'Move it. The lights are changing. We're dealing with the kind of weirdo who turns a corpse into a flower arrangement, so what's strange about sending more roses to the funeral?'

After Windsor Bridge the traffic was moving again, but remained heavy. They progressed steadily along the Lower Bristol Road as far as Widcombe Hill, then made the short cut over Claverton Down only to find another tailback at the bottom of Brassknocker, where it linked with the A36. Diamond was drumming his fingers on the head restraint in front of him. 'Do we have a torch on board?' he asked.

'I haven't looked,' said Julie.

'We're going to need a torch.'

In motion again, they made a detour to the post office in Limpley Stoke and bought a serviceable lamp with a good beam that they tested on the wall of the pub across the street. By now it was pitch dark outside.

'Do you know the way from here?' Diamond asked, as Julie was turning the car.

'I think I can get you to Conkwell,' she said. 'I've often passed the sign on the Winsley Road.'

'There's a good walk to Conkwell,' he said. 'You start at the Dundas Aqueduct and make your way across a field and up a steep track through the woods. Not today, though.'

Another insight into his private life? 'I didn't know you were a walker,' Julie remarked.

'My neighbour,' he explained. 'Boots, knapsack, flat cap, walking stick, the lot. What a pillock!'

They located the turn and started up a one-track lane between high hedges. A mist was making driving difficult; the full beam of the headlight simply exaggerated the effect. Julie settled for dipped lights, giving visibility of twenty yeards or so. Driving at forty in these conditions seemed an act of folly. The lane was so narrow that they couldn't even have passed a cyclist. Summoning some self-control, Diamond was silent, allowing Julie to concentrate. He was playing his own mind-game of willing all other traffic to stay clear of this small lane for the next five minutes, and simultaneously willing Julie to keep her foot on the accelerator.

A mile or so along the lane they reached a cluster of buildings. A sign warned that there was no turning-point in the lane to their left, so they drove on to a verge and got out. The lamp was about to prove its worth.

Conkwell is a hamlet of stone-built cottages stacked a hundred and fifty feet up the steep escarpment of the

Avon valley. By day it is a joy to visit, by night daunting. At this early stage of the evening there were lights at several windows. Diamond knocked at one of the first they came to and asked the elderly man who came to the door to direct them to the recording studio. The old fellow knew what they were asking about. It was a walk of less than a mile, they were told, but he wouldn't advise going through the wood after dark.

They thanked him and ignored his advice, taking a footpath that looked as if it might lead into someone's garden, yet presently brought them into Conkwell Wood. With the flashlight picking out the path, Diamond strode ahead, forcing his feet through inches of leaves. 'At certain times of the year, you can still hear nightingales,' he informed Julie, as if he were leading a nature ramble, then added, 'so my neighbour told me.' The only sound on this particular evening was the steady drone of traffic across the valley cruising along the A36. Occasionally they saw the moving headlights, for the wood dipped sheerly to their right.

Diamond was still on his nightingale theme. 'These days, in this neck of the woods, you're more likely to have your eardrums blasted by rock music.'

'I shouldn't think so,' Julie told him. 'The studio must be soundproofed.'

Every few steps, he raised the torch beam to see what was ahead, but for the present there was no variation in the treetrunks and bushes except that some of the trees were dead and had fallen at odd angles against the branches of others and become festooned with creepers. The path was reasonably clear thanks to regular use by walkers and horse-riders, but there was thick scrub on either side, mainly of brambles. Once they disturbed a roosting bird and sent it screeching in search of a safer place.

After some minutes of careful walking, because hidden

rocks were a real hazard, they passed a six-foot chain-link fence with a triple band of barbed wire along its top. Examination with the flashlight revealed that it was too thick in rust to have been erected by Jake Pinkerton, who had built his studio in the mid-eighties. The path skirted the fence, so they moved on.

Pinkerton's fence, when it came in sight, was taller, clear of rust, and electrified along the top. The name of a security firm was displayed at intervals. They walked around it looking for the entrance. From time to time Diamond waved the flashlight across a section of the interior.

'Looking for something in particular?' Julie asked.

'Maybe,' he muttered. 'But it's going to be well hidden.'

'Difficult with a torch.'

'Yes.'

A moment later, almost at the highest point of the wood, they activated a double set of floodlights. Dazzled and immobilized as rabbits on a motorway, they had found the entrance. A respectably wide road led up to the studio.

'So I needn't have ruined these shoes,' Julie commented in an effort to reduce the whole expedition to basics and restore her nerve.

Diamond wasn't listening. He had found a box with a two-way communication system and a surveillance camera above it. 'Police,' he said after the speaker had crackled, 'for Mr Jake Pinkerton.'

'Mr Pinkerton has left,' came the answer.

'We'd still like to come in.'

'Wait for the barrier, then.'

They passed through a security gate. Ahead, a man in a silver-buttoned black uniform and peaked hat opened a door and asked if he could be of some assistance – but in a manner that made clear that the 'some' was meant as a limitation rather than infinite generosity.

'I'm sure you can,' said Diamond, who in his time had

done a similar job and knew about dealing with visitors without appointments. 'This is Inspector Hargreaves and my name is Diamond. Show him your ID, Julie, would you? How long ago did Mr Pinkerton leave?'

'At least an hour.'

'Was he going home?'

'I wouldn't know, sir.'

'I expect he has a car phone,' Julie chimed in.

'Good idea,' said Diamond, and told the security man, 'Better let him know we're here. Is there anyone else about?'

'Two of the studios are in use. A band is making a recording right now.'

'Regular staff, I meant.'

'The chief sound engineer is in the control room with the studio manager, but they wouldn't want to be disturbed unless it's extremely urgent.'

'We won't bother them in that case. You can show me what I want to see, Mr, em, Humphrey. Are you ex-police, by any chance?' On the principle that you get better service if you address people by name, he had gone close enough to read Cyril Humphrey's identity tag.

The security man flushed crimson. 'I can't help you. I know nothing about the workings of the studios.'

'The studios don't interest us,' said Diamond, in the knowledge that he was speaking only for himself, not Julie. 'I want to see where you park your cars.'

'That's round the back.'

'Then we'd like to look round the back.'

As it worked out, they had privileged views of the studios on their way to the car park, because the modern trend in studio architecture is for huge windows where soundproof cladding was once thought indispensable. The artists need no longer feel enclosed in a bunker. So the recording session and the rehearsal were on display to anyone passing the window; hence, presumably, the elaborate security. However, nobody in the studios seemed to be doing anything; long-haired youths lounged around looking bored, drinking from paper cups.

'The car park's this way,' Humphrey informed them.

About ten vehicles stood on a square of Tarmac with space for three times that number. Diamond flicked the flashlight across them. 'Does the boss leave his car here?'

'Mr Pinkerton? No, sir. He has his private garage round the other side.'

'We'd like to see that next.'

'No chance. It opens electronically.'

'From outside, you mean.'

'Yes, he has a sensor thing in his car.'

'It triggers the mechanism?'

'Yes. We don't have a spare.'

'When the door has opened and he's driven in, does it close behind him?'

'Yes, sir.' Cyril Humphrey seemed smugly satisfied that he had conveyed the principle – and the impossibility of letting them see inside the garage.

'So there must be an interior door,' said Diamond, 'leading to his office, right? Then we'll all go inside and get to it that way.'

'I couldn't take responsibility for letting you into Mr Pinkerton's office. Not without permission.' This was becoming a battle of wills.

'The office doesn't interest us,' said Diamond. 'We want to see the garage.'

'It's empty.'

'I said the garage, not the car.'

'You could phone him,' Julie reminded the man.

Faced with the prospect of informing Pinkerton that the police wanted to look inside his garage, Humphrey backed down. He admitted them inside the building, along a carpeted corridor hung with modern paintings, through a secretary's office and into the sanctum, a room furnished like a set from a Wagner opera, all black and silver, with ironwork thrones (you couldn't call them chairs), a vast round iron table, braziers for lights and the walls hung with suits of armour.

They were shepherded across to a stretch of black wall where a door was artfully concealed. Then down some stone steps to Jake Pinkerton's private garage, a clean, concrete place with space for four vehicles.

'You see?' said Humphrey. 'Nothing here.'

Diamond made a short walking tour and then said, 'Is this the only garage? What about the other top people? Do they have anywhere to leave their cars under cover?'

'This is the only one.'

'Thanks, then. What sort of security do you have outside?'

Humphrey looked uncomfortable. 'What do you mean – the fence?'

'The grounds. Dog patrols? Lights? Alarms?'

He gave a guarded answer. 'It's an effective system.'

'Can I take a walk around the grounds without having a Doberman at my throat?'

Humphrey realized that he was dealing with a real eccentric. 'You want to go outside, in the grounds? That's impossible.'

'Why?'

'Well, for one thing it's uncultivated. Thick woods.'

'We know. We walked around the fence. Let's get on with it, Mr Humphrey. We've got a deadline.'

'Nobody goes there,' Humphrey tried to reason with him. 'There's nothing out there.'

'There will be presently,' Diamond told him. 'There'll be Inspector Hargreaves and me with our flashlight and anyone willing to join us. You'll need a torch if you're coming. In fact, two torches would be even better.'

At a loss to understand why these people had come to torment him, Humphrey capitulated. He led them back to the security control room near the entrance to pick up the torches. 'What exactly are you hoping to find?'

'The Lost City of the Incas,' Diamond muttered.

'Out there? There's nothing there, I promise you.'

'How do you know, if nobody goes there?'

'Well. . .'

'Anything hidden six years ago is going to be well covered by now.' He led them around the building waving the flashlight until they reached the place where the bushes came within a few yards of the car park. Distances can be deceptive in the dark, but he estimated that the studio was sited in an area the size of half a football pitch, and most of the spare ground lay behind the buildings.

The undergrowth was a prickly, formidable barrier. Diamond picked up a stick and beat a space between two bushes. He plunged in, swore a little, and returned with two stout sticks that he handed to Julie and Humphrey. But before the expedition started, more people came from inside the studios wanting to know what was going on. The pop performers had decided that this was a 'good laugh' and opted to join the fun. So did some technicians. Resourcefully Diamond requisitioned three cars and positioned them with their headlamps lighting up the wood. It took on the character of a police search, with Diamond marshalling a line of helpers to make a sweep of the grounds.

The rustle of feet through scrub took over, punctuated by hacking and the occasional shout as someone discovered some piece of rubbish. It was cold, uncomfortable, but good-humoured work; the novelty of the exercise kept everyone going until there was a shout from one of the pop group on the far left side: 'What do I do now?'

'What's the problem?' Diamond called across.

'I'm stuck. Can't go no further.'

'Why not?'

'There's some kind of shed here.'

302

'I'll come over.'

By the time he got there, others had converged on the place. It was indeed a brick-built shed with a corrugated iron roof, abundantly overgrown, quite impossible to have been seen from the recording studio or the perimeter fence. They had to rip away masses of ivy and convolvulus to get at the door. A heavily corroded padlock came away more easily than some of the creepers and the door split into two pieces as they tugged it open.

The torches probed the dark interior. Someone asked, 'Is this what we're looking for?'

The light was picking out a curved surface that enclosed the dented chrome rim of a car headlamp. The glass had been removed except for a few shards. Diamond stooped to wipe the centre of the bonnet. The colour was red and the octagonal MG badge was mounted over a black polyurethane bumper. His pulse beat faster. He bent lower and cleared a layer of muck and moss off the registration plate. The number was the one he'd banked on finding: VPL 294S. This was Britt Strand's car, off the road since 1988.

'Give me more light, someone,' he demanded, squeezing between the wall and the side of the car, brushing away leaf-mould and dust that must have been falling through holes in the garage roof for years. Julie's flashlight gave him a better view.

'There's damage to the nearside wing, you see?' he said. 'It's badly dented here. Is the other side okay?'

Someone shone a torch over it and said, 'There's nothing wrong with this side.'

'Well, this headlamp is smashed and the bumper is out of alignment,' Diamond went on. 'The car definitely hit something.' He looked up at Julie. 'That's it, then. How long have we got?'

She glanced at her watch. 'To midnight? Just under four hours.'

Chapter Twenty-Five

Emerging from sleep, Samantha felt warm air against her face. It was a pleasant sensation considering how cold the rest of her body had become – pleasant until she began to suspect that the warmth she could feel was human breath. She could actually hear the sharp intake of air and the slow exhaling. Horrified, she opened her eyes and saw nothing. The place was steeped in darkness. Impossible to see who the breather was, or how close. But she wasn't mistaken. The quiet, rhythmical rasp of air continued.

She tried turning away and found that she couldn't. She was tied, hand and foot. She remembered why, and where she was. After she had tried to attract attention on the hotel balcony and Mountjoy had wrestled her to the floor, he had dragged her inside and trussed her even more tightly. Enraged, he had turned savage, grunting with the effort of tightening each knot in the flex. This time he'd used a strip of adhesive to gag her. Then he'd left her on the floor, and she'd lain there expecting to be kicked or beaten. She was still naked from the waist up.

But having restrained her, he'd gone away. Some time afterwards, he must have slung a blanket over her.

Now, this silent approach. This was the first time he had crept up on her like this. Up to now he had respected her – if being kept a prisoner could be termed respect. He'd made no sexual advance, never deliberately laid hands on the no-go parts of her body.

The breathing quickened.

She tensed.

She felt his hand on her shoulder.

He spoke: 'You awake?'

She couldn't answer through the gag and wouldn't have known what to say anyway.

'Nod your head.'

She obeyed. Could he have come as close as this just to check that she was still breathing?

He started to peel the adhesive from her mouth, one hand against her cheek to hold her face steady. He warned her, 'You scream and you get no food.'

Her face stung. She took a huge gulp of air. The taste in her mouth was foul.

He untied her hands and she felt something being put into them: a banana. She unpeeled it. She was ravenous.

He said, 'I've been watching them down there. Yes, they know we're here, thanks to your antics. They've stopped the traffic from coming through and they've got people on the roofs of all the buildings.'

Secretly she rejoiced. Someone must have seen her waving the T-shirt. She gulped the banana in three pieces. Her lips were numb where the gag had been. Dabbing at them gently with the tips of her fingers, she said as inoffensively as she was able, 'What's going to happen, then?'

He said, 'How would I know?'

'What do you expect?'

'I'll tell you what I expect,' he said with bitterness. 'I expect that fatso detective to get me the justice he owes me. Where is he? I don't see him down in the street.'

The frenzied note in his voice alarmed her. All she could do was try and humour him, praying that nothing the police did would tip him over the edge into panic. Somewhere he still had a gun.

She thought of her father and sent up a prayer that he

305

would not be directing the police operation. Daddy wasn't capable of being calm and dispassionate. He wouldn't know how to bring a siege to a peaceful end.

Mountjoy said, 'We're going to have to move.'

'Again?'

He must have heard the despair in her voice because he told her, 'Not to another place. Just inside the building. Keep them guessing.'

'Where can we go, then?'

'Somewhere more secure, where they can't surprise us. While you were sleeping I was looking around. Want a drink?'

She murmured a positive response. She would have done so even if she had not been thirsty. Any offer of food or drink had to be encouraged.

He put a can of something into her hand. She felt for the ring-pull, but her fingers were too numb to lift it. She told him she couldn't open it and he did the job for her.

'I don't kid myself,' he confided. 'They're trained for this. Sieges, I mean. They have the latest surveillance techniques. Listening devices. They could be picking up the words I'm speaking to you now.' As if alarmed by his own conclusion, he went silent for a time.

She took some of the drink.

He resumed, 'This old building isn't a fortress. There are ways they can get up here, right up here to the top without using the main stairs. There's an external fire escape round the back and there are back stairs that link up with the cellars. Or they could climb up the balconies at the front. They could use a crane, or a helicopter.'

Samantha judged it sensible to say nothing while he was talking in this vein. In her mind she was replaying the ending of sieges she'd seen on television, when tear-gas was used and special troops went in wearing masks and protective suits.

Mountjoy said with a touch more confidence, 'What

holds them up is that they don't know which room we're in.' He paused, and she was conscious once more of the sharp rise and fall of his breathing. 'Do you know where we are right now?'

Of course she knew. The only thing she didn't know was how to answer a question like that. 'Somewhere near the top?'

'Couldn't get much higher if we tried,' he said. 'If you stood down there in the street and looked up at the front, this is the bit at the left-hand end, with the twin gables. Have you ever looked up at the old hotel?'

'Not often,' she said truthfully.

'Because then you'd know where I'm going to take you. It's at the opposite end. Shaped like a turret, with battlements. That really *is* the highest point. The only way into it is up a spiral staircase. They can send up anyone they like and I can hold them off with my gun. And in case you were wondering, it doesn't have a balcony. Get up.'

He switched on a torch and she saw that he had the gun in his other hand. He ordered her to pick up the pieces of flex and wrap the blanket around her shoulders. She asked if she could first put on her T-shirt, which she found she had been using as a pillow, and he gave his consent. She reached for her violin case; she wasn't going to leave it here. Then she pulled the blanket across her back.

They left the room and crept along a corridor. Thinking that it was a vital opportunity to get her bearings, she looked about her, but with little advantage, because he kept the torch-beam directed low, at a spot near her feet. At the end of the corridor he told her to turn right and then immediately left, where the torch picked out the first steps of the spiral staircase.

Climbing the stairs, she was overwhelmed by despair. What he had said was absolutely right. The turret room was going to be impregnable. No one could surprise them. He could command the one doorway with his gun. The siege was certain to end in a deadly shoot-out. What other outcome could there be?

'The door straight ahead.'

On the stairs he had kept close behind her so as not to allow her to aim a kick at him. He gave her a nudge with the gun. She saw a short passageway ahead of her with three doors. The turret was not one room, but divided into three, like segments.

'Must have been used by servants,' Mountjoy said as they entered the poky little space. In a strange way, he sounded apologetic about the accommodation.

It was the first faintly civil remark he had expressed in some hours. Samantha made an effort to encourage a conversation. 'These days they'd take down one of these internal walls, install a Jacuzzi and call it the penthouse suite.' As the torch flicked across the room she saw that the arched window facing the front was boarded over to well above head height. 'If that was taken down, there must be a wonderful view.'

'We're here precisely because it is boarded up,' he said, hostile again. 'We can't be overlooked from the Abbey or anywhere else. Get your wrists behind your back.'

The socializing was over. He started the business of tying her again, efficiently, though not so viciously.

'Do you have to tie my legs?' she asked.

'That's the whole point, to confine you to this room.' But he didn't gag her this time. When she was seated against the wall with the flex firmly knotted around her jeans, he spread the blanket over her legs. 'I'm going to see what's going on.' He stepped out of the room and across the passage. She saw how right he was about the turret. He could keep her in this room without any risk that she would be seen from the street. Presumably the window in the next room wasn't boarded over, so he could use that for observation.

Presently she heard a shout of, 'Bastards!' from the

308

other room. Her heart-rate quickened; anything that upset Mountjoy was putting her in danger. In a moment she understood the cause of the outcry: a strong beam of light penetrated the room through the arched area at the top of the window that had not been boarded over. Down in the street they were using some kind of searchlight.

He came back into the room. 'They ought to be trying to negotiate, not harassing us with lights.'

She suggested, 'They must be trying to find out which part of the building we're in. How can they negotiate if they don't know where we are?'

He was silent.

It seemed a constructive thing to have said. She was emboldened to add, 'What you need is a mobile phone.'

'Thanks,' he said bitterly. 'Next time I break out of jail I'll remember to have one in my pocket.'

'What I meant is probably they'll get one to you somehow. They'll see the sense of talking.'

'Oh, yes? I can see them doing that.'

'You talked to that man Diamond face to face.'

'Bugger all use it did me.'

She was in two minds about Mountjoy. She wanted the siege to end, but she understood his situation; after all, she was part of it. Frightened as she was, and angry at being hauled off the street and made hostage over an issue she hadn't even heard about, she sensed that he might have a genuine grievance. If so, he'd been wrongfully imprisoned for years. She didn't want him injured or killed for her sake. She didn't want to spend the rest of her life thinking he'd been gunned down so that she could be released.

She could also understand that prison was responsible for his fatalistic moods, but that didn't make them easier for her to endure.

She tried striking another positive note. 'I'm sure Mr Diamond is doing his best to get to the truth.'

'What's that?'

309

'I said I'm sure—'

He cut her off in mid-sentence. 'Listen.'

She could hear nothing, but Mountjoy crept out of the room and stood at the head of the spiral staircase.

Samantha leaned as far forward as the flex allowed. She thought she heard a faint sound. She wasn't sure if it came from inside the building.

Mountjoy stepped back into the room, gun in hand. His voice was pitched on a high, hysterical note. 'I'm going to gag you again. I can't trust you to keep quiet. There's definitely someone inside this place.'

She reacted quickly. 'It could be Mr Diamond.'

'Some chance!' He found the roll of plastic adhesive and clawed at the end with his fingernail.

Samantha said, 'If you use that gun, you're finished, whatever the truth is.'

He ripped off a piece of the plastic, slammed it over her mouth and said, 'I've got to the point when I'm too tired to care any more. The buggers will do for me anyway.' He got up and walked to the top of the staircase.

Chapter Twenty-Six

The kidnapping was public knowledge now. Once the Empire Hotel had been cordoned off, the news embargo could not be sustained. Channel Four News at seven led with still pictures of Mountjoy and his hostage Samantha, followed by live coverage of the scene in front of the hotel and an interview with the Chief Constable of Avon and Somerset, Duncan Farr-Jones, who stressed that although the escaped prisoner was a murderer, and known to be armed, the police were taking measures to bring the siege to a quick conclusion – to which he added, ' . . . ensuring the safe release of Miss Tott.' He said nothing about Mountjoy's prospects of survival.

Several hundred Bathonians had left their living rooms for a sight of some action. Peter Diamond arrived at Orange Grove soon after eight to find police lines where that afternoon there had only been chequered tape. The yellow jackets with reflective stripes were visible stopping the public at every point of access to the open space in front of the hotel façade. The number of police minibuses and coaches parked beside Bog Island testified to the reinforcements brought in from all over the county.

Julie dropped him at the north end of Pierrepont Street and reverse-turned and drove away. At this critical stage of the operation it was necessary to divide forces. Crucial things still had to be checked and Diamond would be checking the most crucial – the state of Mountjoy's nerves.

311

Too many hours had passed without communication. The man was trapped; he would be exhausted and afraid. If he panicked and used the gun, all the good work of the past hours would be undermined. He had to be informed as soon as possible that the new evidence proved him innocent of murder. It was up to Diamond to give him that reassurance, man to man. This wasn't an occasion for loud-hailers or mobile phones.

Meanwhile Julie was given the essential task of following up on the discovery in Conkwell Wood.

At Bog Island, ominously, two ambulances were waiting, their crews outside watching the play of the searchlight across the hotel front. The Chief Constable, dapper in a flak-jacket and Tyrolean hat, was briefing some of the press outside the police caravan that was being used as the headquarters of the rescue operation. Spotting Diamond's approach, he cut short the interview and they went inside the van and it wasn't for a cosy chat. 'Where the devil have you been all afternoon? You should have been in touch.' This was said in the presence of a civilian radio operator, Keith Halliwell and Mr Tott, who got up as if to welcome Diamond and sat down smartly when he heard the rebuke.

Diamond was surprised by the hostility. From long experience of dealing with evasion he decided it had to be a cover for some shabby decision. Side-stepping the Chief Constable's question, which he considered superfluous at this stage, he asked, 'What's the state of play? Are we in communication with Mountjoy?'

Tott said, 'No, we're not.'

Farr-Jones piled on the reproach. 'You're a fine one to talk about communication.'

Diamond was more than willing to tough it out with them; that was one of the perks of being a civilian. 'What's been happening, then? It's a siege. I thought the first priority was to set up some line of communication.'

312

Farr-Jones said acidly, 'The first priority is to establish where Mountjoy is, and where he's holding Miss Tott.'

'Haven't you done that?'

'They're somewhere on the fifth or sixth floor. They moved from the place where they were sighted. We've occupied floors one to four.'

Diamond erupted at this. 'You sent men in? Jesus Christ, you gave me your word that you wouldn't storm the building.'

Farr-Jones checked him curtly, 'Don't over-dramatize. We haven't *stormed* the place. We made an orderly move. That was a decision I took an hour ago.'

'Armed men?'

'Well, I wouldn't send them in with batons and shields when the fellow has a hand-gun.'

'But you gave me an undertaking. I had until midnight to talk him down, you said. You'd stand off until midnight. You bloody agreed!'

Farr-Jones thrust a finger at Diamond. 'Don't tangle with me, Diamond. This is a police operation and I'm responsible, here, on the spot, taking stock from minute to minute and giving the orders. You weren't anywhere about, and you haven't been in touch.'

'What exactly are these orders?' Diamond asked, appalled at the potential for a blood bath.

'To seal every possible escape route and advance as high up the stairs as they can without personal risk.'

Tott did his best to take out some of the sting. 'We're working from maps the City Council have supplied. The problem is that the building is a honeycomb. Most of the rooms on the top floors have access to roof spaces. The plumbing is extraordinary. They say it's like the engine room of a battleship up there.'

'Where's Warrilow?' Diamond asked, as a disquieting thought surfaced.

Farr-Jones said firmly, '*Commander* Warrilow is directing

313

the team inside the hotel. We're in radiophonic communication.'

It was as dire as he had feared. Warrilow could justify any action by claiming he was in the firing line. 'Tell him I'm coming in right away and order him to put the action on hold.'

'You've got some neck, Diamond.'

He kept control, just. 'What I've got, Mr Farr-Jones, is what I promised: the means to bring this siege to an end. I'm ready to talk to Mountjoy, only not with gunmen moving in for a shot.'

'What are you saying – that something has turned up, something relevant to the case?'

'Nothing *turned up*,' muttered Diamond, his distaste for the words made clear. 'We turned it up, Julie Hargreaves and I, through solid detective work. We can prove that Mountjoy didn't murder Britt Strand.'

Tott clenched his fist and said, 'Nice work.'

The Chief Constable was less charitable. 'Who the devil did murder her, then?'

If he thought he was entitled to be handed the name on a platter, he was disappointed.

Diamond said rigidly, 'We're dealing with the siege. Would you tell *Commander* Warrilow I'm coming in and order him to pull back his men to the third floor? I won't talk to Mountjoy under armed threat.'

'You don't seem to understand,' said Farr-Jones. 'This is a high-risk incident.'

'It is now.'

'We have men deployed all over the building.'

'Yes, in disregard of the promise I was given,' said Diamond, and then played his highest card. 'Are you dispensing with my services, Chief Constable? Is it down to Warrilow to end the siege in a shoot-out?'

Tott exclaimed, 'God forbid – no!'

Farr-Jones took refuge in silence.

314

'I'd like to have that confirmed,' Diamond pressed him. 'Strictly off the record, as our friends out there express it.'

The allusion to the press struck home. There was a sharp intake of breath. Then Farr-Jones turned to the radio operator and said, 'Get Mr Warrilow for me.'

Diamond didn't wait to hear the outcome. He headed straight for the front of the hotel, ignoring the press people who trotted beside him, thrusting microphones at his face and badgering him with questions all the way. At the top of the flight of stone steps under the white, wrought-iron portico, he was waved inside by the constable standing guard.

The once-gracious entrance hall that Diamond was seeing for the first time was ungraciously lit by the strip-lights installed during the time the civil service had occupied the hotel. There were armed men in combat suits at the foot of a fine mahogany staircase that must once have been carpeted and now was fitted with lino treads and metal strips. To the right was a modern-looking counter normally occupied by the security firm who patrolled the hotel. Warrilow stepped from behind it like the bell captain, his deportment proclaiming that he was the man in charge.

'I suppose the lift isn't working?' Diamond cut through any tedious preliminaries.

Warrilow astutely decided that obstruction wasn't the best way to deal with this charging rhino. 'If you're serious about wanting to go up, you'll be forced to use the stairs. I hope you're in good shape.'

'And I hope the Chief Constable made himself clear,' Diamond stated firmly. 'I'm not going up there with guns in support and I don't want to be interrupted, however long it takes. My brief is to talk him down, and I want his trust.'

Warrilow threw in a spanner. 'Do you happen to know where he is?' He asked the question as if he, personally, would give anything to know.

'Don't you?'

'It's far from clear. We believe he moved out of that room under the gables.'

'The room with the balcony, you mean?'

'Yes.'

'Taking the girl with him?'

'We assume so. We're getting no sound from that end of the building.'

'Where else would they have gone? Do you have the plans?'

With a world-weary manner, as if going through the motions of co-operating with an awkward hotel guest, Warrilow led him to the desk, picked up a sheaf of papers and handed them across. Diamond leafed through them. The fifth floor, where Samantha had been sighted on the balcony, was a V-shape, with some twenty-five rooms divided by a corridor. One side overlooked Orange Grove, the other Grand Parade and Pulteney Weir. The point of the V ended in a heptagonal shape that he took to be the base of the turret that dominated the eastern end of the hotel façade. 'I reckon this is where they went,' he said.

'I doubt it,' commented Warrilow, taking the plans and flicking over to the sheet that showed the sixth floor. 'Look, the turret goes up to another level and is quite cut off. It's partitioned into three rooms, each with just the one door. They'd be trapped rats in there.'

'Access is by a spiral staircase,' Diamond pondered aloud, ignoring what had just been said. 'He could defend that. And this looks like another set of stairs to the roof. A fire escape, by the look of it. If he kept the girl tied up in one of the rooms, he could stand here' – he touched the point on the plan – 'and have a view of the fire escape and the spiral staircase at the same time.'

'He'd still be trapped,' Warrilow insisted. 'I have men on the roof.'

Diamond took a sharp breath. 'How did they get up there?'

316

'The exterior fire escape at the back of the building.'

'What are their orders?'

'They're patrolling the roof. They won't go in until I radio them. It's under tight control, Diamond. When Mountjoy understands that there's no way out wherever he is, he'll surrender peacefully. He'd better.'

'I'll tell him,' Diamond said in a quiet, implacable tone.

'You still want to do this?'

It wasn't worthy of an answer. He put down the plans and looked about him.

'What now?' Warrilow asked. 'A gun?'

He shook his head.

'You'll need one. Are you armed?'

He said, 'A bat phone.'

'What?'

'Personal radio. Isn't that what you call them these days?'

Warrilow beckoned to one of the constables by the door and had him lend his radio to Diamond, who then needed instructions in how to use the thing. He had such a deep-rooted dislike of mechanical appliances that even those he'd been forced to master were later expunged from his memory.

'You're insisting on doing this?' Warrilow repeated himself with something not far short of actual concern. His hostility had been rather defused by Diamond's ineptness with the radio.

'Of course.'

'And you won't be carrying a gun?'

'No.'

'Then for God's sake use the radio at the first hint of trouble.'

'I'm giving the radio to Mountjoy,' Diamond told him casually.

Having asked for another guarantee that no police personnel were on floors five or six, he started up the

317

grand staircase like a freshly arrived guest, pausing to check the angle of his hat in the triple mirror on the second landing.

At the third floor, a shade less exuberant, he stopped for breath and spoke to a group in combat jackets holding automatic rifles. They told him that sounds had been heard in the tank-loft on the fifth floor, but no one was sure if it was water circulating, because earlier someone had used one of the old wooden-seated toilets.

He met another six armed men on the next flight and they assured him that they were the advance party, the Special Operations Unit, marksmen every one; they had been on the point of occupying the fifth just as Warrilow had given the order to withdraw to level four. To Diamond's eyes, they looked disturbingly young, yet they insisted that they could have 'taken' Mountjoy and freed Samantha. He didn't recognize a single one of them from the old days and they didn't look as if they wanted to be friendly. That didn't stop him from reminding them to stay off the top floors while he was up there.

He wasn't built for all these flights of stairs. As he got higher, breathing more heavily, wishing he'd brought a torch for the dark corridors, he thought seriously of the risk he was taking – principally the risk of being shot by his own side. He would have liked to have cleared the entire hotel of armed police. These young men brandishing their guns made him uncomfortable. They scared him more than Mountjoy did.

Here he was, a civilian, staking his life on his ability to talk an armed man down from a siege. Why? Because it was personal. Because of the mistakes he'd made four years ago. He owed Mountjoy this.

And there was another reason for doing this, wasn't there? It wasn't just altruism. What the hell was it? His memory wasn't functioning too well. Got it! He wanted the damned job back, didn't he? Nobody would have thought so when he was slagging off the Chief Constable; in truth, he'd rather undermined his job prospects then, but Farr-Jones *had* broken a promise, however he liked to put it. He'd handed over effective control to Warrilow. In a short time those eager young men with guns would have located Mountjoy and started firing. This needed to end peacefully. It cried out for the old, unfashionable policing he represented. He wasn't remotely like your chummy old English bobby, Dixon of Dock Green – thank God – but at least he pursued the truth, whatever the cost. That was what had kept him from being kicked off the force all the times he'd traded aggro with people like Farr-Jones. His values were right.

He was approaching the fifth floor. He bent his back as he prepared to go up the last steps. It was an unconscious action and he was annoyed with himself for doing it and instantly straightened up. The right signal to give Mountjoy was openness, not stealth. In fact, he needed to announce that he was coming.

'Mountjoy, it's me, Peter Diamond.' He raised his voice and said, 'I want to talk to you. I promised to come and here I am.'

Midway up the last flight, he paused and listened. He thought he detected a movement.

'Mountjoy, is that you?' he asked.

Someone fired a shot.

He slammed himself against the wall.

Immediately after was a second shot.

The firing had come from just above him, on the fifth floor. The echo was still ringing through the building.

His first thought was that Warrilow had double-crossed him and marksmen were posted up here. He was incensed.

Boneheads.

But presently he decided that they weren't firing at him, or he'd be dead. He was an easy target. The action was in the corridor. They must have spotted Mountjoy.

319

He waited almost a minute without moving, his ears ringing. Then another sound blended in, a high-pitched intermittent beep.

The personal radio. He snatched it off his chest, pressed the switch and heard the crackle of static, followed by Warrilow's voice. 'Control to Diamond. Are you receiving?'

Diamond hissed into the thing, 'You told me there were no guns up here. Someone fired two shots.'

'We heard them. Where are you now?'

'On the fifth floor.'

'We don't have anybody higher than the fourth apart from the team on the roof, and they haven't moved.'

'Someone must have.'

'I'm in communication, for God's sake. I know where the men are. Nobody has moved. Nobody. Mountjoy must be doing the shooting. Listen, I'm sending a team up to you now.'

'Don't,' said Diamond at once. 'I can handle this.'

'That's ridiculous. He's out of control. He may have shot the hostage.'

This crushing possibility had hit Diamond almost as it was spoken. Horrible as it was, it had to be faced. He spoke his thoughts aloud as they came to him: 'There were two shots, so he may have killed himself as well. Hold back your men until I've clarified what happened.'

Warrilow said, 'I don't take orders from you.'

'I'm on the spot and it's got to be my decision,' Diamond told him with passionate conviction. 'Hold everything. Do you hear me, Mr Warrilow? Do you hear me? I'll radio down when I've checked.'

He couldn't rely on Warrilow, but with luck he had bought himself a few minutes. He shut off the radio and shouted into the darkness, 'Mountjoy?'

There was just the echo from the bare walls. The burnt gunpowder lingered in the air.

'Mountjoy, this is Peter Diamond. Where are you? Do you need help?'

No answer, but he expected none. The most likely explanation of the silence was that Mountjoy had cracked under the strain and blown his brains out, but that didn't entirely account for the shooting. It takes one shot to commit suicide and there had definitely been two. A double killing? He had to be prepared for it.

He got up and mounted the last couple of steps and stood on the fifth floor. 'I'm alone,' he shouted once more. 'Unarmed. Can you hear me?'

Apparently not.

But he fancied he could hear a slight movement higher in the building. Possibly it was coming from the men on the roof. He strained to listen.

It had stopped.

Across the corridor he could just make out the angle of the V, where the spiral staircase ought to be. He stepped forward, through a space where the walls didn't run exactly parallel, into what had to be the lower level of the turret. The way ahead was practically pitch black.

'Mountjoy?'

Nothing.

'If you're up there—' He was stopped in mid-sentence by another series of beeps from the personal radio he was carrying. He clasped the thing and fumbled with the controls, wanting just to silence it, but then there was a crackle of static and Warrilow's voice came over.

'Command Control to Diamond. Our monitors are picking up sound from the top floor of the turret. Are you receiving me? The top floor of the—'

The sentence was never completed because he snatched the radio off his chest and crunched it savagely against the wall.

If there was sound, there was life. 'Mountjoy, it's just me, Diamond.'

321

Reaching into the space ahead, he found the hand-rail of the staircase. 'I'm unarmed. I want to help you.'

This time he was certain he heard something. Not a response. More the sound of someone whispering. He dared to hope again.

He located the first step and started climbing. 'I'm coming up to you,' he said. 'I'm not armed. I promised to come back and I have.' Steadily, scarcely pausing, he mounted the steps. At one point he froze when the whole staircase was made visible by a moving light, the rails casting long revolving shadows that threatened to give him vertigo. It was the searchlight beam scanning across the front of the building and it moved away just as suddenly.

The whispering upstairs – if that was what he had heard – had stopped since he had spoken.

The problem about going up a spiral staircase in darkness is that you lose all sense of direction. It was only when the handrail ended that he realized he'd reached the top. At a loss, he tried for a mental picture of the sixth floor plan; there was a landing at the top of the stairs, wasn't there? There were three doors, each leading to a room, a segment of the heptagon.

Choose the right one, he thought grimly, and you must expect to look down a gun barrel.

'I'm at the top,' he said, wishing he sounded more in control. 'In case you didn't hear, this is Peter Diamond and I'm alone.'

He spread his arms. Where were the doors? One should be to the left, one ahead, one to the right. His outstretched fingers didn't make contact with anything. Maybe the sensible thing was to wait for the searchlight to pan across this end of the building again.

No. He'd spoken. Mountjoy expected him now. To wait was just to plant suspicion of a trap.

He moved forward a step. His right hand touched a flat surface that moved away from him with the contact –

certainly the door. He faced it and pushed. 'Are you in here?'

They were not. There was a faint source of light from the window. The room was definitely empty. He could tell without stepping fully inside. To go in would be a mistake.

He stepped back into the corridor and groped for the door at the end. Both hands found it simultaneously. Like the other one, it was already standing slightly open. He expected that. They wouldn't have wanted it closed. He pressed at it gently without saying anything this time. There was nothing sensible to be said. But he thought he heard an intake of breath.

He stood in the doorway, getting a strong sense that someone was very close. This room was darker than the other. The window-space seemed to be screened in some way, because there was a faint semicircle of light at the top, but darkness below. Defensively, he moved his left foot against the base of the door. He tried to decide if the smell he was getting was the smell of unwashed clothes. After some days on the run, they'd be getting pungent. He swayed forward, steadied himself on the door-frame and took another step.

There was a distinct scraping sound to his left, then a gasp, a voiced sound, and the voice was female.

He said, 'Samantha?'

He stepped towards the source of the voice. His foot touched something soft, like fabric. Clothes? A blanket?

Abruptly the room was bathed in light. The searchlight beam thrust through the space at the top of the window and showed him two people pressed against the wall behind the door, one female and frightened, the other holding a gun. Except that the woman was Una Moon, the man GB and the gun a twin-barrelled shotgun.

Chapter Twenty-Seven

The searchlight moved off the turret. Through pitch black, Diamond spoke the same words he had been poised to say to John Mountjoy: 'You can put down the gun. It's me.' He was too staggered to think of anything else. But he didn't doubt what he had seen. It wasn't some trick of the imagination brought on by fumbling about in the dark and getting disorientated on the spiral stairs. He couldn't have mistaken Una Moon's pallid face and scraped-back hair ending in the plait; there was no way he could confuse her with Samantha Tott. And the man holding the shotgun couldn't be anyone except GB; his whole physique was larger than Mountjoy's.

Una spoke out of the darkness. 'For God's sake don't panic, anyone. I'm going to switch on the torch.'

A beam picked out Diamond's feet and cast a faint light over the rest of the room. He saw that GB had obeyed his order to the extent of slanting the gun across his chest, pointing it upwards, though his finger still lingered around the trigger. The crusty everyone treated with awe stood beside Una like a kid caught truanting. They had been waiting in the room with their backs to the wall, hoping not to be discovered.

Diamond stared around the small room, getting his wits together. There were signs of recent occupation on the floor, a heap of blankets and a violin case. 'You fired those shots?'

GB gave a nod.

'Both?'

Una said, 'Yes. And he missed with both.'

'We don't know that,' said GB.

Una rounded on him with scorn, 'Come on – where's the gunman, then? I didn't see him lying on the floor anywhere, did you?'

Diamond said, more as a statement than a question, 'You were shooting at Mountjoy?'

Una was unfazed. She said fervently, as if she were going straight on with the diatribe she'd given him in the market café, 'Someone had to rescue Sam, so I got hold of GB. I couldn't stand it any longer, knowing she was in here and you pigs were doing sod all about it.'

'That's untrue,' said Diamond.

Una overrode the objection by saying, 'Sam is one of us, and we stick together.'

'How did you get in?'

'Through a window. GB is a genius at opening up places. Nobody saw us. We were through the cellars and up the back stairs while you lot were still poncing about in the hotel lobby.'

'With the idea of what – taking on Mountjoy yourselves? Did you run into him?'

'We spotted him in the corridor, the skunk. We'd searched every room on the floor below this and were coming out of that one at the end, where Sam was seen on the balcony this afternoon. They weren't in there any more, but just at that minute we saw a movement at the far end. He stepped right across the corridor. It was him, no question, the scumbag, and GB should have blown his head off, but he missed, twice.'

Already reduced to a support role by the force of Una Moon's invective, GB said in his own defence, 'He was only in view for a couple of seconds, at most.'

Una explained, 'We thought he ran upstairs, so we

looked up here.'

GB said more firmly, 'He was definitely up here not long ago. Look at this stuff. It's Sam's violin case. They were in this room.'

'And now you've scared him out of sight,' said Diamond.

'What's wrong with that?'

'For one thing, I was trying to win his confidence and for another he could seriously harm the girl if he panics. You must be cuckoo, loosing off a shotgun.'

'He's got a certificate for it,' said Una.

'A certificate to shoot people? How long have you been up here?'

'Half an hour. Three-quarters. How would I know?'

'Couldn't you have left this to the professionals?' Diamond rebuked them. The doubts as to his own status didn't cross his mind.

GB said positively, 'With three of us, we can take him. No problem.'

'No, we cannot,' Diamond snapped back. 'You fouled this up. Don't you realize there are marksmen out there looking for a target? You wander about with a torch, waving a bloody shotgun. You're lucky they haven't picked you off already. Your horsing around is over for today.'

'And if we refuse?' said Una.

'I can do you for unlawful entry, using a firearm with intent to endanger life and obstructing the police in the pursuance of their duties,' he chanced it, but with conviction. 'I'm handling this my way. And before you leave, I want that gun unloaded and I'll take any spare cartridges you have.'

'Like fuck, you will!' said GB, and he lifted the butt of the gun and charged.

The advantages were all with GB: his height, his physique, his age and, not least, the weapon. He was as large a man as Diamond had ever handed off, and it wasn't the tidiest of moves, but his years as a rugby forward had left him with some skill and, more important, nice timing. He ducked under the shotgun, thrust a hand firmly against GB's oncoming shoulder and steered him aside. GB cracked his head against the edge of the door, keeled off balance and hit the ground. The gun clattered across the floor.

The big crusty was up immediately and launched himself at Diamond again, this time intent on butting him. It was even more like the loose scrum now, and Diamond dealt with him in a way that no referee would have countenanced, by swaying to the left and bringing up his knee. Bone struck bone and the bone in GB's case was his jaw. His head jerked backwards and he crashed down for a second time.

Then Una clubbed him over the skull with the torch and shouted, 'Birdbrain! You great dumb-bell! What are you bloody thinking of?'

GB wasn't thinking of much after the combined impacts of Diamond's knee and the torch. He rolled on his back and groaned.

The torch had suffered, too. It flickered a few times and went out.

Una composed herself quickly. It was far from certain that she had lost control. More likely she had summed up their situation and started battering GB as a way of cutting their losses. She told Diamond, 'That didn't happen, right? The gun isn't loaded any more and we don't have extra cartridges, but you can take it if you want.'

'Leave it on the floor. Tell him to get up. I'm going to hand you over to the men on the roof.'

She didn't argue. She merely said, 'Are you going to rescue Sam?'

'That's the only reason I'm here.'

She had to be satisfied with that. She told GB to get up. He swore at her and obeyed. Diamond stood back, allowing them to shuffle out and turn left out of the room

327

where the light was slightly better and towards the fire escape, a wooden step-ladder leading up to a fire door.

'Better hold your hands above your heads when you get to the top,' Diamond advised. 'They might think you're someone else.'

He watched as they mounted the steps, opened the door and emerged on the roof. There was a shout up there, the standard instruction to a potential armed suspect to lie face down. The gun crew on the roof took over. If nothing else, it must have relieved their monotony.

He was seething. And the knee that had clobbered GB felt as if it might not hold him up much longer. The stupidity of the crusties had made his mission infinitely more difficult and dangerous. He knew he must dismiss the incident and fix his mind on Mountjoy again. He needed to be certain that the rest of the turret remained unoccupied. There were two extra rooms, each faintly lit from outside. He checked them. Then he felt his way to the spiral stairs and down to the fifth floor, where he took stock.

Mountjoy and his hostage could be in any of the twenty or so rooms along the two corridors of the V, or on the balconies, or the roof-spaces that were accessible through some of the rooms; but he'd go bail on their being somewhere on this level and he did have an idea where to look first. Tott had said something about the plumbing being like the engine room of a battleship; this was the floor where the water tanks for the entire hotel would have to be sited. In the turret rooms he'd seen old-fashioned radiators that must have been installed for the comfort of the Admiralty staff, so there would be pipes and tanks for hot water as well as cold. The tank space had to be large.

More than likely it was sited in the centre of the building, close to where he was. He waited for another swing of the searchlight to give him a long view of the corridor ahead. When it came, he noted the positions of the doors and spotted what he was looking for, a plain door without panels and with smudge-marks around the handle. He crossed the corridor and opened it.

'Mountjoy?'

He couldn't see much, but he could hear the steady drip of water not far ahead and there was a metallic resonance to it that could only mean a cold tank. Leaving the door open, he sidled in, across what felt like wood flooring gritty with dust. His knees touched an obstruction that felt curved and spongy: the insulation around a water pipe.

He said into the darkness, 'Listen, if you're in here, this is Diamond.'

A voice close to his ear said, 'And you're a dead man, Diamond.'

The solid object jammed against his throat had to be the muzzle of a gun.

'I trusted you, bastard,' said John Mountjoy, spacing the words as if every one tasted noxious. If he had sounded agitated the last time they had met, in the Francis, this was a voice on the edge of breakdown.

'I didn't fire those shots,' Diamond was quick to say.

'I imagined it, did I? My back is a bloody mess of torn flesh and pellets and I imagined it?'

After one of the quickest mental adjustments he'd ever had to make, Diamond talked fast and earnestly. 'You're wounded? That wasn't me, I tell you. That was some morons who got into here without my knowledge. They weren't police. I just got rid of them. They've been taken away. They didn't think they hit you.'

Mountjoy came back at him. 'In a corridor, with a shotgun?'

'Are you badly hurt?'

The question was ignored. 'You're lying, Diamond. You were calling my name before the shots were fired. I stepped into the corridor and got shot. You set me up, you bastard.'

'I did not. I didn't know they were up here. I want to end this peacefully. I've got news for you.'

'Yes,' said Mountjoy bitterly, 'the place is swarming with police. Christ!' He groaned in pain and pressed the gun harder against Diamond's neck.

'Your conviction was wrong. I can prove it now.'

There was an interval without words, but it wasn't because of what Diamond had said. It was filled by Mountjoy rasping for breath. He was in real pain. Finally he muttered, 'Double-crosser.'

Diamond said with difficulty, because the gun was constricting his breath, 'We had a deal. You wanted the truth about Britt Strand – by today, you said. I kept my word. I know who did it now.'

'I'm going to blow your brains out.'

'Will you listen?' His mind raced. The man was past reason, in too much pain.

The pressure on his throat eased and it was not a good omen. He was certain that Mountjoy was about to press the gun to his head and fire. In the split second before it could happen, he did the only thing open to him. Blindly he swung his arm upwards to deflect the gun. He dipped his head in the same movement. His forearm made contact with Mountjoy's. The gun blasted.

There is said to be a short grace period after any severe trauma such as a bullet wound, during which the shock to the nervous system results in the victim feeling no pain. Diamond had no idea whether he was wounded. He dived to his left, hit the floor and rolled over several times until the floorboards ended and he dropped into the space over the joists. He knew they were joists because the upper edges crunched into his limbs and ribs in parallel. It took extraordinary self-control not to cry out.

He pressed himself into the space and lay still.

Then white streaks penetrated the roof area and it came alight. The searchlight beam.

A short distance off, Mountjoy was about to pick up the gun. The pain of the pellet wounds must have been severe, because in the act of bending his back he gave a groan and stopped before completing the movement. He was forced to go down on one knee.

Diamond was up and charging at him as the hand groped for the revolver. Mountjoy succeeded in picking it up and partially turning before Diamond flung himself into a diving tackle that crunched into the convict's ribs, bowling him over like a tenpin, still holding the gun. He was no sharp-shooter. He'd missed his opportunity. Diamond flattened him to the floor, gripped his wrists with both hands and hammered them against the boards until his grip loosened and the gun slipped free and out of reach.

Mountjoy gave up resisting.

'As far as you and I are concerned, that cleans the slate,' said Diamond. He reached for the gun and held it against Mountjoy's head. 'Where's Samantha?'

No answer.

'If you've harmed her. . .'

'No,' said Mountjoy, responding to a jab from the gun. 'She's all right. Get off me, will you?'

'Where?'

'Over there, behind the big tank.'

'Where's that?'

The big tank could have been anywhere. The searchlight had shifted again.

'Just a few feet away.'

'Lead me to her,' said Diamond. 'You're sure she's all right? Why hasn't she said anything?'

'She's gagged.'

He eased himself off, allowing Mountjoy to get to his knees, groaning. It seemed unlikely at this stage that he was capable of counter-attacking, but the gun was a wise safeguard. He kept it pressed against the sore back, ignoring the wincing and groaning while Mountjoy got himself upright and started stumbling over joists and pipes. He reached what was evidently the cold water tank and edged around it to the far side, sliding his hands along the surface.

'Here. Careful. Don't tread on her. There's a torch down here somewhere.'

'I'd shoot you,' Diamond warned him. His senses were compensating for the dark. He could hear how close he was to Mountjoy and he was primed for any sudden movement. And he was conscious of the closeness of someone else, whether through body heat or scent he was not sure.

'Got it.'

The light came on and discovered a young girl lying face upwards in the cavity between two of the joists. Her ankles and thighs were tied with white flex and her hands were trapped behind her back. A brown adhesive strip was across her mouth. One of her eyes was bloodshot and her forehead was bruised.

'It's all right, love,' Diamond told her. 'It's over.'

Chapter Twenty-Eight

Of the major players in the Empire Hotel drama,
Diamond was the only one to take part in the final act.
When the crucial interviews were conducted late that
evening at Manvers Street Police Station, John Mountjoy
was face down and naked in a treatment room at the Royal
United Hospital having pellets of shot removed from his
back and buttocks. Commander Warrilow and two armed
officers were in attendance and the patient was in no
doubt that if he made one false move he would require
further treatment.

Samantha allowed her father to drive her home for a
hot meal, a bath and a night between clean sheets in the
family home. Exhausted as she was, she insisted that she
would return to the squat the next day, although she
conceded that busking was not in her plans.

After making statements about the firing of the
shotgun, GB and Una were given a stern dressing-down by
Keith Halliwell and told that a decision would be taken
later about possible prosecution. This was something of a
charade; they knew it wouldn't happen. They left the
police station before midnight.

In the room upstairs with the oval table and the portrait
of the Queen, where the assignment had first been given
to Diamond, the Chief Constable thanked him warmly for
securing the safe release of Miss Tott and the recapture of
Mountjoy.

'It's what I undertook to do,' said Diamond, adding, after a pause, '. . .sir. I think I should address you in the proper manner now.'

'Er . . . really?'

'I mean, in view of our agreement.'

'That, yes,' Farr-Jones said vacantly.

'My part of the deal was to bring the siege to a peaceful end by midnight,' Diamond reminded him.

'True – although Mountjoy might argue with that. "Peaceful" isn't the word I would use to describe the state of his end – his rear end.' Farr-Jones grinned like a shark.

'He's alive, sir.'

'And kicking, I dare say.' Farr-Jones was in cracking form.

Diamond waited.

'Well, I can't say I approve of everything you've said and done in the last couple of days, Diamond, but I certainly gave my word and I'll see what I can do about getting you reinstated. You're quite sure you want to resume your police career?'

'My CID career, sir.'

Farr-Jones nodded. 'The Police Authority will be duly advised, then, with a recommendation from me. You acted bravely. We're not ungrateful.'

Diamond grasped the firm, stubby hand that was extended.

Farr-Jones took the camaraderie a stage further by placing his left hand over Diamond's right shoulder and giving it a squeeze. 'What is more, you reeled him in without any nonsense.'

'Nonsense, sir?'

'About reopening the Britt Strand case.'

'Ah, that's right, sir,' said Diamond smoothly and amiably. 'There wasn't any nonsense about it.'

This cheerful assurance dented the Chief Constable's smile. 'What exactly are you saying?'

'We cracked the case, DI Hargreaves and I. That's why Mountjoy surrendered. I gave him a solemn promise to get a signed confession from the real killer of Britt Strand. Incontestable evidence. We need nothing less to get the original verdict overturned.'

Farr-Jones reddened ominously. 'You're not serious? The man's in custody again. That particular case is closed as far as I'm concerned, and you, too, if you've got any sense at all.'

'It isn't a question of *my* sense, sir. It's about our sense of justice, isn't it? Re-opening the case may be damaging to my reputation, but it's right that justice is done. I'm getting that confession tonight.'

'Like hell you are! Where from?'

'Here, sir. While we were in the spotlight at the hotel, Julie Hargreaves was quietly putting the final touches to our investigation. She's one of your best detectives.'

'I'm aware of that.'

'But I don't think you're aware that earlier this evening she brought in a man for questioning.'

The Chief Constable's eyebrows lifted like the Tower Bridge.

'He's in an interview room downstairs and I understand he's willing to make a statement.'

As if struck speechless, he mouthed the word 'Who?'

'Jake Pinkerton.'

'The pop singer?'

'Producer, sir. His performance days are over.' The low-key style Diamond was employing was deceptive; secretly, he was savouring the Chief Constable's appalled reaction. 'Would you care to observe? I said I'd assist Julie. She seems to think my presence will be useful.'

Dressed this time in a pale blue tracksuit with reflective strips, Pinkerton was waiting in the interview room absorbed in pressing back the skin from his fingernails, giving a fair impression of nonchalance.

'He was at home, making phone calls,' Julie told Diamond.

'Have you said what it's about?'

'I didn't need to. It's obvious someone has told him.'

'Has he put up his hand, then?'

'I doubt if he will,' she said. 'But I think he'll crack.'

In an adjoining room, the Chief Constable watched the interview through one-way glass.

'Mr Pinkerton, I don't believe in prolonging things,' Diamond said after the tape had been switched on and the usual preliminaries spoken by Julie. 'When I interviewed you at your house the other day, you gave me some information about Miss Britt Strand, but you were selective.'

'I thought I was extremely frank,' said Pinkerton in a tone that made clear his intention to meet the challenge. 'I told you we had it away. I said it was great while it lasted. What else do you want – the positions we liked best?' He winked at Julie.

Diamond didn't mind brass; it was preferable to silence. 'You said the affair lasted several months – into 1988. Is that right?'

'I *told* you this,' said Pinkerton with irritation.

'You also told me she drank whisky straight.'

'And you said you heard she was TT, as if I was lying. But I wasn't. She kicked the habit later.'

'I'm sure you're right,' Diamond agreed. 'Everyone else I've asked about her drinking said she didn't touch alcohol. You know damned well why I'm asking this, don't you?'

'You tell me,' Pinkerton parried.

'First, let's talk about the driving. We didn't discuss her driving when we spoke. She *was* a driver when you met her, back in 1987, wasn't she?'

He hesitated, pulling back from the table between them. 'What's behind this?'

Julie said, 'Answer the question, Mr Pinkerton.'

He shifted position in the chair. 'Yes, she had a sports car, an MGB, red.'

'Good, we're making progress now,' said Diamond. 'Did you ever borrow it?'

'The MGB? No, I had wheels of my own. A Merc, I think, at that time. I've had so many.'

'I'm interested in Britt's car,' said Diamond, choosing his words with care. He needed to trap Pinkerton into a lie, and this was his best opportunity. 'She didn't possess a car at the time of her death. Hadn't driven for at least two years, according to people who knew her. I wonder what she did with the MGB?'

'Sold it, I expect.' ·

So that's how you want to play it, Diamond thought. 'No, she didn't sell it. We checked the ownership. The car still officially belongs to Britt, four years after her death.'

'I can't help,' said Pinkerton.

'You can. It's in your possession, isn't it?'

He tried to look mystified. 'What do you mean?'

'We found it this evening, with a little help from your friends.' Diamond grinned. 'Out at Conkwell in a shed in the wood behind the studio. Had you forgotten?'

Fingering the tab on the zip of his tracksuit, Pinkerton sighed and said, 'Totally. It was so long ago.'

'We could see that from the weeds and things growing all over it,' Diamond agreed. 'It's definitely Britt's car. How did it get there?'

'She must have asked me to look after it. Yes, I'm sure she did.'

'This was when you were having the affair with her?'

'Right on.' He sounded casual, but he was looking miserable.

Diamond tightened the screw. 'Come on, Jake. The affair was over by the end of 1988. Why didn't she collect her car?'

'Good question.'

'Answer it, then.'

Pinkerton ran the tip of his tongue along his upper lip. 'The way she told it to me, she wanted it off the street. She had no garage for it. She saw I had this shed at Conkwell big enough to take a car, so she asked me if she could keep it there.'

'Not very convenient when she was living in Larkhall.'

'No.'

'So what happened? Did she ever use the car again?'

'Not to my knowledge.'

'Did you?'

'I answered that already.'

'The reason I ask,' said Diamond, 'is that the car is damaged. It shouldn't be on the road in the condition it's in. The nearside headlamp is shattered, the wing is badly dented and the bumper has been knocked out of shape.'

'So what's the problem?' said Pinkerton, making a good attempt to seem untroubled. 'It hasn't been on the road.'

Diamond leaned forward and spoke companionably. 'Jake, the problem is that you haven't been giving me the whole truth. When she put the car in your shed, it wasn't for convenience, it was to hide the damage, and you colluded with her. She failed to report an accident she caused. You must have seen the state of the car.'

He examined his fingernails again. 'Yes.'

'It could have been repaired,' Diamond pointed out. 'Why wasn't it repaired?'

'Couldn't say.'

'Could the reason be that she was afraid the damage would be reported?'

'I can't speak for her.'

'Speak for yourself, then,' said Diamond sharply. 'That car has been sitting in your shed for six years. It's worth a bit, an MGB. It should have been part of Britt's estate.'

'I'm not into stealing motors, if that's your drift,' said

338

Pinkerton. 'I never wanted the bloody thing.'

'You didn't want it known that you conspired with her to conceal an accident.'

After a pause, he said, 'Is that what this is about?'

'That's why you did nothing, isn't it? Well, isn't it?'

Pinkerton looked away.

This time, Julie followed up. 'You saw the state of the car. You must have asked her how it was damaged and she must have told you.'

Still no response.

'Tell us exactly what she said. At this point,' she added, 'we're looking to you for co-operation.'

Pinkerton was bright enough to recognize a hint. He glanced towards Diamond, then back to Julie, knowing that they wouldn't offer a no-prosecution deal while the tape was running. They sat like two Sphinxes.

He talked. 'Britt came to my house in Monkton Coombe one night, late. She was in a state. She'd been working on a story, as she put it, out at Warminster, and she'd had a liquid lunch.'

'When was this?' said Julie.

'I was working on the Sons of Slade album, so it must have been 1988. October, '88.'

'You're sure of this?'

'Yes. She told me she'd been well over the limit when she started for home and she got on the wrong road and found she was heading for Westbury, instead of Bath. It wasn't too serious because she knew the way back through Trowbridge. But then she noticed a police car in her mirror and she got the idea he was following her. She knew damn well if she was breathalyzed, she'd lose her licence. To shake him off, she left the main road, and then lost her way altogether in the lanes. It was already starting to get dark, so I guess it was around five by then. As she told me, she was driving through a village when a pedestrian stepped into the road suddenly. Britt swerved, but couldn't avoid hitting the person and tipping them over, as she put it. The car scraped against a drystone wall, but she held on to the wheel and got it under control again and kept going.'

'Kept going. She'd hit this person and didn't stop?'

'Right.'

'Man? Woman?'

'She didn't say. She didn't actually drive over them, and she was braking when she hit them, so she thought they couldn't be seriously hurt. But if the shunt was reported, she could be in real trouble. She couldn't leave the motor in the street outside the house. She had to get it out of sight. She came to me asking for help, so I said she could keep the motor there, at least until the incident was forgotten and she could get the damned thing repaired and back on the road again.'

'And she never did,' said Diamond.

'That's right.'

'Did you hear any more about the accident?' Julie asked.

'She never mentioned anything to me.'

Diamond said, 'Didn't you bring it up? I mean, you had her car sitting in your shed long after you split up with her.'

Pinkerton gave a shrug. 'You're going to find this hard to believe, but it's true. I forgot all about the thing. My business was expanding. I was being given new bands almost every month, creating sensational new sounds. Bloody snowed under.'

'You're quite sure she didn't discuss the accident again?'

'Not with me. It was a sensitive area. I mean, she cut out the booze completely, and we both knew why. And as far as I know, she stopped driving.'

'The way you described it when I interviewed you last time was different. You led me to believe that you hadn't the foggiest idea why she gave up.'

He shook his head ruefully. 'Give me a break, man. I didn't want to get involved.'

'We're investigating a murder, and you ask me to give you a break?' Diamond piped. 'You've withheld evidence, put me in risk of my life, and you ask me to give you a break? You're joking. And I'm not satisfied with your answers. I don't believe you forgot about the car's existence.'

'It's gospel truth,' insisted Pinkerton.

'It's bullshit. When she was murdered, and there was all the stuff in the papers, you must have thought of the car.'

He rubbed his face.

'Out with it,' said Diamond.

He sighed. 'OK – I kept quiet about the motor. I'm bloody well known in the biz, Mr Diamond, much bigger than you realize. As it was, I had the press on to me asking questions about my relationship with Britt. I said it was over, history, and that was the truth. If they'd known I still had her car, they'd have put the knife in, and so would you. No one would have believed we broke up.'

'You told me when we spoke before that you kept in touch with her. Was that correct?'

'Sure. We stayed friends.'

'And she never mentioned the accident or the car?'

'I told you it was a sensitive area.'

'When was the last time you saw her?'

'About three weeks before she died. In Milsom Street, by chance. She was alone, shopping.'

'What was said?'

'Nothing much. We got up to date. I gave her the dope on the bands I was working with and she talked about the magazines she was in. That's all. Just a few minutes in the street.'

'Did you speak on the phone after that?'

'No. It was definitely the last time. I've told you everything now, honest to God.'

'What was the point of all that?' Farr-Jones demanded in

an irritated tone. 'I was led to believe you were about to extract a confession of murder.'

'Murder? No. Vital information, yes,' said Diamond.

'Hearsay, most of it.'

'True,' he conceded.

'He did admit to keeping the car hidden,' said Julie. 'He conspired with her to withhold evidence.'

'You're not seriously proposing to charge him with that?' said Farr-Jones. 'I've had a very long day, you know, and it's late. Personally, I'm adjourning until tomorrow.'

'Right, sir,' said Diamond mildly. 'What time would you care to see us?'

'Is there any more to discuss?'

'Some clearing up.'

'Eleven o'clock, then.' The thought of another day made Farr-Jones yawn.

'Fine,' said Diamond. 'Outside the church?'

'Which church? It isn't Sunday, is it?'

'Steeple Ashton.'

'Whatever for?'

When Farr-Jones had left, Diamond shook his head slowly. '*He's* had a very long day. Doesn't it bring tears to your eyes, Julie?'

Chapter Twenty-Nine

By one of those contradictions that enhance the charm of the English countryside, the parish church at Steeple Ashton has no steeple. A storm removed it in 1670. The tower survived and dominated the village and the landscape north of Westbury Hill, for even in its truncated form St Mary's is a tall church. Knobbly pinnacles in profusion compensate for the lack of a steeple, and, if anything, the building looks over-ostentatious rather than incomplete. The lavishness of the decoration is a testimony to the profits of the wool trade in medieval Wiltshire and curiously most of the gargoyles carved on its hood-moulds and battlements have the chunky character of knitted toys.

All this was lost on the group of senior policemen stamping their feet and rubbing their gloved hands while they stood under the south porch like mourners waiting to line up behind a coffin. A hard frost had whitened the churchyard and a sharp east wind was blowing.

Precisely as the hour of eleven showed on the blue and gold dial of the church clock, Peter Diamond and Julie Hargreaves came around the side of the building.

'Good day to you, gentlemen. Is everyone here?'

It was a gratifying turn-out. As well as Farr-Jones and Tott, there were John Wigfull, Keith Halliwell and a pair of uniformed inspectors who had earlier been assigned to Commander Warrilow. The latter, to everyone's relief, had returned in triumph to the Isle of Wight the same morning with his patched-up prisoner.

Diamond and Julie had arrived more than an hour before and made use of every minute; their comings and goings in the frost showed as grey tracks between the graves in the section of churchyard to the west of the church.

'Would you care to follow me, then? This won't take long.' Diamond picked a fresh track over the crisp turf, leading the others in single file towards a layout of graves as regular as an actor's teeth. Eventually he stopped beside a plot with a short stone cross as headstone. On it was the simple inscription:

GEORGINA MAY HIGGINSON
13.9.1981 – 17.10.1988

'Barely seven,' remarked Tott.

'Dreadfully sad,' murmured Halliwell, the most sensitive of the group. Something else had needed to be said, even though words were inadequate.

'You'll have noticed the date, sir,' Diamond said for the benefit of Farr-Jones.

'October, '88. You're assuming this little girl was the victim of the hit-and-run accident?'

'We're certain of it. This is the only child's grave we could find for 1988.'

Farr-Jones blew out a plume of white breath. 'Did this child actually die in a road accident? Have you checked with records?'

'DI Hargreaves just has, on her personal.'

Julie reported, 'A child of this name was knocked down and killed by a car, here in Steeple Ashton, opposite the village stores, at 4.45 p.m. on this date. The driver was never traced.'

Diamond added, 'The next of kin are John Higginson, father, resident in Belfast, and Prue Shorter, mother, who still lives here. She is the photographer who worked with Britt Strand.'

Up to now, each statement had made sense to Farr-Jones. The last one did not, and his face showed it.

Diamond explained, 'Miss Shorter offered to work for Britt some time in the summer of 1990, almost two years after the child was killed. She had a strong suspicion by then that Britt had been the driver of that car, but she wanted to be certain, because she planned to avenge the killing of her daughter by taking the life of the person who caused it. So she worked as her photographer through the summer and autumn of 1990 until she was totally sure, and the right opportunity came.'

'Weren't we aware of any of this at this time?'

'The accident? It was in the records as a hit and run, but we had no reason to link it with the Britt Strand murder. We routinely checked all the witnesses for previous convictions and Miss Shorter was clean. The fact that she happened to be the parent of an accident victim didn't show on the computer.'

'It wouldn't,' Wigfull confirmed.

Farr-Jones asked, 'How did you get on to her, then?'

Diamond unexpectedly tiptoed on the spot like one of the cygnets in *Swan Lake*. 'You'll have to forgive me, sir, but I need to take a leak. It must be the cold.'

'Here?' said Farr-Jones, frowning.

'I happened to notice that Prue Shorter has a fire going in her cottage. What say we nick her now?'

It was the most civilized arrest in the combined experience of all the detectives. The timing couldn't have been bettered. 'How many of you are there?' Prue Shorter asked. 'Eight is it? I'm afraid I haven't got chairs for all of you. Would you like to handle the knife, Mr Diamond? It's the large one in the drawer behind you.'

She passed a steaming Dundee cake across the kitchen

table for Diamond to cut.

Several of the officers looked to the Chief Constable for guidance in this unprecedented situation. He had the good sense to give it his endorsement. 'When I was a small boy, I used to read the Rupert books,' he surprised them all by saying. 'Rupert Bear – the original ones by Mary Tourtel with yellow covers and black and white illustrations. They always seemed to end with Rupert coming home from some adventure to find that homely Mrs Bear had baked a cake.'

There was an uncomfortable silence. Senior policemen rarely provided such insights into their personal lives.

Prue Shorter ended it by saying, 'Personally, I could never believe in animals wearing clothes. I liked the Famous Five.'

'Enid Blyton,' said Wigfull, the walking encyclopedia.

Tott said, 'Wasn't one of them known as—'

'George. Yes,' Prue Shorter said quickly, and added almost unheard, 'Georgina.'

Their arrival at the cottage door had not fazed her. She had asked them in and said, 'Now that you've come, I can't tell you how relieved I am. What do you want first, my dears, a slice of cake or my confession?'

After that, it had seemed churlish to mention that two uniformed officers were posted outside the back door to prevent her escaping. Regardless, she had welcomed them in and made filter coffee for all.

Diamond finished cutting the cake and put the knife into the kitchen sink, out of Prue Shorter's reach. He still had a vivid memory of Britt Strand's lacerated body. This homely Mrs Bear could wield a knife as well as bake cakes. 'Are you ready to talk?' he asked her.

She said with sublime composure, 'Don't you want to tell them how you sussed me out, ducky? Take your applause while you've got the chance. I'm totally gobsmacked by your brilliant detective work, but I'm not sure if the rest of them are.'

346

Farr-Jones, in thrall to this redoubtable woman, said, 'Yes, Mr Diamond, why don't you give us the rundown on your investigation?'

'Not only mine,' Diamond pointed out. 'There were two of us. DI Hargreaves must take a lot of the credit. In fact, she deserves a commendation.'

Julie looked down at her coffee.

Diamond was less modest. 'You want to know what led us here?' he said. 'It was the old, old story of observation and deduction. Some of it didn't mean much at the beginning. For example, when Julie and I first came to this cottage we noticed a child's violin in one of the alcoves in the other room. There was also a drawing pinned to the noticeboard, a stick figure, obviously the work of a young child. Not much to go on, but the next time I visited, the violin was gone. It emerged that Miss Shorter had been married briefly and given birth to a girl, who had died young, at the age of seven. I didn't follow up by asking what she died of, and you may think that was a mistake on my part, but with the benefit of hindsight I doubt if I'd have got the truthful answer. I was straying into dangerous territory. Right?'

Prue Shorter gave a nod.

'Of course,' Diamond went on, 'you're constantly recording things in your memory and ninety-nine per cent turn out to be unimportant. It took some painstaking work and smart deduction on Julie's part and mine to discover that Britt Strand had once owned a car, an MGB. Still does, according to the computer records. She suddenly stopped driving at the end of 1988. We found the car eventually and discovered clear evidence of a collision. Jake Pinkerton, her boyfriend at the time, allowed her to hide the thing in the woods behind his recording studio at Conkwell. Naturally, we questioned him. At the time of the incident, Britt Strand confided to Pinkerton that she'd knocked someone down, but she wouldn't say whether it

347

was a man or woman. Why? I thought. Why did it matter what sex the victim was? The reason she wouldn't even tell her boyfriend was that she was too ashamed to give him the whole truth. She had knocked down a child and done nothing about it.'

'Left her lying in the road with a fractured skull,' added Prue Shorter in a hard, accusing tone in sharp contrast to the genial persona she had projected up to now. 'It was in the papers next day and she still didn't come forward.'

Tott said, 'Deplorable.'

'Even so,' Farr-Jones remarked to Diamond, 'the link between a child's violin and a hit and run accident is pretty tenuous.'

Diamond said sharply, 'There's more to it than that.' He was piqued. 'A whole lot more. There's the drinking. We heard from Jake Pinkerton that Britt had been a whisky drinker in the old days. She gave it up completely after the accident. Went TT.'

'That was a great help after my little girl was dead,' said Prue Shorter acidly.

'Let's come to you, then,' Diamond addressed her directly for the first time. 'A resourceful lady. A whiz at making cakes. A good mixer in more senses than one.'

She laughed.

'I mean it,' he insisted. 'You're a natural at making friends, or what are we all doing here around your kitchen table? You could charm anybody, even your worst enemy, and that's precisely what you did. But not with cakes. You had your expertise as a professional photographer. Local freelance, taking news pictures for the *Bath Chronicle* and the *Wiltshire Times* and sometimes selling stuff to the nationals. Really good pictures. You were nicely placed to show your work to Britt and convince her that she'd be better off using the local talent than some hotshot from London. This was mid-1990, wasn't it?'

Prue Shorter nodded.

'The dates are important,' he said, looking around the table. 'The little girl was killed in October, 1988, so we're talking about a time at least a year and a half later. Quite a long interval.' He turned to Prue Shorter again. 'What I haven't mentioned yet is how you got to know that Britt was responsible. After all, you didn't know that her car was still in existence. You got to the truth by an altogether different route from ours.'

She said, ' "Responsible" isn't the word I'd use for her.'

'How did you discover that it was Britt who killed your daughter?' he pressed her.

'The roses,' she answered in a voice drained of the animation she'd displayed before. 'They appeared on the grave the day after the funeral. A dozen in a plain transparent wrapper. No message. No indication who supplied them. I spent weeks trying to find out, asking at all the florists in Bath, Bristol, Trowbridge, Westbury, Melksham. I guessed they were placed there by the hit and run driver, you see. I *knew*. But I couldn't trace the shop. She must have got them from London. I had to wait a whole year before I got any closer to her.'

'On the anniversary of the accident?'

'Yes. I should have realized and watched the churchyard, but I didn't. A fresh bunch appeared, still with no clue as to who brought them. But instead of doing the rounds of the florists this time, I asked the people who live in Church Road, outside the church, if they'd seen anyone. Not many cars go up there, except at the weekend, unless there's a funeral. This happened to be a Tuesday. Well, one of the people opposite had noticed a taxi draw up towards dusk, and a woman in a headscarf and black coat get out and go into the churchyard. The taxi waited about ten minutes, until she came back. It had one of those illuminated signs on the top. It was from Abbey Taxis, who work out of Bath.'

'Ah. You traced the driver?'

349

'The next day. He remembered her. And she'd had the roses with her. Even better, she had a slight foreign accent and he gave me a good description. She was blonde, attractive, well dressed. The trouble was that he couldn't tell me her name or address. She'd picked up the taxi from the rank outside the station and that's where he put her down at the end. I got him to drive me around Bath several afternoons in the hope that he would spot her, but we had no luck. Then one evening some weeks after all this he phoned me and said he'd been talking to one of the other Abbey drivers who believed he knew the woman. He'd driven her more than once from the station to a house in Larkhall and she was a Swedish journalist.' She spread her hands. 'That was all I had, but it was enough. I asked in the newspaper office. She didn't work for the local rag, but they knew about her. It's their business to know about local people. It wasn't too promising when I discovered that this woman didn't drive or drink, but I'm not easily discouraged. I got to know everything I could about her. I got the job with her, joined her on a couple of stories, at Longleat and the Trim Street squat.'

'You're so good with people that you managed to suppress the anger you felt towards the woman who killed your daughter.'

'No,' she interrupted Diamond. 'You're telling it wrong. I wasn't certain she'd done it. If I'd been certain, I would have killed her before I did. I couldn't have waited.'

The way she stated this was chilling.

Diamond accepted the correction with a nod. 'I was saying that you won Britt's confidence completely, took all the photos she wanted and took them well. Visited her flat in Larkhall. Got to know her routine, her friends, her landlord, and I'm sure this was one-sided. She didn't visit you. She wouldn't. You were the photographer, the junior partner in this team, so you brought the prints to her to see. She didn't know you lived in Steeple Ashton where she'd killed the child. Your phone has a Devizes number, and that was all she needed to know to stay in contact.'

He took some more coffee. No one else spoke. He took a bite at the cake. He had their attention for as long as he chose to go on. 'In September or October of 1990, Britt got on to John Mountjoy's enrolment racket. As usual, she confided in you, gave you the background, the suspicion that he was enrolling Iraqis who had no intention of becoming students, except to satisfy their visa requirements. You took some external shots of the college. And now we come to the day before the murder, October the seventeenth – two years to the day since your daughter was killed in the car accident. This was the day you confirmed beyond all doubt that Britt had been the driver of that car.'

'The roses?' said Farr-Jones.

Prue Shorter nodded.

'You watched her bring them to the grave?' said Diamond.

'And I knew for sure,' she said in a low voice.

'You also had the opportunity to do something about it the next day. Britt had accepted the invitation to the meal with Mountjoy and told you she would take him back to Larkhall and tape the conversation. She aimed to confront him with the evidence that night, and she did. He admits it. But he didn't kill her. Neither did GB, her latest admirer, who was jealous as hell and followed them back to the house. Nor Billington, who came home unexpectedly to collect the key of his car. The murder was committed after each of the men had left. You visited her late that night, when she was alone in the house, around midnight or after, on some pretext you'd given over the phone – maybe even the truth, that you knew for certain that she was the hit and run driver.'

Prue Shorter gave a nod. 'That was the only way I was going to get admitted at that time of night.'

351

'She agreed.'

'Right away.'

'And you went to the house armed with a knife—'

'A kitchen knife.'

Diamond thought fleetingly of the knife she had given him to cut the cake, then banished the idea. 'She invited you upstairs. You also brought with you the roses she'd placed on your daughter's grave. You stabbed her a number of times and filled her mouth with the roses.'

She eyed him challengingly.

'One question,' he said. 'Before leaving the house, did you remove a cassette from her tape-recorder?'

'You won't find it here,' she said. 'I chucked it in the river. She taped almost everything. It could have given me away.'

Speaking more to the police than to her, he admitted, 'The significance of those roses was a real puzzle to DI Hargreaves and me. We hadn't seen them in a churchyard. We only saw them at the scene of the murder. For a time we assumed the obvious, that they indicated a jealous lover. We also made the mistake of assuming that the person who killed her must have bought them. One thing was certain: whoever bought them took care to make sure we didn't trace them to a local florist's. It was only yesterday evening that we worked out that she had bought them herself, to place on the grave of the little girl she had knocked down and killed.'

Prue Shorter slammed her hand on the table. 'You make it sound like an act of sympathy. She did it to salve her bloody conscience, the bitch. On the anniversary of Georgina's death these revolting roses appeared on her grave, my child's grave, defiling it. They weren't placed there for my baby's sake, or mine, oh, no. She left them to convince herself, herself, her bloody self that she wasn't callous and cold-hearted. But she was, or she'd never have left my child dying in the street. She didn't care. Her life went on untroubled, the high-powered job, the glamour, the travelling, the lovers. Buying a dozen red roses once a year was no sacrifice at all. I gave them back to her. Stuffed them into her lying mouth after I'd stabbed her. They ended up on her bleeding corpse instead of my daughter's grave.' She glared red-eyed around the table. 'Don't look at me with your pious faces. None of you knows what I went through. You can't know what it was like to bring up a child alone, trying to make up for the father who abandoned her and struggling to earn enough to keep us at the same time. You didn't nurse her through attacks of asthma and bronchitis. You didn't comfort her when she had nightmares about starting school. And you weren't taken to a mortuary and asked to identify her pathetic little corpse.' She covered her eyes and sobbed.

Farr-Jones glanced towards Julie, who went to Prue Shorter and placed an arm around her shoulders.

Presently she looked up and said, 'My dears, I didn't mean to do that. I'm sorry. Who would like more coffee?'

Diamond phoned Stephanie at lunch-time and told her he would be home that evening. 'In time for a celebration supper,' he said. 'I'll pick up something we'd both enjoy. And a bottle.'

'What's the celebration?' she asked. 'Did you recapture that convict?'

'Yes – but there's more to it than that, Steph. I'll tell you tonight.'

'What's happened? You sound quite like your old self – disgustingly chipper.'

'My *old* self? There's nothing old about me, as you'll discover.'

The line went quiet for a moment. Then she said, 'Are you sure you're all right? That bee-sting hasn't affected you in some way?'

'I'd forgotten all about the bee-sting.'

She asked warily, 'What did you take for it?'

'I'm perfectly okay, I promise you. Just happy at the outcome.'

'Well, that's a relief,' she said. 'I thought you'd be totally knackered by now.'

'Not at all,' he told her. 'It was a challenge, and I was equal to it. In the end, it was a piece of cake.' He laughed. 'A piece of cake, my love.'

Chapter Thirty

When Diamond looked into the makeshift office, Julie was still typing statements.

'How many more?' he asked.

She looked up and sighed. 'Two sheets of this one, and then I've got to start my own.'

'Paperwork,' he said. 'Don't you hate it?' He riffled through a sheaf of papers of his own that he had just collected from estate agents: details of properties for sale in and around Bath. He would be doing his paperwork on the train to London.

She typed another sentence, then said, 'At least she admits everything.'

'Four years too late.'

'I felt quite sorry for her, and she's a murderer.'

He was unmoved. 'She didn't show much sympathy for Mountjoy, stuck in Albany for the past four years.'

'He'll get a quick release, won't he?'

'Don't know,' he said. 'The wheels grind slowly. The CC promises a report will go straight to the Home Office.'

'After I'd taken the statement, I asked her about Mountjoy,' Julie said. 'If he was on her conscience, I mean. She said when she read about him in the papers, the violence he used on women, she reckoned he deserved every day he spent in prison.'

'That misses the point, Julie. Prue Shorter isn't the law.'

'I didn't say I agree with her.'

She went back to her typing.

'We ought to have a drink,' he suggested.

She said, 'If it doesn't seem too ungrateful, I'd like to get this out of the way. I don't want to hold you up.'

'Can I fetch you a coffee before I go?'

'No, thanks.'

'Cheer up. The news isn't all bad,' he said.

'What do you mean – the prospect of you getting your job back?' Oddly she didn't sound cheered up.

He left to catch the next train.

The Last Detective

Peter Lovesey

Detective Superintendent Peter Diamond is the last detective: 'not some lad out of police school with a degree in computer studies' but a genuine gumshoe, given to doorstepping and deduction. So when the body of a woman is found floating in the weeds in a lake near Bath with no one willing to identify her, no marks and no murder weapon, his sleuthing abilities are tested to the limit.

Struggling with a jigsaw of truant choirboys, teddy bears, a black Mercedes and Jane Austen memorabilia, he alienates his superiors, forensic scientists — and many of his suspects. He even persists when 'the men in white coats' decide they have enough evidence to make a conviction. It's just as well: for despite disastrous personal consequences, and by following the real clues hidden amongst Bath's historic buildings and intertwined with its literary past, the last detective exposes the uncomfortable truth ...

'A brilliant performance ... we shall be lucky if we get a more baffling or entertaining crime puzzle to read this year'
Julian Symons, *TLS*

Crime fiction
0 7515 0121 2

Diamond Solitaire

Peter Lovesey

Peter Diamond, the short-fused detective who stormed out of the CID in *The Last Detective*, takes a job as a Harrods security guard and loses it one night when a little Japanese girl sets off the alarms in his section.

The child Naomi is a challenge, for she is autistic and a mystery. Diamond, strongly committed to helping her, arranges a television appeal to discover her true identity, but she is kidnapped. By interpreting pictorial clues left by Naomi, Diamond tracks her to New York, where a murder is discovered, and to Tokyo, where Japan's most famous sumo wrestler helps bring the quest to a sensational climax.

'Lovesey really does turn a neat plot ... it's phone-off-the-hook time'
Independent

'One of the very best of the current generation of crime writers, and he controls his plot like clockwork — everything timed to perfection'
Evening Standard

Crime fiction
0 7515 0160 3

| ☐ The Last Detective | Peter Lovesey | £4.99 |
| ☐ Diamond Solitaire | Peter Lovesey | £4.99 |

Warner Books now offers an exciting range of quality titles by both established and new authors which can be ordered from the following address:

> Little, Brown & Company (UK),
> P.O. Box 11,
> Falmouth,
> Cornwall TR10 9EN.

Alternatively you may fax your order to the above address.
Fax No. 01326 317444.

Payments can be made as follows: cheque, postal order (payable to Little, Brown and Company) or by credit cards, Visa/Access. Do not send cash or currency. UK customers and B.F.P.O. please allow £1.00 for postage and packing for the first book, plus 50p for the second book, plus 30p for each additional book up to a maximum charge of £3.00 (7 books plus). Overseas customers including Ireland, please allow £2.00 for the first book plus £1.00 for the second book, plus 50p for each additional book.

NAME (Block Letters) _____

ADDRESS _____

_____

☐ I enclose my remittance for £ _____
☐ I wish to pay by Access/Visa Card

Number ☐☐☐☐☐☐☐☐☐☐☐☐☐☐☐☐

Card Expiry Date _____